THE BABY PROJECT

AND

SECOND CHANCE BABY

BY
SUSAN MEIER

MILLS
BOON

Susan Meier spent most of her twenties thinking she was a job-hopper—until she began to write and realised everything that had come before was only research! One of eleven children, with twenty-four nieces and nephews and three kids of her own, Susan has had plenty of real-life experience watching romance blossom in unexpected ways. She lives in Western Pennsylvania with her wonderful husband, Mike, three children, and two over-fed, well-cuddled cats, Sophie and Fluffy. You can visit Susan's website at www.susanmeier.com.

THE BABY PROJECT

BY
SUSAN MEIER

All the characters in this book have no existence outside the imagination of the author, and have no relation whatsoever to anyone bearing the same name or names. They are not even distantly inspired by any individual known or unknown to the author, and all the incidents are pure invention.

First published in Great Britain 2011
by Mills & Boon, an imprint of Harlequin (UK) Limited,
Eton House, 18-24 Paradise Road, Richmond, Surrey TW9 1SR

© Linda Susan Meier 2011

ISBN: 978 0 263 88880 5

23-0511

Harlequin (UK) policy is to use papers that are natural, renewable and recyclable products and made from wood grown in sustainable forests. The logging and manufacturing processes conform to the legal environmental regulations of the country of origin.

Printed and bound in Spain
by Blackprint CPI, Barcelona

Dear Reader,

Every once in a while in a writer's career a really great story idea comes along. For me *The Baby Project* was one of those ideas.

With the loss of both her husband and baby daughter, Whitney Ross has suffered the kind of tragedy most of us will never experience. But Darius hasn't had an easy life either. Imagine not merely being ignored by your super-rich father, but also discovering that you have three half-brothers. One of them a baby!

When Darius and Whitney are named Gino's guardians, neither expects to be overwhelmingly attracted. Still, both are positive they're strong enough to handle it—and each other.

But raising a baby and falling in love are equally surprising. Sometimes funny. Sometimes poignant. Darius and Whitney discover that when everything seems to be rolling out of control the best idea is to simply hang on.

Join me for laughter and tears when Darius and Whitney try to raise spunky little Gino, form a family with Darius's two cantankerous adult half-brothers, and unexpectedly fall desperately, breathlessly in love.

Susan Meier

CHAPTER ONE

"THE ANDREAS BROTHERS have arrived."

As the secretary's announcement came through the speaker phone, attorney Whitney Ross turned from the window in her father's law office. The gathering January storm clouds above the New York City skyscrapers concerned her, but the Andreas brothers' visit would be every bit as tumultuous.

Gerard Ross pressed a button on his phone. "Tell them I need five minutes."

"You're enjoying this."

"Not *enjoying* exactly." He grimaced, leaning his round body back in his office chair. He rhythmically tapped the blotter on his cherrywood desk. "How about if we say Stephone used his will to accomplish a few important things?"

Though Whitney had never met Stephone Andreas's sons, the man had been a close friend of her father's. He'd come to dinner at least once a month from the time she was six, and had talked about "his boys" incessantly. So she suspected she knew what was going on. The senior Andreas had always believed his three sons needed a kick in the pants and it seemed he'd finally found a way to give them one.

"You persuaded Stephone to use his will to force them to grow up."

"This is about more than growing up. All three are smart. All three are good businessmen. Any one of them could take over the family holdings. But not one of them has a sense of loyalty or family."

"And this is where the will comes in?"

"Yes. Stephone made his oldest son, Darius, chairman and CEO and left him the Montauk estate. Whether that divides them for good or forces them to unite all depends on whether Darius takes the reins like a true leader."

He rose and headed for the black leather sofa in the comfortable meeting area in the corner of his big law office. After he sat, he patted the spot beside him, indicating that it was where Whitney should sit for their upcoming meeting.

"But before I bring the brothers in, there's something you need to know. Missy had something put in her will for you that Stephone agreed would also go into his."

Whitney took the seat he'd offered. "Missy put something in her will for me?" She wasn't surprised. Missy Harrington had been her roommate from the time they were freshman at university the whole way through law school. With an alcoholic mom and a dad who'd left when Missy was young, Missy had adopted Whitney's family as her own, and they in turn had taken her under their wing. For seven years she'd shared every holiday and most of her vacations with the Rosses. Whitney had hardly seen Missy since she had introduced her friend to Stephone Andreas, but they had still shared a strong bond.

"She didn't exactly leave you something. In accordance with Stephone's and Missy's wills, you and Darius got shared custody of their son."

Whitney's stomach squeezed. "What?"

"Okay. Look. It's been three years since the accident that took Burn and Layla. And though I had never dreamed that Missy and Stephone would die so soon when I let them put this provision in their wills, it's still time you came back to the land of the living." Her dad pulled a small envelope from one of the files in the stack on the coffee table. "She left this note for you."

Whitney wrapped her hand around the envelope, and she paled.

"In the unlikely event of their deaths, Stephone wanted Darius to raise their son, but Missy was adamant about you having joint custody. The Andreas brothers are rich and spoiled. And they don't even know their father had another son. It's anybody's guess how they'll react when they find out. I believe that Missy made you co-guardian to ensure that Gino was also in the hands of someone *she* knew could take the reins and care for her baby."

"But I don't know Gino! When Missy and Stephone moved to Greece, we practically lost touch. I've never even met Gino. I'll be no better for this baby than his brother."

He caught her hand. "You might not know Gino, but Missy knew you. She knew you had a sense of family. A sense of right and wrong. You've also been a mom. You'll get to know Gino and, as young as he is, Gino will grow accustomed to you, too." He squeezed her fingers. "Besides, you need this."

She tried to bounce off the sofa, but her dad held fast to her hand. When she faced him her eyes were blazing. "No! I don't *need* this! I'm fine!"

"You're not fine. Otherwise, getting custody of Gino wouldn't make you angry."

He pressed a button on the phone on the coffee table that sat in the center of the circle made by the sofa and three black leather chairs. "Cynthia, bring in Gino, please."

Whitney's heart stopped. Her stomach rolled. Her head spun. For the past three years she'd avoided even being near a baby. The scent of baby powder, the feel of snuggly blankets, the sight of someone so tiny, so helpless and so beautiful would have been her undoing. And now her father wanted her to take a baby into her home?

The side door opened and Cynthia Smith walked in carrying six-month-old Gino Andreas in a baby carrier, along with a diaper bag and a duffel.

Her father squeezed her hand again. "Your mother and I have been keeping Gino during the Andreas funerals, but it's time you took him." He rose and accepted the baby carrier from Cynthia. "Thank you, Cyn."

She nodded and her blond hair bobbed. "You're welcome, sir."

As Cynthia left the room, Whitney's father set the carrier on the sofa, pulled Gino out and presented the dark-haired, dark-eyed baby boy to her. "He's yours, Whitney."

Knowing there was no arguing with her father, Whitney slid the envelope into her jacket pocket and took the six-month-old with shaking hands. He immediately began to cry.

"Don't cry, sweetie," she crooned, automatically pressing his head to her shoulder to comfort him. "It's okay."

Her instinctive response to his crying amazed her,

but she wasn't surprised by the pain that sliced through her—the memories that flashed through her brain. Her daughter had been a tiny blonde with huge blue eyes. She'd rarely cried, except when she missed her mother. She'd loved bananas and puppies. To Whitney, she'd seemed the smartest baby on the face of the earth.

Tears filled her eyes. Her stomach tightened.

She couldn't do this.

Maybe she needed more time with her therapist, Dr. Miller?

But before she could say anything to her dad, the office door opened. Wearing jeans, cowboy boots and a cable-knit sweater, Cade Andreas entered first. Behind him was Nick, the dark-haired, dark-eyed brother who most resembled the senior Andreas. And finally Darius. Taller than their father, but with eyes and hair as dark as his, striking in his expensive business suit, Darius was very clearly the leader of the group.

Their expressions were solemn, yet strong. Almost arrogant. The head of the Andreas family was dead. They now controlled one of the largest shipping conglomerates in the world.

Or so they thought.

She glanced at the baby in her arms. For the first time in three years she felt a swell of protectiveness only a mother could feel, and she understood why Missy had given *her* custody along with Darius. The Andreas men were strong. Maybe too strong. And babies needed love.

The question was did she have any left to give?

"Are you kidding me?"

Darius Andreas gaped at Gerard Ross, his deceased father's attorney, then at Gerard's daughter Whitney

Ross, a tall, cool blonde with gray-blue eyes who looked nothing like her short, round father. The pair sat on the black leather sofa. The Andreas brothers sat across from them on three black leather chairs. Beside Whitney was a baby carrier and inside the carrier was a baby boy who looked to be only a few months old. His black hair and dark eyes marked him as an Andreas as clearly as Gerard Ross's pronouncement did.

"I assure you, there's no joke." Gerard leaned back, getting more comfortable. "This little boy is your father's final son. There are four of you now."

He picked up the will and began reading again. "It is my wish that the remaining two-thirds share of Andreas Holdings be divided equally among my four sons— Darius, Cade, Nick and Gino."

Gino.

A baby.

His final half-sibling was a baby!

Darius sucked in a breath, forcing that to sink in, but it wouldn't. His brain had frozen. He was stunned, speechless and working not to lose his temper over something he couldn't change. Nick and Cade appeared to be equally shell shocked.

Finally, the business sense Darius had trusted his entire life came to his rescue. "I want a DNA test."

The smooth leather sofa sighed when Gerard sat forward. He looked down at his entwined fingers, then caught Darius's gaze. "Your father might not have married Missy Harrington, but he's named on the birth certificate as Gino's father. Had Missy not died with your father, you might be fighting her for the company right now."

"I still want DNA."

"I understand you're surprised—"

"Surprised? How about shocked? First our father calls us to the hospital after the accident to tell us that he gave one-third interest in the company to someone else. So we'll never fully own our own damned company. Then he tells us *we* have no sense of family and unless we pull together we're going to lose everything he built. Then he dies. Just like that." He snapped his fingers. "Now you're telling us there's a fourth brother?"

"Mr. Andreas, the very fact that you didn't know your father had another child is proof that your sense of family leaves a bit to be desired."

Darius nearly cursed. Who was his womanizing father to tell him that he had no sense of family? His father had abandoned his mother. Hell, Stephone had abandoned *him* until he was in his teens. And then he'd appeared in Darius's life only because he had wanted to ensure that Darius went to a good university so he could be groomed to work for Andreas Holdings.

"For decades our father preached that we shouldn't take family troubles to outsiders." He rose. "Yet it looks like that's exactly what he's done." He reached for the baby carrier. Now that the shock was receding, things were beginning to sink in and make sense. He didn't really need DNA to tell him this was his brother. His father had been living with a thirty-year-old woman. It was no shock she'd gotten pregnant. Gino had all the physical markings of an Andreas. With his father's name on the birth certificate and Gino's name in the will, this little boy was family. And his father wanted him to care for him. So he would. Unlike his two brothers, Darius had always done what their father had asked.

"We'll take our brother and go now."

Whitney held back the carrier. "Dad?"

Gerard said, "There's more."

Darius just barely controlled his rising fury. *"More?"*

"You, Darius, get custody of Gino, but you share it with Whitney."

He turned his heated gaze on her.

Her yellow hair was probably pretty, but she had it rolled in a tight, no-nonsense bun at the back of her head. Her gray suit hid any hint of the body beneath it. He caught the gaze of her blue-gray eyes. In spite of the fact that she dressed to downplay her appearance, Darius felt a click of attraction. And it was mutual. He saw the flicker in her pretty blue orbs.

"It's up to you how you divide Gino's time. If you want to have him three days a week and Whitney four, or if you want to have him for two weeks a month and Whitney two, whatever you choose is up to you two. But she will vote his share at your board of directors meetings."

This time Darius did curse. But he quickly pulled in a breath, struggling to rein in his temper, and glanced again at Whitney. The click of attraction he'd felt when he'd first looked into her eyes turned into a current of electricity that zapped between them. They were definitely attracted.

If this were any other day, any other time, any other circumstance, he would have pursued her. Peel off a few layers of clothes, take down her hair—he was just about certain he'd find paradise.

But those eyes, those pretty Persian-cat eyes, told him to forget it. It didn't matter if they were attracted to each other. They had a job to do. Raise Gino. Together.

Whitney stayed perfectly still under Darius Andreas's scrutiny, though warm, sweet attraction hummed through her. She ignored it. He was a gorgeous man with his dark, brooding good looks, his tailored suit made to accentuate his broad shoulders and trim hips, and his commanding personality. Any woman would react to him. Simply from the way his other brothers hadn't even spoken since introductions were made, it was clear that Darius was the brother in charge. And that was very sexy.

With his piercing onyx eyes boring into hers, she suppressed a shiver. But she wasn't worried about falling victim to the attraction. Attractions frequently grew into relationships and relationships made people vulnerable. The pain that had followed the loss of her husband had been indescribable. She'd never put herself through that again. She'd never even let herself get close. She couldn't be attracted to Darius Andreas. She refused.

Darius squeezed his eyes shut in disgust and popped them open again. "All right. Fine." He motioned for Whitney to follow him. "Let's go."

"Go?"

"If this baby's on the board, he's working for a living."

Whitney's dad laughed. "Very funny, Darius."

"I'm not laughing. My father left the company in a sad state. There's work to do. And nobody's excused. Since your daughter has his vote, she'll pull his share of the duty."

"That's preposterous—"

"Dad." Whitney interrupted her father. "It's okay. I've never been one to shirk my responsibilities." She straightened her shoulders and looked Darius in the eye, accepting his challenge. If he thought he'd intimidate her on day one, he was sadly mistaken. She could handle a little work. "If everybody's working, then I will, too."

"All right," her dad agreed, "but before anybody leaves there's one more thing."

Darius turned. His dark eyes were ablaze now.

Whitney's dad looked from Darius to Cade to Nick and back at Darius again. "With someone else in possession of a one-third share of Andreas Holdings, and four brothers sharing the other two-thirds, you don't have to be a math scholar to know that individually none of you has controlling interest in the whole company." He glanced from Darius to Cade to Nick again. "Your father has instructed me to allow the holder of the one-third interest to remain anonymous until she decides how to handle her position. She's in her seventies, so she may simply want to sit back and enjoy the profits. But if she decides she wants to be active in the company, you had better be united or Andreas Holdings will end up being run by somebody other than an Andreas."

"We'll need a few minutes." Past being shocked by the conditions and warnings coming out of his dad's lawyer's mouth, Darius spoke quietly, with the authority of command. "We'd appreciate the use of your office to discuss this."

Gerard Ross rose. "Whitney and I will take Gino to her office. Have Cynthia call us when you're ready."

Gerard and Whitney left the room through a side door and Darius faced his brothers. "This wasn't exactly how we expected the reading of the will to turn out."

Nick snorted a laugh, but Cade rose. "Frankly, with the exception of Gino, nothing that happened this morning surprised me. You got most of the goodies, Darius. The Montauk estate and the chairmanship, but I think it all evens out with you also getting the baby." He saluted and headed for the door. "Good luck with that."

Right. Cade. The rebel. He should have guessed he wouldn't hang around to lend a helping hand and probably neither would Nick. There was no love, loyalty or unity among the Andreas brothers. They'd gone their separate ways, managed their trust funds individually, made their own fortunes. And each of them had his own life. But after Attorney Ross's warning about the mystery shareholder, Darius was beginning to understand some of the things their father had babbled about on his deathbed. If they weren't unified when that shareholder came out of the woodwork they could end up dockworkers in their own shipyards.

"Come on. You can't just walk away." He motioned for Cade to return to his seat, but instead, Nick rose.

"Sure we can. You're the chairman and CEO. You're the one who has to run things. You might have bullied Ms. Ross into working for you, but we're not buying in. We'll be back for board of directors meetings and for our share of the profits."

"So you really are just going to leave? Even after Dad told us he wanted us to unite? Even after hearing there's another shareholder?"

"You'll handle it."

"This company belongs to *all* of us. I thought you'd both want a part of things."

"Yeah, and I thought Dad would be around when I was a kid. But he wasn't." Nick caught Darius's gaze. "You were the golden boy. The company, the baby, the troubles are all yours."

He left the room with Cade right behind him.

Darius fell to the sofa. Over the years he'd cursed his dad for being a philanderer who had created three very different sons…four now. Today he looked up at the ceiling, finally understanding what had troubled his father for the last ten years of his life. The Andreas brothers truly weren't family. Having three different moms and hailing from three different parts of the United States, they were as divided as they were different. They might share dark hair, dark eyes and a shrewd business sense, but there was no love lost between them.

The silence of the lawyer's office rattled around him. Both of his parents were dead now. He had no cousins or aunts and uncles. He had two adult half-brothers, but they wanted nothing to do with him.

He thought back a few weeks to Christmas. He'd gone to parties galore, but on Christmas morning he'd been alone. His footsteps had echoed in his cold, empty apartment. Unless he did a better job of raising Gino than his father had done with him, Nick and Cade, this would be the sound of his life. Silence.

In a weird way, he was glad he'd gotten custody of Gino. Gino was his family now.

Well, his and Whitney Ross's.

A sliver of excitement slithered through him when he remembered the feeling of attraction that had arced between him and Whitney. Oh, she was tempting. A challenge. A buttoned-down present, begging to be unwrapped. But that would be nothing but trouble. He had to raise a child with her.

He understood why Missy Harrington had recognized that Gino would need a mother figure. Anybody who spent two minutes in the company of any of the Andreas brothers knew they weren't the settling-down kind. So if Missy wanted a mother for Gino, she'd probably known she'd have to pick her. But he didn't have a clue how "shared custody" would work in the real world. Would sharing a child be like being married? Or maybe being divorced? Would they have to draw up a custody agreement that set forth who got the baby and when? Or would they pass the poor kid back and forth like a tennis ball or Frisbee?

He ran his hands down his face. He had absolutely no idea how this would go. Worse, he had no idea how to care for a baby. Hell, he just plain had no idea how to be a dad, since his own father hadn't come around until he was nearly an adult.

Which gave Whitney a second, maybe more important, role in this child-custody venture. Because Darius didn't know how a father was supposed to behave, Whitney was going to have to teach him.

CHAPTER TWO

As WHITNEY AND HER DAD left his office, Cyn caught his arm. "They need you in the conference room right now."

"But I'm still working with the Andreas brothers—"

"The exact words Roger said were, 'The Mahoney case is going to hell in a ham sandwich. The very second Gerry is out of his meeting we need him in here.'"

Whitney's dad faced her. "Will you be okay?"

She forced a smile. "Yes. You go on. When the Andreas brothers are through with their little powwow, I'll have you paged if we need you."

"Thanks." He kissed her cheek, slid the duffel and diaper bag onto her shoulder, turned and raced away from her.

Walking to her office, Whitney looked down at Gino. Sucking a green-and-brown camouflage-print pacifier, he peered up at her. Luminous dark eyes met hers. Her heart stumbled in her chest. Layla's pale-blue eyes had been a combination of her father's sky blue eyes and Whitney's gray blue. Her hair had been yellow. Baby-fine. Wispy. Whitney had never been able to get a clip to hold and she'd become one of those moms who used multicolored cloth hair bands to decorate her baby's head.

Her chest tightened. She'd give everything she had, everything she owned, every day of the rest of her life, for even one more chance to touch that wispy hair.

Gino spat out his pacifier and began to cry. Whitney set the baby carrier on the small floral-print sofa in the right-hand corner of her office.

"Don't cry, sweetie," she said automatically and her throat closed. Her chest tightened. Caring for a baby was something like riding a bike. Unfortunately, all the remembered skills also brought back memories of the baby she'd lost—

The nights she'd walked the floor when Layla was colicky. Her first birthday party when the abundance of guests had scared her. Bathing her, cuddling her, loving her.

Being her mom.

Don't cry, sweetie.

She squeezed her eyes shut, trying to pull herself together, but Gino cried all the harder.

She sat on the sofa, lifted him from the carrier and cuddled him against her chest. Sobbing in earnest now, the little boy buried his face in her neck.

He smelled like baby lotion and felt as soft as feathers from an angel's wings. She closed her eyes again, weakened by longings for her own baby. Remembering treasured events. The plans they'd had for Layla's future. The mom she'd wanted to be.

Shaking with sorrow, she pushed at those memories, trying to get them out of her head. But they wouldn't budge. Instead, they arched in her brain like a rainbow of photos, a cacophony of happy sounds. Baby giggles. Toddler laughs. First words. Mama. Da Da. Nanna. Pap Pap. Kitty.

She knew it was the sweet baby scents that caused her

total recall. So she grabbed a blanket from the diaper bag and laid it on the sofa, then placed Gino on top, putting three feet of distance between them.

She swallowed. The memories receded. Her shaking subsided. The thumping of her heart slowed.

The little boy blinked at her.

"I know you're probably scared," she said, talking to him as if he were an adult because she couldn't risk the baby talk that she knew would soothe him. "I know my mom was very good to you the past few days, but I'll bet you miss your own mama…" She swallowed. Miss didn't even halfway describe the feelings of loss this baby must feel. Even though he probably didn't understand that his parents were dead, *her* heart broke because she *did* understand. She knew exactly what it felt like to lose the two people closest to her. He was alone. Scared. And wanted his mom. Or someone to make him feel safe again.

In three long years, she hadn't felt safe. Everything she believed had been tossed in the air and come down in pieces the day her husband had committed suicide and killed their baby with him.

As she checked Gino's diaper to see if that was why he was crying, a rush of memories of Layla flooded her brain again. Except this time they weren't happy. This time, she heard her baby crying, calling for her, and suddenly she was face to face with her worst fear. The fear that morphed into guilt. The guilt her therapist had told her was pointless.

No one knew if Burn had deliberately put Layla into the car with him when he'd decided to kill himself by sitting in the vehicle while the garage filled with carbon monoxide. Speculation was that he'd put Layla into her car seat to go somewhere, but when he'd gotten behind the wheel he just couldn't force himself out into the world. He'd sat in their garage long enough for the fumes to begin to get to him and was soon mentally too far gone to remember he had the baby with him.

That explanation had soothed everyone but Whitney. If everyone accepted that Burn's depression and mounting mental illness were reason enough to forget he had their child in his car, then shouldn't she have realized he was too sick to care for her baby?

Layla.

Why hadn't she recognized Burn's growing troubles?

Why hadn't she protected her baby?

What had been so important in those months that she'd missed all the signs that Burn was tumbling over the edge?

Tears filled her eyes as Gino began to cry, drawing her back to the present. She wanted to cuddle him, to love him, but her memories of Layla were still morphing into memories of Burn's suicide, Layla's death and the horrible, horrible feelings of guilt.

She couldn't deal with the guilt.

She changed Gino's diaper but rather than hold him, she returned him to the baby carrier. He looked at her with sad dark eyes.

She blinked back tears, hoping for his sake that the trouble she had holding him was only temporary. It wasn't his fault her family had died. Plus, Missy had wanted her to care for this little guy—

Remembering the envelope her dad had given her, she rose from the sofa to retrieve it from her jacket pocket. After fumbling with the seal, she pulled out the slim sheet of white stationery. Pacing in front of her sofa, she read…

Whitney…

It's funny to be writing this because I don't think you'll ever read it. Actually, I hope you never do read it. But we're having wills drawn up today and we have a baby. Plans have to be made for who will care for Gino just in case something happens. Stephone said he wanted Darius to have custody, but I didn't think that was such a good idea. I know Darius will never marry and that means Gino will never have a mom. But I also recognized I couldn't talk Stephone out of naming Darius as guardian. All I could do was suggest making you co-guardian. So that's what we did. If something happens to me and Stephone, Darius will be Gino's dad and you will be Gino's mom.

Love him, Whitney. I'm not sure Darius knows how. Missy

Whitney swallowed and sank to the couch. The note was short and to the point. A mother's simple plea. Love her baby. Because she wasn't sure his older brother knew how to love. Hadn't she already guessed that?

She glanced at Gino. The baby blinked at her dubiously. This little boy had gone from his parents' home in Greece to Whitney's parents' home, and now he was being passed to her. It had undoubtedly frightened Gino to be passed from one set of strangers to the next. He had to get into a stable environment. *She* had to get him into a stable environment. Without her, there was no guarantee Gino wouldn't be raised by nannies or at boarding school. Worse, there was no one to prevent Darius from seeing Gino more as a vote at a director's meetings than as a baby.

She had to do this. She had to be a part of this little boy's life. She had to care for him. She had to *love* him.

She popped the pacifier into Gino's mouth again. "This has been a rough couple of days for you. But you're safe now. I'm going to take good care of you."

An arrow sliced into her heart. How could she promise she'd take good care of this little boy when she hadn't even been able to protect her own child from her husband...the baby's father?

Darius gave himself another minute to collect himself, then stepped into the hall and instructed the receptionist to let Attorney Ross know he was ready.

Pacing the rich red Oriental rug, he waited for Ross to return. When the side door opened, he spun toward it to see only Whitney enter. She held Gino in the basket-like carrier. A big duffel bag and a diaper bag were slung over her shoulder.

"I know I said I could begin working for you today, but I just realized there's no one to care for Gino. Plus, I have no baby things at my home," she announced casually as she stepped inside. "No crib, no high chair, no swing or rocker."

Darius's male senses perked up. Probably because he and Whitney were alone for the first time. He caught the scent of her perfume on the air, noticed her legs were long and shapely.

"I was thinking I should probably make arrangements to get all of that shipped to my apartment."

Darius almost said, "Sure," if only because his immediate reaction was to give her anything she wanted. But that was his attraction talking, agreeing so she'd like him. He had to resist that. He wanted this little boy in his life. He also needed Whitney to teach him how to

be a father. The only way he could see that working out
would be for her and the baby to live with him—at least
for the first few weeks.

"I've been thinking about this deal and I'm not sure
either one or the other of us taking him is the right thing
to do."

She blinked at him. "You want to leave him at a
hotel?"

He chuckled, hoping she was joking. Surely she
couldn't think he was that inept. "No. I'm saying we
need a plan."

"We'll hammer out an agreement of some sort eventually. But he needs somewhere to stay tonight. It's already close to five and neither one of us owns a crib. We
should also hire a nanny." She caught his gaze. "Unless
you've got baby experience I don't know about."

Heat whipped through him. This attraction wasn't
going to be easy to ignore. But he was a very strong
man. "Actually, I'm going to need a little help getting
accustomed to him."

She turned away, fiddled with something in the diaper
bag. "We both will in the beginning."

Rats. She wasn't getting what he was driving at. He
didn't want her to know just how baby-stupid he was,
and he couldn't tell her without putting himself at a
disadvantage. He wasn't accustomed to negotiating from
anything less than a position of strength. But sometimes
the best way to win an argument was to use the element of surprise. Just come right out and propose the
ridiculous.

"Or we could live together."

She spun to face him. "What?"

"Look, I inherited my father's estate on Montauk.
There's a house big enough that we wouldn't even have

to run into each other. This way we'd both see the baby every day and we could discuss any issue that came up the minute it came up."

She didn't say anything. Darius wasn't sure if he'd taken her so much by surprise that she was speechless or if his suggestion was so ridiculous she didn't know how to respond. So he pushed on.

"It doesn't have to be forever. Only the first few weeks. That way the little guy wouldn't be shuffled from one of us to the other before he got to know either of us. Plus, we'd have servants. We wouldn't be doing this on our own."

Whitney surprised him by saying, "How many servants?"

He shrugged. "Well, if I remember correctly there are several maids. My dad also always had a cook. And an estate manager, Mrs. Tucker."

Her expression went from strained to thoughtful to sort of happily surprised. Victory surged through him. But she hadn't actually consented. The battle wasn't over yet. He needed a deal sealer. Something that would put her totally on his side.

On impulse, he walked over to her and glanced down at the baby carrier. The brown-eyed boy blinked up at him over his pacifier.

"He's cute."

"He's very cute." She paused for a heartbeat then said, "Do you want to hold him?"

"Yeah. That'd be great." How hard could it be? Not only was he trying to get on Whitney's good side, but he had to be a dad to this kid. There was no time like the present to begin learning how.

She set the carrier on her father's black leather sofa, unbuckled the strap that held Gino in and lifted him in front of her. Eye-to-eye with the baby, she said, "Gino, I'm giving you to your big brother."

Darius laughed. "Was that an introduction?"

"No. That was me preparing him to be taken by a stranger."

"He'll know?"

Her gaze met his over the baby's dark head. "Of course, he'll know."

Her eyes were the most wonderful color of gray-blue. A sort of sexy, yet innocent shade that sparked his attraction to life again. Something sharp and sweet stabbed him in his middle. He was wishing that he didn't need her so he could follow this compelling urge he had to pursue her, when she presented Gino to him and fear immediately knocked every other thought out of his brain.

But before he had a chance to panic over his first-ever attempt at holding a baby, his hand brushed Whitney's as she gave him the baby and pinpricks of awareness lit up his skin. He'd never felt an attraction this strong, this gripping. A warning stirred in his brain, but Whitney let go and suddenly Darius was supporting Gino's full weight.

"Whoa!" He bobbled him a bit before he got control. "He's heavier than I thought."

Whitney smiled slightly. "Yes. Most six-month-olds aren't quite that…sturdy."

Feeling painfully awkward, but determined to get the hang of this, Darius laughed uncomfortably. "We are a family of big eaters."

She looked away.

Not sure if she was totally disinterested in him and his family or uncomfortable at being so close to him, Darius casually said, "How about if we swing by your apartment and gather some things so we can spend the weekend in Montauk? My dad and Missy might have only popped by the house for a few weeks a year, but after Gino was born they had to have created a nursery. So at least he'll have somewhere to sleep tonight. That way you can take a look around the place and see that I'm right. The house is big enough that we could live together for a few weeks without getting in each other's way."

Whitney's skin pricked with fear, trepidation and possibility. She couldn't picture herself alone with Gino tonight. Well, actually, she could. She saw herself paralyzed with grief as he lay in the crib sobbing. Darius's suggestion that they spend the weekend together would have been the answer to a prayer, except he wouldn't be any better with Gino than she was.

Of course, he had staff and eventually they'd hire a nanny.

Still, it could take weeks to hire someone. Especially since they had to find someone willing to go back and forth between her Soho loft and Darius's estate. If they didn't have a nanny tonight, there would be no hiding the fact that she was having trouble being around the little boy. Trouble holding him. Trouble smelling him. Trouble just being in the same room.

Of course, if she had a breakdown in front of Darius it might be bad for her, but it would be good for Gino, because at least there'd be someone to pick up the ball. No matter how inexperienced. With a few quick baby lessons she could probably turn Darius into a moderately competent caregiver.

As if to confirm that idea, Darius jiggled Gino on his arm, as he cooed and gooed at him, and Gino playfully slapped his face. They liked each other. They almost appeared to have some kind of natural family bond.

Blessed relief swelled through her. It wasn't a perfect idea, but it was better than her being alone with Gino. In the name of teaching Darius how to do his part for the little boy, she could hand over most of the tasks that might cause her to burst into tears.

Plus he had staff. Gino would be surrounded by people who could care for him until they found a nanny. And if Whitney played it right, she wouldn't even have to have a panic attack to get assistance. Gino was so adorable, every maid, cook and butler would want a turn at holding him, feeding him, rocking him to sleep.

She sucked in a breath, caught Darius's gaze, and said, "Okay. We'll spend the weekend at your house."

He smiled at her, reminding her of the other teeny, tiny thing she'd forgotten to add into the equation. They were attracted. And about to live together.

Luckily, his house was huge. And she wasn't stupid. She'd keep a cool head and everything would be fine.

CHAPTER THREE

ON THE DRIVE OUT TO Montauk, Darius called ahead to let the staff know they would be arriving.

Clicking off his call, he faced Whitney. "There's a nursery."

"Really? That's great."

"Yes. My father and Missy had been staying at the house when they were in the accident."

Sadness tiptoed through her at the loss of her friend, but she focused on the job she had to do for Missy. "So there wouldn't happen to be a nanny?"

"No. Their nanny was a young woman from Greece. She went home immediately after the funerals."

"Too bad."

He shrugged. "Not really. I'm sure we can easily hire someone."

Whitney smiled noncommittally, then her gaze fell to Gino who was asleep in his car seat. She should have started Darius's baby lessons the minute they got into the limo. She knew what to do and his hands could be the hands that carried out her instructions tonight. But now Gino was asleep and probably wouldn't awaken until they arrived. And when he awakened, he'd be crying. Then Darius would see her struggle and fumble.

Sucking in a soft breath, she told herself not to borrow

trouble. Everything would work out if she just kept a cool head.

The limo pulled up to an iron gate and the driver used a combination on a keypad to open it. As they drove up the wide, circular drive to get to the enormous house, Whitney's heart kicked into overdrive. With bare tree branches blowing in the January breeze the estate had a cold, deserted feel to it. An ominous mood that almost made her shiver. And definitely made her wonder if this was the right choice. Darius Andreas was a stranger and she'd agreed to live with him.

Whitney unbuckled Gino as the driver opened the door. He helped her out and Darius stepped out behind her, then reached inside for the baby.

Refusing to panic or let her imagination run wild over the cold, empty feeling that surrounded her, Whitney followed him to the front door, where he hit a few buttons on a hidden security panel, then opened the door.

They walked onto white marble tile in the echoing foyer. A curved stairway led the way to the second floor. A huge crystal chandelier awakened with light when Darius hit the switch as an older woman wearing a tidy black suit walked into the foyer to greet them.

"This is Mrs. Tucker," Darius said, turning to Whitney then Mrs. Tucker with a smile. "Mrs. T, this is Whitney. She's Gerard Ross's daughter."

Mrs. Tucker nodded once. "It's a pleasure to meet you, ma'am."

Whitney returned her smile. Though her parents hadn't had servants while she was growing up, and she herself had never had anything more than a cleaning service, her parents now had a full staff for their home on Park Avenue. "It's a pleasure to meet you, too, Mrs. Tucker."

"You're in the guest suite in the right wing upstairs. Geoffrey will get your bags from the limo."

"Thank you."

Mrs. Tucker turned to leave, but a thought struck Whitney and she stopped her. "Where's the nursery?"

"In the left wing beside the master suite and Mr. Andreas."

"Will the nanny also be beside the nursery?"

"Yes, ma'am. The nanny's quarters are on one side. Mr. Andreas's are on the other."

That just didn't sit right. Not because of the unexpected jealousy that slithered through her at the thought of another woman being a door or two away from Darius's bedroom, but because she felt as if she were being eased out. She hadn't questioned Darius talking her into living at the house in Montauk. Her fears had actually caused her to be relieved he'd thought of it. But now that he'd assigned her to a room across the house from the nursery, suspicions rose in her. He wanted the baby at his house, wanted her at the other side of the mansion. What was he up to?

"Why am I not near the nursery?"

Holding Gino in the baby carrier, Darius stepped forward, caught her arm and directed her to the stairway as Mrs. Tucker scrambled away, obviously glad Darius would field the question.

"I thought you'd prefer privacy, particularly since Mrs. Tucker has agreed to sleep in the nanny's room to help with Gino until we get a regular nanny."

He sounded sincere, genuine. But this was a skilled negotiator, a smart businessman, a charming man. And her fears about caring for Gino had blinded her to the way he'd been calling the shots. That ended here. That ended now.

"Isn't there another suite close to the nursery?"

"Yes, of course."

"I'd like that one, then."

Darius stopped walking. His black onyx eyes snared hers, she was sure, in a show of strength, ready to meet her challenge. But within seconds the expression in his dark orbs shifted from serious to sensuous.

As if he only now realized how close they were standing beside each other on the stairs, he pulled in a breath. Tension rose up, shimmering through her. This man was attracted to her. There was no better aphrodisiac for a woman than the realization that a powerful, sexy man wanted her.

Her.

And she'd just insisted she be in a room closer to the nursery, *closer to him.*

She almost told him to forget about her request for a room change, but knew that if she did he'd realize it was because of their attraction. She also remembered it was her responsibility to love Gino and maybe even to protect him from overbearing Darius, and by God, she intended to. If that meant she needed to be close to him too, she'd handle it.

She smiled, hoping to appear to be a woman who hadn't even been slightly affected by the way he'd looked at her. "I take my responsibilities seriously, Darius. Though I'm glad Gino will be close to the nanny we hire, I want to be close too. The will says we share custody. I was given a job. I intend to do it."

His serious eyes suddenly filled with mischief that sent her pulse scrambling. "So you want to be across the hall—" he smiled "—from me?"

She stared into his sexy dark eyes with every nerve ending in her body humming and the blood in her veins virtually singing. Her voice squeaked when she said, "Yes."

"So be it. I'll have Mrs. Tucker tell Geoffrey to put your things in the room across the hall from mine."

With that he pulled out his cell phone, turned and walked up the stairs. Whitney nearly collapsed on the stairway. She heard him speaking on the phone, instructing someone to ready the room across the hall from his, and guessed he was talking to Mrs. Tucker. She hastily climbed the stairs with shaky legs and followed Darius to the nursery. But two steps inside the door, she froze.

A mobile over the cherrywood crib zapped her back in time. She could have been standing in Layla's nursery. The colors of the wall were different, but most of the furniture and lots of the toys were the same. So were the scents.

Darius carried the baby inside. "I think he needs a change. I'd offer to do it," he smiled engagingly, "but I've never changed a diaper in my entire life."

Smothered by thoughts of her baby, Whitney couldn't get her legs to move or her mouth to form words. Memories rolled through her mind. In perfect Technicolor she saw the vision of Layla standing up in her crib, holding the bars, crying for her mother. She remembered the Christmas gifts she had bought and hidden in the closet as if little Layla would somehow know to look for them. It had been almost a year before she had been able to clear out the nursery, if only because she couldn't step inside without crumbling.

But Darius didn't seem to notice her paralysis. Pulling Gino out of the baby carrier, he said, "I'd be happy to do it, though, if you want to teach me."

Whitney cleared her throat. "Sure." Relief swamped

her. For as much as she didn't want Darius taking over Gino's life, with her grief perilously close to the surface she simply couldn't handle touching Gino right now. Whether she liked it or not, take-charge Darius was saving her.

She glanced around until she saw the changing table. She pointed at it. "Take him over there."

Darius carried the sleepy baby to the changing table.

Whitney frowned. "We left the diaper bag in the car."

"Geoffrey will get it. But there should already be diapers here somewhere. I told the staff to make sure the nursery was stocked." With one hand holding Gino in place on the table, he opened the doors of the cupboard beneath it. "Ah. There they are." He reached in and pulled one out with a smile. "The staff is very efficient."

She took a cautious step to the changing table. "So I see."

"Now what?"

Forcing back the memories, she pulled in a slow, cleansing breath. Her grief subsiding, she strolled closer. "Unsnap his pajamas and slide him out."

He unsnapped the one-piece pajamas but was a little rough in getting Gino's arm out. She laid her hand on top of his. "Gentler."

"Okay." He peeked over at her and smiled stupidly. "His skin is soft, like velvet."

She remembered thinking that very thing the first time she held Layla and swallowed back the grief, pushed back the memory of the nurse laying her brand-new baby girl into her arms. "I know."

When Gino was out of his pajamas and wearing only

his diaper, Whitney pointed at the tabs of his diaper and said, "Yank on those to open the diaper."

He yanked on the tabs and to everyone's joy, the diaper was only wet.

Darius said, "Whew."

Whitney couldn't help it. She laughed. "Okay, toss that in the container beside the changing table." She motioned to the available diaper pail. "Slide another diaper under him, fasten the tabs, put him into clean pajamas and you're done."

Darius followed her instructions, needing another reminder about being gentle with Gino's little arms and legs as he tucked them into pajamas. But again he only smiled when she told him.

Her suspicions about Darius came tumbling back. He was too nice. Too eager. Once again she wondered if he wasn't trying to edge her out. "I'm surprised you want to learn all this."

He caught her gaze. "Gino is my family now."

"Oh. So you're really getting into the daddy thing?" Her voice dripped with skepticism as she asked the question, but she couldn't help it. A single man—a single *rich* man—who wanted to care for a baby was more than an anomaly. It was downright weird.

"My dad didn't have a lot of time for me." He peered over at her. "Or my brothers, and I don't want that to happen to Gino. If I'm to be his male influence, I want to do my end of the duties."

"So you're going to learn how to do *everything?*"

To her surprise, he wasn't insulted. He laughed. "Hey, I just changed a diaper. I think my commitment has been proven."

Not even close. Particularly since she didn't understand why he was making such a hands-on commitment.

Sure, he didn't want Gino to grow up without a dad. She got it. But there was more here. Her lawyer's instincts had gone from suspicious to downright positive there was something here she was missing.

"Okay, then tomorrow morning, we'll hit the ground running with your baby lessons."

He laughed, but Whitney wasn't kidding. Not just because she was afraid to touch Gino too much, but because she wanted to push Darius to the wall, give him so much baby time he would own up to what was really going on.

When the baby was dressed, Darius pulled him off the table and gave him a quick hug and kissed his cheek. "Good night, little guy."

Then he handed the baby to Whitney. Preoccupied with his motives, she didn't realize what he was about to do and had to scramble to catch Gino.

But the second the yawning baby was in her arms, the feel of his ultra-soft pajamas and smooth skin kicked her back in time again. Especially, when she brought Gino to her and hugged him. The second the little boy was snuggled against her, sadness overwhelmed her. The hollow, empty feeling of loss. Echoes of Layla's giggles rolled through her brain. Memories of her lifeless body haunted her.

She pulled Gino away from her shoulder and swallowed. Then, for Darius's benefit, she offered the baby a wobbly smile. "Good night, Gino," she whispered hoarsely, hoping Darius didn't notice she was trembling.

Because she wanted to cry. She missed her baby. She yearned for the life she'd lost. Was that so bad? So hard to understand?

She stopped. No. That wasn't so bad. Or so difficult

to comprehend. In fact, the smart way to handle her situation with Gino might be to *tell* Darius about Layla and Burn. She didn't want his sympathy, but it was clear now that she would have difficulty getting adjusted to caring for a baby. Soon Darius would notice. It would be better to get the story out in the open and solicit his help than to have him see her stumble and question her ability to care for his little brother.

But tonight wasn't the night for that conversation. With his motives now in question, she knew she had to wait a bit, see what he was up to before she bared her soul. If he was trying to get the baby away from her, she didn't want to hand him over on a silver platter. She'd wait. See if he didn't tip his hand or, alternatively, convince her that his motives were good.

Once the baby was in bed, Darius caught Whitney's arm and turned her to the door. "It's late. I'll show you to your room then we can have dinner."

Exhausted, confused and aching for privacy, she woodenly said, "I'm too tired for dinner."

"Really?" As they stepped out of the nursery and into the hall, he closed the door behind them. "I instructed Mrs. Tucker to have the cook make chicken and dumplings."

She turned, startled. "Chicken and dumplings?"

He smiled. "Yes."

How could he know her favorite food?

"I called your dad while you were in your apartment packing for the weekend." he said, undoubtedly answering the expression of confusion on her face, and directed her to walk to a door a few feet down the hall. "I figured if you could be kind enough to let me have at least the weekend with the three of us at my home, I could be gentleman enough to assure you ate well."

She quickened her steps down the hall, wishing he hadn't done something so nice when she was so tired, but at least slightly more comfortable with him. "I'll have some for lunch tomorrow."

She wasn't sure why she expected him to argue, but her suspicions were allayed even more when he simply said, "Good enough."

He stopped at a door only a few feet from the nursery. "Your suite?"

Feeling a tad foolish, she retraced her steps and stopped in front of him. He smiled slightly. Sexily.

Strange schoolgirl nervousness swept through her, reminding her of the first time she'd ever stood by a door with a boy, knowing he was about to kiss her good-night. Awareness tingled through her bloodstream. Her breathing went shallow and her legs turned to rubber. It had been so long since she'd reacted to a man that she'd forgotten the wonderful discomfort.

But Darius caught the doorknob and twisted it, opening the door, revealing a soft green-and-yellow room to her. Beyond the sitting room furnished with a sage-colored sofa and chair, accented by a cherrywood armoire with matching cherrywood end tables, was an open door leading to a bedroom. She could see patches of a yellow-and-sage-green bedspread. See the closed yellow drapes.

Her heart skipped a beat. The suite was calm, soothing. So different from her cool aqua and brown bedroom in her condo that she felt as if she was entering another world.

"Is something wrong?"

She spun to face him. "No. It's—" Warm, inviting, comforting. She swallowed. "—Lovely. I'm sure I'll be fine here."

"Let me make sure everything really is ready before I leave you." He stepped inside the sitting room, casually looking from left to right as he made his way to the bedroom.

Confusion buffeted her as she followed him inside. From a cursory glance into the room, it was clear that while she and Darius had been in the nursery, Mrs. Tucker had sent the staff to ready the room. He had no reason to check their work, unless he was stalling. Or unless the staff was so new to him that he didn't trust them?

That had to be it.

When he stepped inside the room she'd be sleeping in, a fresh ripple of unease passed through Whitney. It felt odd, uncomfortable to have a man who'd clearly had a sexual reaction to her standing beside the bed she would sleep in. Her chest tightened. Stupid nervousness rose up in her again, reminding her that it had been a long time, maybe too long, since she'd been alone with a man.

But his gaze was casual, touching the queen-sized bed, the bare dresser, the pale sage club chairs arranged by the window for reading.

After he'd seen everything in the bedroom, his peek into the master bath caused his expression to turn puzzled, and she had no idea why. The vanity was white oak with a glass countertop. The floors were Calcutta marble slab. A separate custom-glass tile shower was utilitarian, but the oversize, extra-deep soaking tub almost caused her to sigh with joy. She could have a bath. A nice long bath to ease away the tension and grief of this long, long day. That tub would be her haven tonight.

He glanced at her then quickly away. His expression was so odd that she peeked into the bathroom again. Her gaze lit on the huge tub and suddenly her face flamed with color.

Of course, a woman saw the tub as a haven. A man saw it as a playground.

Their eyes met and the warm syrupy feeling she'd had when she'd first seen him returned. She reminded herself he was handsome. Reminded herself that being attracted to him made her normal. Even congratulated herself on finally, finally, being attracted to someone again after three long years of mourning her deceased husband. But she concluded with a reminder that she didn't want to get involved with anyone—ever. She'd never again give another person that much power over her life.

Plus, she had custody of Darius's baby brother. The little boy whose vote on his board of directors was hers. All this "attraction" could simply be Darius angling to get on her good side so she'd vote his way at directors' meetings.

Darius rubbed his hand across the back of his neck and pointed at her door. "Since you're tired and I have things to do, I'll be going."

"Oh." That surprised her. Wouldn't someone who intended to use their attraction stay? Flirt? Instead, it seemed he couldn't wait to get away.

Disappointment flooded her, which rattled her. She didn't want him to be attracted to her, but since he was, having him not act on the attraction was the second-best thing. She shouldn't be disappointed.

She forced a smile. "Okay. Great." She headed out of the bedroom too, walking with him through the sitting room.

At the door, he was even more nervous. When their gazes bumped, she knew why. They stood about a foot apart, at the door, saying goodbye. He looked down at her. She gazed up at him. Attraction shimmied between them. The urge to kiss goodbye was like a physical thing. So strong, yet so foreign, it paralyzed her.

For the first time since her husband's suicide, she wasn't thinking about her broken life. In fact, it wasn't even getting half of her attention. His nearness dominated her mind. She couldn't think beyond the fear that he'd kiss her.

Then she realized she didn't fear he'd kiss her. She *wanted* him to kiss her. What she felt was glorious, spine-tingling anticipation. Not fear.

Dear God.

Curiosity and confusion combined and rumbled through her. How could she possibly be so attracted to Darius Andreas that she couldn't ignore it? That she wanted more.

But he didn't kiss her. He didn't even try. Instead he grabbed the doorknob at the same time that she did and their fingers brushed. Though she jerked away, the mere touch sent a maelstrom through her. It had been three long years since she'd been married, and for months before that her husband hadn't been interested in her. She hadn't been touched by a man she found attractive in nearly four years. Sensation after sensation poured through her, almost embarrassing in their intensity.

Darius quickly headed out the door. "I'll see you at breakfast tomorrow."

The door closed behind him before she could even answer. Knowing it was coming, she quashed her confusing disappointment when it was just a wisp, before it had a chance to fully form, because it was ridiculous. Stupid.

She shook her head. After that little episode by the

door, she didn't have any doubt that Darius was attracted to her. After the way he ran, she also knew he didn't want to be.

And that was good.

Wasn't it?

She sighed with disgust at her foolish ambiguity. This weekend was not about an inappropriate attraction. It was about figuring out how they'd raise Gino together, about helping Gino grow accustomed to them as they got to know each other—

Worry gripped her. She couldn't tell Darius about losing her husband and child without making herself look like an empty, sad, still-grieving woman, who wasn't ready to help him with Gino. Though part of her knew that was true and she should be honest, the other part warned her to tread lightly with this man. He was rich, powerful. If she showed her weakness too soon, he could take her to court, seeking full custody, citing her incompetence. Then Gino would be raised by him. Alone. And she wouldn't be able to fulfill Missy's wish that she love her baby.

She couldn't let Missy's son be raised only by Darius. Hadn't he gotten her into his house and almost put her into a room on the other side of the mansion? He'd have poor Gino in boarding school before he was four.

The thought of sweet baby Gino in a boarding school shored up her defenses and she felt herself growing ready to protect him. She would fight to her last breath before she let him put that child in boarding school—ever. And that wouldn't be their only argument. She and Darius would have hundreds of fights over the course of raising his half-brother.

That thought caused her to fall to a chair in complete shock. In the confusion of the day, she hadn't carried this guardianship all the way through in her head. But it was suddenly abundantly clear that whether they wanted it or not, this child bound them forever.

They might as well be married.

Or divorced.

Good God.

What had Missy gotten her into?

Tonight was supposed to have been the night she did her laundry. Instead, here she was in the home of a virtual stranger, with a baby who made her relive the best and worst part of her life and a man she was so attracted to she sometimes couldn't breathe in his presence.

It would be a miracle if she survived the weekend, let alone a lifetime.

CHAPTER FOUR

WHEN THE BABY AWAKENED at about three, Darius bolted up in bed. For a few seconds he was disoriented, then he remembered he was in the hideous floral and lace master bedroom of the house in Montauk. By the time he remembered Gino was in the room next door, the little boy's crying had stopped.

He got out of bed anyway, grabbed one of the pairs of jeans he'd had his staff pack and messenger to the estate and jumped into them. Heading out of the closet, he opened another drawer and snagged a T-shirt.

In a few long strides, he was at the door that connected his room to the nursery. Mrs. Tucker sat in the rocker feeding Gino, who gulped noisily.

He tiptoed into the room, but Mrs. Tucker laughed. "No need to be quiet now. He's wide awake."

Leaning against the crib, Darius crossed his arms on his chest. "And by the looks of things he's starving too."

Mrs. Tucker snorted a laugh. "They always are."

"Always? You mean this isn't an isolated incident? He's going to be getting up at three every night?"

"Maybe not on the dot, but, yes, he'll be waking somebody up in the middle of the night every night until he learns to sleep for long stretches without needing a bottle."

Staring at the dark-haired, dark-eyed little baby, Darius said only, "Hum." Gino was so sturdy that he looked packed into the green one-piece pajama. His hair sort of stuck up in all directions, making him even cuter.

Gino stopped sucking and Mrs. Tucker set the bottle on the table by the rocker. She lifted him up and he suddenly belched loudly. Mrs. Tucker laughed. "Well, now that takes care of that."

She reached for a tissue in the box also on the table beside the rocker and wiped away white gunk from Gino's mouth.

Darius winced. "Am I ever going to get the hang of this?"

"Eventually." She caught his gaze and smiled. "And just when you do the rules will change."

Darius's face fell. "What rules?"

Settling Gino on her lap to rock him, Mrs. Tucker laughed again. "Not exactly rules, but the things you'll need to do. He's a baby now. In a few months he'll be a toddler. Then there are the terrible twos—"

"Terrible twos?"

"You don't want to know about that yet."

He did but he also didn't. Because right now, falling asleep in Mrs. Tucker's arms, Gino looked like an angel. Darius swallowed. Strong, protective feelings rose up in him, feelings more intense than anything he'd ever felt.

He pushed them down. He might intend to be a part of this kid's life, but these feelings were weird. They had to be wrong.

Mrs. Tucker rose from the rocker and settled the

sleeping baby in the crib. "Better go back to bed. Morning comes quickly when you have a baby."

Darius headed for the door. "Good night."

Heading for the opposite door, Mrs. Tucker whispered, "Good night."

In his room, he crawled back into bed. He didn't like the idea that Mrs. Tucker had to do double duty, as his estate manager and the temporary nanny, so he set his alarm for six, hoping he'd get up before the baby.

When it went off a few short hours later, he didn't balk or linger. He quickly pulled on the jeans from the night before and a fisherman-knit sweater and, paying no mind to his bare feet, raced to the nursery.

"Good morning."

Dressed in jeans and a pretty blue sweater that brought out the blue of her eyes, Whitney stood on the far side of the crib, watching Gino, who was still asleep.

"Do you want to learn how to feed him this morning?"

He took an instinctive step back. He and Whitney had shared a powerful few minutes at her bedroom door the night before, but she didn't appear to be any the worse for the wear. Like him, she seemed to want to ignore their chemistry.

And he did want to feed the baby. But before he could say that, Gino's eyes fluttered open. He yawned and stretched and then let out with a yelp.

"That's your cue," Whitney said with a laugh. "Change his diaper, while I get a bottle."

Whitney calmly walked to the small fridge in the room and retrieved a bottle, which she put in the warmer.

Not wanting to jeopardize the peace between them or have Gino wake poor, sleeping Mrs. Tucker, Darius carried Gino to the changing table and simply did the things he'd done the night before when he changed the baby's diaper and put him into a clean sleeper.

Gino wasn't really happy about the arrangement and he began to scream. Darius noticed that Whitney was preoccupied with staring at a bottle warmer that seemed not to need her attention. It confused him that she didn't react to Gino's crying, but he wanted to learn how to care for this kid. He also wanted Whitney's help. He wanted them to get along, be a team. He couldn't complain about the tasks she gave him to do. He had to do them.

When the light on the warmer went out, Darius was already on the rocker, holding screaming Gino over his shoulder.

Whitney winced. "Do you still want to feed him?"

In spite of Gino's screaming, Darius casually said, "Sure. But you're going to have to tell me what to do."

"Arrange him across your lap so that his head is supported by your forearm."

Peeling crying Gino off his shoulder wasn't an easy task. He stiffened his limbs and refused to settle on Darius's lap.

Whitney handed him the bottle. "Here. Take this. Let him see the bottle is coming and he'll calm down."

With both hands busy with the baby, Darius didn't have a clue how to take the bottle, but he secured Gino as best he could with one hand and managed to get the other free to take the bottle.

He would have criticized Whitney for not helping, except as soon as he had the bottle in his hand, Gino began to calm down.

"Now, just press the nipple to his lips and he'll do the rest."

To Darius's complete amazement, as soon as he nudged the nipple against Gino's lips he not only stopped crying, he also started suckling loudly.

He laughed with relief. "Wow. That was different."

"Babies *are* different. They can't talk so you have to understand their crying and sometimes watch their body language."

"There's a lot to learn."

As Gino greedily gobbled his milk, Whitney walked away from the rocker and paced the room. Darius watched her for a few seconds, confused. She was in the room, but detached. Not like someone who didn't want to help, but like...well, a stranger. That was when he realized she might not know Gino any more than he did.

"So why did Missy make you guardian?"

She faced him, her expression rye. "You mean aside from the fact that she wanted to make sure her baby had a female influence?"

He laughed. "Yes. Why you?"

"Missy and I were very close from university until the day she met your dad."

"Really?"

"Her dad had left her mom before Missy was six, and her mom was an alcoholic who went in and out of rehab. Because she had money enough to have a maid, somebody who by default took care of Missy, no one ever realized how alone Missy was. So after we met, she began to come to my parents' house with me on weekends and holidays." She shrugged. "We were like sisters."

"And then she met my dad and none of us saw either one of them again."

She laughed sadly. "Missy really loved your dad."

"And he loved Greece."

"And that's where they lived."

They fell silent again. When the baby was done eating, he showed Whitney the empty bottle. "Now what?"

"Now you have to burp him."

"Burp him?"

"You hold him like this," Whitney said as she lifted Gino from Darius's lap up to his shoulder. "And pat his back."

As she said the words, she demonstrated by patting the baby's back. He burped noisily.

Whitney smiled and set Gino on his lap again. "That feels better, doesn't it, little guy?"

This close, her smoky, sexy voice curled around Darius and he nearly squeezed his eyes shut. That voice would be trouble if he heard it for several weeks with her living under his roof. Even the way she'd refused dinner the night before had been breathy and sensual. And then there was that tub. And the look that had passed between them.

He bounced out of the chair. "So do we take him down to breakfast with us or what?"

"Is there a high chair by the table?"

He nodded. "Yes."

"Then I think we should keep him with us."

"Okay."

After all the time he'd already spent with the baby, Darius didn't feel uncomfortable holding Gino, but that in itself was odd. The powerful feeling he'd had the night before came back full force. Sacred, reverent, it squeezed his heart and made breathing difficult.

Since his father's death, everything had happened so fast that he hadn't had time to think anything through.

But suddenly everything seemed so real. He had a child to raise, responsibilities beyond money and food. This kid would take up his time, change his morning routine, break into his afternoons, want his evenings. The understanding of what he'd taken on was so overwhelming that he felt as though he needed a minute.

He held Gino out to Whitney. "Could you hold him while I grab some shoes?"

She hesitated and Darius nearly groaned. The last thing he wanted to do was give her the impression he didn't want the task of caring for the baby. He wanted her to see his commitment.

"You know what? Never mind. I'll take him into my bedroom with me."

To his surprise, Whitney smiled. "And what will you do with him while you're putting on your shoes?"

He sucked in a breath. "Good question."

She took Gino from him. "Go get your shoes."

Relief poured through him. He raced into his bedroom, slid into socks and shoes and was back in the nursery in less than two minutes.

Noting that Gino was in the playpen, he frowned. "Ready for breakfast?"

"Yes." She reached down and lifted Gino out of the playpen, then handed him to Darius casually, smoothly, but as he took the little boy, she wouldn't look at him.

He hadn't expected her to put Gino in the playpen or to immediately pass him back when he returned from getting his shoes. But her not being able to look at him was actually more perplexing.

The night before, he'd walked away from the opportunity to kiss her without any hesitation, even though she was throwing off you-can-kiss-me signals. He'd hoped that walking away would show her that even though he was attracted to her, he didn't intend to follow through. Yet she still behaved in an overly cautious manner around him.

She strode to the door as if nothing were amiss and held it open while he came through with the baby. Following her down the steps, he stared at her stiff back. He'd never met a woman who was so hot one minute and so cold the next. It was almost as if she could turn her emotions off.

Which, in some ways, was good. They didn't want to be attracted to each other. It didn't work for either of them. And he was turning off his feelings for her every bit as much.

So why did it bother him?

In the breakfast room, which was actually one of several sunrooms along the east wall of the house, she took the tray off the high chair and instructed Darius to set the baby on the seat.

"But don't let go," she said, rummaging along the edges of the seat until she found what looked like seatbelts. "We have to buckle him in."

"Got it," Darius said, eager to learn. Especially when she didn't even seem to realize she was giving him lessons.

Another good reason to persuade her to live here with him permanently, not just for a few weeks.

Cook entered the sunroom with coffee and asked what each would like to eat. Darius ordered pancakes. Whitney chose a bagel and cream cheese.

"And should I make the baby's cereal?"

Darius glanced over at Whitney, who winced. "Wow. It's been so long since I was around a baby that I forgot that some kids start eating cereal around six months or so."

Cook proudly said, "He's been eating cereal for a few weeks now."

"Then get us the cereal." She faced Darius. "Sorry about that."

"Hey, I didn't even know babies ate cereal."

Cook walked in with a small bowl and a tiny baby spoon. As if recognizing his bowl, the baby slapped his hands on the tray. Cook handed the bowl and spoon to Darius who set them on the table then edged his seat closer to the high chair.

He didn't even consider opting out of learning how to feed Gino. He wanted to know everything. "So you're ready for this, huh?"

Gino screeched with joy.

Whitney said, "Just put a little bit of cereal on the spoon and very easily guide it to his mouth."

Darius did as instructed. Gino greedily took the bit of cereal and smacked his lips. The second bite was a little messier, but Darius just used common sense about getting the spoon and the cereal into Gino's mouth. After a few spoonfuls, when Gino tried to blow bubbles with it instead of eating it, Darius knew he wasn't hungry anymore.

"If you're playing in it rather than eating, I'm guessing you're done."

As he set the spoon down, Mrs. Tucker walked in. "Cook didn't want to start your breakfast until you were free to eat it. So, I thought I'd take Gino upstairs and play with him a bit. I'll walk through the kitchen to let Cook know she can make your breakfast now."

Darius rose and helped her get the baby out of the high chair. "Sounds good."

When she left, the little room fell silent.

Finally, Whitney said, "It's beautiful here."

Darius looked out at the steel-gray ocean, the deceptively blue sky. Though the day seemed calm, he knew winds off the sea would make it freezing cold out there. "Yes. I'd forgotten."

"Did you come here often?"

"After I turned eighteen I did."

"Why do I get the feeling you were forced?"

Her perceptiveness made him wince. "Because I was. My father gave me access to a five-million-dollar trust fund when I turned eighteen. He told me it was mine but he wanted me to go to college and work for Andreas Holdings. He hadn't as much as visited after he left my mom, then suddenly he was in my life, ordering me around. Our time here wasn't always pleasant."

She toyed with a salt shaker. "I liked your dad."

He laughed as Cook brought in his pancakes and Whitney's bagel. When she was gone, he reached for the maple syrup and said, "Most people who didn't have my dad for a lover or a parent did like him."

"Yes, I suppose that's probably true."

Surprised by her answer, he set the maple syrup on the table. "I thought for sure you'd sing his praises."

She snorted a laugh. "I know what it's like to deal with a person who has a public personality and a private one. I had a husband everybody loved."

His brows rose. So she'd been married? He hadn't even considered the possibility since she'd kept the last name Ross. But having been married, maybe even having been hurt by a divorce, might explain why she was so nervous around him.

Better than that, though, she'd opened the door for him to question her about her past. He'd been so focused on the baby that he hadn't really given much thought to the woman who shared custody beyond asking why Missy had chosen her.

Pretending great interest in his coffee, he said, "Everybody loved your husband but you?"

"Oh, I loved him. He loved himself too." She reached for the cream. "So what are your plans for the day?"

He recognized a change of subject when he heard it and realized that though she'd opened the door to talk about her past, she hadn't done it deliberately. He was curious about her, but he also knew asking about a husband she no longer had was a tad intrusive. It had no bearing on their situation and was none of his business. And if he wanted to convince her he was harmless, it would be wise to follow her lead and let the subject change.

"Actually, I want to spend as much time with the baby as I can."

She set her bagel on her plate and studied him. Her narrowed eyes were both suspicious and skeptical. "So, you weren't kidding. You really want to be a good dad?"

"I want to be a *great* dad." The words rolled through him. Now that he'd spent time with Gino, they meant so much more than they had even the day before. Now, he knew the cost. He was taking responsibility for another person.

It didn't confuse him as it had the night before or overwhelm him the way it had in the nursery that morning, but he was smart enough that it still sort of scared him. Especially since he'd vowed that he wouldn't be a part-time, no-show dad the way his father had been. Deep down inside, he had to admit he wasn't entirely sure he could do that. The only role model he'd had was a poor one.

Still, that wasn't something he could confide to Whitney. Technically, she was still a stranger. So, taking his cue from her when the conversation turned to something she hadn't wanted to tell him, he also changed the subject.

"What are *your* plans for the day?"

"I'm working on a class action case with my dad. Depositions are in. He's read them. I haven't." She grimaced. "That's never happened before."

Knowing he could get Mrs. Tucker to help him with Gino that morning and eager to make Montauk a comfortable home to Whitney, he turned his attention to his pancakes. "There are three offices in this house. You can have your choice. And you can spend the whole day if you need it. Mrs. Tucker and I will take care of Gino."

Relief saturated her voice. "Thanks."

She worked all day, stopping only to have lunch around two, long after Darius and Gino had eaten so she didn't have to interact with either one of them. But she couldn't get out of dinner. She arrived in the formal dining room at seven, dressed as she had been all day in jeans and a bulky sweater.

Darius, who was already seated at the head of the table, rose.

He still wore the fisherman-knit sweater and jeans he'd put on in the morning. Holding out the chair at the place beside his, he explained, "I assumed you'd be too busy to change."

She sat. "Yes. Thank you."

"My father insisted everything be formal. I'm more accommodating." He shook out his napkin. "I hope you like Italian."

"Actually, I love most foods." She risked a glance at him and fought a quiver of attraction. That morning she'd noticed that he looked very good in the casual clothes, but tonight he hadn't shaved. The scruffy stubble on his chin and cheeks made him sexy in a disreputable, sinful way. The man was simply too handsome for his own good and she was vulnerable. She hadn't interacted with a man like this—single and attractive—since she'd met her husband. She was out of practice, attracted and needy. A deadly combination when three feet away from a gorgeous man. Especially when she didn't want to get involved with another man.

But she couldn't be a total grouch or, worse, an unappreciative guest. "You don't have to worry when it comes to me and food. I'd eat constantly if I didn't have work to keep me busy."

He laughed. Pinpricks of delight raced up her spine. It had been so long since she'd made a man laugh in simple conversation that she'd forgotten the joy of it.

"I don't believe it." His gaze rippled down the lines of her body and lingered on her breasts. "Your figure's too nice."

Good Lord! He was flirting with her!

The desire to flirt back shoved at her. It rattled through the recesses of her brain like a prisoner banging the bars of his cell, longing for release. Especially with the joy of having just made him laugh taunting her, reminding her of what it felt like to be normal.

But it had been so long since she'd done anything even remotely like flirt, and he was absolutely the wrong guy to experiment with—

Or was he? They both needed each other too much professionally to cross any lines. He'd walked away from the perfect opportunity to kiss her the night before, proving that he might be attracted to her, but he didn't intend to follow through. And she was too frightened of relationships to let anything she attempted go any further than flirting. He might actually be the perfect person to practice on.

She smiled, trying not to look obvious, trying not to look self-conscious, trying desperately to look simply like a single woman flirting with a single man. "I'll bet you say that to all the girls."

He laughed again. "Only the really pretty ones."

Joy exploded inside her. She'd done it! Or maybe *they* were doing it. Flirting. Getting her back into the real world. What was a simple conversation for him was turning into a monumental event for her. But she hoped to God he didn't realize that.

A younger woman served dinner, standing off to the side to attend to their every need, precluding any possibility that the conversation could become intimate. The flirting stopped, but the discussion stayed casual, neutral and she relaxed totally.

At the end of the meal, Darius rose. "How about a game of pool?"

"Pool?"

"You know balls, sticks, table with green felt?"

She laughed then marveled that she had. Maybe her dad was right. Maybe it was time. She wanted so badly to be normal again. Real. Honest. Just herself. And Darius seemed to have the power to help her take the steps.

Still, no good would come of pushing things.

"I don't think so, I'm—"

"Tired? Really, Ms. Ross? I'm about to suggest you take some vitamins."

She laughed again, feeling light, young, incredibly

carefree. Memories of her other life, her sadness, nudged at her, but she shoved them back. She needed this. She *wanted* this.

He directed her to the door on the right. "Come on. This house is filled with things to entertain us. It would be a shame not to take advantage. Particularly since we're going to be spending lots of time together over the next eighteen years. We should get to know each other."

Fear and elation collided, creating goose bumps on her upper arms. Getting to know each other didn't have to be something to be afraid of or even something sexual. He wanted the same thing she did. Nothing sinister. Nothing difficult. Just a simple evening spending time together. To get to know each other. Because they had joint custody of a child.

Inclining her head in acceptance, she ignored the fear and tamped down the elation and reminded herself that spending time getting to know each other didn't have to be a big deal. She didn't have to tell him about her family that night. She could wait for a more suitable time. Tonight, he was only asking for a game of pool.

"All right."

The room with the pool table was a huge den. Cherrywood walls and leather furniture gave the space a totally masculine feel.

"Your dad's room, I assume," she said, walking to a wall lined with sticks, as Darius gathered and racked the balls.

"Got it in one." He ambled over to choose a stick. "But before you begin feeling sorry for Missy, take a look around. They might have lived in Greece, but they spent time here. Her influence is all over the place."

"Really?"

"She's redone at least three rooms." He winced. "Including the master bedroom."

"You don't like her taste?"

"If you're asking if I like floral bedspreads and lacy curtains, then no."

She laughed, glad she'd agreed to spend some time with him. Over the next half hour they played several games of pool and he handily beat her.

"You're a ringer."

"Ringers make you believe they're terrible so they can persuade you to bet them, and then they take your money. I haven't done that." He shrugged. "We're just having a nice friendly few games."

"With me getting my butt beaten."

He racked the balls and broke, scattering the colorful orbs across the table with a clack and clatter. In an uncharacteristic turn of events, none of them fell into a pocket.

"Hey! Looks like I get a turn this time."

She walked around the table, sizing up potential shots. When she found one she liked, she angled her stick across the table, levering her body in sync with the stick.

"No. No. You'll never make the shot that way." He strode around the table to her. "Let me help you." He lowered himself over her, his one hand covering hers on the stick, his other circling around her so he could guide her hand on the handle.

Her nerve endings exploded at the contact. Rivers of molten need rode her blood. And she remembered why they had to be careful. Even about becoming friends. Their attraction was like nitroglycerin. One bump and they could go up in flames.

As if realizing how close he'd put them, he turned

his head and caught her gaze. Their faces were only millimeters apart. His warm breath fanned her face. Longing burst inside her. Her fingers itched to touch the stubble on his cheeks and cruise his throat. Just a brush. Just a touch to feel the warmth of another's skin. To feel the pulse of another heartbeat, to know that *she* was alive.

His hands shifted from the stick to her shoulders and he lifted her from the awkward position of leaning across the table. For a few seconds, they stood there, barely a foot apart. She watched myriad emotions play across his face, as if he were arguing with himself about whether he should kiss her. It crossed her mind to say something. It crossed her mind to run. This attraction they felt was nothing but wrong, but curiosity and need warred with common sense. This entire night had been an experiment of sorts for her. A return to life. To people. She didn't want to stop. She almost couldn't stop. She needed him to kiss her as much as she wanted it.

Slowly his head descended, as if he were giving her plenty of time to step back. She considered it, but stayed frozen, mesmerized, hoping, and in seconds his mouth met hers.

A tsunami of need flooded her, a yearning so strong she shook from it. His hands smoothed from her shoulders, down her back to her hips and nudged her closer. The longing to be held, to be loved, to be touched percolated through her. He satisfied it with another nudge that brought her fully against him. Her breasts nestled against his chest, pebbling her nipples. His mouth moved over hers simply, smoothly, and temptation turned into action as her mouth instinctively opened under his and he deepened the kiss.

Desire thundered through her. Warm, wet need. Her

limbs weakened. Her breath hitched. And her brain clicked on again, like a light switch being flipped in a dark, dangerous room.

This is wrong! This is wrong! This is wrong!

The words were a litany in her brain. Not only was she not ready for anything beyond a chaste, experimental kiss, but the night before she'd sensed there was something wrong in his behavior. Something he wanted from her. Or maybe that he was trying to trick her. She shouldn't be kissing him, clouding the issues.

The sound of someone clearing her throat entered the room and Whitney jumped back like a guilty teenager.

Joni Johnson, the girl who had served dinner, stood by the door. "I'm sorry to disturb you, Mr. Andreas, but Mrs. Tucker asked me to get you. The baby is sick."

CHAPTER FIVE

DARIUS AND WHITNEY raced behind Joni, who led them up the back steps. When they reached the nursery, Darius pushed ahead, not caring about decorum, and ran into the room.

Gino lay in the crib, crying. Darius reached down and scooped the little boy into his arms. "Hey, little guy. What's up?"

"I've already called the pediatrician," Mrs. Tucker said, wringing her hands. "He said he'd be here as soon as he can."

Gino snuggled against Darius and cried harder.

"I couldn't get him to drink his evening bottle and now he won't stop crying." Mrs. Tucker's voice was strained and anxious. "I'm not a nanny and my only child is over thirty. It's been so long since I cared for a baby that I have no idea what's wrong."

Whitney peered at Gino over Darius's shoulder. "Can I hold him?"

Darius caught her gaze and the instant he did, he regretted it. Thoughts of their kiss devoured his mind and desire arched between them. He couldn't believe he'd broken the promise he'd made to himself not to kiss her, but he had. Part of him wasn't sorry. They had chemistry that just wouldn't quit and if they were in a position to pursue it they'd probably set his bedroom on fire. He couldn't resist a taste.

But they weren't in a position to pursue it, and there would be consequences. Especially for this little boy if he didn't handle the situation correctly.

He swallowed and handed Gino to her. "Here."

After laying the baby across her arm, she studied his face, pressed her hand to his forehead, looked into his mouth. "I think he's getting a tooth."

Furious that she could be so flippant, Darius pinned her with a hard stare. "I think we should let the pediatrician decide."

"Oh, of course!" she said, handing the baby back to him. "I'm just saying that there's no reason for us to panic while we wait for the doctor to arrive."

Mrs. Tucker visibly relaxed. "I should have thought of that. But it's just been so long since I've had kids." She sank into the rocker. "If I may make a suggestion, sir, I think we should get a nanny here as soon as possible." She sighed heavily, as if having trouble getting her breathing to regulate, and Darius realized just how worried poor Mrs. Tucker had been.

But his eyes narrowed in on Whitney, the woman he shared custody with, and he suddenly wondered how she knew so much about babies. She'd said she'd been married, but she hadn't mentioned children. If she'd had them and her husband had gotten custody, there had to be a reason for that. If there was something god-awful in her past that made her husband a better candidate to have her children than she was, he wanted to know what it was.

"I'll just go back to the kitchen, then," Mrs. Tucker announced, rising from the rocker and heading for the door.

"Sure," Darius said. "We'll be fine." Plus, he wanted some time alone with Whitney. Since the day they'd met at her dad's office, he'd been so preoccupied with getting along with her that he'd let all the inconsistencies in her life slide. That ended here. That ended now.

Darius sat on the rocker. Gino snuggled against him, sniffling, but relaxing against his sweater as if seeking comfort. His heart warmed with emotion. He was falling in love with this kid. In only two days, the little boy was getting to him.

But that was all the more reason to make sure he knew Gino's "other" guardian. His dad might have approved Whitney, but his dad hadn't planned on dying. He might have simply decided to placate Missy and agreed to appoint Whitney as shared custodian. Given that she was the daughter of his friend and the friend of Gino's mom, he might not have checked into her past the way he should have.

"So, are you going to tell me how you know so much about babies?"

She walked away from him toward the window, but didn't answer his question.

"I can have you investigated, you know. Or maybe even guess. A woman who was married but lost custody of her children to her husband probably has a skeleton in her closet."

She sucked in a breath, refusing to look at him. Darius squeezed his eyes shut. Damn it! If he hadn't needed her help so much, he would have realized something was off with her before this. He wouldn't have silenced his instincts, and he would have confronted her.

"You know what? Don't tell me. Go back to your room and pack. Because I'm going to contest that damned will. I'm getting you away from my baby."

"Don't." She turned, her eyes filled with tortured pain. He could easily guess why.

"Why not? Don't want a courtroom full of people to hear why you shouldn't be around a child? Why you don't have your own?"

She swallowed. "It's not what you think."

"You expect me to believe that?"

Whitney's limbs began to shiver, then her entire body began to shake. She had absolutely no doubt in her mind that he intended to check in to her past. When he did, he'd discover she'd had a child who had died. She'd wanted to tell him, but she'd wanted it to be on her terms, so she didn't look incompetent or grief-stricken. But it appeared *this* was the time.

She opened her mouth, debating what she would say, how she would say it, but the only thing that came out was, "I had a daughter."

Darius said nothing, only snuggled his baby brother closer as if protecting him from her, and her heart shattered. "I would never do anything to hurt Gino."

"Really?"

"My *husband* hurt my daughter." Her shaking intensified. Tears filled her eyes. "My husband *killed* my daughter."

Darius stopped rocking.

"He intended to kill himself." Her tears spilled over her lower lids, trailed down her cheeks. Memories of that day and all the days after it when she'd wondered, berated herself, lived in an ocean of guilt, filled her brain, stopped her tongue, clogged her throat with tears.

She swallowed hard. Once. Twice. Three times before she could speak.

"No one knows if he'd forgotten he had the baby in the car seat when he realized he could simply sit in the running car in the garage to eventually kill himself." Her lungs expanded to painful proportions. Sobs screamed to erupt from her chest, but she held on.

"His company had failed and though money wasn't an issue, his pride suffered." She turned, faced Darius, opened her hands in supplication. "It was his third company. He'd bragged that number three would be the charm. But it wasn't. His father was angry with him for wasting his time. His brothers were making names for themselves on Wall Street and Burn did nothing but fail." A sob escaped. "He was the family embarrassment."

Darius swallowed, visibly shaken by what she had told him. "I'm sorry."

Her sob turned to muffled weeping. "Everyone's sorry."

He rose from the rocker. "Maybe no one knows what else to say?"

She turned away as her crying took her. There was a place she went, a soft, comfortable place, where emotion took control of her body. Problems weren't solved. Trouble didn't disappear, but tension eased. Tears and sobs provided a welcome release not just for the pain, but also for her tight muscles and limbs. And she wanted to go there now. She wanted to go to her own room, sink onto the bed and let the crying soothe her.

"You weren't at fault, you know."

She spun to face him as sadness morphed into anger. "Really? I couldn't have noticed my slightly depressed husband tumbling into full-fledged mental illness? There were no signs? You're sure?"

"No, but—"

"You wouldn't accept my diagnosis of Gino. You

insisted on waiting for the pediatrician. So now I'm telling you to stop diagnosing me. Back off."

The door opened and Mrs. Tucker entered with a short, gray-haired man behind her. "Dr. Sullivan," she announced as she stepped aside and let the man shuffle over to Gino.

"Hey, Gino," he crooned, taking the baby from Darius's arms. Obviously familiar with the little boy, he hugged him before he said, "I hear somebody might be getting a tooth."

He laid the little boy on the changing table and began to examine him.

Silently, Whitney slipped behind the group huddled around the baby and out the door.

Darius watched her go, cursing himself for pushing her and cursing her husband.

She'd had a daughter. A little girl. A baby who was probably the light of her life. He squeezed his eyes shut in misery. He'd brought all that back for her, made her relive the worst days of her life.

The doctor examined Gino and told Darius and Mrs. Tucker there was very little that could be done for a baby getting a tooth. He gave them some gel to numb his gums and advised them to get a teething ring.

Luckily, Gino fell asleep almost immediately after the doctor left, but Darius stayed by his crib, angry with himself for forcing Whitney to talk, but more concerned about the baby.

Finally, around midnight, he went to bed. But what seemed like only two minutes later, Darius heard the sounds of the baby waking and he popped up in bed. Glancing at his clock, he saw it was only just after two and groaned.

Still, not wanting Mrs. Tucker to have to deal with a cranky baby alone, he jumped into jeans and a sweatshirt and raced into the nursery. As he entered through the side door, Whitney bolted into the room from the main door, wearing a fluffy pink robe over white pajamas.

Their eyes met across the nursery and everything inside him stilled. He'd forced her to relive the worst days of her life the night before, but at least with that out in the open she had to know he didn't doubt her anymore. He wouldn't be making good on his threat to contest guardianship.

Gino screamed again, reminding him that if he didn't pick him up and tend to him, he'd wake Mrs. Tucker. Beating Whitney to the crib, he lifted the little boy out and hugged him, patting his back to soothe him.

Whitney stood a few steps back. Concern brought her close enough to see what was going on, but not so close that she was actually part of it.

Things would have probably been a bit stilted and awkward between them as they worked through the aftermath of that conversation and her memories, but ultimately they would have been okay—if he hadn't also kissed her.

He couldn't believe he'd done that, but the temptation had been so strong he couldn't resist. He'd thought that one kiss might take the edge off. Instead, the taste of her stayed on his lips all night.

Turning away, she said, "I'll warm a bottle."

She took a bottle from the small refrigerator, set it in the warmer and waited, all with her back to him.

Guilt suffused him. He should have been kinder with her, gentler.

Whitney walked over with the warm bottle, motioning for Darius to sit in the rocker. "Once he drinks this, we'll put the gel on his gums again so he can fall back to sleep."

Panic rose in him. He might have fed Gino before, but he really didn't trust himself to feed the baby when his mouth was sore.

Obviously seeing his hesitancy, Whitney said, "Arrange Gino across your lap, but lift his head a little higher than you normally do."

In three or four movements, Darius had the little boy across his lap and halfway between sitting and lying on his arm.

"Now, put the nipple to his lips and he'll do the rest. His hunger will supersede the pain in his mouth."

Darius did as instructed and Gino latched onto the nipple as if he was starving.

Whitney stepped away. "I understand how his being sick would make you nervous."

Of course she did. She'd had a daughter. He'd brought up those memories for her. In the silence of the nursery where he'd confronted her, the most natural thing to do right now would be to apologize for pushing her to tell him about her daughter.

So he did. "I'm sorry."

She ambled to the side window. Though it was the middle of the night and she probably couldn't see anything, she stared out into the darkness. "For not knowing how to care for Gino?"

"For pushing you into talking before the pediatrician got here."

Her eyes never left the window. "You had no idea. You were worried about Gino. I accept that."

Just as he'd suspected, his mistake was something she'd probably faced before. She wouldn't hold a grudge or make something out of it he hadn't intended. Things might still be awkward for awhile, but ultimately they'd be okay.

The baby nudged the nipple out of his mouth and Darius pulled the bottle away. He sat him up a bit then waited a few seconds before he offered it again. Gino latched onto the nipple, and the room became eerily silent. This time he couldn't blame it on the repercussions of his pushing her into talking about her baby. There was a second elephant in the room and he had to get rid of it, too.

With a glance at Gino to make sure he was still suckling, he said, "I'm also sorry I kissed you. It won't happen again."

She stared out the window, saying nothing, and he wanted to groan at his stupidity. Kissing her had been a ridiculous, in-the-moment impulse that he should have thought through. Instead, he'd let his hormones rule him.

But rather than tell him to go to hell, or that he was an immature ass, she quietly said, "How do you know it won't happen again?"

He had no option but the truth. "Because it's not a good idea for either of us. We have to spend the next eighteen years dealing with each other as we raise this baby. If we started a relationship that fizzled, one of us would end up angry or hurt and that's not good for Gino."

Whitney stared outside though she didn't actually see anything. It was the second or third time he'd given Gino preference in a conversation. It had surprised her the morning before when he'd said he wanted to be a great dad. But after the way he'd behaved while waiting for the pediatrician—protective, strong—she knew he wasn't faking it, wasn't saying these things to make himself look good or get her into his corner. He intended to be a good father to his half-brother.

She peeked over at him. He wore jeans and a baggy gray sweatshirt and looked absolutely gorgeous in a casual, athletic way. His short hair wasn't exactly mussed; it simply wasn't combed as it usually was for a day of work, and wisps fell to his forehead boyishly. His typically stern face was relaxed. Neither a frown nor a smile graced his mouth.

She'd kissed that mouth.

He'd held her against him.

She'd faintly felt his heart beating beneath the fisherman's sweater.

She could have tumbled over the edge the night before, could have done something really out of character, really wrong. But fate had stopped them. He'd said he didn't want it to happen again, and she believed him. Not just because his first priority was Gino, but because of the conversation afterward. He now knew she came with baggage. She might as well have dressed in dynamite. There'd be no way a man who could have any woman he wanted would go near a woman with her kind of past.

Which was good.

Sad, because she'd finally begun to relax around someone; but good because she'd panicked the night before. She hadn't known how to stop. She'd gotten in over her head. If Joni hadn't come in, she could have messed up royally.

Her priority was to uphold Missy's wishes and to do that she had to be objective. Not get involved with her co-guardian. She also wasn't ready for a relationship. Burn had hurt her. No, Burn had cost her her ability to trust. As nice as Darius Andreas seemed to be, as good as he clearly wanted to be with Gino, an intimate relationship was a totally different thing. God only knew *if* he had the ability to have one. And God only knew *when* she'd be ready to have one.

Glancing at Gino's bottle, she saw it was empty, and walked over to the rocker. "Here," she said, easing the bottle out of Gino's mouth and Darius's hold. "You have to burp him now."

Darius sat perfectly still. Didn't let her perfume affect him. Wouldn't let himself wonder if her skin was as soft as it looked. Wouldn't let his mind wander back to the kiss the night before. He'd made a promise of sorts to her that she would be safe in his company, and he intended to keep it.

"Lift him to your shoulder the way I showed you yesterday morning."

He did as she instructed, but kept his gaze averted. They really were like gasoline and a match when they got too close, and the best way to handle it would be to keep their distance. But if he wanted her to teach him about the baby, that wasn't possible. His only alternative was simply to control himself.

"Now, pat his back."

He brought his hand to the baby's small back and lightly patted twice. Gino burped.

Whitney stepped away. "He's a good eater and a good burper. That's usually a sign of a very healthy child. He'll probably have this tooth in before we know it."

Relief washed through him and he rose. But once he was standing, he realized had no idea what he was supposed to do.

"Does he go back to bed now?"

Whitney laughed softly. "Let's hope. Otherwise, it's going to be a long night. First let's put some of the gel on his gums."

Darius winced. "Sorry, I forgot."

"You're new and there's a lot to remember." She found the gel and gently applied some to the baby's gums. He spat and fussed, but she persevered.

As she stepped away, Darius asked, "Should I lay him in the crib?"

"Actually, the best thing to do would be for you to stay on the rocker. Position him the same way you had him while you fed him, so that he's not lying flat but is upright enough that he can breathe more easily, and just rock him until he falls asleep."

Darius sat and positioned Gino on his lap. "Hey, little guy."

As he set the rocker in motion, Whitney leaned against the crib. "Don't talk too much or he'll never go back to sleep."

"What should I do?"

"Just keep rocking him." She smiled. "You could also sing him a lullaby."

Darius winced. "Yeah. Not in this lifetime."

She laughed. "Eventually, you'll sing. Everybody does."

"Not me."

"Just wait. The day will come when you're desperate and you'll sing."

Chuckling softly, Darius shook his head.

In a surprising move, Whitney pushed off the crib and stooped down in front of him. He noticed that she didn't touch either him or Gino, but she started to sing.

"Hush little baby, don't say a word, Papa's going to buy you a mocking bird…"

Her voice was soft, lyrical. Gino blinked his heavy eyelids and rolled his head to the side so he could look at her.

"And if that mocking bird don't sing, Papa's gonna buy you a diamond ring. And if that diamond ring turns brass, Papa's going to buy you a looking glass. If that looking glass gets broke, Papa's going to buy you a billy goat."

As if by magic, Gino's eyelids drooped. Whitney's voice softened even more, and she slowed the song, as if lulling him to sleep.

"If that billy goat won't pull, Papa's going to buy you a cart and bull. If that cart and bull turn over, Papa's going to buy you a dog named Rover." Her voice softened again, the words she sang slowed to a hypnotic pace. Gino's eyelids drooped until eventually they stayed shut.

Her song finished, Whitney rose. She nodded at Gino. "He's asleep."

Mesmerized by the sweet expression on her face and the casual way she'd lowered her voice and softened the song to lull Gino to sleep, Darius only stared at her. "He is?"

"He is." She headed for the door. "Good night."

"Good night."

Darius rose and put Gino in the crib. Sadness seeped into his soul. He'd bet she'd been the perfect mother.

Sunday morning, when Darius heard Gino cry, he popped up in bed again. He jumped into the same jeans and sweatshirt he'd worn the night before and raced into the nursery just as Mrs. Tucker finished changing the baby.

"He's feeling a lot better this morning." She caught

Darius's gaze. "I'm sorry I didn't hear him wake up last night."

"That's okay. Whitney and I took care of him."

Before Mrs. Tucker could answer, Whitney entered the room. Their eyes met across the nursery and all he could think of was her singing to Gino the night before. The sweet motherly affection he'd heard in her voice. The easy way she'd used the song to lull Gino to sleep. And he suddenly understood why Missy had chosen her for her baby's guardian. Whitney was born to be a mom. She really would be Gino's mom. Not a substitute, not a guardian, but a real mom.

Just as he intended to be a real dad.

He could picture them two or three or even six years from now, as the perfect parents. He could see them standing with their arms around each other's waists, waving to Gino who rode his bike along the big circular driveway in front of the house.

He shook his head to dislodge that image. It was one thing to parent a child together. But they didn't need to have their arms around each other's waists. They had to be objective. They couldn't have a relationship. He had a conglomerate to run. A life that kept him so busy he'd barely have time to squeeze this baby in. But he would. Gino would become his family. And after that there would be no time left for anyone else. Which made him the absolute worst choice of men for Whitney to get involved with. Now that he knew her past, he also knew she needed someone to love her, to understand her, and he simply had too much on his plate already. He would ignore signs that she needed to talk, or signs that she was feeling sad, or signs that she simply needed to be held. And he would hurt her.

She broke eye contact and strolled a little closer to the baby. "Good morning."

"Good morning," Mrs. Tucker chirped. "Here's the bottle," she said, offering both the baby and the bottle to Whitney.

Darius raced over, understanding now why she hesitated. Being Gino's guardian was probably a living hell for her, yet she'd accepted the job and planned to do it. "I'll take him."

Mrs. Tucker put Gino in his arms and glanced at her watch. "If you don't mind, I need to go now. Two of the maids are new and we don't really have a schedule yet." She smiled like the happy employee that she was, causing Darius to notice just how weary, how sad Whitney was in contrast. "If you need me, I can be free again after breakfast."

With the baby and the bottle in Darius's hands, Mrs. Tucker turned away and walked out of the nursery.

He sat on the rocker and gave Gino the nipple as he had the other times he had fed him. Gino latched on greedily and sucked down the milk. Whitney walked around the nursery, glancing at toys and knickknacks scattered on the shelves. She didn't say anything and, try as he might, Darius couldn't think of anything to say either.

When Gino was finished with his breakfast, Darius burped him like a pro then rose from the rocker. "So what do we do now? Put him back to bed?"

Whitney smiled slightly. "I'm guessing he just woke up before we walked in. So he should spend some time downstairs."

Panic fluttered through him. "Downstairs? With his gums just waiting to put him in severe pain again?"

"Of course. He still needs his cereal and I'm guessing

he'll want to play a bit. In fact it's good to entertain him and make him happy for as long as we can."

Panic was replaced by fear. Yes, he'd rocked this kid, fed this kid, even changed a diaper—much to his horror—but he wasn't capable enough to be alone with a potentially sick baby all morning.

"Ready?"

He peeked over at Whitney. "You're coming with us?"

"Sure."

That's when he saw it. The sadness that hummed through everything she did was sometimes eclipsed by very normal behavior, but it was still there.

And everything she did for Gino undoubtedly reminded her of the baby she'd lost.

CHAPTER SIX

DARIUS WAITED UNTIL they were seated at the table in the sunroom for lunch, while Gino was napping, before he broached the subject they'd come to Montauk to discuss—how they'd share custody of Gino. The wall of windows brought in the broad expanse of the ocean, sloshing sloppily, with no rhyme or reason or organization, against the shore. The scent of warm clam chowder wafted around them comfortingly, but Darius felt more like the ocean. Disjointed. Uneven. Unable to get his bearings.

Not only did he feel uncomfortable about pushing her to tell him about her family, but he also felt awful for her loss. Technically, he and Whitney would be connected for the next eighteen or so years of their lives, maybe longer. Gino would love her as a mother, and, he hoped, love him as a father. But their lives were so different he wasn't really sure it was possible for them to find common ground.

She'd been married, been a mom and now lived in a loft in Soho and worked at a law firm. He'd spent his entire adult life running from marriage and being groomed to manage a huge conglomerate. He also had an apartment in the city, but Gino had a nursery at this estate, so Darius genuinely believed it was better for him to get rid of his apartment and live here. If Whitney really wanted to make the commitment to Gino that Darius believed she should make, then she should want to give up her loft and live here too.

The three of them living together was the only way to ensure that Gino saw both of his guardians and also lived something of a normal life. Still, he couldn't hit her with that yet—especially not after the way he'd pushed her the night before. The way he had this figured, the best thing to do would be try to get her to agree to stay another week, or maybe two weeks, and then continue to tack on a week or two at a time until she realized, as he had, that Montauk was Gino's home.

Because the following day was Monday, the end of the weekend, there was no time left for delay. He had to persuade her to stay an entire week or maybe two and he had to do it now.

He casually picked up his napkin. "I'm glad we decided to spend the weekend here, getting to know the baby."

She met his gaze, her pretty blue eyes cautious.

"It was good for him to be in a settled environment—especially since this is his home, or had been when his parents came to New York."

She didn't even hesitate. "Absolutely."

"So you wouldn't mind saying a little longer?"

"How much longer?"

With her being so agreeable, it seemed a shame to ask for a week or two, when a month would be better for Gino. "How about a month?"

"A month!"

"Or six weeks." Going with his usual tactic of surprising his opponent by asking for more rather than backpedaling, he forged on. "This is Gino's home. He needs to be somewhere he feels safe. Since he spends half his day sleeping, I also think it's important he be in his own crib. We're adults. I think we can make an adjustment or two for him."

"Okay."

She surprised him so much he forgot they were negotiating. "Okay?"

"Yes. We have to hire a nanny, and I need time to turn my spare bedroom into a nursery. So, yes. It makes sense to keep Gino here where he's happy until I can get some of that done."

Dumbstruck, he said nothing.

She ate a spoonful of soup. "Layla liked being in her own crib. Especially when she was sick."

Layla. Her casual use of the name shook him. But the very fact that she'd said it so nonchalantly told him he had to be every bit as casual. Not make a big deal out of it. Not ask questions that didn't fit into their conversation about Gino. Even though he was burning up with them.

How could a man not remember he had his child with him?

How did a woman deal with the grief, the guilt, of not noticing her husband was slipping over the edge?

Though he tried to hold them back, they tore at him until he couldn't stop himself from asking, "How did you deal with it?"

"What?"

Recrimination roared through him, telling him he shouldn't push her again, but he was unable to stop himself. "Your loss. How did you deal with such a monumental loss?"

She glanced up at him. "Therapy."

He shook his head. "Dear God. It must have been awful. I am so sorry."

She set down her spoon. "Actually, that's one of the reasons I held back from telling you. I don't want you to feel sorry for me. I want you to know. You *have* to know. You have to understand. But if I really want to get on with the rest of my life, you can't feel sorry for me. You can't treat me differently than you would have when you thought I was just a thorn-in-your-side lawyer."

He laughed. "I never thought you were a thorn in my side."

She smiled at him. "Of course you did. You probably always will. We're not going to agree on how to raise Gino. We might as well admit up front that there will be disagreements and maybe set some ground rules for how to handle them."

"I'm not sure what you mean."

"Well, for instance, there could be some deal breaker things. Like I don't think he should get a new car at sixteen."

He laughed, not just at the absurdity of talking about something that wouldn't happen for fifteen-and-a-half years, but also at the absurdity of depriving Gino of something he'd need.

"Really? No car at sixteen? In case you haven't noticed, I'm rich. I can afford to get him any kind of car he wants. And he'll want one. It's the only thing he'll talk about the entire time he's fifteen."

"Doesn't matter. Kids that age aren't good drivers. We should have as much control as possible about when and where he drives. The best way to do that is for him to have to ask permission to take a car."

He gaped at her. "I have ten cars. He could easily take one without my permission."

"Then you're going to be busy keeping track of them. Because, to me, the car is a safety issue. And a deal breaker."

He scowled, remembering his own driving at sixteen, and realized she was right. "Okay, but then one of my deal breakers is pink."

"Pink?"

"No matter that you call it rose or mauve or some other flaky name, I don't ever want him dressed in pink."

She blinked, then frowned, then burst out laughing. "That's your idea of a deal breaker?"

He turned his attention to his soup. "Give me time. I'm sure I'll think of more."

"So will I. But that's kind of the point. We should balance. You know I'm right about the car, so you didn't argue once you understood. I get it about pink." She rolled her eyes. "It's a pet peeve and I respect that. But most things won't be so black and white. We're going to have to learn to discuss issues as they come up and respect each other's viewpoints."

He put down his spoon and motioned with his hand between them. "So this kind of works?"

"The fact that we're both objective parties?"

He nodded.

She smiled. "Give us a few years. We won't be quite so objective. The first time he looks at us with real love, we'll both melt." She caught his gaze. "That'll probably happen within the next day or so, so get ready. You and I are about to become mom and dad to that little boy."

The truth of that swooped down on him, reminding him of the things he'd thought the day before. He sniffed a laugh. "I already figured that out."

"Well, good. That makes you ahead of the game."

"What about you?"

"I've been through this before. I know exactly what I'm in for in the next year and a half. I've even thought ahead to the next twenty-five years. Kindergarten, elementary school, middle school, high school… university…marriage."

Of course she'd thought ahead to the next twenty-some years. She was a planner. She'd probably thought of every special event in her daughter's life, previewed it, then suffered through the memories of her plans when her daughter was gone. He'd love to ask, not because he wanted to know her dreams for her daughter, but just because he suspected she needed to talk about some of this. But they weren't really friends. They were two people bound by someone else's wishes. He didn't feel he had the right to be so personal. Yet he also couldn't think of a way to change the subject or even what to change it to. Nearly everything to do with Gino would remind her of her baby. After that there wasn't much for them to discuss.

They were quiet for a few seconds then Whitney said, "This soup is wonderful."

Ah, food. She'd said she loved food. That was as good a topic as any. "Cook worked for my dad for the past few decades. Every time she tried to quit he doubled her salary."

She laughed. "I can understand why."

Her laughter pleased him and reminded him of how relaxed she'd been the night before at dinner and while playing pool. She actually seemed happy now. Relaxed.

So once again, he talked about food. "You should see what he paid the pastry chef."

Her eyes widened. "You have a pastry chef?"

He laughed. "*My dad* had a pastry chef."

His laughter scared her. She knew he was being kind, but the sound of his laugh filled her chest with syrupy warmth. It wasn't love. But closeness. Companionship. Ease. They'd known each other a few days. Yet they were not only comfortable enough to discuss Gino and his future rationally, but she'd also told him about Burn. About Layla. Now he was laughing with her and making her laugh.

And he'd kissed her.

She shoved that to the farthest corner of her brain. He'd promised he wouldn't kiss her again, so that couldn't come into play. She had to forget all about that, the way he'd promised he would.

"If we stay here a whole month, I'll weigh two hundred pounds before I go home."

"You could stand to gain a pound or two."

His comment reminded her of the way he'd looked at her the night before when she had been practicing flirting. Yearning seized her, but so did the memory of how much trouble that longing had gotten her into.

"No woman believes she can stand to gain a pound or two." She set her napkin on the table and rose. "I need to work this afternoon."

He smiled slightly and rose politely. "Okay."

Walking back to the office, she congratulated herself. She hadn't exactly run away, but there was no point in hanging around when they had no future. She'd sealed her fate with him by explaining her past. He'd even told her he wouldn't kiss her again. Yet she still had crazy feelings around him. Which, now that she thought about it, was preposterous. They didn't even really know each other. So, whatever she felt, it was based purely on animal attraction.

On the up side, the fact that her feelings were wrong gave her a reason or a way to control them. From here on out, every time the attraction rose up in her, she'd simply remind herself she didn't know him. So anything she felt was purely physical. Something to be ignored, not pursued.

On Monday morning, they drove into the city together, leaving Gino with Mrs. Tucker. Reviewing files from his briefcase, he didn't talk. Not even to discuss the job she'd be doing for Andreas Holdings in Gino's stead. She'd been quiet at breakfast, stilted, and he'd gotten the message. She might have agreed to live in the same house, but she wanted her space. Which was fine. Probably smart. He wanted her to be happy. If being left alone made her happy, then he'd leave her alone.

Eventually, she'd come around on her own terms, soften to the baby and to him. When she did, he'd see it. And he wouldn't exactly pounce, but he would capitalize on the moment and suggest that they make their living arrangements with Gino, at his house in Montauk, permanent.

When they arrived at Andreas Holdings, he directed her to follow him to his office—formerly his dad's office. Cherrywood paneling and a wall of bookcases gave the room an old-fashioned, stuffy feel, but there was nothing he could do about that. He hadn't yet had a chance to redecorate.

He walked past the brown leather sofa and chair, directing her to follow him to his desk. Keeping with the all-business tone they'd established that morning, he handed her a stack of files. "These are contracts I'd like you to review and summarize for me."

"Okay."

He pressed the button on his phone and paged his assistant, who was at the door in seconds. "Minnie will show you to your office."

She left the room on the heels of his assistant, and Darius stared at the door that closed behind them, hoping he was doing the right thing.

He met her at the limo for the ride home and immediately retrieved files to review, so they didn't have to talk just because they were commuting together. He even let her go up to her apartment on her own to pack the things she would need for the upcoming weeks.

They talked about nannies at dinner. That morning, she had called the service she'd used when she'd hired a nanny for Layla and they had emailed résumés of potential candidates. She'd narrowed them down and had scheduled interviews with all four the next day. Because Whitney would conduct the initial interviews at the headquarters for Andreas Holdings, Darius had consented to sit in on at least five minutes of each interview and, acknowledging how busy he was, she'd accepted that. Before dessert she excused herself, saying she needed to go back to the depositions from the case she was working on with her father.

At nine when he went into the nursery to say goodnight to Gino, Whitney was already there. He was neither surprised nor concerned when she kept the slightest bit of distance between herself and the baby. He knew why she hesitated.

Still, he and Whitney were the baby's guardians and because of work that day they hadn't spent as much time as either of them wanted to spend with the baby, so he excused Mrs. Tucker.

"We're okay here. So if you want to go to your room, that's fine."

When she was gone, Darius sat on the rocker, bottle in hand. "Hey, little guy."

From her spot beside the crib, Whitney said, "He's really getting to know who you are."

Darius couldn't help it. He smiled. "I know."

"And you're really beginning to like him."

Darius looked up at her. "You were right. It hits you like a ton of bricks."

Her blue eyes softened and became distant. "Yeah."

He hadn't meant to bring her child to her mind, but with the two of them caring for a baby, it was very hard not to. Of course, if he kept the conversation specific to Gino, maybe he could avoid that.

"Remember how we were talking about him not getting a car on his sixteenth birthday?"

"Yeah?"

"Well, that started me thinking about some weird things."

"Like what?"

"Like how am I going to tell him about our dad. Or whether or not I should even tell him about our dad."

Whitney bristled. "You can't *not* tell him about his own father."

"No, but I could be judicious. You know…tell him the good stuff and temper the bad."

She took another step closer. "That won't work if your brothers decide to tell him the truth."

"I've been thinking about that too. My dad wanted us to behave like brothers. And, as you can see, Cade and Nick more or less deserted me."

"So you're going to keep Gino away from them so they don't tell him about your dad?"

He shook his head. "No. I've actually been thinking of inviting them up to the house. Maybe once or twice a year, so they'll have a chance to get to know him. There are four of us who are brothers, not just me and Gino. They might not want any part of me. But they're Gino's big brothers. I think they should be in his life."

She nodded. In front of the rocker now, she stooped down. "In some ways, that's going to make his life tough."

Darius frowned. "Seeing his other brothers only a few times a year?"

She caught his gaze. "No. Having three adult brothers. I know you might not get this yet, but this kid is almost forty years younger than you are. And the distance between his age and that of his other two brothers is almost as great. There are *three* of you who will expect him to meet your standards." She passed her hand lovingly over Gino's soft black hair. "Three of you who will criticize his dates, expect a say in where he goes to university." She shook her head then ran her index finger down Gino's cheek. "I'm guessing he's going to rebel."

Cautious, hardly breathing, Darius watched her. She didn't seem to realize how lovingly she was caressing the little boy. She appeared mesmerized, as if she'd waited all her life for a child and now that she was with one, she couldn't stop herself.

"In one way or another all three of us rebelled."

She looked up at him with a soft smile. "Really?"

"I attended Wharton instead of Harvard."

She gasped as if mocking him. "Wow. I'm surprised your dad survived the blow."

"Hey, to him it was a big deal. Harvard was his alma mater."

"What about the other two?"

"Nick got married at seventeen."

Her eyes widened. "Now, that's more like it!"

"And Cade refused to go to school at all. He bought a ranch with his trust fund and worked it."

"Okay. Cade wins. *That's* rebellion."

"Yeah, but when his oil interests got into trouble, he needed our dad. That still sticks in his craw."

She laughed and rose from in front of the rocker. "'Sticks in his craw?'"

"He's a Texan. It's like they have their own language down there."

With the baby asleep, Darius rose from the rocker and laid the little boy in his crib. After covering him with a green blanket, he leaned down and kissed his cheek.

From the corner of his eye, he watched Whitney lick her lips. He pulled away from the crib. "Want to kiss him goodnight?"

She pressed her lips together and shook her head slightly. "I need to get ready for bed."

He let her walk out of the nursery, but he had seen the longing in her eyes.

Could it be that he'd made a mistake in running interference for her? Could she actually need to be around Gino, not away from him? Would that help her take the next steps in her recovery?

Tuesday morning, he got to the nursery before Whitney, and when she arrived he dismissed Mrs. Tucker again.

As he fed the baby his bottle, Whitney started off standing by the crib, but ultimately gravitated to the rocker. Again, she stooped in front of it, watching Gino as he ate.

He thought about that all morning at work. He didn't know if the change was because she'd told him about her family, or if she was simply growing more accustomed to Gino, but that child drew her. And for every bit she was drawn to the baby, he felt drawn to help her adjust.

If nothing else, they shared custody of Gino. She was his partner. And he needed to help her.

When they stepped into the house that evening, Mrs. Tucker met them to take their coats. "Chinese for supper tonight," she said then walked away with their garments.

"I see your love of food precedes you. I've never had a housekeeper announce the menu at the door, unless she knew somebody was truly interested."

She laughed. "I am!"

Darius pointed up the stairs. "Baby first. Food second."

She didn't hesitate. Not only did they always put Gino first, but she was actually eager to see the little guy. She wasn't entirely sure what had happened, but with Darius in the room, it was no longer excruciating to be with the baby. There were painful minutes. She still made comparisons in her head. But Darius was like a layer of protection.

They walked upstairs together and the second they stepped into the room, Gino bounced up in the crib and held his hands out to Darius.

"Look how cute!" Darius said, laughter bubbling through his voice. "He wants me." He strode over and Gino all but leapt into his arms. The baby squealed, a sound that was half-joy and half-annoyance as if he couldn't wait the two seconds it took for Darius to snag him out of the crib.

Whitney's chest squeezed. Not with pain or fear or even a remembrance of her own child, but with happiness. Staying at this house hadn't been her first choice for how they'd share custody, but it was now clear that being here had been the right thing for Gino.

She grabbed a tissue and gently ran it beneath Gino's runny nose. He squawked and reached for her.

Darius laughed. "Take him."

She shied away. She might have been able to touch him, to experience some of the joy a baby brings into any world it enters, but she wouldn't go overboard. She liked being able to be in the same room without being overwhelmed with memories. She had weeks here at Darius's house to get accustomed to Gino. She didn't have to push. She could take this slowly.

"That's okay. You keep him."

Gino squealed and stretched out of Darius's arms toward her.

Darius chuckled. "I'm sorry, but he wants you. He likes you."

"I know. But he likes you, too." She took a few steps back.

Gino screeched again.

"Right at this minute, I think he likes you more."

Motherly longing laced its way through her. The pure feminine desire to lave love on a needy baby rose up in her. Especially a baby who so obviously wanted her. Her heart swelled with affection so strong it tightened her chest. She *wanted* to love Gino. She might even need to love him. There was a hole in her heart so big that some days she wondered how it managed to pump enough blood to keep her alive.

And standing in the nursery where this little boy belonged, beside the man who shared custody with her, suddenly it all seemed okay. She took Gino from Darius's arms.

Darius smiled. "Look how much he likes you."

She took a soft breath, preparing for panic, as sweet baby scents and the feeling of him snuggling into her assailed her. "I'm glad we came here, glad we decided to share these few weeks so we could all get adjusted."

He shrugged. "It works."

She nodded and turned away to rock Gino a bit as he nuzzled against her neck. The panic she expected didn't come and she realized the memories of Layla floating out of her subconscious were wispy, insubstantial. Not bold and blaring, but still there, soft and sweet. She wouldn't forget her baby as she got on with the rest of her life.

"Yes. Being together does seem to be working."

"What do you say we take the baby down to supper with us?"

She nodded.

He smiled. "Do you want to change first?"

"Yes."

"Okay. You hold him while I change and then I'll come back and take him while you change."

Whitney nodded, feeling herself able to take another careful step. Holding Gino, alone.

Darius left the room and she smiled down at the little boy. "So how was your day?"

He tilted his head as if questioning her.

She laughed. "I get it. Not much happens in the life of a six-month-old."

He screeched as if protesting that fact.

"Then again, Gino, everything that happens is sort of new to you. I mean, you can't even talk yet. Just wait till that happens." She waltzed him around the room, making him giggle. "Then there's walking. You're gonna love that."

She spun around the room again, but stopped when she saw Darius standing in the open doorway between his room and the nursery.

"That was fast."

He ambled into the room. "I'm hungry."

"Me, too."

She handed the baby to him, but couldn't help noticing his still expression. "What?"

"I think we should live together."

"We are living together."

"I mean permanently." He ran his hand along the top of Gino's head, across the shiny black hair so much like his own. "The house is huge. We both love the baby. He loves both of us. Wouldn't it be a shame to divide up our time when we could both see him every day?"

She gaped at him. "You're serious."

He smiled charmingly. "It's the right thing to do for Gino."

All the little warning bells she'd heard the Friday before when they'd arrived at the house, all the little suspicions that had nudged at her, suddenly found their meaning. He'd been leading her toward this from the beginning. Being nice, getting her to agree to one simple thing after another until they were at the point where his real goal became clear. He wanted them to live together.

Well, he could ask, but that didn't mean she had to agree.

"It doesn't work for me."

"Why not? There's plenty of space. We have a cook. We're hiring a nanny." He pointed out the window at the serene ocean below. "You're by the sea. On a beautiful, peaceful estate. You can keep your condo if you want. Spend time in the city anytime you want. And Gino can be here, comfortable and happy with his nanny."

"You mean with *you*."

"I can't always be here either, remember? I have a job that forces me to travel. All the more reason for Gino to have a home base."

"You mean all the more reason for you to keep control. You're afraid that with your schedule, I'll have him more than you'll have him."

He shook his head and laughed lightly, as if they were having a casual conversation, not a monumental one. "That's absurd."

"Then why do you want to live here?"

"Because it makes sense."

"Not to me."

"I can't see why not. Whitney, I don't want this to come out wrong, but you need this as much as Gino does. You're still shaky around him."

Fury rose up in her. She couldn't believe he'd use her fears around Gino against her. Telling him about her baby had been the hardest thing she'd ever done, but she'd trusted him! And he was using it against her.

Mrs. Tucker stepped into the nursery. "The cook wants to know when it will be convenient to serve dinner."

Whitney headed for the door. "I'm not hungry. I'm going to work. Have Geoffrey bring Gino's swing to my office and I'll watch him while Mr. Andreas dines."

Alone.

Alone from here on out because she wasn't trusting him again!

CHAPTER SEVEN

AT EIGHT O'CLOCK THAT NIGHT, after two hours of reading depositions, with Gino splitting his time between the swing and the playpen across from her desk, Whitney asked Mrs. Tucker to bring a bottle to the nursery.

She didn't look for Darius or even let him know she was putting Gino to bed. The mood in the nursery was subdued, as if Mrs. Tucker knew Darius should have been called in at least to say goodnight. Still, good employee that she was, she didn't say anything as she fed Gino his bottle.

But Gino fussed as if he, too, knew something was off balance, and Whitney began to feel a tad guilty for being so angry. Then as she tucked the covers around Gino's neck and his soft baby blankets brought Layla to mind, she remembered that she'd trusted Darius. She'd told him the truth about the reason for her troubles with Gino and he'd used it to further his plan to keep the baby with him. Permanently.

Needing a break from thinking about all this, instead of returning to her office, she headed for the kitchen to make herself a cup of cocoa and maybe an omelet, since she hadn't eaten dinner.

It took her a minute to find the kitchen. Coming from the other side of the huge house, she got slightly disoriented. When she finally found it and pushed open the door, she stopped dead in her tracks.

The space wasn't appointed to be a regular household kitchen, but looked like the kind of kitchen found in a restaurant. Stainless-steel appliances and hanging racks of pots and pans surrounded a long stainless-steel prep table that sat across from a sixteen-burner stove. Only a few cupboards lined the back wall.

Still, big or not, the kitchen had to have cocoa and milk. She headed for the refrigerator and easily found milk. When she spotted the eggs and cheese, she smiled. An omelet was a definite possibility.

She pulled supplies out of the refrigerator and went on a quest for mugs, plates and utensils. Unfortunately, the cupboards didn't hold so much as one mug, one plate or one fork. As quickly as her mood had lifted at the sight of eggs, it plummeted. What good would it do to find the eggs and cheese, if she didn't have anything to eat them with?

Hearing the door open, she spun to face it and saw Darius enter the room. He looked cute and cuddly in a big sweatshirt and sweatpants. Then she remembered he wanted her to live here permanently and her fury returned full force.

She sucked in a breath, told herself not to let her anger rule her. It was better to find out now that he was the kind of guy who would use her confidences against her, rather than later. At least now she knew not to get too friendly with him.

But just as she was about to freeze him out of the kitchen with a cold shoulder and a frigid stare, she realized he might know where the utensils were, and if she wanted food—and she did—she needed him.

Though it galled her, she very quietly said, "Are there any mugs or plates or forks in this house?"

He took a step into the room. "Probably."

"But you don't know where they are?"

He shook his head. "Sorry."

She stifled a curse. "I just want a simple cup of cocoa." She opened and closed two more doors, working to control her temper and not start another fight. "And maybe an omelet."

"If you're hungry, we can call Cook."

"Or I could just make myself something." His spoiled, pampered, rich-guy attitude fed her bad mood. He didn't live a real life. Probably never had. He wouldn't know a genuine emotion, especially not trust, if it came up and bit his butt.

"You rich people." She shook her head. "You're so helpless."

He sauntered the rest of the way into the kitchen. "Hey, I am not helpless. My dad might have been rich, but my mother wasn't. She not only cooked, but she had a job. And she taught me to cook." He pulled a skillet from the arrangement hanging over the prep table. "What kind of omelet would you like?"

Though all that surprised her, the last thing she wanted was for him to wait on her. She wanted to maintain her independence. She didn't want to trust him. She certainly didn't want to depend on him. Hell, from here on out she wasn't even sure she wanted to be friendly with him.

"I'll make my own omelet."

"No. You smeared the good name of Andreas with your snotty comment that I was helpless. I have honor to defend."

Right. Honor. A guy who used her trauma to try to get her to live with him was not a man of honor.

"Okay, how about this? I'll hunt for everything you need and you make your own omelet?"

Unfortunately, she was so hungry that she couldn't turn him down. "All right. Fine."

He rubbed his hands together, as if he were enjoying this. "What should I look for first?"

His enthusiasm only grated on her nerves. "I found the refrigerator so I know where to get just about everything for the omelet. But I have no clue where to find the cocoa."

"I'm on it." Turning to the right, he headed off and disappeared down a short hallway. After a few seconds, he emerged with cocoa but not the mug.

She frowned at it.

He laughed. "Don't get huffy. We eat off plates every day. Drink out of cups. They have to be around here somewhere."

While she broke eggs into a mixing bowl, ignoring him, he glanced around again. Then he disappeared down the short hall to the left. A few seconds later he was by the prep table holding two mugs and two plates.

"Here you go."

"Two?"

"You're not going to share?"

With a sigh, she added an extra cup of milk to the pot on one of the sixteen burners, her ire simmering. If this weren't his house, she'd lambaste him for thinking he could join her when he'd betrayed her trust. But it *was* his house. And he'd helped her find the dishes. If she refused to share, she'd look petty. Childish.

"Sure. I'll share."

Apparently missing the sarcasm in her voice, he smiled, and, spotting the onion and green pepper she'd laid out beside the chopping block, he ambled over to them. While she stirred her cocoa, he cut both the onion and the pepper.

She sighed. "Stop helping me."

"I have to." Chopping the onion and pepper and not looking at her, he added, "Not only will the cocoa get cold while we wait for you to make the omelet if I don't get it started for you, but I have to make up for upsetting you when I suggested you live here permanently."

"Huh!" Damn. She'd said that out loud. Sucking in a breath she turned on him. Since he'd started the conversation, they might as well have at it. "Do you really think you can make up for using what I told you against me? I trusted you. I told you something I don't talk about with anyone else and you used it."

"I didn't 'use' it. I simply pointed out the truth. You're having trouble and the three of us living together helps you. But there's more to me wanting Gino here than just that. Did you miss the part of the conversation where I told you Gino loves us both? He could have us both. Every day. If you'd live here."

"Did you miss the part where I have a life?"

"And you can keep it. You'd just live it from Montauk instead of the city."

"I like my home."

He stopped, caught her gaze. "Now who's being spoiled and pampered and even a little bit prissy?"

Icy pain froze her limbs. *Prissy?* After almost two years of caring for a baby and three years of mourning the loss of that precious child, the word *prissy* rumbled through her like thunder announcing an impending storm.

He winced. "Sorry. That was sort of over the top."

Oh, he wanted her to think he was sorry, but he wasn't. She had his number. He'd apologized only so she'd focus on what he'd called her and not on their real issue. There was no way she'd let him get away with that.

"You apologize for your words, but you skate over the actual problem." Pain rippled through her again. Not because of her anger over being called prissy when she was anything but, but because for some reason or another she believed he should know she wasn't prissy. And the only way to avoid dissecting that would be to force them back to their actual problem.

He dropped the knife and strode over to her. She snapped off the burner under the cocoa. If he wanted a fight, she was ready to give it to him.

"I know you love Gino. I see it in your eyes. You might have agreed to take custody only wanting to fulfill your friend's last wishes. But you like him now."

Once again, he was skirting the issue and she refused to let him. "Of course I do, but that doesn't change the fact that you used something I told you against me."

"I only pointed out the truth." He sighed. Stepped closer. "I thought that since you trusted me enough to tell me, that I could speak honestly about it, too."

That brought her up short and she didn't know how to answer. Had he really only been speaking honestly? Had it been so long since she'd spoken honestly about Layla and Burn that she didn't know what an honest conversation felt like anymore?

The truth of what he'd said rippled through her.

She *did* need help with Gino.

And he *was* Gino's other guardian. He had a right to be concerned.

Her skin burned with shame. Especially since she didn't want to admit any of it. He'd only been speaking the truth, but she was so out of the loop, she hadn't realized it and had accused him of using what she'd told him. And the truth was that she still did need help.

She wanted to turn away, to run, but she couldn't. Behind her was a sixteen-burner stove that ran almost the length of the room. In front of her was six feet of angry man.

"Maybe I'm just not ready to talk about it yet."

He gurgled a sound of disgust. "You won't ever be ready if you keep avoiding it in every discussion."

His angry voice echoed through the room and she realized how upset he was. She could understand his annoyance if he were defending himself against her accusations, but he wasn't. Not really. He was talking about her. Angry about her.

"Why are *you* mad?"

He forked his fingers through his hair. "Because you're a nice woman." He snagged her gaze, his brown eyes sharp, filled with banked fury. "You're a smart woman. I know you didn't deserve what happened to you. But it did and you have to get through it to the other side. Yet you won't."

"Hey! You try losing everything! Your hopes. Your dreams. Your *baby*. Your sweet little blue-eyed baby girl who hadn't done anything to anybody." Her breath hitched. "You try losing that much, being responsible for that loss, and then putting your life back together."

"What do you think I'm doing here…with Gino… with my brothers…after my dad's death?"

She gaped at him. "You think losing your dad compares?"

"No. But when you add the fact that I lost my mom

only a few months before, I think I'm in the ballpark. She was fifty-three. Smart. Funny. Everybody's best friend. My dad's biggest defender. And one day she gets to work, has a heart attack and dies." He grabbed Whitney's shoulders as if forcing her to focus in on what he was saying. "I'm alone except for that little boy upstairs and two brothers who hate me, shouldering the burden of a company that's floundering. Do you think I don't look around some days and want to pack a bag for Tahiti, buy a hut and a bottle of tequila and just say, 'screw it all'?"

"It's not the same."

"No. It's not. But just like my troubles don't give me license to stop living, neither do yours. And they sure as hell aren't going to turn into the reason you expect me always to give you your own way." His eyes sharpened. The anger in them flared.

Instead of being frightened, Whitney felt something sharp and sexual click inside her. They were both strong, passionate, vital people. Though she didn't think his trauma was worse than hers, she did believe he at least had a partial understanding of what she was going through. She was sort of sorry that she'd pushed him, but not completely. The score now felt even. Everything was out in the open.

But they were also toe to toe. Stimulated. Attracted. He'd promised he wouldn't kiss her again, but suddenly that promise seemed to belong to another universe, another time, another two people.

He held her gaze. Their physical attraction vibrated between them. Their anger withered and her breath shivered in her chest.

He was going to kiss her.

She told herself to turn and run. She knew the

outcome of the last kiss. She hadn't been able to control herself. She'd wanted everything from him. Not because she loved him but because her body was desperate for release, satisfaction, closeness.

But making love with a man who was virtually a stranger wouldn't give her the satisfaction or closeness she sought. Sex would be a cold, hollow, empty substitute for affection.

She couldn't let him kiss her.

Yet she had no path of escape.

Even as she thought that, his hands slid off her shoulders. He took a step back, away from her, then turned and walked out of the kitchen.

CHAPTER EIGHT

HE'D WANTED TO KISS HER senseless.

Darius stood in front of the mirror over the double sink in the master bathroom. He'd splashed cold water on his face twice, but he couldn't get rid of the weird, compulsive instinct that he should have kissed her. Not because of their silly sexual attraction, but to shock her. To knock her out of the prison she'd built for herself and into the real world. Not for Gino, but for himself. So he could taste her, touch her.

That was wrong. Or it would be if that were his only reasoning. But it wasn't. He'd also wanted to yank her back into the real world because he liked her. And he just *knew* that beyond her fear was a wonderful, passionate woman. Someone he could really relate to. Somebody he could love.

That had scared him silly. The impulse to connect with her was so foreign, yet so strong, he knew the only way to control it had been to leave the room.

He pressed a towel to his face to dry it and headed into the bedroom. Yanking off his sweatshirt, he tried to ignore the emotions swirling through him. Wanting her for anything more than a partner to raise Gino was foolish. Dangerous. *Selfish*. He was the CEO and Chairman of the Board of a huge conglomerate full of people who depended on him. He'd barely have time to be a father for Gino. How could he expect to have time for a wife—especially a wife who would need a more sensitive husband?

He was not a sensitive man.

He would hurt her.

He had to stop wanting her.

The next morning Darius was already feeding Gino when Whitney walked into the nursery. She said, "Good morning," then stooped down in front of the rocker. "And good morning to you."

Their fight the night before had had a greater effect on her than she'd wanted it to. Not only had she come face to face with how attracted she was to Darius, but some of the things he'd said to her had rattled around in her brain.

He'd called her a nice woman.

Just the thought of it made her smile. In the past three years she'd been called cold, distant, frigid. No one had seen past her pain to the real Whitney hiding beneath the surface. And the mere knowledge that someone had actually seen the real her gave her enough strength to try to be that person again.

She sucked in a breath and caught Darius's gaze. "Let me feed him."

Darius didn't say anything, but his dark eyes asked a million questions.

"Hey, I've got to do this."

He sighed. Breaking his silence with her, he said, "Yes, you do."

"Okay. So I'm ready."

He rose from the rocker and took a few steps away

so she could sit down. When she was comfortable, he handed her the baby first, then the bottle.

Fear made her hand tremble as she slid the bottle into Gino's mouth. Nearly every time she'd touched him, memories had assaulted her. And, after the memories came hours of recriminations. Guilt. Beating herself up for not seeing the obvious.

But Gino took the nipple greedily and this time she didn't see her baby's face as he suckled. She saw dark-haired, dark-eyed, very hungry Gino.

She laughed.

Darius turned away.

Her heart tumbled in her chest. Darius's silence made her feel ashamed. Selfish. He'd mentioned his mother's death the night before. He'd said he was alone. He hadn't exactly reached out to her, but had only told her because it fit into their argument. Still, this morning she knew she had to say something.

Seeing Gino was happily suckling, she drew in a quiet breath, swallowed, then said, "I'm sorry about your mother."

"It's okay."

"No. It's not." She shook her head angrily. "This is what always happens with people when I try to talk to them. Nobody's tragedy is as terrible as mine so nobody really talks with me."

He turned around again. His face scrunched in confusion. "That's ridiculous."

"No, it isn't. Look at you. You won't tell me about your mom."

He busied himself with arranging the items on the changing table.

"See!"

Still occupied with powders and lotions, he casually said, "There's not really a lot to tell."

"But you said you were alone."

"That was a slip. A way to show you that you're not the only one who's suffered a loss." He shook his head, but didn't face her. "I shouldn't have compared my situation and yours. Our losses were totally different. Plus, I'm lucky. I might have two half-brothers who intend to ignore me, but I still have a baby brother, and if I raise him he'll be in my life for at least eighteen years. I have a family."

She glanced down at Gino. "You know, if you really wanted to have a family you should bring your brothers together. You shouldn't hang back, waiting for the right time for them to come up and meet Gino. You should take the bull by the horns and invite them now. Get them involved with him now."

He faced her.

"The longer you wait, the more distance you put between yourself and them, and between them and Gino, and the less chance they'll accept your invitation."

He crossed his arms over his chest. "And you're the expert?"

She shrugged. "Lawyers counsel people. We sometimes can't see what's in front of us in our own lives, but we have this uncanny ability to think really clearly about the lives of our clients." She glanced down at Gino, then back up at Darius and smiled slightly as she caught his gaze. "You're not really a client, but I'm sort of new to your life, so it's easier for me to see the obvious."

"And you think I should invite my brothers here?"

"Yes. I think you need a chance to bond."

He snorted out a breath. "Bond. Like a bunch of

girls at cheerleading camp?" He shook his head. "That's ridiculous."

"No. Bonding is finding a common denominator. Something all three of you care about. So that you can relate to each other."

The baby spat out his bottle and Whitney burped him. But when she tried to sit him on her lap again he squirmed and squealed.

Without hesitation Darius walked over and hoisted him up, into his arms. "You look like a guy who wants to play."

Gino giggled. Darius hugged him and headed for the toy box. Whitney's chest tightened and her heart squeezed. He loved Gino so much. And his reasons for wanting Gino in his life were good. He wanted a family. This time, the guilt she felt had nothing to do with her past and everything to do with right now. This minute. She'd mistrusted him, accused him without knowing anything about him.

Maybe the same was true of his brothers?

Maybe they didn't so much hate the eldest Andreas son as much as they simply didn't know him well enough to like him?

Darius opened the toy box and pulled out four big plastic blocks. He sat Gino on a brightly colored striped rug and lowered himself beside him.

The way Darius so easily, so naturally played with Gino tugged on her heartstrings, and once again she thought of his brothers, of how wrong it was for them to dislike their oldest brother.

"I'm not going to drop the idea that you should invite your brothers here."

Preoccupied with trying to get Gino to take a block,

Darius said, "I've already told you I don't want to 'bond.'"

"So don't look at it as bonding. Look at it as getting a chance to talk about the company, about your dad, about the things you have in common."

"And you think talking will fix everything?"

"No. I don't know for sure that there's a way to fix your family. But I think it's a start. And I think you owe it to yourself and Gino to try."

He shuffled the blocks in front of Gino, who batted at them before he picked up the yellow one and inspected it.

When he didn't answer, guilt from their argument in the kitchen rose up in her again. At a point when he would have spoken about his mom, she'd been so wrapped up in her own troubles that she hadn't reached out to him. Every day they'd been here, he'd reached out to her. She owed him.

"If you can get your brothers to come up for a weekend, I'll stay here with Gino until the Monday after that weekend."

He glanced up sharply. "Their schedules aren't going to be any easier than mine. It might take eight or ten weeks before they can come."

"I'm fine with that."

He studied her for a few seconds. Finally he said, "I guess I do have enough room here that we could easily invite my brothers for a weekend."

Darius spent the first few hours at work on the phone with his brothers. He didn't actually speak with each of them all that time. He used most of it calling various numbers he had for them before reaching secretaries who could have given him Cade and Nick's private numbers, but didn't. Each opted to have her boss return Darius's call. Luckily, and somewhat unexpectedly, both did. Immediately.

Though Nick and Cade were reluctant to accept his invitation, he reminded them of their childhoods without their father. He asked them if they really wanted the fourth brother to be raised that way—never really knowing the rest of his family. And suddenly the tones of the conversations were different. Both brothers agreed that Gino needed to know his half-brothers and both agreed to spend a weekend.

He hung up the phone satisfied, happy that his brothers would be at the house in three weeks, until he realized that not only did he have to spend three days with two brothers who hated him, but also that Whitney would be spending three days with them.

Cade the rich, rebellious cowboy and Nick the brooding Southern gentleman.

Jealousy speared him.

He actually stopped walking.

He'd never been possessive of a woman before, never been jealous. Plus, he'd already figured out he was all wrong for Whitney. He had to get over this.

Before he could take his thoughts any further, his phone rang. His first impulse was to ignore it, then he remembered Whitney would be interviewing nanny candidates that morning and he'd promised to spend five minutes with each of them to determine which of the four would get interviews at the house, with Gino.

He picked up the receiver. "Yes."

"I'm sitting here with Mary Alice Conrad," Whitney said happily. "If you have a few minutes, I'd like you to meet her."

* * *

After Darius's five minutes with Mary Alice Conrad, Whitney had a very good idea of the kind of nanny Darius envisioned for Gino. She didn't invite him in on any more of the interviews and simply chose Liz Pizzaro and Jaimie Roberts for interviews at the house.

On the drive home that evening, Whitney informed Darius that the following night they'd be conducting the home interviews with Liz and Jaimie. So, Thursday night, they set themselves up in the den. When Mrs. Tucker escorted Jaimie in, Darius sat behind the big desk in the corner. Gino chewed on a block in the playpen and Whitney stood by the double-doored entrance.

"Come in," Whitney said, shaking Jaimie's hand as Mrs. Tucker discreetly exited and closed the door. She pointed at Darius, who rose. "This is Mr. Andreas, Gino's half-brother and other guardian." She turned and motioned to the crib. "And that's Gino."

Jaimie, a tall redhead wearing tight jeans and a red leather jacket, gasped. "Oh, he's darling!"

Darius dryly said, "We think so, too."

He walked from behind the desk over to the playpen. "Would you like to hold him?"

Jaimie turned and smiled at Darius. "Yes!"

He directed her to take him out of the playpen and she eagerly did so. But he also watched her like a hawk. Through the one-hour question-and-answer session, Jaimie didn't miss a beat, but Darius still didn't seem to like her.

When tall, blond, gorgeous Liz Pizzaro arrived, Darius brightened.

"Come in!" he said, rising from the leather sofa where he'd been sitting to chat with Jaimie.

Whitney's chest tightened oddly. It was such a cliché for the woman of the house to be jealous of the nanny that she refused even to let her thoughts wander to the possibility.

"That's Gino," Darius said, pointing to the baby who was now growing restless in the playpen.

Liz didn't wait for an invitation. She reached in and lifted Gino out and into her arms. "What's the matter, little guy," she crooned.

Gino screeched. But Liz only shook her head and smiled. "He's tired. Yet he's not very fussy. I'm guessing he's a really good baby."

Darius laughed. "Well, we think so, but we're prejudiced."

Liz jostled Gino and made him giggle. "Daddies are supposed to be prejudiced, aren't they?"

Darius winced. "I'm Gino's half-brother. Not really his dad."

Liz blinked innocently. "Of course, you're his dad. I can tell by how protective you are that you take the job as his guardian seriously." She smiled. "And that's what dads do."

Whitney suppressed her own smile. She didn't even have to wait for Liz to leave to know what Darius's choice would be.

"Gino just seemed more comfortable with her."

She nudged his foot with the toe of her high heel. "It didn't hurt that she called you Gino's daddy."

Darius raised his eyes until he snagged her gaze. "Is that so bad?"

Whitney's heart expanded to painful proportions. "No." Guilt assailed her. It suddenly seemed abundantly wrong to take Gino away from Darius, even for visits. Yet it seemed equally wrong for her to simply drop her life and move in with a man she barely knew.

There didn't seem to be a middle of the road to this

problem unless Darius could mend the rift with his brothers and get close enough to them to ensure that Gino wasn't his only family.

CHAPTER NINE

SUNDAY NIGHT, when dinner was over, Whitney rose from her seat and motioned for Darius to follow her.

"I took the liberty of having my secretary gather some information about your bothers, just to get some background details."

Darius also rose from the table. "You investigated my brothers?"

"No. I just had my secretary run a quick search. I told her to get only background information. Nothing serious. Just enough that we would know some basic things."

His eyes narrowed. "I have no desire to poke into my brothers' lives."

"We're not poking. We're just looking. Lawyers never go into a courtroom or a meeting unprepared."

"CEOs don't go into meetings unprepared either."

She turned and smiled. "Exactly. So my secretary got enough background information that we won't feel at a disadvantage when they're here."

They stepped into the office. She directed him to sit on the sofa in front of a low coffee table. Carrying the thin file she retrieved from the desk, she followed him and sat beside him.

The second she sank into the smooth leather, his

nearness overwhelmed her. He'd taken a walk outside after spending time with Gino when they got home from work and he smelled like fresh air and baby powder. A week ago that would have sent her into a tailspin of despair. Today, it only reminded her that she was attracted to this man. It didn't scare her. It didn't make her crazy. It was simply a fact.

She licked her suddenly dry lips and forced her mind back on the info her secretary had found.

"Okay. We'll do Cade first." She glanced down and read aloud, "Cade Andreas, age thirty-one, net worth—" She paused, forcibly told herself not to gape, and read the number on the page.

Darius snorted. "I see that little oil thing worked out for him."

She cleared her throat. "Yes. I guess it did." She returned to her reading. "He's a loner who doesn't really socialize too much, except with the employees of his ranch."

"All of which I already knew."

"Okay." She rifled through the sheets until she came to the first page for the information on Nick. "How about this? I'll read Nick's sheet. You read Cade's. If either of us finds anything noteworthy we'll tell the other."

Darius leaned back, got comfortable and began reading.

Whitney almost mimicked him, until she realized that leaning back into the soft sofa they'd be side by side, almost touching. Sort of close and cuddly.

Arousal sparked, sharp and sweet, at just the thought. It leaped through her, awakening the more dangerous longings. To be held. To be loved. But, luckily, her common sense rose up. It might not frighten her anymore to be attracted to Darius, but a relationship between them wasn't practical. No matter how much they now understood each other, they still had a baby to raise together. If they tried a relationship and it didn't work, Gino would suffer.

So she leaned forward, away from him.

"Here's something interesting. Cade is married."

That perked up her senses. "Really?"

"Yes." He glanced up at her, obviously confused. "But he didn't bring a wife to the funeral."

"Do you think he's the type to leave his wife at home?"

Darius shrugged. "Who knows? A man who says 'sticks in my craw' could do just about anything."

"Should we plan for a wife?"

"Nope, if he didn't mention bringing a guest, I'm not planning for her."

"Okay." She went back to her reading, then had a change of heart. "Maybe we should plan for a guest."

"We have plenty of extras. If we need something Mrs. Tucker will find it."

"You're sure?"

He pierced her with a look. "Positive."

"Maybe we should check?"

"No. He should have told us he'd be bringing a guest. Since he didn't, I'm not going out of my way. If he wants to be inconsiderate that's his choice."

At his snippy tone, Whitney laughed. "I see that hits a nerve."

He set the paper down again. "It doesn't hit a nerve. I think he has the right to behave however he wants to behave, but if the tables were turned I'd be more consid-erate. That's why I don't expect a lot out of him. Frankly, I'm surprised he's interested in Gino. He's busy with his oil company. He's got a ranch so big I'm not sure even he knows how many acres he has. And he doesn't really like people."

"He's going to be our tough nut to crack then."

Darius merely snorted a "Humph."

"Says here in Nick's report that he owns a factory." She shuffled through the papers. "His net worth is about one quarter of Cade's."

"Yeah, considering Cade's net worth, that brings Nick in at around half a billion dollars." Darius caught her gaze. "Don't ever underestimate Nick. He'll come here all Southern-gentleman charm and manners and he'll leave with the silver."

Her eyes widened. "He's a thief?"

"No, he's a sweet-talker."

Whitney couldn't help it; she laughed. "So you have a sweet-talker and a grouch for half-brothers?"

"Yeah, great, isn't it? I've got a grouch, a sweet-talker and a baby." He snorted in derision. "Which makes me crazy to think I can unite them."

"Or a tower of strength."

"Right."

"Oh, come on. You know you're strong."

He gave her a confused look, then a grin bloomed on his face and he nudged her playfully. "You think I'm strong."

She sucked in a breath. Even casual contact with him sent her senses reeling. But she understood why. Not only was she needy, but he was awfully good-looking. Now that they were getting to know each other, it was sometimes difficult not to simply fall into what seemed to be happening between them.

But, remembering Gino, remembering how difficult it was just to be able to hold him without thinking of Layla, she knew getting involved in a sexual relationship would be every bit as traumatic. She couldn't risk this newfound peace between her and Darius.

She got up from the sofa and walked to the fireplace. "Don't get too excited. I'm just saying that anybody who runs a company as big as yours has to have his attributes."

"Like what?"

"Like you're vain and arrogant." She smirked at him. "Do you really want the list to go on?"

He rose from the sofa and ambled over. "I like the other list better. The one where you talk about the good things." He paused and studied her eyes as if he'd been thinking the same thing she had been while sitting beside him on the sofa—how easy it would be to fall into whatever was happening between them.

Trying to get them back on point, she said, "Okay, you're strong. You're a good leader. And when push comes to shove, you always try to do the right thing."

He grinned. "See. I knew you could come up with a better list."

"You're making me want to go back to the one that starts with vain and arrogant."

His features shifted, his expression became serious again. "Don't."

Awareness bubbled through her. She wanted to believe it was only their sexual attraction, something she could deal with by always staying a few feet away. But gazing into his eyes, that excuse didn't work. In a few short weeks, she'd come to see what a good man Darius Andreas was. Were she not wounded, were she not afraid, she would be falling head over heels in love with him because he was the kind of man a woman couldn't help loving.

She sighed playfully as if put upon. "All right. I'll

stick with the list that reminds me that you always try to do the right thing."

"I'd appreciate that."

His expression was so intense she suddenly wondered if he wasn't telling her something more. That he seriously wanted her to see his good points because he wanted her to like him.

Her heart leapt with hope. But she squelched it. No matter how good he was, she was weak. She was broken. He deserved better.

She swallowed. Scrambling to get them out of their personal conversation, she pulled away. "I'll bet it seems odd for you to have brothers who are so different."

Watching her walk back to the sofa, apparently accepting her return to their original topic, he said, "Yes and no. We never met until we were adults, so I spent most of my life growing up as an only child. When we did meet, we didn't like each other. I was the product of a marriage. They resented me because our father didn't marry either of their moms. And Nick's mom had a long-term relationship with our dad. It was a surprise when he walked away rather than marry her."

"That is kind of awful."

He took the poker from beside the fireplace and stirred the logs, creating a shower of sparks.

"If you dislike that story, you'll really hate Cade's. His mom was a one-night stand. Stephone simply refused to return her calls until she got a court order for a DNA test after Cade was born." He shook his head. "He didn't think enough of Cade's mom to call her back. I don't know Cade, but if someone treated my mother that badly, I'd hate him, too."

"No wonder they're bitter."

"And don't forget, our different mothers taught us

different things. Mine always loved our dad. She taught me to respect him." He shook his head. "I wanted to hate him." He caught her gaze. "Not for me, but for her. He loved her, yet he couldn't stop cheating."

She understood Darius's anger, but she'd handled enough divorces to be a realist. "For some men, fidelity is impossible."

He looked at the ceiling. "Do you really believe that?"

"Yes." She answered unequivocally, knowing that would bring some sort of meaning to his childhood suffering. It didn't exactly smooth it over, but it did somewhat explain it and take the burden off the women who bore the Andreas brothers and put it where it belonged. On Stephone.

"With some men an affair is the best a woman will get. Lots of women go into them with their eyes open." She shrugged. "I know Missy did. She hadn't expected anything from your dad but what they had in the moment. I'll bet she never spent a sorry day because her expectations were real, honest."

Darius turned to face her and his gaze slid over to hers. His dark eyes held hers, as if there was something else he wanted to say, but instead he turned away and headed for the bar.

"So we get beer and steak," she said, snatching the opportunity to return them to their intended subject because the silence in the room was strained. Awkward. And she wasn't sure why. Especially since they had been getting along, relating normally, for several days.

She couldn't risk losing that. "Since Nick is from the South, I'd say some Tennessee whiskey would probably also be in order."

"Some shrimp."

"And crab legs."

Darius laughed. "Are you still trying to please Cade's potential mystery wife or yourself?"

"Hey, if I have to be here, I'm making the most of your money and connections to get some really good fresh fish."

Chuckling, he pulled a bottle from beneath the bar. "How about a glass of wine?"

"Actually, if our work here is done, I want to go talk with Cook and then call my dad."

"Why?"

"I have a fabulous recipe for jambalaya and my father has the name of a whiskey I think both your brothers will like."

"You don't have to do that."

She smiled. "I want to."

The funny part of it was she did. She liked taking charge. She liked the spike of adrenaline that formed when she had a plan to work and was working a plan. She'd been hiding in the background for so long she'd almost forgotten what a formidable force she could be. After a brief smile, she left the room.

Darius watched her leave, not missing one sway of her soft hips, one step of her long, curved legs. He leaned on the bar and rubbed his hand across his mouth. He wasn't sure if it was wishful thinking on his part, but could she have just told him that she wouldn't mind an affair?

Could it be that in the same way she'd gotten comfortable with her role in his house, she was also getting comfortable with their attraction?

He replaced the wine on the rack and poured himself two fingers of whiskey.

There was only one way to find out.

* * *

Saturday afternoon, after the baby had awakened from his nap, Darius and Whitney set him on the nursery floor. Strong, happy Gino crawled to a stray block that had missed being put into the toy box.

"Did you see that? He crawled!"

Whitney laughed. "You need a video camera."

Darius pulled his cell phone out of his jeans pocket. "Until I get one, this will do."

He aimed the camera at the little boy who slapped the block on the floor by the toy box. Whitney slipped behind him, lifted the toy-box lid and began tossing other soft plastic toys to Gino, who giggled with delight. Darius moved his cell phone to her.

She held up her hand. "Don't!"

"Why not? You look great."

"Yeah, but I don't want to be in your pictures."

"Why not?"

"Because we're...we're..." She wanted to say they were only co-guardians. She wasn't family and didn't really have to be a part of his life. But that was wrong. They were working together for Gino. Both were committed to raising him right and well. Like it or not, they were connected. Maybe for the rest of their lives.

She threw her hands up in defeat. "Whatever. Get me in the video if you want."

He laughed. "Such enthusiasm, right, Gino?" He said, catching the baby's attention. Gino patted his thighs and spouted a bit of gibberish.

"Wish we could get him to crawl again."

Whitney stooped beside the toy box and tossed a colorful ball a few feet away from the baby. "Hey, Gino. See the ball?"

He slapped his chubby hands on his thighs.

Whitney tossed another toy over by the ball.

Gino screeched.

This time she tossed a little stuffed frog she knew was one of Gino's favorites. Finally, he rolled to his knees and crawled after it.

Darius's face blossomed into a broad smile. "Got it."

She lifted herself from the floor. "You need a real video camera. Come on. We'll take Gino to your office, get on the Internet and have one delivered."

Darius scooped Gino from the floor. "Sounds good to me."

They trooped to the second-floor office Darius used. Whitney was not surprised to see he had a second swing set up beside his office chair. When Gino wasn't napping, Darius usually kept his baby brother with him.

He slid the baby into the swing and turned the knob at the top that not only set the swing in motion but also activated the music box. Then he dropped to the chair behind the desk, hit a few buttons on his keyboard and brought his monitor to life.

At first they went on a generic search that led them to the websites of a few well-known brand names of cameras.

When bending down to view the screen became awkward, Whitney leaned her hip on the arm of Darius's chair, half sitting so she could see better. After reviewing the websites for the brands with five-star recommendations, Darius ordered the camera he wanted and clicked off the website.

"We should have it tomorrow."

He looked up at her and she suddenly realized how close they were. At first she was surprised their attraction hadn't sprung up. Then she realized something amazing. She was sitting so close their arms had brushed yet she hadn't panicked. Hadn't noticed, really. She was bless-edly comfortable with him. Relaxed. Content. Almost... happy.

No. She *was* happy. She *liked* him. And not just as a friend or co-guardian. She *liked* him.

She bounced from the arm of his chair. "Okay. Now that that's settled," she said, trying not to sound confused or angry or even weepy and scared. Liking him, seri-ously liking him, meant taking steps, doing things.

Kissing for real.

Getting to know each other.

Making love.

The thought caused her heart to stop. She could see them making love. And why not? They were attract-ed and they were already getting to know each other. They'd flirted. They worked together. Hell, they'd al-ready kissed.

How had they gotten beyond her barriers?

It didn't matter. She wouldn't couldn't get involved with another man again, especially not someone to whom she was committed because of a baby.

CHAPTER TEN

FOR THE FIRST TIME since getting Gino, Darius felt his world righting. He had grown more than comfortable with his role as Gino's father. Plus his feelings for Whitney had taken a sudden, unexpected turn. Now that he realized she might be agreeable to an affair, their attraction no longer seemed wrong. It was just part of the picture. Part of who they were. And if they continued to grow in friendship as they had been, pretty soon he was going to act on it.

As they drove home from the city the following Tuesday evening, he realized "pretty soon" might come sooner rather than later. There she sat, long lean legs crossed, her soft yellow hair tumbling over her shoulders as she worked, tempting him. Over the past few weeks, she'd slowly changed the way she dressed from oversize suits to simple sweaters and skirts. She'd also relaxed her hairstyle, as if she was returning to her normal self. And she was captivating. Gorgeous. If he didn't stop staring at her, he'd be in sad shape by the time they reached the estate. So he did the only thing he could to get his mind on something else. He started talking.

"Nick's flight has been moved up. He'll be at the house on Friday afternoon of the weekend he and Cade are staying, instead of Friday evening."

Whitney looked up. Her pretty Persian-cat eyes warmed with humor. "So are we going home early to meet him, or are you risking the silver?"

"I told you. I'm not worried about the silver, but I'm not so sure I want to leave him alone with Liz."

She burst out laughing. "Oh, come on."

"No, you come on. He's a womanizer."

Her head tilted. "Really?"

He scuffed the toe of his shoe in the limo carpeting. He'd just called his brother a womanizer as if it was a bad thing when *he* intended to try to get Whitney into bed.

"He's got thirteen years on her."

She nudged his shoulder. "Stop acting like an old man."

He glanced up, caught her gaze. "I *am* an old man."

"At thirty-eight?"

The question came out on an airy giggle and everything inside of Darius thundered to life. He hadn't flirted with anyone in weeks. Maybe months. But there was something about flirting with Whitney that was more fun than normal. Maybe because only a few weeks ago this kind of conversation would have been foreign to her. And he'd helped her get to this place.

Surely that meant he could be allowed to enjoy it?

"Maybe I'm not so old as I am experienced."

She snorted and glanced down at her papers again. "I'll bet you are."

He knocked the toe of her high heel with the toe of his oxford. "Wanna find out?"

She looked up, her eyes filled with fear. But in a blink the fear was gone, replaced by curiosity.

Oh, yeah. She wanted to find out.

The mild tingle of arousal in his gut suddenly became

a raging river. He could have ravaged her right there in the limo.

And not been sorry.

That shocked him. He really wouldn't have been sorry. In his mind's eye he saw nothing but pleasure with her. No sadness or fear for her. No guilt or recrimination for himself.

This really was going to happen.

Finally, she said, "Don't flatter yourself," and returned her attention to her paperwork, but he knew she was lying. She wanted him as much as he wanted her.

It was a milestone for her. One he wouldn't take lightly. He would make sure the moment was right when he seduced her. But he would seduce her. Not just for his own pleasure but for hers, and to bring her wholly back to the woman she was supposed to be. He couldn't bring back her child. Couldn't change her memories. But he'd been helping her take steps to recovery all along. He could help her take the next one.

After dinner, he would lure her into the den and they'd have 'the' conversation. He wouldn't risk any misunderstanding. They both had to be clear about this or it wouldn't work.

Because they were now getting down on the floor with Gino, Whitney changed into jeans before she went to the nursery to play for the hour before dinner. After they ate, Darius rose from the table and immediately walked to her chair, which he pulled out for her. "Can you spare a few minutes to talk with me in the den?"

"Sure."

He led her back down the hall. Once in the den, he pointed to the sofa as he headed for the bar. "Wine?"

Because she still had two hours of reading to do, she shook her head. "No. Thanks."

"I was kind of counting on you having a glass of wine before our talk."

"Really?" She laughed. "You want me tipsy?"

"Yes. No." He winced, then pulled out a bottle of wine and popped the cork. "I want you relaxed."

She laughed again. "I thought we were past being nervous around each other."

"Not quite. There's one more thing we haven't discussed. Something we need to discuss and then we'll have everything out in the open between us."

"I'm ready."

He sucked in a breath. "Okay, Whitney, I don't have to tell you that we're attracted to each other."

That was the last thing she'd expected him to say. Rather than sit on the couch as he'd indicated, she took a step back toward the door. "And?"

"And I know I told you that I wouldn't kiss you again, but I've changed my mind. I now think we should do something about this thing between us."

Looking at his full lips, the gleam in his dark eyes, she felt a longing that she hadn't felt in years. Oh, she was tempted, but she'd already worked all this out in her head and decided it was trouble. She laughed nervously and, as casually as possible, took another two steps back. "I'm not ready for a committed relationship."

Unfortunately, he came out from behind the bar and easily caught up with her. He stepped close, toyed with a strand of her hair. "Who says that's what I want?"

Her breath froze in her lungs. Temptation rose up like the morning sun, bright and full of promise. But they weren't the only two people in this equation.

"Have you forgotten, we're parents…raising a child together for the next eighteen years?"

"We're also mature adults who understand ourselves.

You were hurt, nearly destroyed by a man you trusted. I had a father who couldn't remain faithful if he tried. I saw how he hurt my mom. I won't hurt a woman that way."

"And you think having affairs doesn't leave women hurt?"

"Not if you go into the relationship knowing the score. You said yourself Missy was fine with what she had with my dad."

"I know but—" Though that was true, she hadn't meant it in the context he'd taken it. "That's different."

"How?" He snagged her gaze, his eyes bright and serious. "Why? Neither one of us wants a marriage. Why are we any different than my father and your friend?"

"It's just that you seem so sure." She frowned. "Weirdly sure." As if an affair, not a relationship was the obvious choice, undoubtedly because she was the kind of woman no man would ever want to settle down with. Burn might have wanted her, but now she was damaged goods.

She tried to step away, but Darius caught her hands. "Look, I'm the son of a man who couldn't be faithful. I'm pretty sure I inherited those genes. But even if I hadn't, I've had enough experience to know that being wealthy changes everything. I'm tied to my job. I'm tied to this life. I don't have time for a marriage. If you married me, I'd only hurt you more. But there's more to it than that."

Seeing the expression of sincerity on his face, she reeled back her own insecurities. "Like what?"

"My dad blamed sudden riches ten years into his marriage to my mom for making him unfaithful. So he gave me and each of my brothers five million dollars when we turned eighteen, so we'd have a chance to see what it was like to have money. His theory was that when the right woman came along, we'd have all our playboy-bachelor days out of the way, and we could settle down the way he couldn't."

"But it didn't work?"

"No." He snorted a laugh. "Actually, it made things worse. I didn't get my playboy-bachelor days out of the way because I didn't want to run around. I didn't want to gamble. Or skip school or do any of the things kids that age usually want to do. I went to class, worked hard and fell in love with a girl who was one of my study partners. She was from an average family and we were in Wharton, so I knew she was only eking by. It wasn't long before I realized living with me would make her life easier, so we moved in together and pretty soon I was paying her tuition."

"This ends badly, doesn't it?"

He blew his breath out on a sigh. "About a year later, I rushed home early one day to surprise her and I found her with another man. She claimed she'd loved me at first but her feelings had died." He shook his head. "She quite honestly told me she hadn't left me because she needed the tuition."

She could picture idealistic, smitten Darius being so coldly dumped and her heart ached for him. "Maybe she was a little too honest. Cold-hearted even?"

He laughed. "You really haven't been around the block a lot, have you? Lots of life is about money. Your own husband committed suicide because he didn't measure up. It's how we keep score. It's how we keep safe. It's certainly not the root of all evil, but if you've got a weakness it will bring it out in you or make it worse, the way it did with Jen."

"So you're telling me you want an affair for my sake."

"I'm telling you I want an affair because I think that's the best way for us to remain honest with each other. We've come a long way in a couple of weeks. And I believe we've come this far because at a certain point we stopped hedging the truth and looking out for our own agendas and started being honest. It's why I didn't simply seduce you. It's why we're having this discussion now. Honesty might hurt in the moment, but real honesty keeps people from going over the edge."

Surprisingly, what he said made sense. Burn had never been honest with her, and, as a result, he'd delivered the ultimate pain. Even now she didn't know the truth of what had happened with him and the baby. Why he'd killed himself. Why he'd killed their little girl.

"You need this. You need to come back to the land of the living. I can bring you back. I can help you become whole again. No strings attached. Nothing to scare you. Just a nice slow romance to remind you of what it feels like to be a woman again."

She swallowed and turned away. It was too easy to believe him when staring into his sincere eyes. "And what about Gino?"

"What about Gino?"

"You don't think he'll be hurt when our affair fizzles?"

"First, I don't think we'll fizzle. I think we'll morph."

A laugh escaped her. "Morph?"

"Right now we're hot for each other, and you think that will burn out. I think it will simply temper. We'll always want each other." He turned her around, caught her gaze. "If we play this right we could be something like friends with benefits forever."

"Don't you mean parents with benefits?"

He laughed. "Maybe."

When she didn't reply, he leaned in and nibbled her ear. "Don't you want this?"

When her entire body tensed then softened, it was useless to pretend she wasn't attracted—maybe even overly attracted—to him. "Some parts of me."

He chuckled.

"We can't hurt Gino."

"We won't hurt Gino." He pulled away, forcing her to look up at him. "And we won't hurt each other. You've been hurt. I've been hurt. And I had a dad who couldn't stick with one woman if his life depended on it. I can't see myself being faithful forever. I won't make that promise. But I can tell you I'll always be honest and I'll expect you to be honest. When the time comes to shift or morph or maybe even call it quits, you won't be surprised. Or hurt."

"You can't tell me I won't be hurt."

"You might be disappointed, but you'll never be stung or shocked or even surprised. Because you and I will be nothing but honest, up-front, fair. And because what we have feels strong."

"But not strong enough to last forever?"

"Nothing lasts forever. And not always because people can't be faithful." He caught her gaze. "You would have stayed with your husband forever, but you had no control over that. With so many things that can go wrong in a relationship, people are foolish to think they can make one last forever. You're smarter if you go in eyes open. Brain engaged."

She laughed. "Why are you making so much sense?"

He slid his arms around her waist. "I'll give you a

choice of two reasons. First, I'm right. Second, you want me enough that it's easy to agree with me."

She laughed again, but this laugh was tinged with expectation, anticipation.

"Plus we're smart enough to put on the brakes when it feels like we're making a commitment we can't keep. Or when we want something that goes beyond the scope of what we know through experience is nothing but an illusion."

"Yeah." That was why she believed him. Permanency was an illusion. That's the big lesson losing Burn and Layla had taught her. "So what do we do now?"

He pulled away. "What? You think I'm going to seduce you tonight?"

Part of her almost wished he would. Soft and pliant, deadly nervous and hopelessly attracted to him, she knew she wouldn't change her mind, or freeze and run away. "Sort of get this over with?"

"So I'm a get-this-over-with?" He chuckled softly and moved away from her, walking back to the bar where he'd left his wine. "I was thinking more in terms of sweet seduction. A little time. A little flirting." He swirled his wine in the crystal glass. "A little cat-and-mouse."

She swallowed. "You'll have me a nervous wreck."

"Or I'll make you so eager maybe you'll seduce me."

She laughed. "Not likely."

"Oh, you don't know my powers of persuasion."

Friday night, Liz had just finished changing Gino into a fresh sleeper when Darius and Whitney entered the room.

"You guys are either too early or too late. I was just

about to take him downstairs for cereal before I bring him back for a bottle before bed."

Whitney frowned. She knew Liz was a stickler for keeping Gino on a schedule, and she agreed. Babies were much happier when things were always done at the same time of day. But there was no reason she and Darius couldn't spend time with him tonight.

"How about if Darius and I feed him his cereal and rock him to sleep?"

Liz clutched her chest. "No! I didn't mean to sound like it was a problem for me to feed him."

Darius chuckled and took the baby from Liz's arms. "We know that. We also respect your schedule. But we know you have classes tomorrow and you probably want to study. Since we want time with Gino anyway, we're the logical choice to feed him."

Liz cast a wary eye in their direction. "You do know he's already bathed and in his pajamas."

"I've fed him before," Darius said, the voice of authority now that he had almost two weeks of caring for Gino under his belt. "We'll be fine."

Liz was still wary. "I don't want to have to bathe him again."

Whitney batted a hand. "We're fine. Honestly."

Liz grinned. "Okay! I do have some studying to do."

She skipped out of the nursery, eager to get to her books and Whitney and Darius followed her out. She turned to the left. They turned to the right and took the back stairs to the kitchen.

"She's funny," Darius said, heading into the room filled with so much stainless steel and copper pots that it had something of an echo.

"I see her point," Whitney said, going to the cupboard

that she knew contained the cereal. Since her night of struggle to find a plate, spoon and mug, all the things she and Darius might need for themselves or the baby had been moved to a front cupboard. She grabbed the box of cereal, a bowl and Gino's tiny spoon. "She doesn't want to have to do double duty."

"We're virtually pros at this," Darius scowled.

She laughed. "I'm a pro. You're still a beginner."

"Ha!"

"Just go. Get Gino into his high chair."

Shaking his head, Darius left the room. Whitney quickly prepared Gino's cereal and by the time she brought it to the dining room the little boy was already pounding on the tray.

"He knows what this means."

Whitney took a seat beside the high chair. "Of course he does. Sit any human being in front of the table where they've eaten their entire life and they'll want food."

Darius took the bowl and spoon from her. "Good point."

"I'll feed him."

He shook his head. "I'm doing this. Liz maligned my good name."

"Your good name is very sensitive."

He set the bowl on the tray in front of the baby. "I just like it when people trust me to know what I'm doing."

"Liz also likes being good at her job."

He frowned. "I never thought of that."

"She didn't question us because she thinks we're idiots. She just likes being the one who calls the shots with the baby—"

Gino screeched loud and long and Whitney realized they'd all but forgotten the poor kid. But when she looked down at him her mouth fell open in horror.

He'd taken the bowl of cereal Darius had set on the tray, pulled it close to him, and had slathered it all over his face.

Darius gasped. "Liz is going to kill you."

"Kill me!" She grabbed a napkin. "Twenty seconds ago it was your good name being maligned." She pulled in a breath. "This isn't anything to panic about. We'll just make a new bowl of cereal, feed him and then bathe him ourselves."

Taking the bowl and spoon from the tray, she said, "Can I trust you to watch him while I'm gone?"

"Now, you're maligning my good name."

She shook her head and went to the kitchen where she prepared a second bowl of cereal. This time, she didn't give Darius a chance to intervene. She simply sat, fed the baby, and then took the bowl and spoon to the kitchen.

When she returned, Darius stood staring at the baby, who was still in the highchair.

"I'm not sure how to pick him up."

"You pick him up normally."

"I'll get cereal all over me."

"You're going to have to take one for the team."

He laughed at that, drew Gino out of the high chair and winced when the baby's cereal-covered sleeper met his sweater.

Whitney pushed on the swinging door to get out of the dining room and into the hall to the stairs and looked both ways before she turned back to Darius. "Okay. Coast is clear. All we have to do is race up the stairs and down one short hall and we'll be behind closed doors. Liz won't have to know any of this happened."

"I'm right behind you."

They made it up the stairs and into the nursery

without running into Liz and were laughing hysterically when they closed the door behind them.

No longer out of his element, Darius took Gino to the changing table and stripped him out of his one-piece pajamas.

Whitney walked over and cooed at Gino who lay on the changing table playing with a rattle. "Looks like you've got your work cut out for you."

Darius stepped back. He didn't remember volunteering for this duty. Plus, he'd been the one to carry the kid upstairs. "Or you could have your work cut out for you."

She playfully punched his arm. "Hey, you said you wanted to learn everything there was to know about caring for him. Baths are part of that. You've probably never bathed him before."

"But he'll be naked."

"So?"

"So I'm not entirely comfortable with his bladder control."

Laughing merrily, Whitney lifted Gino from the changing table and headed into the nursery bathroom. Seeing how happy she was with Gino sent a surge of pride through him. He'd done that. He'd helped her through her fear and guilt and grief and now she was happy.

Cocky and proud, he followed her into the bathroom, which looked surprisingly like a normal bathroom except instead of two sinks in the vanity, there was a little tub beside the lone sink. Beside the tub was a bin filled with soaps and shampoos and washcloths.

Holding Gino with one hand, Whitney turned on the tap for the tub. As it filled with water, she removed his diaper and set him inside. Gino all but purred with joy.

"Oh, so you like the water?" Darius said, leaning against the doorjamb.

"Oh, no you don't!" Whitney said, laughing when Gino patted his hands in the water and splashed her. "We're both doing this! I need the soap, a washcloth and some shampoo."

Darius stepped inside and handed her the things.

"Thanks."

He took a step back.

"Uh-uh," she said, grabbing the bottom of his sweater with her wet hands. "It takes two hands to hold a big, energetic baby like Gino. So I'm going to give you the choice. Either hold him in the tub or wash him."

"I think I'd be better at holding."

She motioned for him to shift to her left and he did.

"Now, slide your hands around his waist from behind."

He did. Gino squeaked and slapped the water again, this time splashing Darius. Whitney giggled.

"I think you just wanted me to get wet."

"No," Whitney said. "I just want you to share the joy."

"Right."

The bath took little more than five minutes, but before Gino was clean Darius was totally wet. Whitney, however, was suspiciously dry.

When he asked her about it, she gasped in mock outrage. "I just have an instinct about knowing when to step back."

As she bundled Gino in a terry-cloth towel that looked something like a baby blanket, Darius said, "Right."

"I'm serious. Knowing when to step back and when to move in with the washcloth is an art."

She carried wriggling Gino to the changing table in the nursery and pointed at the door to Darius's bedroom with her chin. "You can go change if you want."

"Okay."

He turned and went into his bedroom, but decided against closing the door. It might seem like dirty politics or maybe even a little bit tacky to strip off his shirt in front of her, but he hadn't forgotten their conversation about becoming more than friends. He itched for tonight to be the night, but he hadn't done nearly enough flirting yet. Every time he tried to flirt, the baby would squeak or squawk or want to be fed or just need time.

Actually, he'd seriously begun to wonder how parents ever had a second kid if the first one took up this much time.

Then Gino laughed as if Whitney had tickled him. The sound drifted to him followed by Whitney's happy laugh and something tightened in his gut. He wanted to make love to her in a way he'd never wanted to make love to another woman. Out of joy. Weird joy. A joy that sort of celebrated their lives.

He checked that thought. Not that it was all bad. He still wanted to make love to her out of joy—the joy of finally doing something about their attraction. He'd meant what he said about keeping a certain distance between them. Not just for himself, but also for her.

He would keep that commitment.

He would make love to her.

They would have a relationship.

He would never hurt her.

But he didn't want either of them to have their feelings confused. He didn't believe in permanent relationships.

His dad had taught him that. It was a lesson he'd learned the hard way, by being one of the people his dad frequently ignored.

Days later, Whitney still tingled every time she thought about seeing Darius changing his shirt that night in the nursery, and that, of course, took her back to the discussion they'd had about becoming more than friends. She'd known all along he was attracted to her and she was attracted to him, but it wasn't smart for them to get involved. They had a child to raise.

But, oh, he'd made some really good points for a casual affair. And every day that he flirted with her, touched her hand or looked into her eyes, his arguments seemed even more compelling.

When they found themselves alone in her office again the following Saturday night, her senses scrambled to red alert. He'd told her he intended to seduce her and she knew he wasn't a man to make statements he didn't intend to keep. In a way, it was exciting. Like a game.

Would this be the night?

Would he sweep her off her feet and carry her to the master suite?

Or would he woo her? Seduce her with kisses until she felt dizzy?

In other ways it was terrifying. What if this was the night? Could she handle a relationship that was only about sex and friendship? She'd never had casual sex. She'd only ever made love with a steady boyfriend and a fiancé who had become her husband. She liked commitments.

So could she have a relationship that was only about today? No mention of tomorrow? Burn had promised her tomorrow then snatched it away like a lie. Did she really even believe in tomorrow anymore?

Was Darius right when he said permanency was only an illusion?

"Anyway, when my brothers get here, I think we need to make sure one of us is in the nursery at all times with them."

She set her pen down on her desk. "Refresh my memory. Are we making sure neither one of them snatches Gino, or are we protecting Liz?"

"Protecting Liz!" He sighed. "You're not paying attention."

She winced. "I was working when you came in." Lounging on the couch in his jeans and sloppy T-shirt, looking so comfortably sexy, he had to know he was a colossal distraction.

"Well, stop. My brothers will be here next weekend. We have to make sure we have a game plan."

He seemed so nervous about his brothers' visit that she rose from the chair behind the desk and headed for the conversation area to give him her full attention. She then realized she'd put herself in a terrible position. If she sat on the chair, she'd appear distant and cool. If she sat on the sofa, she might as well tell him she wanted tonight to be the night.

She decided to pace. She'd look perplexed, thoughtful. Actively involved in their discussion.

"What part of the plan do we not have? We've decided every menu and activities for every day. They're going to want to leave just to get some rest."

"I'm not talking about big things. I'm talking about little things. My mother always said you can't be too prepared."

It didn't surprise her that he'd brought up his mother,

but it did relax her. As long as they kept the conversation on concrete things, he wouldn't be thinking about sex. Or maybe she wouldn't be thinking about sex?

"It sounds like your mother was a smart woman."

He sat forward on the sofa. "Oh, she was great. Seriously."

"I'll bet she was proud of you."

"She was." He bounced off the sofa, walked over to her and turned her to face him. "And I get the distinct impression you're bringing up my mother because there's something else you don't want to discuss."

"No! I'm fine."

"Then why are you pacing?"

She shrugged. "I don't know. Bored maybe?"

"We have sort of been stuck here for the past several weeks." His solemn expression shifted into a grin. "Maybe tonight should be the night I seduce you?"

Her breath froze. Her limbs liquefied. As she looked into his sharp, dark eyes, her vocal cords went numb. She couldn't have spoken if she'd tried.

"I promised you flirting and we've been doing that every day. What we're up to is kissing." He brought her right hand to his lips, kissed it lightly, then smiled. "Soft. Just as I expected."

She swallowed as a million pinpricks of excitement raced from the back of her hand up her arm and straight to her heart.

"You're beautiful, Whitney. The day we met, your eyes intrigued me. Such a beautiful shade of blue." His soft, seductive voice trembled through her, heating her blood, fogging her brain. "But your lips are magnificent. Soft. Kissable." His head slowly descended. "I'm going to kiss you now."

She didn't even try to muster an objection. Her

breaths shivered in and out of her chest. Her limbs had weakened. Her brain had shut down. No one had ever spoken to her like this. Listing her attributes. Silkily, sexily telling her he wanted her. How could she possibly argue with that? Resist that?

His lips met hers and Whitney closed her eyes. Dark, delicious sensations tumbled through her. Warmth filled her middle and coiled through her. Unlike their first kiss, this time she wasn't just kissing someone. She was kissing Darius. Someone she knew. Someone she liked. Someone who liked her.

They were really expressing emotion.

But he didn't make a move to deepen the kiss. Instead, he pulled away.

Their gazes clung. She could see the debate raging inside him by the look in his eyes, but he didn't kiss her again.

"We should do that more often."

A happy laugh wanted to escape, but nothing could get past the lump in her throat, the wonderful shivery feeling that held her captive.

His hands slid down her arms until he could catch her fingers. Gazing into her eyes, he said, "Good night." Then he dropped her hands and headed for the door.

He was gone before she found her voice enough to remind him it was only eight o'clock, too soon to go to bed. But it didn't matter. Tonight might not be the night they made love, but it was the night she began to feel again. Really, genuinely, feel. She hadn't even thought of her past. She'd made no comparisons. She had been fully in the moment with Darius.

Was she scared? Absolutely.

Especially since he could want to take the next step at any time, and that would be the real test of whether or not she was moving on.

CHAPTER ELEVEN

THEY DIDN'T GO TO WORK the Friday Darius's brothers were to arrive. Instead, Darius spent the morning in his office fielding calls for work that absolutely had to be handled, while Whitney saw to the last-minute details for the weekend.

She reveled in the job. In the week that had passed, Darius had kissed her every time he'd gotten the chance. He hadn't pushed her to make love, but she enjoyed his kisses enough that she was more than accustomed to their growing feelings for each other. They took care of Gino together and now they were entertaining his brothers together. She'd never felt more at home. She belonged here, in this house, with this man.

When the driver called to inform Darius he had Nick and was ten minutes away from the house, Whitney rose excitedly. "Everything is ready."

Darius wrapped his arms around her waist loosely. "I've decided I was making too big a deal out of this visit, worrying about nothing. My brothers aren't that complicated. Cade's a beer drinker and Nick is such a charmer that you could set raw skunk in front of him for dinner and he'd praise you for it. He'd sweet-talk his way out of having to eat it, but he'd still praise you."

With a laugh, she pushed at his shoulder and eased out of his embrace. "We'll see."

She headed for the main entryway and Darius scooted after her. "I'm serious."

"No. You have a poor opinion of your brothers. I'm hoping this weekend changes that."

The words were hardly out of her mouth before the door opened and Nick walked inside.

Darius stiffened.

Nick's eyes narrowed.

Whitney held back a sigh. She'd give anything to have a sister. Hell, she'd give anything to have a brother. She was an only child who longed for a blood relative to share life's trials and tribulations with. That's why she'd gotten so close to Missy. She wasn't going to let the Andreas brothers ruin this chance to get along.

"You know, I don't expect you to hug. But you could shake hands."

Darius stepped forward, his hand extended. Whitney's mouth fell open slightly at his immediate obedience, then she smiled. Everything she'd been telling him must have sunk in. He'd not only listened to her; he was taking her advice.

Narrow-eyed Nick took Darius's hand. "This isn't a truce."

To Whitney's surprise, Darius laughed and slapped Nick's back. "Right to the point, huh?"

"There's no other way to negotiate."

"Dad's rule number thirty-six."

"Offset by rule number seventeen. Never let the other side know what you want."

Darius laughed again. "I thought I was the only one who realized his rules contradicted each other."

He pointed toward the den on the right. "How about a beer?"

Whitney gasped and caught Nick's arm, turning him toward the dining room. "Or how about lunch? Cade's not supposed to get here until six, so we waited lunch for you."

Nick faced her. His brown eyes narrowed again, only this time it wasn't in suspicion as it had been when he'd looked at Darius. His gaze drifted from her face down to her toes, as if inspecting her.

Then he smiled. "Ms. Ross, right?"

She nodded and stepped back. "Sorry, we should have made introductions."

His smile grew. "We met at your dad's office, remember? I never forget a pretty face."

Darius caught his arm and turned him toward the den again. "Wait until you meet Liz."

"Who's Liz?"

"Gino's nanny."

Nick stopped walking. "Oh?"

Whitney stared at them. First, she wanted to swat Darius for throwing Liz to the lions when he'd told Whitney his goal was to protect her from his brothers. Second, he kept yanking Nick toward a beer, when all three should be having lunch.

"Lunch, remember?" she said, all but stomping her foot to get their attention. "By then Gino should be done with his nap and Nick can meet him."

Nick faced her again then looked at Darius. "She's a lawyer, right?"

Darius said, "Unfortunately."

Nick cocked his head. "Pushy?"

"Absolutely. This weekend was her idea." He motioned for Whitney to lead the way to the dining room.

Nick chuckled and shook his head. "Wait till Cade gets here. It's gonna be an interesting weekend."

The whole way through lunch Darius fielded questions Nick intended for Whitney. Never before in his life had he been so possessive and jealous, but he and Whitney were on the verge of sleeping together, and he had a sixth sense that his brothers were somehow going to ruin all the progress he'd made in the past week. Whitney was a sensitive, only-now-healing woman. One wrong word, one wrong action on his brothers' parts could send her scurrying back into hiding.

This close, there was no way Darius was going to let that happen.

When they went to the nursery, Liz was just finishing changing Gino after his nap. Because he felt bad for the comment he'd made about Liz when Nick first arrived, Darius dismissed her and fed the baby himself. He hadn't intended to throw her under the wheels of the bus, but he'd been jealous of the way Nick was looking at Whitney, and he'd panicked. Dismissing Liz was his way of making up for that.

After watching Liz as she exited the nursery, Nick put his attention on the baby. "He's cute."

"Very cute," Darius agreed. "Once I feed him, you can hold him."

Nick stepped back. "Great." He rubbed his hand along the back of his neck, as if debating something, then said, "You do know about Cade's wife, don't you?"

Darius rolled his eyes. "Yes, if he brings her we're prepared for the extra guest."

Nick shook his head fiercely. "No. I was asking if you knew his wife had died."

Shock took Darius. "His wife is dead?"

"She got sick a few years ago. She fought and fought, but didn't make it." He paced over to the window. "I just don't want you to stick your foot in your mouth by saying something you'll regret."

The urge to thank Nick rose in Darius, but he stifled it. First, it seemed weird to thank someone for telling him Cade's wife was dead. Second, he knew Nick. There was a reason he'd told Darius about Cade's wife, beyond sparing Darius embarrassment. His brothers were cool and calculated. If he wanted to keep the upper hand, he couldn't show weakness.

Gino finished his bottle and Darius rose from the rocker and held out the baby to his brother. "Here."

Nick took the baby with a practiced ease that surprised Darius until he remembered Nick's mom ran a daycare. He let Nick goo and coo and talk baby talk to Gino to his heart's delight. Then at three, he had Mrs. Tucker show Nick to his room and gave him time to unpack.

The second he and Whitney were alone in the den, he caught her by the waist, hauled her against him and kissed her soundly.

"What was that for?"

"I've been wanting to do that all day."

She giggled, and intense, primal need punched at him. At first he considered it arousal, then he realized it wasn't physical as much as emotional. When she giggled she looked young, cheerful, as if he'd all but erased the horrible years she'd just gone through, and that knowledge brought a lump to his throat. She was beautiful, happy, wonderful and his for the taking. He didn't know how long they'd last, but he did know they were good for each other. He was as good for her as she was for him, and that made him proud in the weirdest male way.

A way he'd never felt before. A way that sent an odd niggling of something cruising through him. Not fear. Not doubt. But *something*.

Before he could think it through, Mrs. Tucker walked into the room and Whitney jumped back, the way she always did when they got caught.

"I'm sorry to disturb you, Mr. Andreas, but you received a call from your brother, Cade, during lunch. He didn't want to ruin your meal by forcing you to come to the phone, and simply asked me to let you know he'll be arriving earlier than he'd planned."

"Okay, that's great."

Mrs. Tucker left the room and Whitney laughed. "There wasn't a lot of enthusiasm in your voice."

There wasn't. Not just because his half-brothers were a trial, but because he and Whitney were right on the edge of taking their relationship to the next level and his brothers were ruining it.

He caught her by the waist and pulled her to him again. "Gino's asleep and Nick's occupied." He kissed her neck. "What do you say we go to the master suite and relax?"

She pulled away and smiled. "Relax?"

He pulled her back. "Making love is the ultimate relaxation."

This time when he kissed her, he didn't waste time on preliminaries. He wanted her. She wanted him. They'd already proven they were good for each other. It was time. He kissed her deeply, his tongue delving into the sweet recesses of her mouth, and she kissed him back. They were both more than ready—

Then Nick cleared his throat.

Once again, Whitney jumped away like a guilty teenager. Darius held back a curse.

"I thought you were taking a nap."

Nick laughed. "Not hardly." Having changed out of his trousers and oxford-cloth shirt, he wore jeans and a cable-knit sweater. He strolled to the pool table. Running his hand along the smooth mahogany rim, he said, "So, play much?"

Darius shrugged. "A little."

"A little," Whitney gasped. "He—"

Darius nudged her, telling her with his eyes to stop talking. "I beat Whitney. She thinks I'm a pro."

Nick smiled wolfishly. "Really? I'm not very good either."

Darius racked the balls. "Right."

Nick turned to Whitney. "Want to play?"

Whitney glanced from Darius to Nick, then back at Darius again. "I think I'll sit this one out. I have some filings to read to catch up on my work." She nodded at both men. "I'll see you at dinner."

Darius watched her go. When he faced Nick, his brother was studying him. "I'd have thought the nanny was more your type."

Darius walked over and chose a stick. "The nanny is nineteen."

"That's my point."

Rattled, Darius broke, sending the multicolored orbs in all directions. Four balls fell into pockets. "I'll take striped." He caught Nick's gaze. "And I don't chase babies."

"Just babes."

Darius set up another shot. "Something like that."

Nick leaned on his stick. "So you're staking a claim on Whitney?"

Darius took the shot. Another striped ball fell into a pocket. But he hardly noticed. Nick's question reverberated through his brain. Was that what he was doing? Staking a claim? It seemed so permanent, so settled. And he wasn't the kind to settle. He'd figured out a way to make this situation work for both him and Whitney, and he wouldn't deviate. He didn't give women false hope, or make promises he couldn't keep. That was the rule.

Yet, he didn't want his brother flirting with her, either. Even the thought sent his blood screaming through his veins.

He caught Nick's gaze. "Let's just say that for the weekend I'm staking a claim."

If Nick surprised Darius, Cade shocked him. Instead of bounding into the house in boots and trademark Stetson, he wore a tailor-made suit, white shirt, blue tie. When it came time to change for dinner, he simply took off his jacket and tie, and rolled up the sleeves of his white shirt. He raced to pull out Whitney's chair at dinner before either Darius or Nick could get to it. And he engaged her in genuine conversation, not asking about the baby, but about her job.

Darius had never asked her about her job. Yes, he knew more about her personal life, her history, than Cade did. But Cade had asked about her present and her future. What she wanted. Darius never thought beyond the day they were living.

"So someday you're going to be a partner?" Cade's question slid into the conversation as easily as the chocolate mousse slid down Darius's throat.

"Actually, someday control of the firm will probably be mine. Not only does my father own most of the firm, but I'm the oldest of the junior partners. I'll choose who rises up, who falls."

Cade laughed. "Oh, interesting. I love a woman who's not afraid of a little power."

Whitney blushed endearingly and Darius's blood pressure rose. Having both lost spouses, Whitney and Cade had a lot more in common than he and Whitney did. If Cade kept flirting, eventually he and Whitney would talk for real and they'd realize Cade was the better choice of Andreas brother for Whitney. And Darius would—

Would what? Lose her? He'd never cared if he'd lost a woman before. Why would he care now?

She dabbed her lips with a napkin and said, "It's just past eight. If we go upstairs now, we can all say goodnight to Gino."

Though Cade was closer to Whitney and beat Darius to her chair, Darius was beside her in an instant. He slid his hand to the small of her back and led the way with her to the nursery.

The next morning, breakfast was peaceful. Whitney had eaten early and was out of the dining room by the time the brothers came downstairs. She knew her presence was a distraction, causing them to avoid talking to each other. Instead, Cade and Nick had kept bringing the conversation back to her and her life.

However, she wouldn't have been able to have the kind of serious, honest discussion that Cade had initiated if Darius hadn't pushed her out of her shell over the past few weeks. Standing in the kitchen, peeking through the crack between the door and its frame, watching the brothers, her heart swelled. Darius's half-brothers were rich, powerful, overconfident men who weren't making Darius's task of bringing them together easy. Yet he wasn't backing down. He might be on the brink of losing his temper, but he held it back and held his ground, trying his best to get to know his brothers without an argument ensuing. Still, it was easy to see he was tense. Tight. She wished Nick hadn't strolled into the den the day before when Darius had kissed her and asked her to go to the master suite with him.

He'd been teasing about making love relaxing him, trying to lure her upstairs, but she knew that if they'd gone upstairs, if they'd made love, they would have talked afterward. She would have leaned her head on his shoulder and brushed her hand through the hair on his chest. With their thighs entwined and their bodies sated, they would have talked. About Gino. About his brothers. About how he felt. And she would have soothed him. Because that's what she did best. She soothed him, just as he had calmed her about Gino and brought her back to the real world so she could love again—

So she could love again.

She *could* love again.

The picture of them together, tangled in sheets in the master bed, formed in her brain again, and not an ounce of fear whispered through her. Only joy. Bubbly, happy, joy.

She swallowed. A new fear trembled through her.

She loved him.

She *loved* him.

And that wasn't their deal.

When she came down to dinner that evening, Darius stood by her chair and pulled it out, not giving either of his brothers the chance to one-up him as a gentleman. She didn't know whether to smile or cry. He liked her. He absolutely wanted to sleep with her. But love? In the scant weeks they'd spent together, she doubted it. She'd fallen hard and fast because he'd brought her back from the black pit of despair. He'd shown her tenderness, kindness. She might soothe him, but that was hardly noteworthy. She'd given him no reason to *love* her. As far as Darius was concerned, except for their friendship, they were exactly where they'd been six weeks ago. Physically attracted.

Dinner was spent the same way it had been the night before, with her fielding questions. Somehow or another, both Andreas brothers seemed to know to stay away from the subject of her past. Which didn't surprise her. A few minutes on the Internet could net a person the basic facts of her life. And both were kind enough not to question her about her loss.

Cade's questions were conversational. He asked about her likes and dislikes. Nick was a lot more obvious, asking if she'd been to Europe, if she'd considered visiting the Orient. All but hinting that he'd take her anywhere she wanted to go if she only said the word.

So she bowed out of the pool game to take place after dinner. "Darius and I have spent so much time with you that I'm afraid Liz hasn't had ten back-to-back minutes to study." She made a move to rise and Cade immediately was at her back, pulling out her chair. "Plus, I don't really need dessert." She laughed softly.

All three men said their goodbyes, but Darius was looking at her curiously. Halfway up the stairs, she stopped dead in her tracks. She'd casually, happily, chosen to care for Gino. Alone. And she wasn't afraid. Memories of Layla didn't hammer through her brain. The ones that did come were soft, sweet. Easy. The kinds of things she wanted to remember. There was no pain, just sadness. She'd always feel the loss. She'd always miss her baby girl. She'd always wonder what

Layla's life might have been like. But blessed acceptance had finally come.

Tears filled her eyes and she swallowed hard. A new segment of her life had begun.

Thanks to Darius.

The man she now loved.

In the den, Darius wasn't happy when Cade turned the conversation to Whitney.

"So what's the deal with you and Ms. Ross?"

"We're co-guardians."

That made Nick laugh. "Don't even think about making a move. He's already staked a claim."

Cade laughed. "Really? You're dating?"

"No."

Cade walked up to Darius, close enough to be a silent threat. "So technically you haven't really staked a claim."

Darius's blood pressure rose again. Anger thundered through his system like fighter jets. Standing in Darius's personal space as he was, Cade might as well have come right out and said he was looking for a physical fight, not just a verbal one. And, tonight, after two days of watching Cade and Nick flirt with Whitney, Darius wasn't about to back down.

"Stay away from her."

"Why?

"Because she's only now healing from a loss. She doesn't need to hear about yours and be sad again," Darius snarled.

Nick pushed between Darius and Cade. "Hey, hey, hey! That's enough. Cade, you're here to get to know Gino. Nothing else. And, Darius, get a grip. I can understand why you're sappy—"

Darius stopped his brother with a piercing stare. "Sappy?" He was blistering mad, macho, territorial, *anything* but sappy. And he couldn't believe Nick had said that. "Is that how you see me?"

Cade chuckled. "If you mean jealous and angry and an easy mark, yes." He walked over to the wall and chose a pool cue. "If Nick or I ever need leverage, we now know that all we have to do is talk to Whitney."

Realizing the truth of what Cade said, Darius got his pool cue, cursing himself for being an idiot. Cade wasn't interested in Whitney. He'd been testing to see what pushed Darius's buttons.

"Don't make so much out of what you think you've seen. Ms. Ross and I will eventually sleep together, but you know us Andreas men. Nothing's ever permanent. If one of you stole her, I'd move on. That's our dad's legacy to us."

Taking aim at a shot, Cade said, "So she's a fling?"

Darius snorted a laugh. "What else?" The words tripping off his tongue sounded like him again, reminding him that all the jealousy, the funny feelings, the weird connections he felt with Whitney hadn't been him at all. He didn't know who he'd been when he'd said and thought that crazy stuff. But this was him. It had taken a visit from his brothers to remind him that the soft, syrupy guy he was becoming not only wasn't him, but also that guy wouldn't stand a chance with his two brothers. If he wanted to get along, he couldn't be a sap. He had to be as strong as they were.

Having changed her mind about spending the evening alone after Gino was asleep, Whitney stopped outside the den door just as Cade said, "The next time just say you want Whitney to be off limits."

Darius simply said, "I thought I had."

"Snarling and getting jealous doesn't count." Nick slapped him on the back and the pool game resumed, but Whitney stayed rooted to the spot. Darius had just told his brothers he wanted her to be off limits.

Ridiculously, her heart rose. All this time she'd been worried that Darius hadn't fallen in love the way she had, but now she wasn't so sure. The events of the past few weeks rolled through her mind. Not just the kissing, the conversations. The way they'd compromised over Gino. The way they were creating a family with Gino.

Yes, they had agreed to an affair, but today she'd realized they'd grown so much closer, gone so far beyond that, that she'd fallen in love. So maybe he was feeling it, too?

He had to be. Why else would he be jealous and snarl? She stifled a giggle. She would have loved to have seen him snarl.

She turned around and went to her bedroom where she rummaged through the things she'd brought from home, looking for something cute, something sexy, something that would tell him in just one look that she was ready. Tonight they would make love.

Unfortunately, she didn't find anything. So she settled for a silky camisole and pajama bottoms.

Opening her door, she peeked into the hall, saw no one around and tiptoed to the master suite. She hadn't heard him come upstairs yet, but when he did she would be waiting for him.

An hour later, Darius headed for the master suite. Though they seemed to have come to terms about Whitney, he and his brothers were no closer to getting along than they had been the morning of his father's death. It was frustrating and irritating, and made him so angry he wanted to ask them both to leave. They weren't really trying to get along. Each appeared only to have come to Montauk to get a closer look at Gino.

He snorted a laugh. What purpose did it serve to have them here except to raise his blood pressure?

But when he opened the door and saw Whitney sitting on the corner of his bed, like a sweet present waiting to be unwrapped, everything about his brothers fell out of his head.

She was making the move. *She* was going to seduce *him*.

"Hey."

She peeked up at him and smiled shyly. "Hey."

He wanted to rip off his sweater and jump out of his jeans on the way to the bed, but he remembered her sensibilities so he simply ambled to the bed, sat beside her.

"How'd your night go?"

"Aggravating as hell. My brothers are morons."

She laughed. "I think they both have their good points."

"Oh, you would! They fawned all over you. They're making mincemeat out of me."

She laughed. "They're testing you. That's all. It's like you're playing a real-life game of king of the mountain. You might be the oldest brother, but they've lived their lives without you. They want to make sure you know you can't push them around."

He ran his hand along the back of his neck. "Right." The urge to confide in her rose up in him. He wanted to tell her everything they'd said, all the pushing they'd done, all the ways he'd had to hold his ground.

But, with his brothers in the wing on the other side of

the house, the infernal need to tell her everything only served to remind him that they thought he was sappy. Weak. Vulnerable.

So if he really only wanted a fling with Whitney, he couldn't tell her everything. There were pieces of himself he'd have to keep to himself.

"They're cautious about the three of us becoming friends," he said simply, sliding his hand across her back. "But…I'd rather not talk about them."

He said this as he lowered his head and kissed her. Because he'd taken her by surprise, the kiss she returned was instinctive and sweeter than any he'd ever experienced.

He stopped. He didn't want sweet from her. Not tonight. All he'd ever wanted from Whitney was untamed passion. Something he could easily label. Compartmentalize. Forget.

Forget?

The word brought him up short. Angered him. He pulled away, rose from the bed and began to pace. Planning to forget Whitney pierced an arrow through his heart. Yet, how could he deny that was what he was doing? All short-term relationships were forgettable. That was why they were so easy. So uncomplicated.

But he knew Whitney was neither easy nor uncomplicated. Plus, Gino would keep them together for the rest of their lives. Still, they'd made their agreement to start an affair keeping those two things in mind. They'd planned for this. Carefully.

"I take it you're here because you're still good with a temporary relationship?"

"Yes and no."

He spun around. "Yes and no?"

"Yeah, I…um…"

Nerves took Whitney as reality sunk in. A man who'd changed his mind about an affair because he loved her wouldn't be pacing by the bed. He wouldn't be nearly crazy with nerves or confusion. He'd tell her he loved her, kiss her and seduce her.

Somehow she'd gotten all the signals mixed.

She combed her fingers through her hair. "You don't love me."

His face registered shock, then dismay. But he blinked both away before he sat beside her on the bed again.

"That wasn't our deal. But this isn't a cold, calculating thing for me either. Otherwise, we'd be naked and tangled in sheets right now. I care deeply about you. I feel so many more things than I usually feel for a woman that it scares me."

Another woman might have taken his words to heart, seen them as a stepping stone to love, but she knew Darius. He made decisions quickly, easily. If there was even a chance that he loved her, he'd know it. He'd say it.

"You have feelings, but you don't love me."

He said nothing. But the fact that he wouldn't speak spoke volumes.

Confusion overrode pain, mostly because confusion could give her the strength to walk out of the room before she burst into tears.

He caught her chin and forced her to look at him. "I thought you wanted what I wanted."

"I did."

His gazed locked with hers. "But now you don't?"

"I thought we were on the same page."

Realization sparked in his dark eyes. "You thought we were falling in love."

"I *did* fall in love."

"Oh." He squeezed his eyes shut. "Whitney, I...
I..."

She sucked in a shaky breath. "Don't stutter. Don't
stumble. Just say it. You don't love me."

He swallowed hard.

She shook her head and sprang from the bed, racing
to the door, eager to get away as tears rimmed her
eyelids.

He jumped up and followed her. "This isn't about you
or me. My father—"

She spun around. "Don't!" Her sharp voice stopped
him. "Don't come after me and don't blame this on your
family, your genes. This isn't about genes. It's about
choices. Your dad might have been a runaround, but
that was his choice. You said we were going to build
this relationship on honesty. Then you can at least be
man enough to say you don't like me enough to choose
me."

"You don't understand—"

"No. *You* don't understand. If you loved me, you
wouldn't be able to resist. A commitment wouldn't scare
you. So, no, Darius, you do not love me."

With that she walked out of the room. Pain dulled her
senses, but not her brain. She slipped into the nursery
where she quietly packed Gino's duffel and diaper bags.
She gathered his bottles and cereal from the kitchen.
Then she woke Darius's driver and Liz. Before the sun
rose, she and Liz were in the living room of her Soho
loft and Gino slept soundly in his carrier.

CHAPTER TWELVE

DARIUS WOKE THE NEXT MORNING feeling like a man with a hangover. His head ached. His eyes thumped. Every muscle in his body hurt. He knew he hadn't had enough to drink to make him feel like a man who'd been run over by a train. Lack of sleep most likely had caused the aches and pains and thumping.

After his fight with Whitney, after she'd stormed out, he'd gone to the shower, hoping to give her twenty minutes or so to calm down before they talked again. He stood under the cold water for God only knew how long. But he'd had to spend a lot more time than he'd anticipated for the arousal thundering through his blood to dissipate. By the time it had and he returned to his bedroom, the house was quiet.

Relief had fluttered through him. He'd hated having hurt her, but he knew that if she'd fallen asleep that easily she'd be fine. Of course, he'd also realized that she could be awake across the hall and he wouldn't hear her. So he'd paced, listened for sounds that she was awake, listened for any indication that she'd gone downstairs for cocoa. Hoping they could talk again. But he'd never heard a sound.

That's when he'd started dealing with memories. She'd been everywhere in his house, even his bedroom.

He could picture her laughing, frightened, courageously walking over to take Gino from Liz. And every memory seared his heart, made him feel like a bastard for leading her on. But he hadn't led her on. He'd been honest. Fair. She was the one who'd broken their deal.

Now, *he* had to deal with the mess that caused. All the while she'd be two steps away, or a few rooms away. And the pain evident on her face would be his fault this time. Not a dead husband's.

He slid out of bed and into sweatpants and a T-shirt and forced himself into the nursery. Liz was nowhere around and the crib was empty. He hated the relief that flooded him at the obvious reprieve he was getting, until he saw an envelope leaning against a stuffed bear on the dresser. He walked over to it and opened it.

I've changed my mind about living at Montauk. I've taken Gino and Liz to the city. You may, of course, visit any time. Simply call before you want to see Gino. We'll see my father to get a custody agreement drawn up.
Whitney

Darius expected anger to roll through him. How dare she take the baby? Instead of anger, though, something squeezed his heart.

Before he could even think about that, the nursery door opened. Nick stepped inside and immediately walked to the crib. "Where's the baby?"

The nursery door opened again. This time Cade walked in. "Hey." He glanced at the crib. "Where's Gino?"

Darius waved the note. "Apparently Whitney took him back to the city."

Both Nick and Cade glanced over at him. Nick's eyebrows rose. Cade frowned. "What did you do?"

Darius tossed the note to the dresser. "What makes you think I did something?"

"Because that line you fed us last night about only wanting to sleep with her was pure rubbish."

Nick laughed. "Right. That was really kind of priceless."

Cade all but rolled with laughter. "I know! Any idiot could see he was smitten."

Fury at both of them rumbled through Darius like thunder before a dangerous storm.

"I was not smitten."

Nick said, "You were."

"And what makes the two of you experts? We are all three Andreas men. I know how we are."

Nick shook his head with a chuckle. "You keep telling yourself that. You keep telling yourself that you can't love her or be faithful or whatever it is you tell yourself and see how far that gets you."

Whitney awakened around ten to sunlight filtering in through the wall of windows in her condo bedroom and the sound of Gino crying. She popped up and was at the drawer-made-crib beside her bed in seconds, hoping not to disturb Liz.

"Hey little guy," she crooned, reaching for a clean diaper. "Just let me take care of this and we'll get a bottle."

Liz groggily walked into the room. "I'll get the bottle."

"I'm fine. Why don't you go back to sleep?"

Liz looked at her compassionately. "We're both exhausted. So why don't we share duties until we can both get a nap?"

Whitney smiled. Now that Darius had helped her out of her grief, it didn't seem wrong to accept another person's help. "Okay."

Liz left the room and Whitney changed Gino's diaper. Knowing Liz would need a minute to warm the bottle, she lifted Gino out of the drawer and held him. Close. Because she could. Because she was stronger now.

But memories of the days she'd spent with Gino and Darius assaulted her. She couldn't believe a man who'd so sensitively brought her back to life could believe he wasn't capable of fidelity...of love.

It made no sense, but she wasn't a dewy-eyed school-girl anymore. Darius had been very plain and very clear in his intentions. She was the one who'd gone too far.

And now she was paying the price. She might be stronger. She might finally have the ability to love again. But being able to love had put her in the line of fire for another kind of heartache.

Different from having lost Burn and Layla, this pain rattled through her like a restless ghost with a chain, called her a fool, reminded her that loneliness took many forms, reminded her that when Darius could have chosen her, he'd stepped away, not even wanting to try.

CHAPTER THIRTEEN

SUNDAY MORNING, after walking his brothers to the limo that would take them to the airport, Darius stepped into his huge house and closed the door. The front foyer echoed around him. Empty. Hollow.

He knew the feeling because it mimicked the one in his chest. He swore that without Gino in the nursery and Whitney working in the first-floor office, there was a hole where his heart should be.

Which was foolish. He was damned near forty. With the exception of Jen, he'd never had a relationship that had lasted over four months. He was a scoundrel. A louse. He'd hurt Whitney because he'd selfishly assumed they were on the same page romantically. True, they'd had an agreement but he should have seen the signs that she wanted something more. He should have realized she was falling in love. He knew she was delicate. He knew she deserved something more. Yet, he'd selfishly barreled on, seeking only what he wanted.

He should be shot. Not coddled. So he forced himself to work that afternoon. He took his dinner in the office because after trying to eat lunch alone, with only the ocean view for company, he felt like a man who'd been beaten with a club. He didn't want to miss Whitney, didn't deserve to miss Whitney, but he did.

Monday morning in the limo, he thought about the day he kept bumping toes with her and he laughed, then his chest seized with pain. She brought out the stupidest damned urges in him. He should be glad she was gone. Glad he'd dodged the bullet. Glad he hadn't actually slept with her and really hurt her.

Instead all he felt was lonely. Hurt. Alone.

On Thursday, after having spent the week at the office avoiding her, he realized he could get Gino for the weekend. That lifted his spirits, but the fact that he'd have to talk to Whitney to get permission lifted them more.

He told himself that was stupid as he walked down the hall to her office. It was best for the two of them to stay out of each other's way until the whole heartache thing was over with. He shouldn't want to see her. Still, he wanted Gino for the weekend and he was halfway to her office.

So he continued down the corridor, but as he stepped into her office he saw her desk was empty.

Her assistant walked up behind him. "She now works afternoons for Montgomery, Ross and Swaggart."

"The deal was—"

Maisey Lenosky, a tall brunette who'd worked for his dad for decades, looked at him over the top of her glasses. "If you're not happy, take this up with her. I'm not your go-between. But trust me, had I been in her shoes I'd have gone, too."

Fear sliced through him. "She told you?"

"She didn't have to. I could see for myself you hadn't given her any work all week. So she went back to the job that did."

Relief replaced the fear in a dizzying wave. "Oh. Okay. I'll call her."

He didn't wait for Maisey's reply, simply headed for his office. He dialed the number for Whitney's cell phone and immediately went to voice mail. So he dialed the firm and asked to be put through to her. Instead he got her assistant.

If it were anyone other than Whitney, he'd wonder about getting the run-around. But she was too serious, too honest, to dodge him. She would know he was calling to make arrangements for Gino and she'd accommodate him.

"I'd like Ms. Ross to call me back."

"May I ask what this is about?"

He wanted to say no, if only because it annoyed him to be jumping through hoops with staff, but he said, "Yes. We share custody of my half-brother. I would like to take him to my house in Montauk this weekend."

"That's great. I'll give her the message."

Ten minutes later, Whitney's assistant called back. "She says you may pick up Gino at six on Friday night and keep him until Sunday at about six."

Affront charged through him that she hadn't called him back, but he remembered that he'd hurt her and decided that this was the treatment he deserved. But on Friday night he intended to talk to her. To tell her he was sorry. Truly sorry. So that she could move on. So *they* could move on.

Friday night, Liz answered the concierge call that let him up to Whitney's apartment. He tried not to be on pins and needles about seeing Whitney again, but it was no use. He desperately wanted to ease the pain of the hurt he'd caused her.

So when he stepped into the apartment and Liz immediately handed him the diaper bag and headed for the door, he stopped dead in his tracks. "Where's Whitney?"

"Dinner with her parents. She just left." Liz smiled patiently. "And I'd like to get going so I can get a few hours to study tonight."

He took the hint and left the apartment, following Liz to his limo. But the weekend without Whitney was strained. Though Liz was bright and perky and very happy to stay and play with Gino and Darius the way Whitney had, it wasn't the same.

At night, he stared out the window at the dark ocean, brooding, angry with himself. What made him different from his father was that he didn't hurt the women he romanced. And he hadn't intended to this time, but he had, and that knowledge kicked around inside him. His chest ached. His soul mourned. He wasn't the kind of man who hurt women. Knowing that he had hurt Whitney was killing him.

Sunday night, Whitney wasn't around when he returned Liz and Gino to her apartment. He'd expected that. If he were angry with himself for how he treated Whitney, then how could he expect Whitney to be any less so?

Monday morning, he dressed carefully. Dark suit, white shirt, red tie. It was the first time in his adult life he could remember being worried about his appearance, but concern over the way that he'd hurt Whitney was eating him up. He longed to apologize, to make things right, and this morning he would so that he could get rid of this awful pain.

But when he reached Whitney's office, Maisey sat behind her desk.

"Where's Whitney?"

"She switched her schedule." Maisey sat forward,

smiling at him. "In fact, even she isn't sure what days she's working mornings and what days she's working afternoons."

"She's avoiding me."

"No, actually, her father has given her lead chair in a civil suit. She's very excited."

So was he. He knew how much she loved her work. "Really! That's great."

"She's like a kid at Christmas."

That did not hit him as happily as the first comment did. She wasn't missing him. Didn't care that he was out of her life. Not that he wanted her to be suffering. So this news should have made him feel better. Instead, he felt worse. Rumpled. As if he were an old shirt she'd taken off, rolled into a ball and tossed into the laundry.

Which was foolish. He wanted her to be happy. So why did the news that she was moving on make him feel worse?

Tuesday, he didn't go to work. He took the important phone calls at home and spent most of his day reading financial reports. He didn't shave. He didn't eat. The dining room was now an unholy place of torment. There was no baby to amuse him, no conversation to offset the sound of the pounding surf.

Wednesday morning, he was again in his home office, supposedly reading, but actually alternating between staring at the fire and staring at the ocean. It took him completely by surprise when Mrs. Tucker entered the room.

"You have a phone call."

"I told you I'm not taking calls."

"It's your brother." She smiled. "The sweet-talker."

Darius sighed. "That would be Nick."

She left the room and he yanked the phone from the cradle. "What do you want?"

"Oh, touchy."

"I don't have time to horse around Nick. I have—" Actually, he had nothing. He couldn't focus. He didn't want to focus. He didn't know what he wanted.

"You miss her."

Of course he missed her. What an asinine statement. "I hurt her."

Nick had the audacity to laugh. "Oh, Darius. It sounds like she hurt you more."

"I feel bad because I know I made her feel bad."

"Really?"

"Yes."

"You don't feel bad yourself?"

"Of course I feel bad. I just told you. I hate that I hurt her."

"And that's what's making you stay home?"

"That and the fact that I don't want to shave."

Nick laughed merrily. "Darius! Have you never had your heart broken before? You sound just like me when my ex-wife Maggie left. I couldn't eat. I couldn't sleep. I stared at the damned ocean all day."

Darius said nothing.

"Is that what you're doing?"

Darius scowled.

"Darius?"

"Yes, all right!" Darius snarled. "I've been at home for two days, not shaving, not eating, staring at the ocean. Let's not make a big deal out of it."

"Why not?"

Why not? Darius was just about to slam down the phone or thunder a retort, until he realized he had no retort. He ached. He missed Whitney. Not the way he'd miss a girlfriend who couldn't make it to the house for a weekend. Not the way he missed a lover who'd brushed him off. But like…like part of his life. When she'd walked out the door, his future had changed. He hadn't realized it, but in the weeks they had lived together, he had begun to picture Whitney helping him raise Gino. He'd seen them as Gino's parents. He'd seen them together, happy, for years…without even realizing he was doing it.

He missed her, longed for her, because she was the part of himself he'd been missing. And he finally saw that maybe, just maybe, he hadn't been a philanderer because he liked women—well, that was part of it. But in reality, after Jen had hurt him, he hadn't wanted to go through that pain again, so he'd been biding his time, entertaining himself, until he found the right woman. Someone he could trust with his heart.

And he'd found her.

He'd found the right woman.

And he'd lost her.

"Go get her."

Nick's advice sounded so simple, so easy. But Darius knew better. Or maybe he didn't. After Jen, he'd never wanted a woman back, never tried to get one back. He had no frame of reference for what to expect. She could welcome him with open arms. She could slash him to ribbons. Worse, she simply might not want him. She'd said she loved him, but what if he'd killed that love?

Intense pain rumbled through him. Seized his lungs. Burned his soul. He'd never gone to a woman without the confidence of knowing she wanted him. He'd be laid bare. Defenseless. He wasn't sure he could do it.

"She's lead chair in a big civil suit. I can't just walk

into a courthouse and pluck her out. Especially since I haven't shaved."

"How about this?" Nick said, his voice unexpectedly kind. "Shower, shave and stop at a florist. Buy an armload of roses. Then go to her apartment. Liz is there with the baby, right?"

"Yes."

"Well, Liz will let you in and Whitney's got to get there sometime."

That was true. "If I know Whitney, she won't work late. She might bring two armloads of files home, but she'll get home on time, relieve Liz, spend time with Gino, then she'll work."

"So now you know what time to go. Don't spend the rest of the day brooding. Think about what you'll say, but don't over-rehearse." Nick paused. "And call me tomorrow and let me know how it went."

Darius blinked. Had Nick just asked him to call him?

It had never occurred to Darius that having his brother's support would lift his spirits or give him a weird kind of courage, but it did. "Okay. I will." He stumbled over the agreement, but when it came out it was surprisingly easy. "Thanks."

Whitney took a cab from the office to her home. She yanked out two briefcases full of work, set them beside her on the sidewalk and paid the driver.

When she turned, Jake, the young concierge, was lifting her briefcases. "Evening, Ms. Ross."

"Good evening, Jake."

There was a gleam in his eye. An unholy sparkle. The force of it hit Whitney in the stomach and sent little pricks of misery through her. Jake liked Liz. Liz liked

Jake. They were about the same age, both attending university. They were a good match. She should have been happy.

Instead, their attraction reminded her of how foolish she'd been.

"I'll ride with you," Jake said, when Whitney attempted to take the briefcases as they reached the elevator.

She smiled. "Of course. Thank you." She wouldn't punish Jake for being a good guy who'd found a girl he really meshed with. But she would continue to remind herself that it had been stupidity to think the likes of Darius Andreas would fall for her and commit. She'd genuinely believed he'd fallen. But he hadn't. She had to get over that.

And she would. After she wallowed in misery for a few weeks over Darius. But that was good. It would teach her not to be so naive again.

When she opened her apartment door, the scent of clam chowder greeted her. Her mouth watered. By the time she turned around to thank Jake, he was gone. Her two briefcases sat in the open doorway, but he was nowhere in sight.

She grabbed the briefcases and pulled them into the condo, toward the table where she would work. "Liz?"

No answer. She walked to the kitchen area and snapped off the burner beneath the bubbling soup.

"Liz?"

No answer again.

Panic struck her heart. There hadn't been food bubbling on the stove when she'd arrived home the night she'd discovered Burn and Layla in the garage. But she had walked into a silent home when she'd been expecting to enter a house filled with the noises of a toddler and her overworked dad.

Terrified now, she pivoted and would have raced back to the bedrooms, but as she turned, Darius came out of her bedroom, Gino on his arm.

"Sorry."

Her heart stopped. Her brain turned to mush. Intense relief flooded her, but before it fully registered, the sight of Darius turned her knees to rubber and her heart to a swampy pool of emotion. He looked tired. Awful. His hair went in four different directions. He hadn't shaved—for days, she would guess from the growth on his chin and cheeks.

"Don't worry. I showered."

His comment was so unexpected that a laugh burst from her chest. But she caught it after one quick giggle. This man had hurt her. True, it was partially her fault—okay, mostly her fault for assuming things he'd never said—but she didn't want to get hurt again. She wanted to recover. Which meant he couldn't simply come into her home and take over the apartment.

"I thought you were supposed to call and arrange visits?"

"I did. I called Liz. She actually needed some time to go to the library. She was happy I could watch Gino this afternoon."

"You've been here all afternoon?"

"And I brought soup from Cook as a peace offering." He strolled a little farther into the apartment. "She also gave me a pan of lasagna for tomorrow."

Her mouth watered, but she caught herself. Even if his motivation was good—happy, healthy Gino sat on his arm like a contented angel—and he'd brought food, she couldn't pretend everything was okay between them.

Yes, she knew eventually she had to get along with him. But it was too soon. She wanted the time to heal, and by God she was taking it.

"I'm sorry, but—"

"Nick suggested I bring roses," he said, talking over her as he walked to the stove. He winced. "Thank you for catching the chowder before it boiled over. I'm not good at cooking." He winced again. "My mom would be so mad that I forgot everything she taught me." He produced a small piece of paper. "Cook wrote out instructions for how to heat the lasagna tomorrow."

It finally struck her that he intended to be here tomorrow and righteous indignation roared to life inside her. Her heart hardened. She would not let this man worm his way into her life when she needed time to heal.

"Oh, no. No. No. No. You are not tricking me into letting you live here for the next year. I left Montauk for a good reason—"

"I know." He interrupted her tirade and came a little closer.

Her heart rate sped up. The breath in her lungs shivered. Every nerve ending in her body rose to the top of her skin and all but glowed with awareness. Still, her heart was hard, her determination to get over him strong. If he thought he was going to touch her and have her turn to putty in his hands—

He passed her and she spun around to see him sliding Gino into the swing behind her.

Color bloomed on her cheeks. Why couldn't her hormones realize this man didn't want her? Why did they always jump to wrong conclusions with him?

He faced her. His words were soft and sincere when he said, "I am sorry for hurting you."

Her heart melted a tiny bit. There was nothing wrong with accepting a sincere apology from a guy she had to deal with for the next eighteen years. But she also had to take care of herself. She couldn't let him work his way too far into her life or her good graces.

"That's okay. I—"

"It wasn't okay." This time when he stepped closer, she saw the hesitation in his approach.

Her head tilted in fascination. She'd never seen him fearful before. Even when he'd never in his life as much as held a baby, he'd jumped in and tried things with Gino. To see him wavering now was odd, a curiosity.

"I am so bad at this because I have never done anything remotely like it before."

Her heart melted a bit more. She'd loved him because he was strong, but she also loved him for his honesty. And right now that honesty was costing him. How could she not melt a little inside?

"I love you."

That took her so much by surprise that her heart totally stopped, her chest seized, her mouth fell open.

"I thought I couldn't love." He snorted a laugh. "I thought I was like my dad." He met her gaze. "Turns out I'd just never met the right woman."

She swallowed.

"Nick told me all this." He glanced at her. "He was married, you know? She left him. He told me I have all the symptoms of a broken heart, but that I was lucky." He sucked in a breath. "He thinks it isn't too late for me to apologize and ask for a second chance."

"Second chance?"

"We had a bad first chance. I did everything wrong."

"I wasn't exactly Mary Sunshine."

She saw the spark of hope blossom in his dark eyes. "You're agreeable?"

"You did say you loved me."

"So much my heart hurts."

She laughed. He opened his arms and she stepped into them. Giddy joy flooded her. Relief felt like a warm blanket. Tears welled in her eyes. She'd never believed she would feel this again. Never believed life would be so kind as to give her a second chance. But it was. A chance fresher, brighter, better even than her first, because she now knew the fragility of life upped the importance of real love.

She'd never take him for granted.

"So isn't there something you want to say to me?"

She leaned back so she could look into his eyes. "I forgive you."

"Thanks, but I was hoping for something a little better than that."

"Better than forgiveness?" she asked, teasing him because she still needed a bit of reassurance that this wasn't a dream or a trick, and that they weren't misinterpreting their situation again.

"A lot better than forgiveness. Something that stands the test of time, means we'll be there for each other... means we'll raise Gino together."

She blinked. Shock and joy crashed in her heart. "Are you asking me to marry you?"

"Depends. Are you going to tell me what I need to hear?"

Her lips trembled. She smashed them together. She refused to cry—didn't want to cry. This was without a doubt the happiest moment of her life, the precipice of a new beginning, a second chance at everything, not just love, but babies, a soul mate, a home…an adventure.

She sucked in her breath, raised to her tiptoes, and said, "I love you, too, as her lips met his."

EPILOGUE

THE WEDDING TOOK PLACE in June at the house in Montauk. Darius's two brothers stood up for him as groomsmen. Whitney's two closest friends were at her side. She wore white—a simple strapless silk dress that caressed her curves—and carried roses. Her blond hair had been piled into a careless stack of curls on top of her head with tiny roses scattered between the loops.

Liz and Jake sat in the front row with her parents. Gino arched from her mom to Liz and back to her mom again until he realized Darius and Whitney were only a few feet away from him. Then he screeched and howled until the preacher stopped the service.

Darius laughed. "I'll get him."

He took the few steps over to Whitney's mom, and Gino all but flew into his arms. At nearly a year old, he was a handful, especially when he preferred walking to being held. Dressed in a little tux that matched those of Darius and his brothers, Gino easily could have been the most handsome brother.

Except to Whitney there was no one more handsome, more attractive, more wonderful than Darius. As she thought that, tears filled her eyes, but Gino picked that precise moment to launch himself at her. She caught him just in time.

The hundred or so guests in the ballroom of the Montauk house laughed.

Darius turned to the crowd. "Does anybody have a cookie?"

Mrs. Tucker bounced out of her chair. Wearing a pretty yellow suit, with her hair tucked into a French twist, she looked more like an aunt than his house manager. She produced a cookie from her suit pocket.

"I'm always prepared."

The crowd laughed again. Gino took the cookie and Darius settled the little boy on the crook of his arm.

"We can go on now."

The preacher smiled. Whitney slid her hand into the crook of Darius's elbow. The papers had been filed for Whitney and Darius to adopt Gino. They'd no longer be custodians, but parents. As Gino contently munched on his cookie, Whitney and Darius said the vows that officially made them man and wife.

Gino's parents.

Gerry and Julia Ross's daughter and son-in-law.

Nick and Cade's brother and sister-in-law.

A family.

Darius would never spend another Christmas alone.

SECOND
CHANCE BABY

BY
SUSAN MEIER

First published in Great Britain 2011
by Mills & Boon, an imprint of Harlequin (UK) Limited,
Eton House, 18-24 Paradise Road, Richmond, Surrey TW9 1SR

© Linda Susan Meier 2011

ISBN: 978 0 263 88880 5

23-0511

Harlequin (UK) policy is to use papers that are natural, renewable and
recyclable products and made from wood grown in sustainable forests. The
logging and manufacturing processes conform to the legal environmental
regulations of the country of origin.

Printed and bound in Spain
by Blackprint CPI, Barcelona

Dear Reader,

The cast of characters for my *Babies in the Boardroom* trilogy was determined when I wrote book one, *The Baby Project*. But imagine my surprise when I began hammering out chapter one of Book Two, *Second Chance Baby*, and I discovered that the heroine, Nick Andreas's ex-wife, was pregnant.

A million questions popped into my head. Who is the father? Is she married? What's going on here? Worse…how is Nick going to handle this?

Sometimes writing a book is like that. The characters get minds of their own about how they want their stories to go, and Maggie isn't the kind to sit around waiting for Nick to show up in her life again. She's got married, got pregnant, and then discovered her husband has been cheating on her.

Nick and Maggie are two of the most fun, most romantic characters I've ever created. Maggie just sweeps you away with her absolute determination to be a person everyone can lean on, when she's a person who could use a little help herself.

Turn the page and step into a fun, heart-warming story about a love that certainly deserves a second chance—if the characters can get beyond their past hurts and heal.

Susan Meier

CHAPTER ONE

"YOUR ex-wife applied for the job as your assistant."

Nick Andreas glanced up at his current assistant, soon-to-be-retired Julie Farnsworth. He'd just flown back to North Carolina after six weeks in New York City. He was exhausted and wanted nothing more than to go to his beach house, get out of his monkey suit and take a nap on his hammock. He'd only popped into the office because he had a huge bid due to renew the government contract that was the bread and butter of his manufacturing plant. He had to get an assistant in now.

He just wasn't sure hiring Maggie Forsythe as Julie's replacement was the best way to go. When he had a bid due, his assistant worked with him—*directly with him, at his side*—ten hours a day, six days a week. No man wanted to spend that much time with his ex-wife. Not even an ex-wife he hadn't seen in fifteen years. An ex-wife he barely remembered.

He tossed his pen to his desk. "You wouldn't be telling me this if she wasn't qualified."

"She's qualified. Overqualified in some respects."

"And she actually applied?"

"Well, we certainly didn't drag her in off the street."

He laughed and leaned back in his chair. So Maggie wanted to work for him? He smiled skeptically as weird feelings assaulted him. He hadn't thought about Maggie Forsythe in over a decade. Now, suddenly, he could vividly recall how the sun would catch her red hair and make it sparkle, her wide, happy smile, the sound of her laughter.

"Sorry if I'm finding all this a little hard to believe, but we didn't exactly part on the best of terms. Andreas Manufacturing should be the last place she wants to work."

His sixty-five-year-old assistant caught his gaze with serious dark eyes. "She needs the money."

She was broke? The way he'd been when they'd met?

Memories of his childhood and teen years cascaded through his brain like water spilling from a waterfall. Maggie at six, toothless in first grade, dividing her morning snack with him before they went into the building so no one in their class would see he hadn't brought one. Maggie at twelve, fishing with him so he and his mom could have something for supper. Maggie at sixteen, hanging out in the souvenir shop where he worked, entertaining him on long, boring afternoons before the tourist season picked up. Maggie at eighteen, swollen with his child.

A long-forgotten ache filled his chest and made him scowl. The woman he was remembering with such fondness had dropped him like a hot potato when she'd lost their baby. She hadn't loved him. She'd only married him because he'd gotten her pregnant one reckless night. Twenty minutes after they'd returned from the hospital after her miscarriage, she'd been out the door of his mom's house. Out of his life.

"She should have as many reservations about working with me as I have about working with her."

"Her stepmom died while you were in New York. Rumor has it, she came home for the funeral and decided her dad needed her. She quit her job and moved back permanently but in three weeks of looking she couldn't find work—unless she wants to commute to the city." Julie peered at him over the rim of her glasses. "Aside from tourism, you're the only real employer in Ocean Palms."

He picked up his pen again. "Hire her."

Julie gasped softly. "Really?"

"Sure. We were married as kids. Fifteen years have gone by." He wasn't such a selfish, self-centered oaf that he'd let someone suffer because she had the misfortune of having a history with him. He knew what it was like to have no options. He'd spent his entire childhood living hand-to-mouth. He wouldn't ignore the person who, as a child, had shared with him, helped him, even rescued him a time or two.

Plus, if Julie said Maggie was the person for the job then she was.

Julie rose. "Okay. She's in my office. She said she can begin today. I'll bring her in and we can get started."

Nick sat up in his seat. Today? He didn't even have ten minutes to mentally prepare?

Julie walked to his office door and opened it. "Come in, Maggie."

A true Southern gentleman, Nick rose from the tall-back chair behind his huge mahogany desk. Ridiculously, he couldn't squelch the pride that surged up in him as he took in the expensive Persian rugs that sat on the hardwood floors of his office, the lamps from China, the heavy leather sofa and chair in the conversation area, the art from the broker in New York City. He was rich, successful, and his office showed it. He'd fulfilled the promise of his youth. He had brains and skill and he'd parlayed those into wealth beyond anyone's expectations. One look at his office would tell Maggie he wasn't the eighteen-year-old boy she'd deserted anymore.

The click of high heels on the hardwood announced her arrival two seconds before she appeared in his doorway. Her gorgeous red hair flowed around her, but it was shaped and curled in a way that framed her face, not straight as she had worn it when they were married. Her once sparkly green eyes now held soul-searching intensity. Her full red lips rose slightly in a reluctant smile.

Just as he wasn't the eighteen-year-old she'd left behind anymore, she didn't look a thing like his Maggie.

He relaxed as his gaze involuntarily fell from her face to her dress. A simple red tank dress that showed off a newly acquired suntan, but also couldn't hide her slightly protruding stomach.

She was pregnant?

He gave her tummy a more thorough scrutiny.

She was pregnant.

And suddenly he *was* that eighteen-year-old boy again. Seeing his woman, the love of his life, swollen with his child. More memories washed over him. The dreams he'd had for the kind of father he would be rose up as if he'd been lost in them only yesterday. Love for her, the woman bearing his child, burst in his chest.

But this wasn't his child. She'd lost their child.

And she didn't love him.

Hell, he no longer loved her.

"Come in," he said. His voice was tight with a bit of a squeak but he ignored that, motioning to the chair in front of his desk.

Maggie took a few hesitant steps inside. Now trim instead of lanky, she wore her pregnancy the same way another woman would wear a designer dress.

That was when he realized she was probably married.

Happily married. Not scared and hesitant, with no other options because her stepmom had kicked her out of the house. But happy. Having a child with the man she loved.

He swallowed the knot that formed in his throat, reminding himself that these emotions churning through him were ridiculous. He was over her. Plus, they hadn't even seen each other in fifteen years. The feelings weren't really feelings. They were residue. Like cobwebs that had clung to the walls of his brain and would disappear once he got to know the adult Maggie.

"Julie wants to hire you but I have a few reservations."

He didn't even try to stop the words that flowed from his mouth. Though he'd already told Julie to hire her, now that he saw she was pregnant, he had some concerns. Not about the "feelings" seeing her pregnant aroused, but about her ability to do the job.

She gracefully sat on the chair in front of his desk, smiled softly. "You mean because we were once married?"

He snorted a laugh, but Julie's hand flew to her throat. "You know, I think I'll just go get us some coffee."

Nick said, "She can't drink coffee," at the same time that Maggie said, "I don't drink coffee."

Julie said, "Then I'll get some coffee for myself." She fled the room, closing the door behind her.

Nick sat back in his chair, reaching deep inside himself for the calm that was his trademark. He had to treat her as any other employee and speak accordingly.

"For the next four weeks I need my assistant to work ten-hour days."

"Six days a week. I get that. Julie told me."

"Can you keep up?"

"Of course I can keep up. I'm pregnant not sick."

The room plunged into eerie silence. Memories of

the day she'd lost their baby haunted him like menacing ghosts.

As if recognizing where his thoughts had gone, Maggie sighed. "Nick, I'm fine. Really. And I need this job. If you don't hire me I'll have to get work in the city and commute an hour each way."

"An hour commute might be better for a pregnant woman than racing around the plant looking for documents I need, assembling information from different departments—"

He paused to catch her gaze and when he saw green eyes sparking with fire, everything he intended to say fell out of his head. He remembered that look very well, remembered how many times it had taken them straight to bed.

"I already told you I can keep up."

He took in a quiet breath, reminding himself that Maggie was a married woman who wanted to work for him. The last thing he needed to be thinking about was how her fiery need for independence had played out between the sheets.

"Yeah, well, maybe I want some kind of proof."

She smiled sweetly, calmly. "In a couple of months, I'm not going to be pregnant anymore. Then you're going to be sorry you lost the chance to hire me."

A laugh escaped. Dear God. This really was his Maggie. Fiery one minute, serene the next. And the common sense, logical Maggie could be every bit as sexy as the impassioned one.

But she was married.

And he was a runaround now.

Having a father who'd abandoned him had made him want commitments, but Maggie leaving him had set him straight on that score. And he'd changed. He wasn't simple Nick Roebuck anymore. The guy who hadn't taken his father's name. The guy who wanted commitments. A wife. Family. Nope. Nick Roebuck was gone. He was now Nick Andreas, playboy.

"Besides, my father needs me."

Shifting in his chair, Nick blew his breath out in a gusty sigh. Who he was didn't matter. Who she was didn't matter. She was off-limits. "I'm sorry about your stepmom."

"Thanks."

"I was out of town or I would have paid my respects."

Her gaze dipped. "I know."

"Was everything—you know—okay?" He nearly bit his tongue for his clumsiness. But what could he say? How could he ask if she and Vicki had mended fences? If they'd ever gotten beyond the fact that Vicki had favored Charlie Jr. over her? If Vicki had ever forgiven Maggie for getting pregnant? If Maggie had ever forgiven Vicki for kicking her out of the house?

"It was fine." She shrugged. "Losing someone is always hard."

Which told him nothing. Not that it was any of his business. He scrambled for something safe to say, but the only thing he could think of was, "Yeah. My father died last January. I know how hard these things can be."

She smiled and her eyes brightened. "Oh, so you met your father? You had a relationship?"

"Yes and no." He tapped his fingers on the edge of his desk, tamping down the sudden, unexpected urge to tell her everything. They weren't friends anymore. She might act like the girl he'd known and loved, but she wasn't. And he wasn't the lovesick boy she'd married.

Still, he couldn't ignore her question. "I met my father but we didn't really have a relationship. Unless you call having dinner every other year a relationship."

"That's too bad." Genuine regret colored her voice. "So how's your mom?"

He chuckled. "She's just like a little general at the day-care. Loves the kids, but keeps them in line."

Maggie's laugh was quick and easy. "God I've missed her."

"We missed you." The words slipped out and he knew why. He was getting comfortable with her. And that was wrong. If they were going to work together, he had to draw lines. Be professional.

She looked away. "No point in staying once I'd lost the baby."

Hearing her say that now hurt almost as much as it had the day she'd left. "Right."

"Before I got pregnant, we both had plans."

"Is that what you were thinking about while I was talking to my father's attorney?" For years he'd wondered. What kind of coincidence could it have been that the dad who'd ignored him his entire life suddenly wanted to give him a trust fund? Had it been a gift from fate to Maggie, or a curse of fate for him?

She caught his gaze. "Yes."

When his heart squeezed, he swore at himself inwardly for asking the stupid question. He'd already reasoned all this out in his head. Gotten beyond it. There was no point going over it again. Certainly no point rehashing it with her. Fifteen years had passed and he loved the life he'd built without her.

If they were going to work together, the past would have to be forgotten. His only goal should be to make sure she really did have the education and experience to do the job.

"So you have a business degree?"

"Yes." She shifted on the chair. Her shoulders went

back. Her expression became businesslike. "But I'm not looking down on this job. I think there are a lot of ways I can help you."

"What did you do at your last job?"

"I was an analyst for a firm that put venture capitalist groups together with struggling businesses looking for investors or a buyer."

"Do you know much about manufacturing?"

She laughed. "Most of the businesses looking for investors or buyout are manufacturing companies."

He tapped his pen on the desk. He needed somebody and, as Julie said, Maggie was qualified. Now he and his ex-wife would be spending ten hours a day, six days a week together.

He looked over at her just as she looked at him and the years between them melted away. Her eyes weren't as wary as they had been when she'd walked in the door. Her smile was genuine.

Doubt rumbled through his soul. In the sea of women that he'd dated since he'd hit puberty, she was the only one he'd loved. It had taken almost five years to really get beyond her leaving; years before he stopped hoping every ring of the phone was her calling; years before he stopped looking for her in crowds. One five-minute conversation had already brought an avalanche of memories. This was not going to be easy.

Suddenly the door opened and Julie walked in. "Human Resources called. Before Maggie can actually begin working, she's got to spend the afternoon with them, filling out papers. You won't get to work together until tomorrow."

Maggie said, "Oh."

Nick said, "I hadn't planned on starting on the bid until tomorrow anyway."

Julie motioned for Maggie to follow her and she rose and walked out the door.

He dropped his head to his hands. After weeks of running the multibillion-dollar shipping conglomerate owned by his family, he needed this day out of the office to relax before he jumped into the intense work of the bid.

But the hammock was out. Stirred as his memories were, he'd never sleep. His best bet would be to take a long drive down the coast.

When he was sure Maggie and Julie were halfway to the Human Resources office, he rose from his desk, grabbed his keys and cell phone and headed out.

Five hours later, Maggie Forsythe walked out into the scorching June day and took a quiet, measured breath to calm herself. She'd been so confident when she'd applied for the job as Nick Andreas's assistant. Fifteen years had passed. Plus, her ex-husband, Josh, had done a number on her. The absolute last thing she wanted in this world was to get involved with another man. Yet, when she'd looked at Nick her heart had stopped. Her breathing had stalled. It was as if she was eighteen again and he was hers.

She blew out a frustrated sigh and reminded herself that one person could not possess another. Nick had never really been hers. Just as Josh had never really been hers. Oh, her ex had made the commitment with vows before a clergyman, but he'd cheated on her. And when she'd confronted him, he'd simply left, saying he liked the other woman better.

The sting of the pain of the loss of her marriage rose up in her hot and fresh. She pressed her key into the ignition of her car. She should be immune to men. Forever. But spending a mere five minutes with Nick had caused her brain to fill with memories of happier times. In the fifteen years that had passed, she'd forgotten how much she'd loved him. How gorgeous he was with his curly black hair and nearly black eyes. How commanding.

Calling herself every kind of fool, she pulled her gearshift into Drive. It didn't matter how attracted she was to Nick Andreas. If she couldn't keep a forty-year-old balding lawyer, she certainly didn't have to worry that she'd somehow attract a thirty-three-year-old gorgeous Greek god. Especially since she'd dumped Nick. For all the right reasons, but she'd still dumped him. Broken his heart. There was no way his pride could get beyond that.

She reached her dad's farm and climbed the front porch steps. After a few seconds of searching, she found her dad in the kitchen.

"How'd it go?" His wet hair had been slicked back as if he'd just come from the shower. His plaid shirt and jeans appeared to be clean. The fact that he'd come in from the fields and showered was a good sign. But there were still shadows in his eyes. Just because he'd had a good day today, it didn't mean he would have a good day tomorrow. That's why she had to stay. His good days might be good, but his bad days were awful.

She smiled. "I got the job."

Surprise flickered across her dad's weathered face. "Well, of course you did. You and Nick have always been friends. There's no reason to believe you wouldn't be friends now."

She turned away. Her dad had always believed that she and Nick had only married because she'd gotten pregnant and when she'd lost the baby there was no reason to be married anymore. He didn't know—no one knew—that the day she'd left Nick, she'd overheard his father's lawyer offer him a five-million-dollar trust fund, as long as he ended their marriage, and overheard Nick refuse.

Emotionally overwrought over losing their baby, she'd made a decision she'd known would hurt him. At the time, she'd believed it for the best, and she actually still believed that. Nick had become the man he never could have been if she'd selfishly let him throw away his trust fund by staying married to her. So she'd packed her bag and gone.

Grabbing an apple from the bowl on the table, she pushed all that out of her mind. It was ancient history. Of no consequence and certainly not something she'd tell a man who'd just lost his wife.

"You should see his office. Everything's sleek, sophisticated, wonderful."

"That's the rumor." Her dad ambled to the refrigerator and pulled out fresh vegetables for a salad. "He's got more money than the rest of the people in town combined."

Pride swelled within her. He'd become as successful as she'd known he could be. Her only real regret was that she'd had to lead Nick to believe she hadn't ever loved him, only married him for their baby. Otherwise, he wouldn't have let her leave. She'd never had a doubt she'd done the right thing, but she also knew her choice meant he'd never again love her.

But she didn't want him to love her. Thanks to her ex, she knew the truth about love. Most of the time it wasn't love at all; it was lust. And even if it was real love, real love died. And when real love died, people were left alone.

Except she wasn't really alone. Her father and new baby needed her. She had a job. A real second chance at a life in the small town she'd loved.

It was smarter to appreciate those things, than to pine for what couldn't be.

CHAPTER TWO

NICK's cell phone rang just as he pulled his Porsche into the garage beneath his beach house. Though it was only a little after five, he'd taken a two-hour drive, made a stop at a crab shack for a late lunch/early dinner, spent another hour walking on a rough, undeveloped stretch of beach and then made the drive home.

And he still didn't feel any better about hiring Maggie.

He turned off the ignition and snatched the phone from the seat beside him. Glancing at the caller ID he saw it was his older brother Darius.

"Hey, old man. What's up?"

"I need you to fly to Saudi Arabia and meet with the prince."

"Me?"

"Since you took my place while Whitney and I were on our honeymoon, you're up-to-date on everything. Plus, you're family. The prince will only meet with family and I can't go right now. Gino is just getting accustomed to having me and Whitney home again. I can't leave him."

Climbing out of his car, Nick winced. He understood that Gino, their one-year-old half brother in Darius's custody, had missed Darius and Whitney, but he couldn't do anything for Andreas Holdings until he got his own bid done.

"You're going to have to call Cade."

"Cade?"

Nick smiled at the resistance in his older brother's voice.

"He hates me."

"Nah, he just doesn't subscribe to Dad's theory that the eldest should rule the family empire." He rifled through his trouser pocket for his keys and unlocked the door that led him to a short flight of stairs. "Being a pain in the ass is his way of keeping you in line."

"What? Raising our baby brother, being newly married and running a global entity isn't enough?"

Nick laughed and tossed his briefcase onto the counter of the butler's pantry that led to the kitchen. Black granite countertops offset by a shiny metallic backsplash and sleek oak cabinets greeted him.

"No one said deciding to be brothers for real would be easy."

Darius sighed. "Yeah, and I guess it's better than all of us pretending the others don't exist."

Nick grunted in agreement. Their dad had been a runaround. Unfaithful to Darius's mom with both Nick and Cade's moms. Only Darius had been acknowledged and that had made things very sticky when their dad had died. But they'd pushed through it.

"That's why I feel free to call you for help," Darius said, bringing the conversation back to his point.

"I can't get away now. The bid is due for the contract that keeps my company afloat. Plus, I just hired a new assistant."

"So you finally hired someone."

"Human Resources hired her."

Darius laughed perceptively. "You don't like her."

"I do like her. At one time I loved her. She's my ex-wife."

Darius coughed loudly as if choking, then said, "Only an idiot would hire an ex-wife."

"We were married as kids, remember? I was eighteen. She was pregnant. It was a long time ago. We hadn't seen each other since the day she left."

"Still, there's got to be baggage there."

He opened a cabinet, found his whiskey and a glass. "No kidding. But my back's up against the wall and she's qualified. I have to deal with it."

"Do you want my advice?"

"Do I have a choice?"

"If I were you I'd talk about the past with her. Get it out in the open and discuss it, so you don't have to waste time tiptoeing around feelings."

Pouring a glass of Jack Daniel's, Nick scowled. Just what he needed. A wonderful conversation wherein Maggie told him about finding the love of her life, getting married and now having a baby. Yeah. Right.

"Fifteen years have passed. We don't need to rehash what happened."

"It's your call, but if you find yourself doing things like drinking in the afternoon, you'll know you're in trouble."

He stopped the glass of whiskey halfway to his mouth. It was after five…sort of still afternoon but close to evening. Ah, hell. Who was he kidding? He was drinking in the afternoon.

Nick threw back the shot of Jack anyway.

Darius laughed. "You know I'm right."

Nick poured another glass of Jack. "Yes, big brother, I know you're right. But that doesn't mean I have to like it."

The next morning, Maggie was standing at a filing cabinet near the window when she saw a black Porsche pull into the front parking space and Nick climb out.

"He's here."

Julie came to attention. "Okay. Don't worry about a thing. You sort of stay behind me. Let me take the brunt of his mood today."

Maggie smiled at Julie. "You already know he's going to be in a mood?"

"An assistant doesn't work with a boss for ten years without knowing when he's going to come in in a mood."

Maggie laughed.

"He's been out of the office for six weeks. Our bread and butter contract is about to expire and we have to rebid it. I'm assuming he thought about that all last night so today he's going to be cranky."

The door of Julie's office opened and Nick walked inside. Sunglasses hid his dark eyes but that only accented his generous mouth and the scruffy day-old growth of beard he hadn't shaved. Dressed in jeans and a T-shirt with sleeves that cupped his rounded biceps—hinting to the muscled chest beneath it—he was as built as an adult as he had been as a young man.

He took off his sunglasses and his dark eyes narrowed as he looked at her. His gaze traveled from her head to the toes of her pumps. Heat suffused her. Especially when she realized he was probably looking at her because she'd been ogling him.

"You don't have to dress like that."

She cleared her throat. "Excuse me."

He waved his sunglasses at her tidy blue suit, flowered blouse and white pumps. "We're five miles from the beach. Half the staff goes surfing before work. I don't think you'll find another pair of high heels in an eight-mile radius. Wear jeans."

With that he put his sunglasses back on, pivoted and walked into his office.

Maggie turned to Julie who was having difficulty stifling a smile. "I told you he'd be in a mood."

Maggie scowled. "In Pittsburgh some women still wear panty hose to work."

Julie's face froze in an expression of pure horror. "Good God."

Maggie shook her head and laughed. "I've been Northernized."

"Well, let's at least lose the jacket. Honey, it's June. It's hot and this is a casual company. And obviously Nick feels uncomfortable with you dressed too formally." She picked up a steno pad and a stack of files and walked toward Nick's office. "Follow me."

After quickly shrugging out of her jacket, Maggie scrambled to get in step behind Julie.

"Those stacks," Julie said, pointing at six tall stacks of files on the conference table in the corner, "are everything you need to work on the new bid, but that's not the priority."

Nick nodded in acknowledgment as Julie took one of the two seats in front of his desk. Maggie quickly sat on the other.

"These," Julie said, waving her stack of files, "are the things we've ignored for six weeks. Today, they're the priority."

One by one, she handed the files in her lap across the desk to Nick. One by one, he addressed the issue. A few times he dictated emails. Once or twice he kept the file saying he'd dash off the email himself. But he never once took off the sunglasses.

When they got through the stack, Julie rose to leave. Maggie followed suit.

"Not you," Nick said, pointing at Maggie. "You stay."

Julie scurried out of the office and closed the door behind her. Nick opened the top drawer of his desk, grabbed a small bottle of over-the-counter painkillers and popped the lid. He shook some into his mouth.

"Headache?"

Raising the sunglasses, he peered beneath the lenses at her. She swallowed. In all the years they'd known each other, he'd never quite scowled at her like that. Which was good because it reminded her that they were now different people. And maybe she shouldn't be taking liberties by asking him if he had a headache.

He dropped the sunglasses to his eyes again. "Hangover. I had a—"

She held out her hand to stop him. "You don't need to tell me. I'm sorry. I'm not a nosy person. I'm not a pushy person. I don't know why I said that. It was rude."

He turned his chair sideways and leaned back. "If I didn't have a rip-roaring hangover, I'd probably lambaste you about now. It might have been fifteen years since we've seen each other, but we can't pretend we don't know each other. We do." He pulled his sunglasses down his nose and caught her gaze. "Intimately."

The way he said *intimately* caused her breath to shiver into her chest. Memories popped up like flowers in a bountiful garden and her cheeks heated. That was when she realized he'd probably said that on purpose. Trying to get a rise out of her.

"So what are you doing? Pushing us to the point where we'll yell at each other?"

"Maybe."

She gaped at him. "Really? I was being sarcastic."

"Yesterday when I told my brother I'd hired my ex-wife, he suggested we needed to talk everything out. I disagreed, but he's right. If we don't talk some of this out, we'll spend weeks being miserable, tiptoeing around each other." He leaned back in his chair. "I don't like it."

"What? You don't want to be uncomfortable so you're making me uncomfortable?"

"Think of it more like ripping off a bandage." He turned his head to look at her, but with the sunglasses on she couldn't really tell if he was looking at her or not. "You can either pull a bandage off slowly and be in pain the whole time or rip it off and be in excruciating pain, but only for a few seconds. I'll take the few seconds."

"And I don't get a vote?"

"Nope. I'm the boss. My rules. We have a bid due in four weeks. Clock's ticking. We can't afford to be miserable or even slightly uncomfortable."

"So we're going to talk?"

"I thought we'd start off with what you've been doing for the past fifteen years."

"I told you I worked for a firm that put venture capitalist groups together with struggling businesses."

"I mean personally."

Her mouth fell open. The last thing she wanted to do was tell him about her miserable marriage. But she had a feeling there was no way out of this. He was the boss. They did have a past. They couldn't pretend they weren't curious. The best she could hope for was that he had a worse story. "If I talk, you talk."

"That's actually the point."

A man who had a worse story than a miserable divorce wouldn't be so quick to agree. She glanced around at his exquisitely decorated office. "Right. I don't think you need to tell me what you've been doing. Your office sort of speaks for itself."

He grinned. "It does, doesn't it?"

Pride reared up inside her. Her marriage might have been a failure, but she wasn't. "I haven't exactly been unsuccessful. I gave up a great job in Pittsburgh to come home and be with my dad."

When she stopped talking, he made a rolling motion with his hand. "And?"

"And?"

"And what else?"

She scowled. Damn it. She didn't want to do this. Her most recent life details were not happy or even positive. She was going to look like an idiot compared to him. Maybe the best thing to do really would be Nick's bandage technique. Tell him about her life quickly, concisely and get it over with.

"Okay." She sighed heavily. "I went to college, got a job in Pittsburgh, married a lawyer—"

He winced. "Really, Maggie? A lawyer?"

Her chin rose. "Not all lawyers are cutthroat. Josh was a very nice man."

He pulled his sunglasses down again. "Was?"

"We're divorced."

His nearly black eyes searched hers, but he didn't say a word.

Still, she could see the wheels turning in his brain. The honest woman in her knew she couldn't race through the truth or even sugarcoat it.

"You want to ask how two people who created a baby could get divorced."

"Yes and no. I just sort of realized that we should have set some ground rules for this discussion. I suddenly feel like I'm prying. Overstepping boundaries." He rubbed his forehead. "I'm going to kick Darius's butt for this idea."

"It's okay." And it was. If only because it forced her to realize that she was foolish to try to pretend she could hide her bad divorce. This was a small town. People would talk. If she didn't give them the real version, they might just make up something worse. Sometimes it really was best to stick with the truth, the whole truth—

Actually that wasn't a good idea either.

Because the bottom line truth between her and Nick was that she had loved him, but led him to believe she didn't. When she'd left him, he'd asked her if she loved him and she'd avoided the question. She hadn't lied. Simply let him draw the conclusion for himself that she didn't love him.

No wonder he was having trouble dealing with her. She'd broken his heart—hurt him—by making him think everything they'd shared in their two-week marriage had been an act.

But they'd been so young.

And he'd been so broke.

They'd just lost their baby. She'd had no more reason to hold him down—hold him back.

She'd genuinely believed she was doing the right thing.

She glanced around his office again. He'd done very well for himself with the five-million-dollar trust fund his father had given him. She wouldn't apologize for making the choice he'd refused to make for himself.

"No. It's not okay." He tossed the sunglasses to his desk, an indication that the painkillers were probably beginning to work on his headache. "I'm going to call tech support and tell them to set you up so that you can go into the accounting system." He swiveled his chair until he was facing front again and picked up the receiver of his phone. "Julie will give you directions to their office. Once they get you set up, just do whatever Julie tells you to do."

He punched a few numbers into the phone. "This is Nick. I'm sending my new assistant down for passwords and access into the accounting records."

He hung up the phone and she rose.

But she paused. Her heart clenched with the achy pain of realizing that he might trust her with passwords, but personally he was wary of her. He'd given her his heart and soul and she'd rejected them. Actually by misleading him into believing she hadn't loved him, she'd made herself look like an opportunist. Making him think she didn't love him was the same as saying she'd only married him because she'd needed a place to live. That wasn't true, but that was how it appeared to him. And now he was wary of her.

Even if she told him she had loved him that wouldn't fix anything because she'd be admitting she'd deliberately misled him. If she didn't, there would always be an odd void between them.

But she had done what she believed was for the best.

She turned and walked out of his office.

Nick worked cloistered behind his closed door all day, but he couldn't concentrate. The last thing he'd expected to hear was that Maggie was divorced. Not because he'd created the image in his head that she was happily married. But because she was pregnant. When she'd told him she was divorced, his first thought had been what kind of husband—what kind of man—leaves a pregnant wife? And he hadn't been able to contain or hide his anger. So he'd hustled her off to tech support.

But almost immediately after she had gone, he remembered that Maggie had left him. He couldn't rule out the possibility that Maggie had been the one to leave her marriage. But why? Even though she hadn't loved Nick, she'd stayed with him for the sake of their baby. Hell, she'd only married him for their baby. He didn't want to believe she'd leave her husband when she was pregnant. Unless her husband had done something—

Damn it! He had to stop thinking about her! It was stupid. Ridiculous. And he shouldn't care. She was now only his assistant. Nothing more.

When Julie popped her head into his office at five and announced she and Maggie were leaving unless he needed some help that evening, he simply said goodbye. There were tons of things they could have worked on that night. Projects to get the facts and figures together for the new bid, but he hadn't been able to get himself out of the emotional frenzy he'd created. He hadn't organized anything enough to be able to assign any of the tasks.

Darius was right. Working with Maggie was going to be hard. Every little step of her past that he learned had the potential to drag him back in time and destroy the focus he needed to work. He should have kept the conversation going. He should have endured her entire story. Hell, the entire story probably would have reminded him he had no right to feel anything for her. Good or bad. Fifteen years had passed. He shouldn't even be angry with her anymore.

But he was.

Damn it.

He was.

Forty minutes after Julie and Maggie had gone, he stepped out of the building and headed for his Porsche. But he saw a tow truck loading a Chrysler Sebring. The poor sap who owned the car would be walking at least a mile because Nick had located his plant as far out of town as he could. But, in a way, finding a stranded employee was good. Doing a favor for somebody was exactly what he needed to get his mind off Maggie.

He slid inside his Porsche, tossing his briefcase behind him. After putting down the top, he drove over to the stranded driver.

"Hey," he yelled over the low hum of the Porsche's powerful engine. "Can I give you a lift?"

Maggie peered around the tow truck driver. Nick almost groaned. This is what happened when a man hired his ex-wife.

"You wouldn't mind?"

He leaned across the seat and opened the car door. "No. Come on."

Maggie said a few things to the tow truck attendant who gave her his card, then she slid onto the seat beside Nick. He waited the time it took for the driver to get into the tow truck and pull away before he followed him out of the parking lot.

"Wow. Nice car."

Stuck behind the slow tow truck, the Porsche wasn't going fast enough for the noise of the air swirling around them to impede conversation. He'd not only heard her comment, he had to answer it.

"Thanks. It was a present to myself for my thirtieth birthday."

"I hope you thanked yourself."

"Driving the car is thanks enough." He sucked in a breath. Questions bombarded his brain. And so did Darius's advice. He and Maggie would have a terrible time working together if they didn't get comfortable with each other. Fate had intervened and handed him another opportunity to be alone with her. He could either take it—and attempt to help them ease beyond their past and the awkwardness between them—or he could spend the next several weeks unable to focus or concentrate. With a bid due that wasn't an option.

"It looks like you could use a new car yourself."

"I could, but I can't afford anything like this."

"So what can you afford?"

She winced. Because they had picked up speed, she had to shout to be heard above the wind whipping by them. "Whatever I can get a loan for."

Julie had told him that Maggie was broke, but that was before he'd found out she was pregnant and divorced. Now the word *broke* took on an entirely different meaning.

"How does a woman who was married, and probably had a house and a two-income family come out of a divorce with nothing?"

"House was mortgaged. Everything else had been bought on credit or leased. Plus, my ex had run up private credit card bills. So we had to sell the house and use the equity to pay off the balances. Technically I'm not in debt, but I don't have any money, either. I'm sort of at even."

The casual way she said it teased an unexpected laugh out of him.

"Why do you think that's funny?"

"I don't think it's funny." He picked up speed. Air punched through the car now. His voice rose the way Maggie's had. "I think the way you said it is funny. You're awfully damned casual about it. I'd be spitting nails."

She caught his gaze. "I had my nail-spitting days. I really loved my ex and he didn't give two cents about me." She put her head back and for a few seconds soaked in the warm sun and the cool air that floated around her, reminding Nick of how she'd been when they were young.

Spontaneous. Full of life. "But that's over now. I'm not going to brood. My baby will be my family."

Relief rippled through him. If he was reading her correctly, she was perfectly fine. Divorced, pregnant and penniless, but fine. He had no reason to worry about her. And, even more amazing, now that they'd talked a bit, he actually felt comfortable around her. The cascading memories of their childhood had stopped. The fear that she might have been hurt and abandoned subsided. So much had changed in her life that she really did seem like a different person to him.

They wound along the stretch of road into town, then drove down Main Street. Seafood restaurants teemed with tourists eating an early supper. Souvenir shops displayed their wares on sunny sidewalks. Past the tourist district, brightly painted houses with blooming flower beds took them out of town. In what seemed like seconds, they were on the stretch of road to Maggie's dad's farm.

Sunshine poured down on them. The scent of the sea air swelled around them. They didn't speak and Nick's mind wandered back to the days when they'd ridden their bikes along this road. Happier days. When they were two kids who were friends. Real friends. Back before that one magical night when they'd gotten carried away and made love.

Love?

He nearly snorted, but caught himself. What did two eighteen-year-olds know about love? The fact that she'd left him had proven to him love didn't exist. That belief had led to a very comfortable dating life. He didn't make false commitments as his dad had. He didn't promise to be around forever and then scramble away when his current mistress got pregnant. He was honest, fair. No strings. No messy involvement. Just good times.

Which was why he'd loved being in New York the past six weeks. The boredom he'd been experiencing in a small town that didn't offer much in the way of nightlife had melted away. Thanks to Darius, he had access to a Park Avenue penthouse and an estate on Montauk. As soon as his bid was in he intended to take full advantage by flying up every weekend.

They reached the lane for the farm. He downshifted and slowly cruised to the house. As soon as the car stopped, she hopped out.

"Thanks."

He said, "You're welcome," but she was already halfway to the porch.

He frowned. She certainly was eager to get away from him. *She* was the one who had hurt *him*. Yet she was mad? Eager to get away from *him*?

He shook his head, telling himself that in a few short weeks he would be spending weekends in New York where there were plenty of women who would remind him of why he'd moved beyond the love of his life.

He rocketed out of her driveway back to the main road and the huge beach house that seemed oddly empty that night.

CHAPTER THREE

THE next day blurred into a stretch of boredom for Maggie. Nick began reviewing data for the new bid, but only called on Julie and Maggie to pull files and search for reports. Time should have passed unremarkably, except Maggie's father couldn't seem to wrap his mind around the fact that he was supposed to drive her to work and pick her up after. She'd had to trudge into the field to find him that morning, and she spent the day fearing he would forget her. At four-thirty, she called to remind him, but, of course, she got the answering machine.

But when she called again at five, she got really lucky and he picked up the phone. She arrived home at a normal time, made a quick supper of salads and hamburgers then suggested they go to the Ice Cream Shack for a treat.

As eager for a break as Maggie was, Charlie Forsythe started his old rattle-trap truck and they rumbled into town.

"Are you ever going to get a new truck?"

"No need."

"It's going to shut down completely one of these days and we won't even have basic transportation."

Her dad glanced over at her. The wind coming in through the open window tossed his graying auburn hair to the side. His green eyes sparkled. "Sure we will." He grinned. "When your car gets fixed."

She rolled her eyes. "I haven't heard from Jimmy yet. I get the feeling I'm bottom of his list."

"When did you take your car there?"

"Monday."

"You should get a call next Monday, telling you what's wrong. Then it'll probably take a week or two to fix it."

"A week or two?" Maggie groaned.

The noisy truck chugged into the overflowing parking lot of the Ice Cream Shack. Because it wasn't on the main drag, but in the back of town, tourists rarely found it and the place was packed with locals. Wooden picnic tables were set up in a cozy arrangement to the left, giving patrons an area to socialize in as they ate their sundaes and cones. In a grassy field to the right, parents and small children played Wiffle Ball, a game just like baseball except with a lightweight plastic bat and airy plastic ball. In a town filled with fun and games for tourists, it was a quiet, normal, small-town respite.

Maggie filled her lungs with the sea-scented air coming in through the open window and suddenly felt like she was home. There was no place that epitomized their small town more than the Ice Cream Shack. The sounds of kids at play on rich green grass. The sight of parents licking cones with one eye on their children. Teens hanging out, getting to know each other.

Pure, unadulterated joy filled her. She was home. Finally home. Really home. No nagging husband. No bills. Just a dad who needed her and a baby to fulfill her.

A real second chance.

She rolled out of the truck. Though she was only six months pregnant and her tummy was barely round enough to be noticeable, she felt like a whale. Knowing she really shouldn't be eating ice cream and adding unnecessary weight, she had a plan. Before she indulged in a vanilla cone, she'd play ball with the kids.

"Are you coming, Dad?"

"Are you kidding? I worked a twelve-hour day in the field. I don't need more exercise to deserve an ice cream cone."

As her dad made his way to the ordering window, Maggie laughed and headed off for the ball game. The sounds of childish giggles drifted to her, resurrecting her joy. Someday she'd bring her little boy or girl to this ice cream stand for a sweet treat and some fun with kids his or her own age.

Standing at the edge of the grassy field, she shielded her eyes from the sun with one hand as she surveyed the group, hoping to find a parent she knew so she could figure out which team to play for.

She didn't see a parent, but spotted Nick's mom, Becky Roebuck. Standing behind home plate, wearing pink capris and a simple white blouse, with her curly blond hair floating around her shoulders, she looked about forty of her fifty-five years.

A little boy stood beside her, getting ready for his turn at bat. Positioning his hands on the bright red plastic bat, Becky said, "Okay, so when the ball comes toward you, you just swing at it like this."

With her hands on top of the little boy's she demonstrated the swinging motion. He giggled.

"See. Simple as pie."

"Yeah, Timmy. Simple as pie. You can do it."

That booming encouragement came from Nick. Maggie followed the sound of his voice, and there he stood. No shirt, cutoff jeans and flip-flops.

The urge to turn and run competed with the urge to

simply take in every beautiful bronze inch of him. The joy of being home was instantly eclipsed by sheer unadulterated lust. His biceps flexed as he scooped up an imaginary ball, practicing while his mom coached the obvious newbie to the game. His tanned skin gleamed in the sunlight.

Her breath caught and pulse scrambled. Her Pittsburgh friends had warned her that pregnancy would send her sex drive off the charts, but she'd barely noticed that particular side effect until the day she'd seen Nick again. Still, she wasn't giving him credit for making her weak with longing. It was safer to believe it was wayward hormones.

But good excuse aside, she still quivered, and she knew getting involved in the game would be just a tad foolhardy. Like tempting fate by dipping your toe into shark-infested waters. Nick hadn't yet noticed her. She could slip away.

She turned to go just as Becky yelled, "Hey! Maggie! Is that you?"

Embarrassment flooded her at the same time that the sound of Becky's voice resonated through her, reminding her of the happy two weeks she and Nick had lived with his mom. The peaceful breakfasts, lunches and dinners. Fun evenings eating popcorn in front of the TV. As a family. A real family. Not a third wheel as she'd always been in her own home.

She stopped and faced Becky with a smile. "It's me."

"Did you come here to play some Wiffle Ball?"

She instinctively glanced back at Nick. His smile was gone. In its place was the wary expression he wore at the office.

Not giving her a chance to reply, Becky jogged over and enfolded her in a huge, motherly hug before she kissed her cheek. "Of course you came to play!" She pulled away and held Maggie an arm's distance so she could inspect her. "I have missed you!"

Tears filled Maggie's eyes. "I have missed you, too."

"So why didn't you ever visit?"

That was a loaded question. Where would she start? She could fall back on the truth that everybody knew. She and Vicki had never gotten along. Or she could state the obvious. She'd hurt Nick and hadn't wanted to face that, either. Or she could say the convenient. Her husband hated what he called her grubby little North Carolina tourist pit town.

In the end, she said only, "There never seemed to be time. I had a busy job. My husband was always at the beck and call of his clients."

Becky glanced around. "Where is your husband?"

"We're divorced."

That caused sweet Becky's face to fall in sadness. "I'm so sorry."

The freedom she'd felt when she and her dad had first pulled into The Shack wove through her again. Her marriage might have seemed okay, but in the past few days Maggie had come to realize her ex-husband was a spend-aholic narcissist who'd never been particularly affectionate and who had ruled her. The truth was she'd never been what anybody would call happy. The sweet knowledge that she had a chance to start over, in her hometown, as herself, with no one telling her what to do filled her again.

Her lips tugged upward into a smile. "Don't be sorry. The more I'm divorced from him the more I'm coming to see it might not have been such a bad thing."

Becky looped her arm through Maggie's. "Since it brought you back to Ocean Palms, I'm afraid I'm going to have to agree." She nudged Maggie's shoulder. "Now what position do you want to play?"

Considering that Nick had already seen her—so there was no hiding from him—and noticing that the kids were getting antsy, she didn't argue. She glanced at the field and saw most of the important positions were filled by parents with a smattering of little kids in between, probably learning the ropes of the game. "How about shortstop?"

Becky patted her arm. "Perfect. We haven't had a shortstop in decades."

Maggie laughed and walked to her position. Taking a quick look to get the lay of the field, she noticed Nick was only a few yards behind her and waved. "Hey."

What else could she do? He might be her boss, ex-husband, first lover, but this was a small town. They were bound to run into each other.

"Hey."

His deep, gruff voice drifted to her just as a big bruiser of a boy stepped up to the plate, took a swipe at the first pitch and sent the ball flying to Maggie.

She held up her hands. "I've got it!"

But two seconds before the little plastic ball would have slapped into her hands, Nick cut in front of her and snatched it from the air.

"You're out, Timmy," he called, tossing the ball back to the pitcher, a freckle-faced girl who wore her dark hair in pigtails.

Nick turned to flounce away, but Maggie caught his arm. "That was my ball and I had it."

He glanced at her hand holding his magnificent biceps. Myriad emotions passed through his eyes. The anger blew right by her in favor of the little glimmer of attraction that sparkled in the dark depths of his nearly black eyes. She sucked in a breath. That one little glimmer lit a match under her overactive libido again. Her tummy tightened. Her blood sang in her veins. Her muscles melted. A very familiar sizzle arched between them.

She dropped his arm like a hot potato.

Stepping back, she calmed her voice, as she said, "You shouldn't have jumped in front of me."

He snorted and turned to go back to his place in the outfield. "Right."

"Hey!" She nearly grabbed him again to keep him from dismissing her, but she remembered the sizzle and fisted her hands at her sides. "I'm a good player."

"You're stale."

"And this is a pickup Wiffle Ball game, Mr. Macho! Not the World Series." Memories of how her ex had bossed her in the past two years filled her with righteous indignation. If she was here to be free, then she intended to be free. "You don't have to cover for me."

The next three kids hit low ground balls. Two whizzed right by the pitcher and both kids got on base. With two outs and two kids on, the next pitch could result in either the necessary out to end the inning or a run scored.

Maggie wiped sweat off her brow. Though it was after seven, heat still held the tiny town in a vise grip.

Nick called for a time-out and ambled over to her. "Are you okay?"

She looked around. "Yes." Her face scrunched in confusion. "Did you just call time to check on me?"

"You look awful."

She laughed. "Thanks."

"No. I'm serious. You look terrible. Like you're going to faint from heat."

Her gaze involuntarily fell to the sweat glistening on his pecs. She shook her head. "You should talk. You look hotter than I feel."

Too late she realized how that sounded and she clamped her mouth shut.

But everything inside of Nick stilled as he felt himself being slapped back in time. Back to when comments like that could set his blood on fire and make him want to take her right where they stood. It infuriated him that she still had that power, but when he saw her face heat with embarrassment, a thrill of male pride raced through him. Well, well, well. Sweet little I-don't-love-you Maggie wasn't so unaffected after all. If nothing else, she remembered how good they had been in bed.

He laughed and winked at her. "So I guess I've still got it."

She grabbed his shoulders and turned him around, giving him a shove to send him back to the outfield. He scooted off, pretending to be unaffected and not wanting to make a scene or call too much attention to them, but the skin she'd touched tingled. His body had tensed in anticipation. His blood shimmered in his veins.

He rationalized it away. He would always equate Maggie with sex, sex appeal. Because she was the first woman he'd touched, the first woman he'd tasted, no one had ever compared.

But he'd had lots of women since Maggie and intended to take advantage of the new group he'd begun meeting in New York City. He didn't need to flirt with Maggie. Not even out of boredom.

A little girl with a yellow ponytail got up to bat and hit a line drive right to Maggie. As naturally as if she'd been doing it every day for the past fifteen years, she bent and scooped up the ball. Unfortunately Nick was treated to a picture of her perfect butt and long, shapely legs.

He blinked a few times then spun away as she wailed the ball to the first baseman, who caught it effortlessly, getting the third out that retired the side.

Maggie jumped for joy, whooped and hollered, as she high-fived the dark-haired boy manning first base.

Unimaginable joy hit Nick like a freight train. Memories

of their past collided with the knowledge that she was home. Really home. He couldn't stop it. He couldn't fight it. He couldn't rationalize it away. The truth of it took hold and wouldn't let go. Not even when he reminded himself that he didn't like her anymore and had a good plan for his life that included meeting new people, going to clubs, entertaining in a penthouse. Out in the bright sunshine, doing the things they used to do as children, then teens, then lovers, he couldn't stop the memories, the feelings that erupted like a geyser.

Angry with himself, he took his time walking to the bench that served as a dugout. The team of six-, seven-, eight-, nine- and ten-year-olds continued to high-five Maggie as they grabbed their juice boxes and talked smack about how good they were.

Unofficial coach, Bill Taylor, Bobby Taylor's dad, wrapped her in a bear hug that speared Nick with unwanted jealousy and sent his anger with himself into the stratosphere. Calling himself an idiot, he took a juice box from the metal tub his mom provided and sat at the end of the bench.

Maggie scooted over to him. He pretended not to notice by taking a long drink from the child's juice box that seemed to get lost in his adult-size hand. But there was only so long a man could drink. When he pulled the box away, Maggie stood in front of him. Her long legs peeked out from white shorts. Her huge grin charmed him.

"I told you I didn't need help."

Annoyance skittered through him. She didn't seem to have the same problem he did with being together. While he suffered the torment of the sexually aroused damned, she appeared perfectly content to be around him as a friend.

Of course she wasn't the one who'd been in love. She

was the one who'd left. And maybe if he would continually remind himself of that he could get rid of the weird feelings that filled his gut every time he looked at her.

"I didn't really think you needed help."

Her green eyes sparkled and the fire in his belly sent a shower of sparks through him. "Then why bounce in front of me to catch that fly ball?"

This was not working.

He rose from the bench, inched away from her. "I didn't want you to get hurt."

She gaped at him. "Hurt?"

"You're pregnant," he said, stupidly, as if she needed a reminder.

Her face fell. The sparkle in her eyes morphed into a look of confusion. "It's Wiffle Ball. The ball is so light we don't even need mitts." She laughed. "The worst that could happen is that I'd get a sting."

Her laughter raced through him like a potent drug. The desire to flirt with her, to kiss her, just to enjoy her, exploded and sent longing skittering along his nerve endings.

"Right." He turned and walked away. But all his senses were engaged. His brain, too. He'd always loved sparring with Maggie. Tussling. Playing. Now, he didn't even feel he was allowed to talk to her and somehow it made the temptation even stronger.

He almost snorted a laugh, but caught it. Wouldn't he look like a pathetic sap if she realized he still had the hots for her?

He got into his car and headed down the coast, then slapped the steering wheel. This was ridiculous. He couldn't take an eighty-mile drive every time he saw her. Why couldn't he get ahold of himself? He whipped his car around and headed home.

As soon as he turned onto his street, he saw the big black SUV parked in front of his house. Leaning against the driver's-side door was his brother Cade. Wearing his usual Stetson, jeans and boots, he looked like an indolent cowboy, not the billionaire oilman that he was.

As Nick had pulled his car beneath his house, Cade slipped under the garage door and opened his Porsche door for him.

"I thought you were on your way to New York to talk to Darius before you flew to Saudi Arabia."

He slapped Nick on the back. "That's the thing about a private plane. I can stop where I want. And I wanted to kick your behind for telling Darius to send me to Saudi when you were the one he called first."

He motioned for Cade to precede him up the steps into the kitchen. This was exactly what he needed. A good scrap with his brother to work off some of the emotion simmering through him.

"Sorry. I'm busy."

"Like I'm not?"

"You probably are, but I just spent six weeks in New York, babysitting Andreas Holdings while you sat in your comfy chair in your ranch house probably watching reruns of *Lost*."

Cade snorted.

And Nick relaxed. They'd sit on old lawn chairs beneath the deck, watch the ocean, drink some beer.

"Yeah, well at least I didn't hire my ex-wife."

His dying irritation with himself for hiring Maggie burst into flames again. Still, there was no way he'd let Cade see that. He opened the fridge, pulled out two cold ones and tossed one to Cade. "I'll have to thank Darius for being able to keep a secret."

"Hey, when we decided to be brothers for real, we agreed there would be no more secrets."

"Right." When they were talking about Darius and Gino that had been a great idea. When it came to himself, Nick wasn't exactly thrilled with the no secrets policy. He pointed at the French doors that led to the deck. "That way. We'll pull the old lawn chairs out of the garage, stick them in the sand and watch the ocean and the stars."

Cade nodded and led the way. But the second they were comfortably settled with their chairs in the warm summer sand, Cade said, "So what's she like?"

There was just no changing the subject with a persistent half brother. He sighed and decided to be honest. "The same. Pretty. Tall, but sort of delicate."

Cade laughed. "Delicate? What guy in his right mind says delicate? I don't even use the delicate cycle in my washer."

Fresh annoyance rippled through Nick. Once again, she had him thinking of flowers and girlie words. Just like the sap he'd been at eighteen.

"You still have the hots for her or what?"

"Buzz off."

Cade hooted another laugh. "You *do!*"

"Great. Fine. Whatever. I'm still attracted to my ex-wife. Something like that doesn't just go away."

Cade took a slug of beer. "Sure it does. I have two foremen who cross the street rather than walk by their exes." He peered at Nick. "You should just sleep with her."

Nick almost spit out his beer. "You're crazy."

"I'm serious. Get her out of your system."

"Right."

"Okay, think it through. You have some sort of idealized picture of her in your head. Like she was the special love of your life or something."

Nick scowled, but what Cade said made sense. He hadn't thought about love or even commitments in fifteen years, and Maggie comes back and suddenly it was all he could think about.

"Over the years, you've probably forgotten all the bad stuff, all the stuff that makes her human and you only remember the good."

Nick peered over.

"So what you're remembering isn't true."

Sucking in a breath, Nick said, "I can't just sleep with her."

"Why not?"

"Because I'd be using her."

"How do you know she's not feeling the same things you are? Darius said she's divorced. Maybe she got divorced because her husband never measured up to *you* and now she's back, conveniently working for you—"

"And coming to the pickup Wiffle Ball game at the Shack."

Cade squinted his eyes in question.

"My mom runs the daycare. Knows all the kids. So every other night or so she goes to the Ice Cream Shack, gathers the local kids and entertains them with a game of Wiffle Ball so their parents can have a few minutes of peace."

Cade smiled. "And your ex was there?"

Nick nodded.

Cade laughed triumphantly. "I'm saying she's just as curious about you as you are about her." He took a long drink of beer, then said, "Test the water, bro, and you'll see I'm right. She's here to check you out."

The purely male part of Nick ate that up like candy. The male ego she'd battered needed to hear it.

"Chances are you both built the other into something

you're not," Cade continued, looking out at the ocean as if what he was saying was of very little consequence. A simple answer. An easy way to get both him and Maggie back to normal. "You sleep together once. You both realize you're not the wonderful demigods you've built each other into. And you move on."

CHAPTER FOUR

MAGGIE tossed and turned that night, upset because Nick was upset. She hadn't come home to remind him of things. She wouldn't even be working for him if there were other options. But she was working with him and they were both going to have to deal with it.

She woke late Thursday morning and couldn't seem to pull herself together in her usual forty minutes. Then she had to find her dad in the field and wait for him to change his boots so he could drive her to work in his old beat-up truck.

At the entrance to Andreas Manufacturing, she jumped out and raced to the building. When she plowed through the door into the office, Nick was waiting for her, leaning against the edge of Julie's desk. She saw his feet first, tanned toes wrapped in the thick straps of his leather sandals, then the long length of jean-covered legs, then his bright orange T-shirt, then his scowl.

Great. "Sorry, I'm late. I forgot I didn't have a car. Had to find dad in the field—"

He stopped her with a short, terse motion of his hand. "Julie called this morning. One of her friends has been taken ill and she flew to Vegas to help care for her."

A burst of fear raced through her. "She's gone?" *No go-between? No safety net?*

"She said she'd put in her time and was done."

"I don't get a training period?"

His gaze caught hers. "Do you need one?"

"No." She lifted her chin. She was fine with the work. It was the go-between they needed. But it would be a cold, frosty day in hell before she'd admit that to him. "No. I'm okay."

He pushed away from the desk. "Good."

Heading into his office, he turned away from her and she couldn't stop her gaze from skimming down his back and nearly perfect butt.

Good Lord. Would she ever be able to look at him without thinking of those two weeks they were married? Without thinking about making love, discovering sex… discovering each other? How proud she was to be married to him? How happy she'd been?

She shook her head. Being attracted to him was crazy. Not only had fifteen long years passed, but also she was living a second chance. Second chances did not come along every day. She did not intend to screw up by falling for a man who might be attracted to her but wouldn't really "want" her because she'd hurt him. So why she was having these thoughts was beyond her.

At his office door, he suddenly stopped and pivoted to face her. "Well, come on. Stow your gear then bring a pad and pen into my office and we'll get started."

Grateful that she'd brought her eyes away from his butt before he'd turned, Maggie nodded. She tossed her purse and sandwich into her desk drawer, grabbed a pad and pen and followed him.

He pointed at the conference table which was piled high with files and loose papers, including mail and messages. Julie had called them the information he'd need to write the bid, but though Nick had been reviewing information all week, he hadn't touched these stacks. So it appeared this was the day she and Nick jumped in.

"You sit there." He indicated a chair on the right side. "I'll sit here." He grabbed the back of the seat at the head of the table, pulled it out and sat, putting them catty-cornered from each other. Close enough to touch.

She almost groaned. She didn't understand the ridiculous temptation that continually rose up in her when he was around, except to blame it on pregnancy hormones unleashed the night before when she'd seen him shirtless. Actually, that made sense. Now all she had to do was stifle it.

Looking at the stacks, he drew in a deep breath. "Now the question is where to start."

"I'd go with the files. They're thicker. It'll feel like we're getting more work done."

He scowled, but reached for the files. He pulled a green one off the stack, opened it and began reading.

"Okay," he said, tossing the opened file in front of her. "This is our engineer's analysis of the differences between the product specs from five years ago and the current bid."

He rose and retrieved a cylinder of drawings from his desk. He unrolled it on the conference table. "The part we manufacture has been changed significantly."

She raised her gaze to meet his. "Which will change our bid."

He quickly looked away. "While I was gone, I'm guessing the estimating department already put together the materials numbers. They're waiting for us to call for them. So you do that."

She grabbed her notebook and pen and scribbled the instruction. "Who do I call?"

"Talk to John Sprankle. He's lead estimator. He'll have done the work himself since this is our primary bid."

She smiled. "Great."

He looked away again.

Okay. The first glance away she could think was normal. The second not so much. She didn't have to ask why he was uncomfortable around her. They'd had an awkward time at the ice cream stand. He'd left because of her. She could let it go, let him work through it on his own, but as he'd already said this project was too important for them to be tiptoeing around each other. They had to talk about this. At the very least she had to apologize.

She cleared her throat. "Uh…about yesterday."

He glanced over, his expression guarded. "What about yesterday? Did Julie say something needed to be done?"

"No. I just feel bad that you left the game last night."

He looked away. "Don't be. My younger brother Cade was waiting for me at the house when I got there. He wanted to surprise me."

Happiness bubbled up in her. Nick had always hated being alone. It was wonderful to realize he was getting close to his brothers.

"So what happened?"

"What happened when?"

"With your brother, you dolt." She playfully tapped his forearm. A current of electricity raced up her arm and she was transported back in time. This was how it had started the night they'd gone from friends to lovers. A touch that should have been playful had turned electric. They'd looked into each other's eyes and the spark of electricity had become an avalanche of desire.

He'd kissed her and she'd melted.

Wow. Not a good thing to remember when she was already overheated with pregnancy hormones.

"Is your brother here for a week or the weekend or what?"

Ignoring her, he read over the plans. She should have let him work. She should have been glad he wasn't having the memories she was, should have been glad for the reprieve. But her curiosity was like an overeager child jumping up and down inside her. Questions spilled out before she could stop them.

"Is he tall, is he thin, is he grouchy, is he fun?"

He rolled his head to the side to catch her gaze again. "Why? Want an intro?"

Pain speared her. How little did he think of her? "Are you kidding me? I'm just plain curious and I'm curious for you." She tapped his hand again then held back a groan. He was warm. Solid. His skin rough. Masculine. A magnet for her itching fingers.

He glanced down at her fingers, then back up at her face. Their gazes caught and clung. His eyes sparked with the same need that tormented her.

"Why are you here?"

Caught in his magnetic gaze, she could barely think let alone comprehend a question. "Here?"

"At my company. Working for me?"

"I couldn't get a job anywhere else."

"You wanted to know about Cade…well, he thinks that answer is baloney. He thinks you're here because there's still something between us."

The fire in her belly roared to aching life again. If she said yes, would he kiss her?

Stifling another groan, she reminded herself of the pregnancy hormones. Told herself she was too smart to long for a guy whom she'd jilted, a guy who shouldn't want anything to do with her. But she knew both excuses were, as Cade had so aptly said, baloney. She was attracted to

Nick. Always had been attracted to Nick. And working together had been a foolish, foolish decision.

Except neither of them wanted the attraction and if she nipped this in the bud now, she wouldn't lose her second chance.

"There's nothing between us."

"You're sure."

"I'm sure."

"You lie."

She burst off her chair and paced behind it. "Of course, I'm lying! Dear God, Nick! What purpose would it serve for us to be attracted to each other? None." She laid her hands on her stomach. "I have a baby who needs me. He or she needs me strong and smart. Not caught in a relationship that might only be us trying to recreate something that hadn't worked the first time."

Her reminder was like a bucket of cold water in Nick's face. What an idiot Cade had turned him into. He'd gotten him so stirred up that he'd forgotten the most basic fact about their relationship. *She'd* left him.

She hadn't loved him.

Sleeping together wouldn't solve or prove anything. Except that they found each other attractive. He'd never doubted that. In fact, that was what had shown him the way for his current lifestyle. He and Maggie were so good in bed, she left no doubt that people didn't have to be in love to enjoy each other.

But a smart man also didn't sleep with an assistant he needed.

"You're right. I was out of line. Let's just get back to work." He turned to the specs. "I'm going to dictate language to you that I want you to put into the narrative portion of the bid. Do you take shorthand?"

The relief on her face told him he was right. They

might be attracted to each other but she didn't want to experiment…didn't want him. She only wanted this job.

"No. But I can write really, really fast."

"Great."

He dictated slowly and concisely, his mind fully taken by the complex task. But when Maggie left his office, he ran his hands down his face.

Now he had a reason to want to kick both his brothers' butts.

Amazingly, Maggie's dad remembered to pick her up that night. Nick had been so busy that he hadn't even looked at the clock. But when Charlie Forsythe strolled into her office, still wearing his jeans and work shirt, his hat rolled in his hands, Nick glanced at his watch and saw it was a quarter after seven.

Glad to see her dad, especially since he hadn't yet had a chance to pay his respects, he rose from his seat just in time to hear the old man say, "Charlie Jr. called today."

The eagerness in her dad's voice caused Nick to sit back down.

As Maggie gathered her things from her desk, she said, "That's great."

"Yeah. Still the same old, same old with him, though. Busy. Busy. Busy. Work. Work. Work."

Nick frowned. The old man was picking up his daughter after she'd worked a ten-hour day, yet he didn't seem to notice that as he bragged about the son he'd always adored.

"He's busy," Maggie replied cheerfully.

Nick shook his head, closed his eyes, told himself not to get sucked into Maggie's problems. That was how it had started the last time. She'd always been there for him, so when the tide had turned and he'd realized how alone and abandoned she'd felt in her own family, he'd taken her into his.

He couldn't do it again.

Wouldn't do it again.

But despite his fierce denials, the urge to defend her, to care for her, to comfort her, rose up in him like an angry beast.

"Nick." She poked her head into the office and smiled at him. "My dad's here. So unless you need me, I'm going home."

No matter how much he wanted to take care of her, he couldn't. Hell, she'd yelled at him for stepping in front of her to catch a fly ball. There was no way he could run interference with her dad. He resisted the impulse. "Go." He waved her on, letting her know that her leaving was fine.

But after she had left, he raked his fingers through his hair.

Damn it! He shouldn't care, but the reminder of young Maggie, sad Maggie, needy Maggie, broke his heart.

It was ridiculous. She hadn't thought for more than two heartbeats about leaving him, after she'd lost their baby. She'd hurt him.

So why did he care that she might be lonely?

CHAPTER FIVE

NICK barely slept. He woke early Friday morning and took a quick shower, calling himself every kind of fool for being upset for her when she didn't care about him. Deciding that the sooner he got the bid done, the sooner he could go to New York, help Darius and enjoy the nightlife, he raced to work, and there she sat. Looking like a ray of sunshine at her clean desk.

"Good morning!"

He cleared his throat. "Good morning."

"I got in an hour early this morning and cleared up everything I hadn't gotten through last night so we could get started as soon as you arrived."

"That's good."

When she looked crestfallen at his lackluster response, little shards of pain, like glass, pricked his skin, demanding that he be nicer to her. So he reminded himself that as soon as he got this bid done he could go to New York and he smiled broadly.

"That's great. We have a lot of things to do today. So bring your notebook in and we'll get started."

"Okay." She grabbed her pad and pen and followed him into his office.

Nick tossed his keys and cell phone onto his desk, feeling better, stronger than he had all week. Now that he had himself anchored, nothing she said or did could break his good mood.

This was going to work, Maggie thought, happily scampering behind Nick as he walked into his office. Being honest with him the day before must have really worked. For the first time all week, Nick wasn't grouchy. He wasn't moody. They were finally getting their footing in dealing with each other and could now act like a real boss and assistant.

She happily scooted to the conference table when he motioned for her to sit. As he had the day before, he took the seat at the head of the table, catty-cornered from her. He said nothing. She said nothing. He picked up a file and began reading.

When a whole minute had passed with Nick engrossed in the contents of the file, she set her hands on her lap to keep from fidgeting. After another minute, she knit her fingers together. After the third minute, she glanced around the office.

Sitting close enough to read the framed degrees on the wall, she was surprised to see he not only had his masters but he also had a Ph.D.

"Wow."

He glanced up. "What?"

"You have a Ph.D?"

He turned his attention back to the papers. "Why does that surprise you?"

"Because you started a company at eighteen."

"And went to school at night."

"A lotta nights," she said, unable to keep the admiration out of her voice.

"You have to have knowledge to make a company successful."

"Yeah. Otherwise, it would have been a waste of your five-million-dollar investment."

He stopped reading again, glanced over again. "Excuse me?"

Too late she realized her mistake. He'd never told her about the trust fund his father had offered him. She'd overheard him talking with his dad's lawyer about it.

But what difference did it make? Fifteen years had passed. They'd both moved on. She might as well admit she knew where he'd gotten the money to start his business.

"Your trust fund. I overheard the lawyer telling you about it the day we lost the baby."

He set his pen down, caught her gaze. He said nothing, but his expression compelled her to explain.

"I heard you turn it down. I didn't think it was right for you to lose it."

His eyes narrowed, his gaze turned to stone. "Please do not tell me you left because you heard my dad's lawyer tell me that I couldn't collect the trust since I was married."

"You wouldn't have taken the money otherwise."

He shoved his back against the wall and leaped to his feet. "I didn't want the money!"

His face was a picture of disbelieving horror that sent a shot of uncertainty through her. She refused to give in to it. He might not have wanted it, but he and his mom had needed it. "Oh, come on, Nick. You and your mom had spent your entire life scraping to get by. I was supposed to just stand there and let you turn down five million dollars? I couldn't have lived with myself."

He snorted a laugh. "You couldn't have lived with me not getting the money? Well, live with this." He slammed his hands against the edge of the table and leaned toward her. "I didn't take the money."

"What?"

"I didn't take the money. I didn't want it. I wanted to prove to my dad that I could make it without him and I did."

Shock rendered Maggie speechless.

"So, consulting me before making such a huge decision would have been a good thing."

Unable to process what he was telling her, Maggie swallowed the lump in her throat. "You seriously didn't take it?"

"No." He shook his head as if in total disbelief of what she'd done. Then, without another word, he headed for the door of his office and barreled through hers. She heard the door slam then a minute later the roar of his car's engine, but didn't bother getting up.

Too many emotions roiled through her. Too many thoughts competed for attention.

She'd sacrificed their love so he could collect the money due to him—

And he hadn't taken it.

Nick was halfway through town when his cell phone rang. Shaking with fury, he wanted to ignore it but he noticed the caller was his mom.

He picked it up, sucked in a calming breath and said, "Hey, Mom. What's up?"

"The toilet in my office is overflowing!"

"Get a plumber—"

"I called one but he can't come this morning. Oh, my God, Nick! It's going to run over into the new hardwood and warp it—"

For a woman who had turned into a very shrewd business owner once he was able to give her some financial backing, his mother's lack of understanding of simple things usually made him laugh. Right at this very minute, he wasn't in a laughing mood.

Still, that wasn't his mother's fault. "Okay. Calm down. I'm in the car anyway, I'll be right over."

He made an illegal U-turn and headed for the daycare, the whole time telling himself that Maggie's admission meant nothing. Yes, he'd been too angry to stay in the office with her. And, yes, he hoped she'd leave a note on his desk saying she'd resigned. But the knot in his gut and the pain in his chest were ridiculous. Maggie had left him so long ago, and he was such a different person now, that it shouldn't matter why.

But it did.

And when he let his brain tiptoe into forbidden territory, he knew why it did. But he hauled his thoughts out of there. It served no purpose to consider the fact that she might have loved him. Might have always loved him. Might have left him *because* she had loved him.

He tightened his fingers around his steering wheel as he pulled into the driveway of the neat, redbrick building he'd bought for his mom's daycare when he'd gotten his first multimillion-dollar contract. He counted to four hundred as he walked up to the front door, calming himself, telling himself not to think of Maggie—

The door opened before he could grab the knob. His mom caught his arm and yanked him inside, her floor-length accordion skirt swishing with every move.

"Hurry!"

She dragged him down the hall, past the brightly painted rooms filled with toddlers, elementary school kids and preteens, separated for ease of discipline. Energetic music poured from the toddler room. Three-foot-high kids formed a circle in the elementary age room. Computer monitors blinked in the preteen room.

"Relax, Mom. The water's not going to reach the hardwood unless you've got about eighty gallons gushing out. And even if you did, I think by now you probably have towels sopping up the mess."

Stepping into her office, he could see he was right. She had a mountain of towels in front of the office door, protecting her beloved hardwood.

He stepped over the towels into the bathroom. "See? Everything's fine." He leaned down. "I'll just tighten this knob here that turns off your water and we'll call another plumber."

She leaned against the doorjamb, crossed her arms on her chest. "Why? Can't you fix this?"

"Probably. But I can also afford a plumber."

"And you have to get back to work?"

Not able to lie to his mother, he shrugged.

"Ah. Not going back to work. Hmm. Let's see." She ambled over to the open bathroom door, her skirt moving gaily around her. Bracelets jangled merrily on her wrist. "This is your first week back after being away for six weeks, so you need to be there. But you also hired your ex-wife as an assistant so that might be the problem."

"That certainly didn't take long to get around town."

"A good piece of gossip never does." She smiled. "Once Maggie left the Shack last night, Mary Bryant told us you'd hired her."

He carelessly lifted one shoulder, trying to look unaffected. "It's not a big deal. Maggie and I haven't seen each other in fifteen years. Working together won't be a problem. I'm fine."

She laughed. "No, you're not. I saw you leave the Wiffle Ball game the night before last. You played one inning with her then bolted. I'm not stupid. I figured you didn't like being around her."

Boy, he just couldn't keep anything from his mother. "All right, Kreskin. I'm not fine."

"So what happened this morning that you left?"

He rolled his shoulders, loosening the tightness. "She told me she overheard Dad's lawyer the day she lost the baby. She left so we'd get the money."

His mom blinked then she tilted her head. "But you didn't take the money."

"I know."

"Wow."

"Yeah, wow."

They were quiet for a few seconds. Nick stood perfectly still as his mom studied him, his face, his body language. Finally she said, "You're not just angry. You're surprised."

"I didn't know she'd overheard. So, yeah. I'm surprised."

"Oh, Nicky! Are you lying to me or yourself?" She shook her head, sending her curls bouncing. "It's not the surprise of finding out she overheard the lawyer that bothers you. It's the surprise of hearing why she left."

He squeezed his eyes shut in misery. As if it wasn't bad enough he had to face this, he had a perceptive mom who just wouldn't stop until she'd dragged every damned detail out of him. "Look, Mom. I've got to go."

She caught his arm. "We were in trouble, and Maggie had a big heart. You couldn't expect her to sit by and do nothing when she overheard you turn down five million dollars."

Nick's jaw tightened. "I *loved* her."

"And she loved you."

He forked his fingers through his hair. "No kidding."

She framed his face with her hands and caught his gaze. "That's what's really bothering you. That she loved you?"

The truth of that flashed through him like lightning illuminating a stormy night. He'd forced himself to go on after the loss of the one woman he'd ever truly loved by telling himself that only a schmuck pines for a woman who doesn't love him. Now, realizing she had loved him, everything changed. His heart broke again, only this time for an entirely different reason.

Still, he wouldn't tell his mother that. He wouldn't tell anybody that.

"We were a team. She should have consulted me." He stepped over the mountain of towels again, away from his mom and her penetrating glances and on-point observations. "Have Bernice keep calling plumbers until she finds one who can take an emergency call," he instructed, referring to his mom's office manager, as he walked toward the door. "Have the bill sent to me."

"I can pay my own bills now. But that's besides the point. You're hurt. You're furious. And you shouldn't be."

He rounded on her. "Really? I feel like somebody took my whole life, tossed it in the air and it came down in disjointed pieces that don't make sense."

"Oh, this makes perfect sense. Nick, Maggie had just lost a baby. She was grieving and tired and only eighteen years old."

He pressed his fingers to his eyelids. He hated thinking of Maggie being scared, alone, aching from the loss of their child when he should have been there for her. He *would* have been there for her.

"And now you're going to have to deal with it. Fifteen years have passed. You're a success. She's moved on. Life has gone on. You have to deal with it."

* * *

Maggie spent the morning sitting in her office chair, waiting for Nick to return. He didn't.

In the afternoon, she turned on her computer and cruised the various software, stopping to analyze the accounting programs since she knew that's where most of her responsibilities lay. At five, she packed up, hoping her dad remembered to pick her up. He didn't.

So she called, but no one answered the phone. Assuming he was outside, she waited until five-thirty to call again. Again no answer. Six. No answer. Six-thirty, he picked up the phone, apologized and headed out to get her.

She was waiting by the front gate when the shake-rattle-and-roll truck pulled up. It stopped in front of her, she climbed inside and they headed home.

"I'm sorry I forgot you."

She mustered a smile for her dad. "You're busy. I understand."

"It's just that being outside is so much better for me. Inside reminds me too much of Vicki."

Maggie swallowed and tears welled in her eyes. She'd kept her composure all day. All damned day. She'd sat at her desk, pretended nothing was wrong, prayed that though Nick had left angry—furious—he would spend the day thinking things through and realize she'd done what she'd done because she had loved him and it was the right thing. They were too young to be married, too young to be committed to one person or one course of action for the rest of their lives. He had to see she'd done the right thing.

When he hadn't come back or even called, her gut told her he didn't agree. And she'd faced the possibility that he'd be firing her the next day. And the worst part of it was, she knew Nick was right. They shouldn't be working together. She shouldn't have gotten a job with him. She should have sucked it up and stayed in Pittsburgh.

But her dad needed her.

"I know it must be hard to lose the love of your life." She swallowed. Why did saying that hurt? She'd lost Nick so long ago she'd gotten over it. She'd married someone else. She was pregnant with that man's child. Losing Nick was so far in her past it shouldn't hurt.

He sucked in a breath. "Harder than you'd ever believe. We were a team—"

The tears in her eyes spilled over. She and Nick had been a team. Until that one final decision. A decision she'd made on her own because she knew he'd never choose money over her. No matter how much he and his mom struggled.

Her dad glanced at her. "Are you okay?"

"I'm fine. Hot. Tired." She forced a watery smile. "Pregnant. I cry at the drop of a hat now. You know how hormones are."

"Alleluia. I sure do! I remember how funny Vicki was, pregnant with Charlie Jr. She cried at everything." He laughed as the old truck puttered down Main Street. "But I also know it's probably hard having to get a job while you're pregnant. Still, I think it was a real blessing that you got to work with Nick."

"Really?" That popped out before she could stop it. How could this be a blessing? Only five days in his employ and she'd not only been tossed into a sea of confusion, but she'd hurt him.

Again.

"Well, sure, he's a great guy. Everybody loves him." He glanced over again. "I've heard rumors about year-end bonuses large enough to pay off car loans. The money's great. And let's face it. You need money."

She swallowed. She did need money.

"And health care. You won't get on Nick's insurance before this baby's born, but you will have health care. You just need to save enough to pay the bills when this little one comes."

She did indeed.

"So you're lucky."

No. She wasn't really lucky. She was stuck.

CHAPTER SIX

SATURDAY morning when Nick arrived in the office, Maggie was waiting for him. His curly black hair had been blown around during the drive in his convertible. His red eyes told her he probably hadn't slept.

Their gazes caught, clung. A million questions arched between them. Silence stretched.

Finally Nick broke it. "It's Saturday."

"I know. Julie said we work ten hours a day, six days a week when you have a bid due. You have a bid due. So I'm here."

She didn't know why she'd been optimistic, but she'd honestly thought it would please him that she'd not only remembered he worked Saturdays, but that she'd come in.

Instead he looked away. "Is your car fixed?"

Disappointment trembled through her, followed by a wave of fear. If she said yes, would he fire her because she had a way home? Would she have to go searching for a job in the city? Hope somebody would hire a six-month-pregnant woman knowing she'd need a leave of absence in three months?

Her dad was right. It was a blessing Nick had hired her. She had to keep this job.

"My car isn't fixed. I caught my dad before he went out to the field."

He combed his fingers through his tangled hair then turned and headed for his office. "Okay, bring in a notebook and we'll get started."

Relief forced her breath out in a rush. She grabbed her steno pad and a pen and scrambled after him. As he tossed his cell phone and keys on his desk, she slid onto the chair at the conference table where she'd sat the day before. She glanced at the framed degrees and shame rode her blood. Memories of the expression on his face rolled through her brain, made worse by the disbelief in his voice when he'd told her he hadn't taken his dad's money.

The tension in her tummy jumped three notches.

He ambled over, sat at the head of the table. Reaching for the file he'd been reading the day before, he cleared his throat. "These are production reports." He flopped the open file down in front of her. "Every day we print out a report of how much each employee got done in his or her shift."

He grabbed the next red file and the next and the next, opened each and then stacked them on the table in front of her. "I use them to determine our labor costs and to estimate delivery dates for bids like the one we're working on."

"Okay." The reminder of the bid heartened her. With Julie gone and something so important due, he genuinely needed her. Her spirits brightened a little more. If she could help him, she could prove herself as an assistant and their past would become irrelevant.

"I like to review these in hard copy first." He glanced down at a tablet in front of him and crossed something off on the handwritten list on the top page. "So I want you to go through these files and make sure there's a report for every week."

"Why don't I just run the numbers?"

He didn't look at her, just sarcastically said, "You want to figure the labor costs and the delivery dates?"

She shrugged. "Sure. Why not?"

He sighed. "Just check the reports, print out what isn't there."

Panic tightened her chest. How was she going to prove herself if the only work he'd give her was barely even secretarial?

"Are you refusing to let me run the numbers because I'm a woman? Or because you're mad at me?"

"I take care of the numbers."

"Can't handle a little competition?"

He glared at her. "Competition?"

"Or maybe you just don't like the idea that your assistant can probably do everything you can do."

He set the file down and raised his gaze until it met hers. "Now who's pushing us to have a fight?"

Her heart tripped over itself in her chest. His dark eyes sparked with fury. His mouth was a grim line. The urge to turn and run gripped her, but pure nerve, the kind she hadn't had since she'd left Ocean Palms at eighteen, chased it away.

She was Maggie Forsythe. She was smart. She was strong. And she needed this job.

She leaned forward, invading his personal space. "I'm not pushing us to fight. I just want to do my job."

He leaned forward, too. His eyes a shiny, angry black now. "Sounds to me more like you're taking over."

She edged forward again, daring him to say what was really making him mad, so they could fight it out or just let her do the work she could do. "I always was better at planning than you were."

"You mean you were always pushier."

"If that's what it takes to get things done, then, yes, I'm pushier."

He yanked the rest of the red files from the stack and shoved them at her. "Great. Fine. You run the numbers."

Heart pounding, she rose from her seat, took the files and marched to her desk. She hadn't stood up for herself like that in fifteen years and, by God, it felt good. Not just because she'd won the battle, but because she could do this job. She shouldn't have to fear being fired. Her abilities, not their past, should be all that mattered. If it killed her, she would prove herself to him.

When she was gone, Nick rubbed his hands over his eyes. He was supposed to be furious with her, so why had he just found her bossing him around sexy?

Because it reminded him of *his* Maggie. That was why.

Just like at the ice-cream stand a few nights before, her hair was sleek, straight and youthful. She'd stopped wearing makeup and was wearing jeans and simple T-shirts. She bossed him around. Wanted to get to work. Didn't like foot dragging. Didn't like the tension between them.

Yeah. She definitely was his Maggie.

But his Maggie had left him. Maybe for good reason, but she'd gone. And now, when he was furious, only now learning and dealing with things she'd known for fifteen years, she was casual. Able to work. She'd moved on. He hadn't.

What the hell did it all mean? She'd left because she loved him, not because she hadn't? Was that supposed to make everything better? At least before she'd told him why she'd left, he could justify his lifestyle. He could blame his broken heart for the new man he'd become. The man who wouldn't commit, who refused to fall in love, who thought love was for losers and people like his brother Darius who needed a good woman at his side.

What had made perfect sense now seemed shallow, wrong.

And it shouldn't.

How could she come home, tell him she'd lied to him, and somehow make him feel like the one in the wrong?

Maggie spent the day reviewing the labor reports and the corresponding software, and by three o'clock had generated the numbers Nick needed. He barely thanked her. Instead he rose from his desk, ambled to the conference table and retrieved a yellow file.

"These are the résumés for the individual supervisors and admin personnel involved in the project, along with the education and experience stats on the machinists." He picked up an enormous white binder. "This is our final bid document from five years ago. Read the segment on education and experience and create a document that mimics what we did five years ago using the new information."

She looked at the file, looked at the bid document and looked at him. A real project.

She smiled. "Okay."

"Don't get cocky. There's a lot of work to do. I can't do it all. You're hired to help me and you want to do your job. So do it. Get to work."

Joy bubbled through her. "Okay."

Happier than she'd been in years, she read the appropriate section of the bid document then read all the résumés in the folder. At four-thirty she wasn't anywhere near ready to start putting together the new information, so she called her dad intending to tell him to wait for her call before he came for her. He, of course, didn't answer. At five-thirty she tried again, but again no answer.

At six, she turned her chair so she could watch for him out the window, as she continued to read. But she needn't have bothered. True to form, her dad didn't show up. At seven, he finally picked up the phone.

"Oh, kiddo! I'm sorry."

"Don't worry about it. We seem to be working later than I thought we would."

"Seem to be?"

"We're not actually speaking yet, so I don't know for sure. All I know is that I'm not leaving until he does."

"He's still mad?"

"Either that or he's turned into a real pain in the butt over the years."

She expected her dad to laugh. Instead he sighed. "Years ago you should have told him the stuff you told me last night about his trust fund."

"Uh, Dad. We didn't see each other for fifteen years."

"Then maybe you should have told him the day you left."

She squeezed her eyes shut. Hindsight was always twenty-twenty. But even if it wasn't, she knew in her heart of hearts that Nick never would have let her go if she'd admitted she was only leaving so he could get the trust fund.

Of course, he hadn't taken the trust fund.

She rubbed her temples. Picking apart something that had happened fifteen years ago would not make it any better. "I'll call you when we're done."

"How are you going to know when you're done?"

"When he leaves, I'll call you."

"Okay. Sounds like a plan."

She hung up the phone, proud of herself for staying, but still aching over the awkwardness between her and Nick. For fifteen years she'd considered paving the way for Nick to get his trust fund a noble sacrifice. Now that she knew her leaving had been moot, she had no idea how to handle it in her brain. She could no longer be proud of the decision that had seemed so right, but how could she be angry with herself when she hadn't known Nick wouldn't take the money?

The only thing she could think to do to make it up to him was work. Work hard. Work long. Save him some time and effort.

At eight Nick came out of his office, keys in hand. Surprised to see her, he stopped dead in his tracks.

"What are you still doing here?"

"We work ten-hour days. I'm staying as long as you are."

With any other assistant he would have admired her tenacity. But he just wanted Maggie gone. He knew it wasn't fair. He knew it wasn't right. Especially since she was such a hard worker—a qualified worker. But that was what he felt. Discovering she'd left him so he'd get money that he hadn't taken had turned his very sane, very comfortable life upside down. Every time he looked at her, knowing she'd loved him enough to give up everything she'd wanted, something horrible happened in his heart. It ached. It mourned. It started generating visions about what might have been.

Might have been.

He could have snorted in derision. There was no might have been in life. There was only what was—what had happened. And what had happened was that she'd made a decision they should have made together. She'd betrayed him by not talking to him. She'd made the mistake, but somehow he'd ended up paying for it and he was paying again. With questions that had no relevance. Questions that rattled around in his brain every time he looked at her.

He wanted her gone.

But she wasn't leaving. And he was going to have to learn to deal with this.

With a put-upon sigh, he said, "Gather your things and I'll take you home since we have now officially worked an eleven-hour day."

"That's okay. My dad—"

"Gather your things."

He hadn't meant for his voice to be gruff, but it had been and she quickly grabbed her purse and headed out the door.

They walked to the car in silence. Slid onto the seats in silence. And would have ridden the whole way to her dad's farm in silence, if she hadn't said, "I'm nearly done with the employee stats."

Frustration buffeted him. Did she have to be so good? Couldn't she drop the ball a bit so he could direct some of the anger racing through him to something tangible, something he could deal with?

"It took me about two minutes to find the files for the résumés in the computer. So I didn't have to retype anything, just organize the information." Strands of red hair that sparkled in the setting sun blew across her mouth and she pulled them away. "While I had the original bid, I took the liberty of perusing the whole thing. I saw the amount of work you have to do to get the bid ready and I know you need more help than you're letting on. So you can't fight me at every turn. You need to let go of the past and accept that I can help you."

The cheek! If she thought a little verbal lashing would

get him to forget that she'd betrayed him, she was crazy. He understood what his mom had told him about her miscarriage impacting her thinking that day, but making decisions alone wasn't how they operated. They had been a team and she'd broken their pact. Now she was virtually acting as if nothing had happened, which made him feel crazy, or as if he wasn't keeping up with the program. He didn't want her to be capable and smart. He didn't want her help. He wanted to nurse his anger. He wanted to be mad. He'd mourned her loss for five long years before he could push beyond it. He deserved his anger. He had earned it.

They finally reached her dad's farm. Maggie jumped out and he was just about to pull away when her father stepped out of the house and onto the porch.

Tall and slender, with a thick crop of hair that had darkened over the years from fire-engine red to auburn streaked with gray, Maggie's dad looked vibrant and healthy. He waved. "Hey, Nick!"

He waved back. "Hey, Mr. Forsythe."

"Come on up. Have a beer."

Eager to get away, he called, "No, thanks. It's late. I have to get home."

"Late? It's eight-thirty. Come on! It's been years. Give an old man a few minutes of your time."

It seemed downright wrong to ignore the request of a man who'd just lost his wife. Especially when Nick still hadn't paid his respects. He glanced at Maggie who'd stopped dead in her tracks on the grass. She didn't look happy at her dad's invitation. More like resigned.

Her dad waved again. "Come on! Please."

Nick turned off the Porsche's ignition, got out and headed up toward the house. Birds chirped. Flowers drifted in the breeze. In the distance a horse whinnied.

Maggie led the way to the porch. When she reached

the top step, her dad said, "Get us a few beers, would you, kiddo?"

She smiled slightly and nodded then disappeared behind the screen door. Charlie sat on the swing and Nick ambled over to the porch railing and leaned against it.

"What's it been?"

"Fifteen years."

Charlie shook his head. "Wow. I'm getting old." He shook his head again. "So damned old. Everybody I remember as a kid isn't a kid anymore."

Nick laughed. "We can all say that."

Maggie stepped out of the house and handed a beer to her dad and one to Nick. He refused to meet her gaze, but did say, "Thanks."

She said, "You're welcome," then headed to the door again. "I'm getting out of these jeans."

Her dad laughed. "Good idea."

She pulled open the screen door and walked inside.

"I'm sorry about Vicki."

Charlie nodded. "Thanks." He waited two beats, then peered around until he could look into the house. He quickly faced Nick again. "She married a louse."

In the middle of taking a swig of beer, Nick nearly choked.

"She won't tell you that because she's got a lot of pride. But she spilled the beans the day after her stepmother's funeral. Her ex had an affair with some bimbo at his health club and left Maggie. Then got her pregnant one day when he came back to pick up a few things. Maggie thought they were reuniting. He just wanted one last tumble for old-time's sake. When she told him she was pregnant, he told her he didn't want the baby. He'd pay support, but he never wanted to see it." He took a drink of his beer. "She's been through a lot. I'm grateful that you hired her."

Because he wanted to fire her, shame flooded Nick. The story of her marriage was abysmal, but from the sounds of things Maggie was lucky to get away from that guy. Even better, though, Maggie's dad might brag about Charlie Jr. but he also loved his daughter. And maybe he should focus on that, instead of her lousy marriage.

"You don't have to thank me. She's smart and educated." Wanting to make sure her dad understood Maggie was every bit as good as her half brother, he said, "She's helping me a lot more than Julie ever did." Though it pained him to admit it, he also added, "We're already over half done with the bid. Instead of taking four weeks, it's probably only going to take us three. With her experience, things may even run smoothly when I need to take trips out of town to help my brother."

"You do seem to be gone a lot."

"My dad neglected his companies in the last two years of his life. My brother needs me in New York to help him get the conglomerate back in shape."

Charlie grunted. "Doesn't make a whole lot of sense to me to fix one company by ruining another."

Upstairs in her room Maggie heard her father's comments through her open bedroom window. She fell to the bed, not sure if she should laugh or cry. Not only had her father told her biggest secret to her former husband and new boss, but he was also chastising Nick for being away too much.

"Things are fine."

"Right, I'll bet your dad said the same thing the years he was letting his company go to hell in a ham sandwich."

The sound of Nick's laughter surprised her. He was angry with her, furious. He didn't even want to be around her, but he was stuck with her. Yet he wasn't taking that out on her father.

"Hell in a ham sandwich?"

Her dad grunted. "I never really understood what a handbasket was. Figured a ham sandwich makes more sense, what with the cholesterol and all. The heart attack that gives you will send a person to hell quicker than some damned basket."

Nick laughed again. The sound of it filled her with warm, sweet delight and wrapped her in memories. In some ways it was good that Nick had matured out of the silly boy she'd married and become a serious adult. It helped Maggie keep her perspective. But in others, it seemed a shame that the happy Nick Roebuck was gone. Replaced by Nick Andreas, businessman.

"Anyway." Nick's voice drifted up to her again. "Thanks for the beer. I'd better get home."

"Why don't you stay for supper?"

A pause. "Actually I've got to call my brother, get the rundown on what happened at Andreas Holdings this week."

The swing creaked. "Okay, then. I'll see you on Monday morning when you pick up Maggie for work. Seems to me it's easier for you to pick her up than me to drive her in, since you're going there anyway."

Maggie's face fell in dismay. If she weren't in her bra and panties she probably would have leaned out the window and told Nick her father was a silly old coot who shouldn't be asking for favors. Instead she could only squeeze her eyes shut in misery.

"Unless you're picking her up tomorrow to work on Sunday? I don't like people working on Sundays, you know. Everybody needs a rest. You come by Monday."

Pure mortification turned her face to scarlet.

But Nick said, "Yeah, sure, I'll pick her up."

CHAPTER SEVEN

NICK thought about Maggie's crappy marriage the whole way home. She'd told him about her husband running up debts. Add that to the fact that he'd left a pregnant wife and the guy wouldn't rate high in anybody's book. But the situation hadn't entirely come together in his head until Charlie had told him he'd had an affair. Then the facts snapped in place like puzzle pieces and a picture formed of Maggie struggling, Maggie being at home alone at night, Maggie suffering in silence.

When he got out of his car, he punched the wall of the short stairway leading to his kitchen. He didn't understand the feelings swirling inside of him. He was angry with her. Furious. He shouldn't care that she'd married a cretin who didn't treat her well and left her pregnant and penniless.

But he did care. He didn't want to see Maggie hurt just because she'd hurt him. Only an idiot thought like that and he wasn't an idiot.

He called Darius and got a rundown on the week at Andreas Holdings, but he kept the conversation brief, telling Darius he still had things to read before he went to bed. He didn't want his perceptive brother asking questions he couldn't answer.

Sunday morning he raced to work, knowing he'd have the office to himself and desperately in need of something to think about to get his mind off Maggie. He stayed until eight o'clock that night and grabbed a hot fudge sundae as his dinner on the way home. He fell into bed and slept like the dead.

Monday morning he felt marginally better. Working alone all day Sunday in the silent office, he'd gotten a lot of organizational tasks done. He headed for Andreas Manufacturing ready to tackle some of the more difficult aspects of the bid with Maggie then remembered he was supposed to be picking her up.

As he drove out to the farm, the things Charlie Forsythe had told him flashed to the front of his brain again, and he groaned in misery. As long as he worked with Maggie, he would be trapped in an emotional vortex. He hated what she'd done, but he didn't mean to punish her. Didn't want to see her unhappy. He just wanted away from her. But because of the bid, he was in as much of a bind as she was. She might need the job, but he also needed an assistant. He was simply going to have to figure out a way to deal with her.

When he pulled up to her house, the front door opened and Maggie ran out. She jumped into his car so fast he'd barely rolled to a stop.

For the first time in days, he laughed. "You don't want to risk your dad talking to me again, do you?"

She turned wary green eyes on him. "Would you?"

"He's lonely. He wanted a few minutes of my time. That's all."

Blessedly the conversation stopped there. But remembering the things her father had said, he shifted uncomfortably on his seat. Lord, he wanted to be furious with her. She'd broken his heart because she hadn't consulted him before making a decision that had changed their lives. But he'd become a very rich man, dated lots of women, had a great life—

And she'd been hurt, taken for granted, cast aside.

"I'll be glad when my car is fixed."

All right, already! Fate didn't have to rub his nose in her troubles. He got it. Not only was she a divorced, abandoned pregnant woman, who had to take a job with her angry ex-husband, but her car had broken. Surely to God he could muster enough sympathy to engage in small talk.

He looked over. "I hope you're not angsting about me driving you to work."

"Yes and no. I'm embarrassed that my dad sort of cor-ralled you into this."

"It's fine."

She glanced out the window. "I know. Everything's *fine*. But you and my dad aren't the ones living without trans-portation. There's more reason to have a car than going back and forth to work. There are times that I'd like to be able to just go. Get out of the house. Get some fresh air."

He thought about his drives along the beach. "I hear that."

"Really?" She peered over at him, her eyes sad, tired. "You live alone. You can have all the privacy you want at your house."

His heart tried to crack open. He wouldn't let it. "Maybe too much privacy. Sometimes it's so quiet I think too much."

She laughed. "That would be the day."

"Oh, come on. It's just you and your dad. How much noise can one fifty-five-year-old guy make?"

"None most of the time." She shrugged then peeked over at him. "He's so preoccupied with keeping himself busy so he doesn't miss Vicki that sometimes we pass like ships in the night."

He forced his attention back to the road, but it was too late. One basic, all-important question had fallen into his brain. How could she want to take care of a dad who'd ignored her once his son was born?

With a sigh, he gave in. If he didn't get the answer, she'd preoccupy his thoughts and he wouldn't get a lick of work done all day.

"So are things okay with your dad?"

"Things?"

"No Charlie Jr. troubles?"

She laughed. "Charlie Jr. troubles?"

Her voice dripped with such incredulity that he grimaced. "I'm remembering the past. You know? How your parents sort of favored Charlie Jr."

"Ah. You're going the whole way back to high school." She smiled. "All that went away when I left for university. Because I worked, I didn't come home for breaks, so they visited me. I sort of had an identity. Was my own person. Had my own place." She shrugged. "I can't explain it. But it was like everything that didn't work at their house, suddenly worked at mine."

He eased back. "So all that stuff from our teen years is gone?"

"Yep." She smiled. "Vicki even made trips up to Pittsburgh without Dad so she could shop at our outlets."

They were quiet for a minute, then she faced him again. "So what about you? You said you and your dad only had dinner once every other year, yet you changed your name from Roebuck to Andreas and even used that name for your company."

Nick grimaced. "Actually it was supposed to be a slap in his face."

"Really? How?"

He glanced at Maggie. The wind tossed her hair. Her

eyes were soft, but serious. Old memories surfaced. Times they'd talked. Confided. He'd never done that with another person. He hadn't even really talked with his brothers about this. And now he couldn't stop himself.

"Think it through. You're Stephone Andreas, known all over the world because you run a multibillion-dollar shipping conglomerate, then suddenly you're not the only Andreas business that comes up when people look you up on Google. There's a tiny company in North Carolina…and guess what? It's run by the son you don't acknowledge."

"Ouch."

He shrugged. "I was young. Angry. I'd thrown my dad's five million dollars back in his face and I wanted him to know I hadn't needed it."

"You regret it."

A statement, not a question.

"Yes." He glanced at her again. "Not refusing the trust, but being such a lunkhead. In my twenties it felt wonderful to be a thorn in his side. But when my company really took root and became well-known in my industry, I started to see what an idiot I was. He might have abandoned my mom and never acknowledged me, but he was trying to make up for that."

"So you forgave him?"

How could he explain to Maggie that he'd become his dad—not completely, but in some ways—so he had no real right to be angry?

He couldn't. So he said simply, "I forgave him."

"I never did hear the story of how you got started without any money."

Eager to be off the topic of his dad, Nick answered without thinking. "I met up with a guy who knew a guy who knew a guy who was not only selling some old equipment, he also had the balance of a contract to finish. So we did the deal on a profit sharing basis—the seller wouldn't get money until the profits were official—and I was in business."

"Smart."

Pride lifted his mood as they reached Andreas Manufacturing. He was smart. He had made it. No one could take that away from him. He pulled his Porsche into his reserved parking space and followed Maggie into the building.

But as they stepped into her office, reality returned. A fierce pang burst in his chest, shoving his pride into another dimension, reminding him she wasn't his friend, only his employee, yet they'd talked. As if she hadn't left him, and there weren't fifteen years between them, he'd told her things he hadn't ever told another person.

Something like fear laced with a warning stole through him. What the hell was he doing? She needed this job. He needed her help. And he also didn't want to hurt her. Nick Roebuck had been the love of her life. Not Nick Andreas. Nick Andreas didn't want to be the love of anybody's life and he had better remember that.

After giving her time to put her lunch bag in a drawer and get settled at her desk, he called her into his office and quickly dictated a few things he needed to be done that morning. Then he went back to work on the bid. He closed the door, kept himself set apart and got back into Nick Andreas mode.

When Maggie returned to her office after eating her sandwich in the employee cafeteria, Nick wasn't back from lunch yet. Bored, she perused the labor files again and was surprised to notice something intriguing.

When Nick suddenly strode past her desk, her head snapped up.

"Hey! I just found the most interesting thing in the labor reports."

He stopped, hesitated then faced her. "What?"

His guarded expression told her that all the goodwill they'd built that morning in the car was now gone. He was back to being angry with her. She had to be okay with that. She had no right to his friendship, only to this job, and she intended to keep it by wearing him down with her abilities.

"This employee Jake Graessle?" She tapped the paper. "Look how the productivity of the person on the machine beside his goes up."

For that, Nick took the few steps over to her desk. He tried to read the paper upside down, but apparently was unable to because he walked behind her desk and stood beside her.

Woodsy aftershave invaded her nostrils. His pure masculine heat wafted to her as he leaned in and read the lines she'd pointed out.

"Interesting."

Forcing herself to ignore his nearness, she said, "If his supervisor is having trouble with another employee's production, he could try an experiment and put him beside Jake. If that employee's stats go up, then we'll know Jake's one of those people who just naturally exerts a sort of positive peer pressure."

With a "Hmm" Nick straightened away. "Call his supervisor in."

She reached for her notepad. "What time do you want to talk to him?"

"You found the data. You have the honor of telling him. And helping him figure out the best way to use it."

Pleasure warmed her blood. "Really?"

"Sure." He didn't look at her as he spoke and his words

were dull, lifeless. "This job can be whatever you want to make it. Julie preferred the secretarial end of things. You're trained differently. I'm not going to stifle you. Go with your gut. Do what needs to be done. Stretch yourself."

Reminding herself that his anger with her was justified, yet he was no longer holding it against her professionally, she let him walk away and called Jake's supervisor to her office. She spent a half hour going over the labor reports and her findings. Liking her recommendations, George Wyman left her office a happy camper. Unfortunately when he had gone, Maggie had nothing to do.

With a deep breath, she pushed herself out of her chair, picked up her steno pad and a pen and walked into Nick's office.

He didn't even glance up. "Yes?"

"I don't have anything to do."

He hesitated, but eventually looked up and pointed at the conference table. "Sit. I'll be right over."

She took her normal seat, but Nick didn't take his. Instead of sitting catty-cornered from her, he sat across from her.

A weird sensation enveloped her. The distance between them felt so wrong, yet what right did she have for things to be anything but strained between them? She shouldn't feel weird. She shouldn't be unhappy. She shouldn't feel anything but gratitude that he kept her in his employ.

He pulled the next file off the stack. It contained hard copies of reports that Julie had generated from the accounting software. He quickly explained that he got some of the reports monthly, some weekly, some daily. Printing all of them and having them on his desk was her duty. Filing hard copies where he could find them when he worked late was also her responsibility.

From there he dictated some correspondence, most of

which he wanted her to send as emails. His voice never wavered from a crisp, efficient monotone. He said nothing nice, nothing personal. In spite of her best efforts to accept that, the temperature in the room went from cool to frigid in the half hour it took him to get through the stack.

Finished, he rose from his seat. "That's all. I think you have enough to keep you busy until quitting time."

She said, "Yes. Thank you," and left his office.

At her desk, she dropped her head into her hands. She might have impressed him enough with her finding about Jake, but he was back to giving her only secretarial tasks again. The good impression she'd made had only been temporary.

She sighed. What did she expect—

Actually she'd expected him to take the damned five million dollars. She'd expected him to be smug about his success, while secretly she could be equally smug about her sacrifice. Instead he'd succeeded without her "help" and was angry that she'd made a decision without him.

She was the loser in all of this.

At five, she didn't even bother letting Nick know she was leaving. He might still be working on the bid, and working ten-hour days, but the work he'd given her that afternoon was his regular assistant day-to-day work. And she was finished. She had nothing else to do. No reason to stay.

She called her dad and left a message on the answering machine to remind him to come and get her before she gathered her things. She had her cell phone. There was no reason to wait twenty feet away from a man so cool icicles were forming on the doorway between them.

She ambled out to the warm, sunny parking lot. That's when she remembered her dad had asked Nick to be her ride to and from work. Even if he listened to the message she'd left on the answering machine, he'd think it was from the week before. She was going to have to go back inside.

She groaned and turned toward the building again but didn't take a step.

Couldn't fate give her a break here? Did she have to embarrass herself by going back to the office and either sitting there with nothing to do or tapping on Nick's door frame begging for work?

She waited a minute. Hoped someone from another department would be leaving and she could ask for a lift. But no one came out of the building. It had taken her long enough to gather her things that everyone from day shift was already gone. The parking lot was silent. Only the hot breeze stirred around her.

She waited another minute or two not sure if she was expecting a fairy godmother to show up with a coach or a coworker to return for something they'd forgotten. But no one appeared.

Straightening her shoulders she headed back inside. It was ridiculously unfair of fate to put her in this disgustingly humiliating position, but there was nothing she could do about it.

She breezed into her office. They were supposed to be working ten-hour days. So she was supposed to stay. And work. Not just sit at her desk waiting for Nick to emerge from his office and grace her with something to keep her occupied.

Angry, she rapped on his door frame. "Hey. I'm sorry, but I don't have anything to do again." She said the words in a rush before she could lose courage. "Could you give me something—anything—to do until you're ready to go?"

"We can go now." He rose from his seat and grabbed

his cell phone and keys from beside a stack of papers on his desk.

Embarrassment flared, fueled by humiliation. If she ever met fate in person, she swore to God she was going to kick its butt.

"You don't have to take me home right this minute. Just give me work to do until you're ready to go."

"I'm ready now." The truth was Nick had been watching her outside his window. He'd seen her stride out to the parking lot as if expecting to see her dad, then turn and look at the door as if finally remembering *he* was her ride. He should have simply left his desk right then and there and taken her home. Instead he'd sat in his office, watching her, because he just wasn't ready to deal with her.

When she'd asked him for work that afternoon, he'd barely been able to sit at the table with her. She smelled good. She looked fantastic. Her soft voice tickled along his spine. It had taken a monumental effort to stay in the same room as they sifted through the files on his conference table. And now he had to drive her home. In his little car, where she'd be six inches away from his fingertips. Somehow or another his hormones had not gotten the message that she was still the enemy. And that made him even angrier with himself.

"I didn't mean for you to drop everything for me—"

Her conciliatory answer turned his anger into disappointment in himself. Wasn't he a better man than this? He could understand not wanting to be friendly with her, but why was he so angry?

"It's fine."

"Thanks."

As he rounded the desk, she turned and, from the side, the protruding stomach that was barely noticeable totally changed her profile. Wounded male pride crackled through him like the sting of a whip. They hadn't just lost each other the day she'd left; they'd lost a baby. They'd lost plans and dreams and hopes…and everything. Had she stayed, there would have been other babies. He'd be a dad now. Not a womanizer. He'd have a houseful of kids and a devoted wife, something to come home to other than silence, something that would have him so grounded he wouldn't long to go back to New York City on the pretense of helping his brother, but actually to enjoy the nightlife.

He'd be a dad.

But she'd made their choices. And he'd made his. Changed who he was. Changed what he wanted. Now he had to live with them.

He motioned for her to precede him out of the office and followed her to his car. The sleek line of her back caught his attention. Just as with their pregnancy, she hadn't gained a lot of weight. The taut muscles of her back curved slightly at her waist then flared into perfectly rounded hips. She'd always worried that she was too thin, too much of a tomboy to be sexy, but he'd loved her exactly the way she was. Her skin felt like velvet, tasted like honey—

He stifled a groan. Really? Was he going to let his hormones rule? Was he going to let himself remember things that might be nothing more than an idealized vision he created because she was his first? Was he that confused or that much of a sap? Fifteen years ago, he might have loved her, might have wanted to be a dad, but after five years of mourning and ten years of being a very happy, very rich bachelor, that part of him was dust. He was who he was. Somebody halfway between his unfaithful dad and superfaithful, supertrusting, eighteen-year-old Nick Roebuck.

He was Nick Andreas. And Nick Andreas wasn't a sappy kid.

She jumped into the passenger side and he slid behind the steering wheel.

"I really appreciate this."

"It's not a big deal."

They were silent as he maneuvered out of the parking lot and through town. This drive, he wouldn't be so foolish as to engage her in conversation. He'd already told her too much about himself. He wouldn't give her false hope that everything between them could be okay and they could be friends. They couldn't.

When they arrived at the farm, she glanced over, smiled and said, "You know, I just really want to say one thing then we can never talk about personal things again."

He didn't reply. Let his silence tell her that if she wanted to speak that was fine. He'd listen. But there was no guarantee he'd answer her.

"I'm proud of you. You really did everything you set out to do."

Another man might have preened under her praise, but the final layer of his emotions peeled off, revealing the real source of his anger. Pain shimmered through him.

He nodded quickly, nothing more than an indication that he'd heard. Then she hopped out and Nick drove out of the dusty driveway.

Far enough away that she couldn't see him, he slapped his steering wheel. Now he knew why he was so angry with her. Why it still hurt so much that she'd left him even though fifteen years had passed.

She hadn't just left so he'd get a trust fund. She'd left because she hadn't believed he'd succeed. At least not without help.

And that was the real bottom line. She hadn't trusted him. She hadn't believed in him.

The one person he'd always thought would stand by him hadn't.

Because she hadn't believed in him.

CHAPTER EIGHT

THAT night, Nick made his typical call to Darius. But when his older brother didn't answer, he left a message asking him to return the call the next morning.

He didn't want to talk to Darius that night. He was too perceptive. He'd hear something in Nick's voice and he'd drag this part of the story out of him, too. Nick was getting just a bit tired of his entire gloomy past being revealed bit by bit for his brothers' entertainment. It wasn't a matter of keeping a secret; it had become an issue of privacy, of pride.

By the time Darius called the next morning, Nick was in control. Now that he understood the real bottom line to his hurt over Maggie leaving, it was easy to keep his anger under wraps. Also easy to put everything into perspective. He wasn't a sap who hadn't gotten over being left by the woman he'd loved. He was a hardworking, ambitious man who'd been blindsided. The woman he'd put his trust in didn't trust him to become the man he'd known he could be and she'd cast him aside.

There was a reason to be angry. But not stay angry forever. He wouldn't get involved with Maggie again. Not even as a friend. But he could work with her. Hell, he needed her. And with his new perspective, he wouldn't have to fight that anymore.

The balance of the week went smoothly. She didn't force them into any more private conversations and he didn't hesitate to give her work. Hard work. The good jobs she wanted. Not only did that free Nick to do the more complicated tasks only he could handle, but also that seemed to please her. Which meant there were no more questions, no more awkward conversations. Even Saturday flew by without a hitch. They were a happy assistant and a busy boss and life returned to normal.

On Sunday morning, when Darius called and said Andreas Holdings needed him in New York bright and early Monday morning, he didn't hesitate to call Maggie at home. With everything sorted out in his head, she was nothing but an assistant. The work for the bid was ahead of schedule. He could afford a day or two out of the office.

Her dad answered. "Hey, Nick!"

"Hey, Charlie. I have to be in New York first thing in the morning so my brother Cade's sending a plane for me this afternoon. I thought I'd come over and give Maggie instructions for what I need her to do in the two days I'll be gone."

"Well, sure. Come on over. I'll save some lunch."

"Don't save lunch. I'll have about two minutes to talk to her before I have to get myself to the airport."

He hung up the phone and, with a legal pad on his bed, he made a list of things for Maggie to do as he hastily packed.

Flying down the driveway to her dad's farm, he raised a layer of dust that barely had time to disburse before he jumped out of his Porsche.

Instruction sheet in hand, he headed for the front porch steps, but the sound of someone jumping off the diving board of the pool in back of the house caught his attention. He remembered swimming in that pool with Maggie when they were about six, after her mom had died but before Vicki came into their lives. Charlie always acted as lifeguard and at least once did a belly flop, trying to dive. Now that he felt better about the whole situation with Maggie, he could spare two minutes to tease lonely Charlie about his dive.

With a happy snicker, he snuck around the side of the house and stopped dead.

Rather than see Charlie, Nick watched Maggie pull herself out of the pool. Water ran from her long red hair, down her arms and legs, and made rivulets down her chest to her breasts. The top of the bright blue bathing suit she wore fluffed out around her middle, effectively hiding her pregnancy. The bottom was cut high enough that every inch of her long, smooth legs was exposed.

His breath shuddered in and out of his lungs. Good God.

He hadn't forgotten how beautiful she was. How sexy. But he had forgotten that nobody did a bathing suit justice the way Maggie did.

She turned in his direction and surprise registered on her face when she saw him. She rubbed a towel across her head to absorb the excess water. "Nick? What are you doing here?"

As she spoke, she took in his black suit, white shirt and striped tie. When her gaze drifted down to his Italian loafers, then roamed to the puddles on the blue and white tiles around the pool, she winced. "I'll come over to you."

"No. It's fine," he said, sidestepping the little bits of water. "I called your dad to let you know I was coming."

She grimaced. "He must have forgotten to tell me."

His gaze involuntarily fell to her long legs again but he immediately jerked his eyes up to her face. "He must have. I need to talk to you about some things for work tomorrow."

Dropping the towel to a nearby chaise lounge, then stretching out on top of it, she said, "Have a seat."

She pointed to the chaise beside hers, and, not sure what else to do, he walked over. Not wanting to wreck his suit or look like an idiot sprawling on a chaise dressed the way he was, he sat sideways, only to realize that put him only about a foot and a half away from her long, lean body.

She blew her breath out and closed her eyes as if enjoying the sun as she got comfortable.

Glad her eyes were shut, he ran his finger beneath his collar, stretching it away a bit so he could breathe. "I… um… My brother Darius called last night. I'm needed in New York."

She opened her eyes. Peered at him. "But you have a bid due."

"I know, but we got a lot of work done last week. We're ahead of schedule. Plus, you've got a really good handle on what we're doing. So I made a list of things that need to be done." He waved the paper at her. "At the bottom is my cell phone number, along with Julie's number in case you have any questions or can't find anything."

She took the paper from him, scanned it then smiled up at him. "Okay."

The hot Southern sun had turned her normally pale skin a soft brown. Her green eyes sparkled. Her full lips curved smoothly, naturally upward. And all he could think about was how he used to be able to kiss those lips. Run his fingers through her smooth, silky hair. Touch all that soft, soft skin.

Reminding himself she hadn't trusted him, hadn't believed in him, and she was nothing but his assistant—an assistant who really could handle things while he was gone—he cleared his throat. "You're sure? No questions?"

She nodded. "I'm fine." She waved the paper again. "And if I'm not, I can call you."

"Or Julie," he hastily reminded. "She's back from Vegas. If there's anything you need that you can't find, she's the one to call because she'd be the one who filed it."

"Great."

Rising, he inwardly cursed himself for sounding like an idiot. "Great."

Unfortunately she also rose, putting them toe-to-toe.

Heat and need roared through him. He didn't want it. He'd thought he'd dealt with it. From Wednesday through Saturday they'd worked together like a well-oiled machine, any thought of their attraction seemingly forgotten. But here it was. Heating his blood, scrambling his pulse, shifting his breathing.

In the past fifteen years, he'd had girlfriends and lovers. Plenty of them. But no one had ever compared to Maggie. He'd always believed that was because she was his first. His first love. His first lover. His first everything. But the desire currently stealing his breath was different, stronger—

Ack! Why the hell was he thinking like this? Sure, she was gorgeous, and, yes, he was attracted, but she wasn't somehow superior to every other woman on the planet. And they seriously needed to move on.

Hell, twenty minutes ago, he'd been absolutely positive he *had* moved on.

He pointed stupidly toward his car. "I'll just get going then."

"Okay, great."

Unfortunately she was directly in front of him. If he

stepped back, he'd trip over the chaise. Step forward, he'd bring them flush against each other.

The thought brought a vision of her soft breasts meeting his chest, their thighs brushing, their lips meeting and suddenly he realized what was going on. These feelings racing through him weren't about Maggie, but about sex. And why not? She was gorgeous. She was sleek. She was his first. So of course he had a special attraction to her. But it wasn't about feelings. It was about a fantasy. Nothing more.

He stepped sideways.

"I'll be back Tuesday afternoon or Wednesday morning. Not sure which."

"Okay."

He headed for his Porsche.

"And Nick?"

He turned. "Yeah?"

"Thanks."

"For?"

She waved the paper at him. "For having faith in me. I know all this has been hard for you, but I need this chance."

He cleared his throat as unwanted emotion clogged there. Every time he had the situation between them narrowed down to just sex, she reminded him that it had never been just about sex between them. Even if she hadn't loved him, they'd been friends. Best friends. Friends who took care of each other.

But in the end that had actually backfired. She'd taken care of him for so long that when a chance to let him stand on his own two feet had arisen, she hadn't trusted him.

He said, "You're welcome," and walked away.

When he was gone, Maggie snatched her towel off the chaise with a curse and went into the house. In eleven years of working in offices she'd never seen anybody who looked as good in a suit as Nick did. Nothing could add to his dark, brooding handsomeness, but the suit reminded her—and the world—that he was somebody. Somebody important. Somebody to be respected.

And she'd just behaved like a fool. Nerves had had her sitting on the chaise lounge and offering him the seat beside her. If she'd stopped there, she could have almost felt okay about it. But, no. She'd stretched out. Nervously closed her eyes. Then stood up too quickly when he'd tried to leave.

But that was because he hadn't been able to take his eyes off her.

That was the part that made her so nervous she'd acted like a damned fool. The part that made her want to shiver. No one but Nick had ever looked at her that way. As if he was starving and she was a feast. She'd forgotten how much she liked the shimmery, shiny look in his eyes when he couldn't stop his gaze from touching every inch of her.

She'd also forgotten the heady surge of power that coursed through her when his eyes simmered. She'd never felt that with any other man, so she'd always believed she'd imagined it. Or maybe that the burst of feminine power that had raced through her was the reaction of a woman being noticed by a man for the first time. Yet, here she was, fifteen years later, feeling it all again. The rush of adrenaline. The shivers of anticipation. The longing for his touch.

She groaned.

She had better get over this soon because from the way Nick raced away, he wasn't having wonderful, positive feelings about being attracted to her. If he was attracted at all. For all she knew he had only been looking at her to check out the differences in her from when they'd been married.

Or maybe the difference two short weeks had made in her tummy. Her stomach was more pronounced now. Though it wasn't the size of a basketball yet, it had grown. The changes might not be noticeable when he was around every day, but seeing her out of the office he might be noticing different things.

That had to be it.

Even if he had been attracted to her, he wouldn't follow through. Time had passed. And he was rich now. Rumor in town was that he dated constantly. While she'd married the first guy she met at university, he'd become a real playboy.

She glanced down at her tummy. What would a playboy want with her?

Nothing.

"So Cade tells me the whole ex-wife thing isn't working out."

Sitting in the backseat of Darius's limo, Nick looked from Darius to Cade, who snickered. "No secrets, remember?"

"I've thought that pact through and I've decided there's a thin line between not having secrets and giving a person his privacy. And we're crossing over into my privacy, so we need to stop talking about Maggie."

"You're just mad because you still like her and you're not sure how to make a move."

Nick gaped at Cade. "I do not still like her. I do not want to make a move. I want an assistant. I want to be able to go to work and be a boss again, not an ex-husband. Not an ex-lover. And I think we're getting there." He deliberately left out the feelings that had rumbled through him at her pool. There was no point to telling anybody about that since he had no intention of pursuing it. He'd rather tell his brothers about the good week of work they'd put in together. That made them both seem normal, sane.

"She's the best assistant I've ever had. Good enough that I left my bid in her hands without having to worry that my company will go to hell in a ham sandwich—" He paused, remembering that was what Charlie had said, then almost groaned when he realized how much the Forsythes were insinuating themselves into his formerly comfortable life. "I like being able to come up here to work without worrying about Andreas Manufacturing."

Darius's long black limo pulled up the circular driveway in front of the family's Montauk estate. As eldest, he had inherited it and the chairmanship of the company, as well as their half brother Gino, but the house was so big there was plenty of room for all of them. Cade and Nick never stayed anywhere else when they came to New York.

"So, it's working out well," Darius said as he climbed out after the driver opened the door. "Not poorly, as Cade had said."

"Cade wasn't off the mark. The day he visited things were bad, but the tide has turned. She's amazing. Perfect." There. He'd said it. Now his brothers could stop riding him.

Darius headed for the front door. "I'm hoping this means we can start talking about making your work for Andreas Holdings official. Get you a title, an office, responsibilities you can take off my plate."

Not waiting for a reply, Darius walked into the house and Cade caught Nick's arm, stopping him before he could follow Darius into the mansion.

"Okay. Here's the deal. Darius won't tell you this flat-out, but he really needs you here full-time. The chairmanship's enough for him. Add CEO of Andreas Shipping to that and he's working twenty-four seven. He thinks you only want to work part-time, so that's all he's offering, but he needs you here full-time and I think you should step up."

"Step up?"

"Sell your beach house and bring your butt to New York permanently."

"Permanently?" Something like terror gripped his heart. "Sell my beach house?"

"Or keep it for weekends. You're probably going to have to fly down once a month to check on your ex anyway after you put her in charge—"

Nick's head was spinning. "Put Maggie in charge?"

"Sure. I'm not saying you give up your job as CEO. I'm just saying that with fax machines and email, you don't need to be in North Carolina to run your company. You give your ex a title like general manager and let her run the day-to-day stuff and instruct her to send the really important things to you by fax or email."

Nick's head spun even more. First, it had never been his plan to move to New York permanently. Or to sell his house. Second, he couldn't see passing off that much responsibility to a pregnant woman—

"I can't pass everything off to her. She's pregnant."

"So? She's already working. You're just giving her the good office. Your comfy chair. The nice sofa. Hell, put a TV in there and she'd practically have an apartment."

"And what happens to the company while she's out on maternity leave?"

"You run it. You take a leave of absence from Andreas Holdings and I'll fill in for you here."

"Or we could just split the extra work at Andreas Holdings as we have been."

"That's not working out for me. I can shift my schedule

to accommodate a few months while your ex has her baby, but being away one week a month as I have been is wrecking my system. And I can't hire somebody to replace me. I run a ranch and an oil conglomerate. I'd need to find at least two people. Maybe four. You own one company. One person can replace you. You yourself just admitted you left your prime bid in the hands of your ex-wife. You trust her."

Nick rubbed his hand across the back of his neck. Not only had he made this mess by bragging about Maggie, but also he suddenly realized he did trust her with his company. Really trust her. What the hell had happened in the past week?

When Nick only stared at his brother, Cade sighed. "Come on. You love clubbing. You like being out and about. Plus, you love being around Gino. Why not do us all a solid and just make the move?"

Not anywhere near able to wrap his mind around Cade's idea, and absolutely, positively not wanting to argue with his younger brother about something that wasn't any of his business, Nick said, "I'll think about it."

"Think fast." Cade angled his chin to point into the foyer, nudging Nick to look at the happy scene just beyond the front door. Pretty blond-haired, blue-eyed Whitney kissed Darius before she handed one-year-old Gino to him. The little boy wrapped his chubby arms around Darius's neck and hugged him.

"We can't put all the pressure of Andreas Holdings on him anymore. He's got more responsibilities than making us money."

When Nick returned late Tuesday afternoon, Julie was sitting at Maggie's desk. His heart sank before he could stop it. Fear caused his pulse to race. Maggie had gone? She'd quit?

After two days of torment while he considered Cade's plan of leaving his business in Maggie's hands, it just didn't seem right that she'd simply quit. He was literally considering giving her the job of a lifetime. How could she leave? Why would she leave?

The answer to that popped into his head without hesitation. He'd been a crappy boss. A crabby boss. She'd been nothing but eager to please and he'd sniped at her. But they'd gotten along and worked together so well the week before—

Of course, he'd also ogled her by her dad's pool. They couldn't stand within two feet of each other without generating enough electricity to power a small city. And she was pregnant. Broke. Maybe juggling it all was getting to be too much for her? God knew he was having trouble keeping up.

He started to ask, "Where's Maggie?" but before the question was fully formed, Maggie came running into the office. "I saw Nick's car—"

She stopped, caught his gaze.

In his mind's eye, Nick envisioned her pulling herself out of the swimming pool, dripping with water, stretching out on the chaise. The feelings he'd had standing toe-to-toe with her slammed through him. His breathing stuttered. His pulse sped up. All his nerve endings went on red alert.

Oh, yeah. He could absolutely understand why she'd be tired of dealing with this—

Except she hadn't quit. She was right here, ready to work. And he was ogling her again.

Maggie took a step back. Her gaze dropped to the floor. "I couldn't find a few things and called Julie."

"That's fine." He had to stop this. She was a capable, dedicated employee, who was clearly uncomfortable with the fact that he was still attracted to her. Unless he wanted to lose her, he had better rein this in and treat her like the good employee she was. "Actually that's great."

Julie peered around Maggie to catch his gaze. "I sort of figure I owed you a week."

Nick didn't argue. "You did."

Bottle of water in hand, Maggie motioned for him to follow her into his office. Files and papers were strewn across the desk. His computer monitor blinked. Without a second's hesitation, she sat on his chair, hit a few keys on the computer and brought up a new document.

She looked so right, so perfect in his office, sitting at his chair that Cade's suggestion of making her general manager suddenly didn't sound so ridiculous. He set his briefcase on the desk.

"This," she said, proudly pointing at the screen, "is your finished bid."

He slowly rounded the desk. *"Finished?"*

"Sure. It was a piece of cake." She glanced back at him worriedly and quickly said, "Not that your system wasn't working, but you were asking departments to update the old forms and then you were matching the info to the new bid package. It was a lot easier to create the new forms in the computer and add our narrative and numbers from scratch. Especially since I had each department handle its own individual section of the bid."

"A lot easier," Julie said from behind him.

He turned. "You were party to this?"

She grinned. "I just monitored. Maggie's the one who gave out assignments, had the staff create the new documents and plug in their own numbers."

He faced Maggie. "So you're responsible."

Her face reddened. "Only if you're pleased."

"I'm flabbergasted." He caught her gaze. "But I won't say I'm pleased unless the bid is correct. I'm not going to take your word for it."

"Oh, absolutely," she said, jumping from his chair. "Here, you can start reading now."

Giving him the seat, she edged around him. But the space behind the desk was narrow and with her baby bump she couldn't slide through gaps as easily as she could if not pregnant. As he tried to get to the seat and she tried to maneuver away from the seat, they found themselves face-to-face again. Inches apart.

She looked up.

He looked down.

She couldn't disguise the spark that lit her green eyes or the hitch in her breath. The reaction caught him off guard. She was as attracted to him as he was to her?

He gazed into her eyes again.

She *was*.

Now neither one of them could deny it.

They held each other's gaze a moment too long and something strange passed between them. In some ways they were the Maggie Forsythe and Nick Roebuck who'd grown from friends into lovers. In others they were two totally different people. But the new people they'd become were still attracted. Very attracted. And connected. Which explained why he was so angry about the way her ex-husband had treated her. He'd always felt connected to her, responsible for her. Not just like the guy who was supposed to protect her, but also as if she were the other half of the whole they were supposed to create. In some ways over the past fifteen years, he'd always felt just a little lost without her.

But that was wrong.

Completely wrong.

Only a fool felt lost over a woman who hadn't believed in him. Especially a man in his position where confidence was sometimes the most important weapon in his arsenal.

He quickly shifted to the right as she shifted to the left and scrambled around the desk.

Julie headed for the door. "It's close enough to five that I'm leaving for the day." She turned and faced Nick. "Actually, with the bid done, I can't think of a reason to come back tomorrow. Unless you want me to work the other few days I owe you."

"No. That's fine." He smiled at her. "Thanks for coming in. For helping out. I think your debt's paid."

"You're welcome."

With that she left. Nick glanced over at Maggie. She smiled sheepishly and sat on the chair across from his at the desk.

Tension tightened his muscles. Understanding what was happening between them helped him to dismiss it. But it also resurrected his anger. He refused to feel connected to a woman who hadn't believed in him. What kind of a man even considered being attached to a partner who didn't share his vision of himself, didn't believe he could reach his dreams? She'd long ago left him. Her baby wasn't his. Her troubles weren't his.

Plus, his brother needed him. And he wanted a new life. As Cade had said, he loved clubbing. He loved nightlife. He wanted everything New York had to offer. If Maggie really had finished the bid, she might have proven herself qualified to take over as Andreas Manufacturing's general manager. He could leave and she could become the new day-to-day boss, saving only the really big executive work and decisions for him.

Everybody won.

That is, if she'd really gotten the bid done.

Turning his attention to the computer, he tried to read the pages on the screen, but he couldn't focus. He shifted on the chair. Peeked up to see Maggie eagerly awaiting his verdict. And then heard the door close behind Julie who was leaving them unchaperoned.

All right. So they were alone. They might not have a person between them, but they had a nice solid desk. And he had more reason to stay away from her than a man needed. Not just their pasts, but their futures. He was on the verge of offering her the job of a lifetime. In a way, he'd be satisfying the fury that rose inside him every time he thought about how life had cheated her, even as he tucked her away with a good job and a good income so he'd no longer have to worry about her. He wouldn't jeopardize that by letting their attraction get out of hand.

Everything would be fine.

Attempting to ease the stiffness of his muscles, he rose and shrugged out of his jacket. He hung it in a closet and walked back to his chair, unbuttoning the cuffs of his white shirt.

"You don't happen to have a paper copy of the bid, do you?"

She jumped out of her seat. "Sure."

She ran to her office and returned with a document about the size of a ream of paper. She walked over and handed it to him.

Once again they were toe-to-toe. But at least this time there was a ream of paper between them. When their gazes met, the air tightened. Synapses fired, but he simply reminded himself that he had found a way to take care of her, so he'd no longer have to worry about her. If he gave in to the hormones riding roughshod over his emotions, he'd spoil all that.

"Okay, great. So I'm just going to jump right in and start reviewing."

He headed for the conference table where he'd have room to spread out.

She picked up her notepad and followed him. "I'll sit here so that every time you find a mistake, you can tell me the section and page number and I'll make note. We can email our line items to the department that created the page and get it fixed."

He sank to his chair and peered at her dubiously. He'd actually been trying to get her to leave. He'd seen her car in the parking lot. She had a way home. Instead he'd somehow fixed it so they were reviewing the document together.

"It really worked to have each department write its section of the bid?"

"Supervisors were thrilled for the opportunity."

He snorted a laugh.

"I'm serious. Everybody said you do too much. That you could delegate and have more time for yourself."

He snorted again. Fate seemed to be pushing him out the door of his own company.

As she sat on the chair catty-cornered from his, he read the first few pages of the bid, the easy pages, introduction and narrative that answered basic questions about the company, and had to admit he was impressed. The answers were short, concise. No rambling.

He pointed at the sheet. "Who wrote these?"

"I did."

Well, no wonder they were short and concise. She didn't have the knowledge others in the plant did. Of course, that also meant she hadn't muddied the waters with unnecessary information.

He went back to reading. With her legs crossed, her sandal-covered foot swung a centimeter away from his shin. Awareness caused his toes to curl. This wasn't going to work, either.

He stopped reading. "Did the department heads give you backup documentation for their numbers?"

"Yes!" She popped out of her seat, ran into her office and returned with a stack of files—so many files, and such thick files, that it looked like he'd be in the office until the following morning reviewing all the data.

But that was good. He could use that excuse to send her home, telling her he'd make the notes of any problems he found himself because not only was this going to take a long time, but also he needed privacy and quiet to read.

Yeah. That was it. He'd tell her he needed silence to read the bid.

She set the files on the table in front of him and he rose. "Okay, then. Since I have everything I need to review this, you can go."

"Go? I thought I'd be taking notes on the problems you found?"

They weren't exactly standing toe-to-toe, but they were close. He thought to take a step back but refused to be that fussy. Surely he could stand a foot away from her.

"No. I don't want you here. You helped create this. You're prejudiced. I'm sort of an independent proofreader. So you can go home." He waved his hand. "You've obviously worked hard for the past two days and it's after five. Go. I'll be fine."

She looked up at him with big green eyes filled with fear.

His insides twisted. He hated to see her afraid. Especially since she had nothing to fear. He was considering promoting her. Trying to take care of her.

"You did an excellent job," he said, seeking to reassure her, but she didn't stop staring at him. Her green eyes softened, as she studied his face. And pretty soon he realized she wasn't afraid anymore. She was caught. Staring at him because she was as tormented as he was about them. About this thing between them. The attraction that just wouldn't quit even though they were the worst possible two people to be attracted.

He shouldn't like her. She hadn't trusted him.

She shouldn't like him. He was still angry with her.

But his head lowered.

She tipped her face up and stepped closer.

And their lips met.

Sweet memory poured through him. This was Maggie. Sweet, sweet Maggie.

Placing his hands on each side of her head, he tilted it back, deepening the kiss, drinking from her like a thirsty man took water. Her lips parted slightly in what could have been a moan of pleasure. He didn't notice, didn't care, but took advantage and slid his tongue into her mouth.

That time she did moan. The feminine purr drifted to his ears and filled him. Sensation after sensation bombarded him and each one flash-connected to a memory. The roar of the ocean. The brilliance of the sun. The heat of innocence.

He let himself indulge, enjoy. He let his thoughts go back to the idyllic time he'd thought would last forever. But when his hand drifted from her face to her shoulder and down to the opening of her simple blouse, common sense awoke in him. A kiss was one thing, touching quite another.

He broke away. They drifted apart slowly. Their gazes bumped. The sound of their breathing filled the air.

He didn't know what to say. What to do. He felt alive inside. But was he really? Or had that kiss taken them on a trip down memory lane? Was everything he felt simply a reflection of what he expected to feel from the past?

It had to be. He didn't know the new Maggie well enough to want her like this. Kissing her hadn't tested out their attraction. It had only proved they once had chemistry. It was a mistake that did nothing but screw up an otherwise perfect plan.

"I'm sorry."

She blinked. "Sorry?"

"You know we can't be attracted to each other."

"Because we work together."

He took a step back. He couldn't tell her about his thought to promote her until he checked out the bid and dug a little deeper into her credentials. So he clung to the reasonable excuse she'd just offered and even added to it.

"And because we really don't know each other anymore. And it might not be smart to get to know each other. You need this job and I need you. We have a past we probably wouldn't be able to overcome even if we did grow to like each other. So what do you say we just forget this happened?"

She studied him with sad green eyes, and he felt like a heel, a fool. He'd been the one to initiate the kiss. Then he'd dismissed it as if they'd been equally guilty.

Hoping to ease the sadness, he said, "Okay. The kiss was my mistake. I don't know what got into me but I was wrong. We need each other." He stepped away, rounded the conference table to get to the chair he intended to sit in and pulled it out. "Go home. I want to review this without interruption. We'll talk in the morning."

CHAPTER NINE

WEDNESDAY morning a torrential downpour sent rain cascading in sheets along the Carolina coast. By the time Nick made it to the office, Maggie had already shed her raincoat, put her sandwich in the desk drawer and started her computer.

"You might as well just bring your notebook in," he said as he breezed through her office into his. "I got through only half of the bid, but there are problems. Not big ones, just things that need to be addressed and we'll be doing that this morning."

She grabbed paper and pen and followed him inside. Taking the seat at the conference table, she watched him dump his keys and cell phone on the desk.

Confusion and sadness met and mingled in her middle. He'd kissed her the night before out of curiosity. They had so much chemistry crackling between them that it was difficult sometimes to not wonder about it. She'd expected the kiss. She'd also expected the fire that ignited her blood when their lips had touched. What puzzled her had been the sudden hope that burst inside her.

If only for the span of that kiss, she'd believed in miracles. She'd hoped and even prayed that it hadn't been curiosity that had pushed him to kiss her, but an uncontrollable impulse. She didn't care if that impulse had been spawned by memories. Now that she was home she was very much like the Maggie she'd been in her youth. If he'd loved her then he could love her now—

Except she'd hurt him. And that was why he'd pulled away. He'd never get beyond the fact that she'd left him. He was too strong, too proud, too *Nick* to simply forgive her.

The hope in her heart was ridiculous.

Wrong.

He took his seat. "When I got tired of reviewing the bid last night, I checked your résumé. You've never done anything like this bid before. How did you know what to do to pull this thing together?"

She shrugged. "I've analyzed hundreds of bids. Maybe thousands. If a company isn't winning contracts, nine chances out of ten there's either something wrong with the business itself or there's something wrong with their bid numbers."

Not exactly sure how to behave around him, she smiled tentatively. "Your bid was great. All I did was streamline your process. I can see why you win the contract every five years. Andreas Manufacturing is a fabulous company."

He coughed as if uncomfortable with her praise, reminding her so much of the old Nick that she didn't think through the nudge she gave him. It was purely reflex.

"You've got to know you're good."

Their gazes met. The wariness in his expression sent sadness trembling through her. He clearly regretted kissing her the night before. The flickering light of her hope dimmed a little more.

"I made a list of questions or problems I found last night. I want to speak directly with the department supervisors to get the answers but I'd like you to sit in on the sessions."

Her gaze snapped to his. *He wanted her around?* "Really?"

He looked away. "This is a list of department heads I'll need to see." Leaning in, he set a paper with a list of names in front of her.

The scent of sea air and man drifted to her. Combined with memories of their kiss, it filled her with longing. Desire rose up as quick and as sharp as it had when his lips met hers the night before.

"Your assignment is to call everybody and set appointments."

To get her mind off wanting Nick, she leaned in to look at the sheet he held and their shoulders bumped.

He automatically pulled away.

The dying flame of her hope struggled to find footing, but it couldn't. He might be attracted to her, but he didn't want to be. And he was a strong, determined man. He could ignore a stupid physical attraction.

But he still had it.

After fifteen years apart, *they* still had it.

"Schedule an hour with each department. Stop at noon, then pick up again at one. That way we'll have spoken with all seven supervisors before the end of the day."

At her desk, she picked up the phone, but as the first extension rang, she peeked into his office. Head bent, he labored over the papers in a file, looking smart, capable, and so handsome. The bittersweet ache returned. Except now that she knew he hadn't accepted the trust fund, the ache made her wonder what might have been. If his father hadn't offered him the five-million-dollar trust fund. If she hadn't overheard him refuse to divorce her to qualify for it. If she hadn't felt so guilty over Nick giving up his legacy for her.

If.

If.

If.

Thinking about ifs was foolish.

But it was difficult not to. They were still attracted after fifteen years. Fifteen years. She could only imagine what their marriage might have been like if they'd stayed together, only imagine what they'd be like if they could set aside their differences and sleep together now—

"Yeah, Maggie? What's up?"

Maggie jumped as Mark Nelson's voice boomed to her through her telephone.

Placing a hand on her galloping heart, she said, "Nick wants to see you in his office." She glanced at her schedule. "He's meeting a department head every hour. Since you're the first person I'm calling, you get your choice of time."

"I'll take the first slot."

"Great," she said, penciling him in. She disconnected the call and her gaze slid into Nick's office again.

Why couldn't she get over him?

Because of the meetings, Nick stayed until eleven o'clock that night. He sent Maggie home at seven, telling her he would be leaving right behind her, though he knew it was a lie.

Cade was right. He was still attracted to her. The pull of her was so strong that soon he wouldn't be able to resist it. Eventually he'd seduce her—and then what? Hurt her? Lose her as an assistant? Lose her as a potential general manager?

He couldn't hurt her or take away the job she needed. He had to be the one who moved on. Darius needed him and as Cade had said, it would be much easier for him to find one CEO or general manager to replace him than it would be for Cade to find the small army it would take to shift control of his oil business and ranch.

Finally home, he sank into a leather chair in the game room and turned the TV to a baseball game before dialing Darius's number.

"Late night."

Relieved to hear Darius's voice, Nick relaxed. "Yes. I hope I didn't wake anybody."

"Gino's the only one asleep. Whitney's on the sofa across from me reading depositions."

"Hey, Nick!" she called, her voice loud enough to come to him through the phone.

"Tell Whitney, I said, hey, too."

Darius laughed. "Nick says hey, too." Then his voice turned serious. "So what's up?"

"Cade is right. I should come to work for Andreas Holdings full-time."

"Wow."

"I've been thinking it over since I was in New York on Monday. But more than that, I came home to find my bid is done. Except for proofing and final checks on the numbers, Maggie pretty much got the thing finished."

"She wrote it herself?"

"She had the staff write it."

Darius chuckled. "Well, I'll be damned."

"I know. Cade thinks she could replace me. At the very least, take over as general manager, leaving the executive stuff to be handled by me through phone, fax and email."

"So what's the problem?"

"She doesn't have any experience for this. She was a glorified analyst at her last job."

"But she did your bid."

"Exactly. She knows theory, but has no actual experience running the plant."

"So train her."

"I don't want to tell her that I'm considering her for a job if it doesn't pan out."

"There are never any guarantees with any employee. You've got to jump in and take a risk."

"I know. But this situation is delicate." He rose from his comfy chair, passed his hand through his hair. "I'm worried that I'm seeing things in her that aren't really there because I want so badly to promote her—to give her a chance."

Darius harrumphed. "That's funny. When you were here, you were telling us you felt nothing for her."

He squeezed his eyes shut. As much as he wanted to confide in his brother, he wouldn't. There were some things a man had to handle on his own.

"She's a penniless pregnant woman. I'd be heartless if I didn't feel something for her."

"Pity?"

The word tightened his gut. Maggie would hate it if she thought he pitied her. "No, more like righteous indignation. She didn't deserve what happened to her after we split. I'd like to see her succeed."

"So bring her up for Gino's birthday. I'll check her out. I can run her through her paces without her even realizing I'm backhandedly interviewing her."

That was true. Darius would be objective where he couldn't.

"That sounds great, except how do I get her there? Say my older brother who's never met you would like you to come to our baby brother's first birthday party?"

"Make an excuse about needing her to take notes at a brothers' meeting. Tell her my assistant can't do it because she works for Andreas Holdings and this is a family thing. It would be a conflict of interest because we'll be discussing our plans for our shares of Andreas Holdings."

It was a great idea. Plus, the thought of attending his one-year-old half brother's first birthday party cheered him. He was at a point in his life when he'd realized he'd never have kids of his own. That was the one drawback of his lifestyle. But with one-year-old Gino in the family, he had no worries about an heir or even someone younger to amuse him from time to time. He could teach the kid how to play basketball, teach him to fish, tease him about girls. In general get out all of his pent-up parenting needs anytime they arose.

He loved having a baby brother.

"Okay. Sounds good. We'll be there."

When Nick arrived at Andreas Manufacturing the next morning, Maggie was walking to the entrance. He hurried out of the Porsche to catch up with her and held the building door open for her.

"Thank you."

"You're welcome."

He followed her inside, making her just a tad paranoid. Should she wait for him? Walk beside him? Make small talk?

She wanted to. God knew the hope that sprang to life inside her every time she saw him. That hope wanted her to believe that if she just gave him time, he'd come around.

And then what? Was she ready for this? Was she over Josh?

In some respects, the answer came quickly. How could she pine for a man who not only didn't want her, but had also refused to acknowledge their child? It wasn't exactly easy, but it had definitely been possible for any love she'd had for Josh to die.

But was she ready to move on?

Her smarter self laughed. At this point it didn't matter if she was ready to move on. Nick might give her ten signs a day that he was attracted to her, but he gave her eleven that he didn't want to be. And today would be no different. He'd hold the door, maybe let his gaze linger a little too long on her face or unwittingly stare into her eyes, but he'd snap out of it. Cloister himself in his office. Not say goodbye when he went to lunch.

Any hope she had was foolish. So it didn't matter if she was ready to move on or not.

They entered her office. She turned and walked to her desk. He continued toward his office. But he stopped, faced her.

"I…um…was talking with my brother Darius last night."

"The older one?"

"Yes. The one who lives in New York and runs Andreas Holdings. He's having a birthday party for our one-year-old brother over the weekend and he'd like you to come."

Her heart stopped. Her breathing stuttered to a halt. His family was inviting her to a party? All the way in New York?

"We've having a brothers' meeting Saturday morning and no one from Andreas Holdings can take notes because there'd be a conflict of interest. Darius suggested I bring you up so you can be our stenographer for the meeting."

The pain of stupidity froze her tongue. When would she learn this man didn't want her?

"I…I…"

He glanced at her tummy. "Oh, God, I'm sorry. I forgot you might not be able to travel."

"I can travel."

"Oh."

She heard the awkward tone of his voice. He didn't understand why she hesitated. She was, after all, *his* assistant. An employee who could take the meeting notes without a conflict of interest.

She straightened her shoulders. She was his assistant. If he wanted her to go to New York, she would go to New York.

"I'd love to go. Thank your brother for inviting me."

"Great." He turned to his office door again. "We'll leave tomorrow morning and be staying at the family estate in Montauk. Pack for the beach."

The beach! That perked her up. She might only live a few miles from the shore herself, but between work and not having a car for the first weeks she was in town, she hadn't even gotten close to it yet. Maybe the weekend would be something like a vacation?

Wearing flip-flops, white capris and a sunny yellow tank top, Maggie met Nick at the small private airstrip a few miles outside of Ocean Palms. Only one airplane sat on the tarmac and Nick stood in front of it. She made her way over, carrying her overnight case.

Approaching the plane, she said, "Wow. So this is how the other half lives."

He took her small bag and handed it to a man dressed in a blue pilot's uniform, then motioned for her to climb the short column of steps. "This is how my brother Cade lives. He's the family multibillionaire. He put this plane at my disposal for the next year."

She stopped, faced Nick. "The next year? That's awfully generous."

He batted a hand. "He has seven planes. He won't even miss this one."

Seven planes? The magnitude of the changes in Nick's family situation never ceased to amaze her. Or to remind her that he was so different now that it had been totally wrong for her to think—even for the fleeting few seconds of one blistering kiss—that they fit together anymore.

She stepped inside an area that looked more like a comfy living room than a seating area for a plane. White leather sofas lined both sides. A shiny wooden bar took up the back.

Amazed, she stopped.

"If you're wondering why the space looks so small," Nick said from behind, "that's because there's an office and a bedroom in the rear."

She spun to face him. "Holy cow."

"I know. Only a guy who never stops working would think a plane ride a waste of time. I'll bet he's never once sat up here and just looked out the window. He probably either works or sleeps. Never wasting a minute."

They sat across from each other, each on one of the long sofalike lounges. They buckled up and fell silent as the plane taxied and took off.

In the air, Nick unbuckled his seat belt and headed for the bar. "Drink?"

She glanced down at her tummy. "I don't think so."

"We have orange juice, apple juice and water. Not just alcohol."

She still shook her head. "It's a long flight. I'd rather not be jumping up and down running for the bathroom."

He shrugged. "Suit yourself."

When he sat again, soft drink in hand, Maggie glanced around. After the quick brush with conversation about the plane, they'd run out of things to say. But she refused to sit silently for over two hours.

"So, you have a baby brother."

Nick surprised her by laughing. "It was the damnedest thing."

"I'll bet."

"Oh, you have no idea. Not only did we not know our dad had another son until Dad's lawyer handed him to Darius at the reading of the will, but also the kid owns an equal share of Andreas Holdings."

Because he chuckled when he said it, Maggie tilted her head in question. "That doesn't bother you?"

"Not really. I don't 'need' the money I get from Andreas Holdings. It doesn't matter to me how many ways it's split." He smiled stupidly, fascinating Maggie. She'd never quite seen that expression. "It doesn't hurt that the kid is adorable."

Ah. That's right. Nick loved kids.

"Of course, he's also pure Andreas. Dark eyes. Dark hair. But he's built like a little truck. Big shoulders and arms. If I wasn't absolutely positive we'll be training him to take over Andreas Holdings when we want to retire, the kid could easily be a football player."

Hearing the pride and love in his voice, Maggie smiled. "He sounds cute."

"You'll get to meet him. It's his party we're going to. Plus, since we're staying at the estate, he'll probably be underfoot." He pointed at her tummy. "Maybe you can persuade Whitney to let you get in some practice."

She smiled again. "Maybe."

It almost hurt to see how happy he was. How in love with the little boy. She thought back to their baby, to how she'd always known Nick would be a great dad, and sadness enveloped her. They lapsed into silence. After a few minutes, he opened his briefcase.

Seeing how he'd been forced to spread papers and file folders around him on his seat, she said, "You should just go back in the office if you want to work."

He peered over. "Are you sure?"

She shrugged. "Yeah. I'm fine. In fact, if you need me, I might only have the notebook I brought for the brothers' meeting, but I could probably still put some of your notes in it."

"With the bid done and in, I'm primarily reviewing things to catch myself up." He rose. "But if I need you I'll call."

"Okay."

Ten minutes later she fell asleep and didn't awaken until Nick jostled her shoulder. "Hey, you have to get up. We're about to land and you have to be in a seat belt."

She opened her eyes and found herself staring into his. Crouched in front of her, he was eye level. His hand on her shoulder was comforting. His dark eyes were warm. The softness of his voice was sweet, soothing.

As if he realized she'd caught him in an unguarded moment, he got to his feet and looked away.

Maggie told herself not to make too much out of the expression she saw on his face. Lots of people looked with love upon sleeping people—

That wasn't true. She was reaching, trying to make something that wasn't innocent seem innocent. She didn't know how long he'd been watching her sleep, but he'd been watching her sleep and it had put a soft expression on his face. And he'd invited her to his family's home. Yes, she had to take notes at a meeting, but they could have hired an outsider for that.

Maybe it was crazy-just-waking-up brain, but she

couldn't stop the feeling that something more was going on here.

Again, they landed at a private airstrip. A long black limo was parked close to where the plane stopped. A beautiful blonde dressed in a black sheath and a wide-brimmed black hat stood beside a tall, dark-haired man, wearing a black suit, holding a baby. All three of them wore black sunglasses. That made her laugh. Though she wasn't sure why. They looked rich, sophisticated, so far beyond her world that Maggie wasn't even sure she could comprehend it.

Nick got out first and held up a hand to help Maggie navigate the stairs. As they deplaned, the trio came over to meet them.

"Darius, Whitney, Gino," Nick said, "This is Maggie."

"Hi." She glanced at Gino. Chubby, happy, with the trademark Andreas dark hair, he was so cute she could have squeezed him. "He's…well, he's so adorable he's breathtaking."

Gino laughed, an airy giggle that warmed Maggie the whole way to her soul. That was what she currently lived for. The day when she'd hear baby giggles. Have someone to guide and love without condition.

"We like him," Darius said, jostling Gino, who jabbered something that contained the word *Dad*.

Whitney stepped forward, glancing at Maggie's tummy, as she took her hands. "You're pregnant."

"Yes. A little over two months to go."

Whitney slid her arm across Maggie's shoulders and began to lead her to the limo. "How exciting for you! Darius and I are talking about having a baby before Gino gets accustomed to being an only child and too spoiled."

Maggie glanced around at the quiet, private airstrip. The area was spotless, silent. There were no other people, no other planes. She'd bet her bottom dollar the Andreas family owned it.

"I don't think there's a snowball's chance in hell that Gino could grow up anything but spoiled."

Whitney laughed merrily. "Oh, you'd be surprised how good I can be at caring for a baby so he doesn't get spoiled."

The driver opened the limo door and Whitney entered with the ease of someone accustomed to luxury, but Maggie glanced around for Nick.

He was at her side in a second. "Everything okay?"

She blew out her breath, feeling a little crazy for having a near panic attack. She'd simply never been around so much luxury before. Her best capris and top felt like rags. Though Nick sensing her distress and racing over eased that odd sensation, it created another.

She hadn't even spoken and he'd come.

Were they getting that much attuned to each other again?

Yes.

The answer came quickly and her heart tumbled in her chest. They'd always had something. A click of recognition. Something.

And she was only kidding herself if she thought she could fight it. Whether she was ready or not, she and Nick were tumbling headfirst into a relationship. She, at least, saw it. Nick—

She glanced around. He'd invited her to meet his family. He'd been by her side every step of the way—

Maybe there was more to this trip than he'd let on? And maybe she was the one lagging behind, not sure she was ready when the truth was it didn't matter if she was ready. She and Nick were a force of nature and if he was falling in love with her again, then she wanted it.

Wanted him.

"Yeah. I'm fine. Just wanted to make sure I wasn't getting into the wrong limo."

He laughed and guided her into the car. "Funny."

She sat on one of the luxurious leather seats. The windows were tinted. The bar discreet. The seat so comfortable she could have happily drifted off into another nap.

As soon as the doors closed and the driver headed toward the front of the vehicle, Darius said, "So, Maggie. Thank you for agreeing to come up and take the notes from our meeting tomorrow morning."

"You're welcome. It's my pleasure." She winced. "Actually I can't wait to see your house." She hoped that hadn't made her sound too much like a penniless bumpkin. "I live five minutes from the beach myself, yet I never get there. I just want one really nice walk on a private beach tomorrow morning."

"Well, that's a given," Whitney said. "If you like, I could come with you."

"No. That's fine. A beach is a beach. I won't wander far enough that I'll overtire or get lost. It's not like I can make any unexpected turns on a shoreline."

Darius laughed. "Sense of humor. I like that."

She smiled, but she also noticed Nick sending Darius some kind of message with his eyes.

Okay. Now this was getting weird. Because Nick had never had much in the way of family when they were dating, she hadn't gone through a screening process. But she had with Josh's family. And she recognized it when she saw it. She might have ostensibly been invited to take a few notes and attend a birthday party, but these people were checking her out.

Oh, God!

These people were checking her out!

The truth of that burst inside her. Something Nick had said caused them to believe there was reason to be worried about her being around him—

Well, she had hurt him. So okay. She got that. But they couldn't be checking her out to make sure she didn't hurt him again. He'd consider that an insult and he'd deck them for that. And he was in on this.

Oh, God!

He *did* have feelings for her.

CHAPTER TEN

AS THEY stepped into the Andreas family's magnificent mansion, people bustled back and forth, in and out and through the entry. Nearly everyone wore black or white and they looked like chess pieces scrambling across the black and white blocks of the foyer floor.

"What's going on?"

Whitney faced Nick with a beaming smile. "Prep for Saturday's party."

"You need a staff for a one-year-old's birthday party?"

"No, silly," Whitney said, taking a clipboard from a woman who had appeared at her side and signing off on something after she read it. "The kids' party is Sunday afternoon. On Saturday night, their parents make big donations in Gino's name to one of three charities we've set up to take gifts. And we thank them with a ball."

Nick watched Maggie's skin grow pasty-white.

He caught her arm. She peeked at him with an expression that totally defied explanation. He couldn't tell if she was scared, sick, shocked...or all three.

"There's a ball?"

"Only about two hundred people," Whitney said, her eyes skimming Maggie's face as she checked her out, obviously seeing the same things Nick had. "It's really not a big deal."

Maggie huffed in a deep breath and laid her hands lightly on her stomach.

Nick nearly had a heart attack. Fear that there was something wrong with her clenched his stomach. He remembered the night she had lost their baby. No warning. Just sudden pain.

"Maggie?"

"I don't…actually, I didn't…well…I packed for the beach."

Relief washed through him as Whitney turned to Darius. "You didn't tell them about the ball?"

He winced. "Sorry. I got everything crossed up."

Whitney faced Maggie with a sunny smile. "No worries. You and I will just go shopping."

"But I—"

"Do it for me. I never get to shop with a girlfriend." Whitney took her arm and began leading her up the stairs. "First, we'll get you settled. You can have a nap or take a long bath or even walk on the beach. When you're ready, we'll shop."

Ten minutes later Maggie was alone in her bedroom, unpacking the few things she'd brought for her stay. The entire room was ivory satin. Chunky bed pillows layered with more delicate throw pillows sat on top of an ivory satin bedspread. The simple hue counteracted the rich cherrywood headboard to make the bed elegantly inviting. Ivory satin drapes were pulled back to reveal a stunning view of the sea.

In front of the bedroom was a sitting room done in soft sage-green. A sage and ivory striped sofa sat by a solid sage Queen Anne chair. Cherrywood tables and an armoire made the room rich, luxurious. The sitting room, bedroom and bath were bigger than her first apartment had been.

Taking out shorts and tank tops, capris and T-shirts and one scrappy pair of jeans, she groaned. There had been no arguing with Whitney about the shopping trip, which in some ways was good because she couldn't exactly wear a scrappy pair of jeans to a ball. But bad because she was about to spend money she didn't have on a dress she'd wear once.

When was she going to get invited to a ball again?

She snorted a laugh just as someone knocked on the door.

Thinking it was the maid with fresh towels or lush scented soap or some kind of expensive, imported chocolate, Maggie sucked it up and said, "Come in," as she walked into the sitting room.

The door opened and Nick entered. "I am so sorry."

Knowing he was talking about not telling her about the ball and deciding to just take it all in stride, Maggie said, "That's okay. I'd have never assumed there'd be a charity ball attached to a one-year-old's birthday party, either."

"Whitney had a child who died. She's very big on charities that involve children."

She pressed her hand to her chest. "Oh, I'm so sorry."

"She's fine. The best thing to do is not mention her past, but she loves to raise money for children's charities. If I'd been on my toes I would have guessed this."

"No harm done."

"Except that you don't have a dress." He stepped closer.

And Maggie noticed something odd.

In a sea of people she didn't know, Nick was the one she did. The one she was comfortable around. And he seemed comfortable with her, too.

"Your sister-in-law has volunteered to rectify the situation."

He laughed.

Maggie smiled. Pinpricks of delight pirouetted across her skin. It was nice to be alone with him, in a neutral environment. He wasn't avoiding making an impression he'd have to live with if the town gossips got a hold of it. She wasn't worried about embarrassing herself in front of people who knew their history. Here where he could be himself, it was clear he really cared about her. She wasn't imagining it because she wanted it so badly.

She remembered the "scoping out" being done by his brother. Though panic tried to rear up, she stopped it in favor of reason. This was what she wanted. Josh was a distant memory. Her marriage to Nick fifteen years ago seemed clearer in her brain than her marriage to Josh. They might have a bumpy road ahead. Some things to iron out. But if he was taking steps to try, then she wanted it, too.

True, it wasn't exactly comfortable to know Nick had brought her here for his family to check her out. It also wasn't fun that she didn't fit in this environment, but she and Nick didn't live in this environment. They lived in a small town, by a beach, with people who said good morning even if they didn't know you and didn't dress in black and white serving uniforms.

If they could get close, admit their feelings, maybe it would hold when they got home?

"I'll be fine."

"Still—" He reached into his pocket and pulled out a money clip. He flipped through the bills until he came upon a credit card, buried in the cash. "Take this. I know Whitney's taste. You'll never be able to afford what she wants you to buy."

This time it wasn't panic that reared up, but disappointment. She wasn't sure which of them she was disappointed in. Him for offering her money—making her feel cheap—or beneath him. Or herself for not having the money to afford a simple party dress—

Well, all right, it wasn't just a dress. It was ball gown for an elite New York event. But she was an adult. She'd worked her whole life. She'd scrimped and saved and her ex-husband had squandered—

She tugged her fingers through her long hair. Yet another gift from her ex-husband. Humiliation in front of someone she wished she could impress. "I have a credit card."

"Yeah, but we don't want to run up any balances."

She laughed. How could she not? He didn't even realize he was talking about them as a "we" a team.

So many emotions tumbled through her. Regret for having married a cretin and for putting up with him for ten years. Fear about what she would be getting herself into if she and Nick really did get together. Pure love for him for being so sweet.

Pure love.

Simple love.

The kind a person only came across once in a lifetime.

She almost gasped. It had never left. She had always loved him.

And maybe that was the thing she needed to face. She loved him. There was no "falling" about this. She was already in love.

And he…well, she had no idea what he felt. He might be falling. He might be testing her. His family might be checking her out. Or she could simply be imagining all this.

She pushed away his credit card. She wouldn't take

money, gifts, *anything*, from him until she understood what
was happening between them.

"I'm fine."

He frowned, glanced at his card, then back at her face.
She tried a wobbly smile.

It worked.

He sighed and tucked away his credit card.

"All right. You handle this. But you have my cell phone
if things get dicey."

"They won't."

In the first floor office, Nick flopped on the sofa.

Darius sat at the desk, talking on the phone. He finished the conversation in only a few minutes and rose.
"Drink?"

"No. Too early."

Darius laughed. "Well, that's a good sign. The day
Maggie started you were drinking in the afternoon."

Nick scowled. "It was after five."

"Whatever." Darius dropped to the sofa beside Nick. "I
like her."

"Everybody does."

"A man could do a lot worse."

"Excuse me?"

"Come on. You know you like her. You fawned all over
her in the limo."

Nick gaped at him. "She's pregnant and in a strange
land. I'd do the same for any assistant."

Darius snorted a laugh and rose from the sofa. "If you're
not going to talk about the fun stuff, I have three contracts
here I'd like you to review."

He ambled to the desk and got the contracts, but Nick
couldn't focus. He hadn't fawned all over Maggie. He'd

done a few nice things. He *would have* done the same for any assistant.

Still, he'd given his brother the wrong idea and that could mean he was giving Maggie the wrong idea, too.

That would have to stop.

"So what's the deal with you and Nick?"

Seated in the limo, nearly in the city, having exhausted all potential conversation about where they'd gone to school, their parents, their lack of siblings—except for Maggie's brother who was never around—Maggie lounged against one bench seat while Whitney relaxed against the other.

"You mean aside from the fact that we were married?"

Whitney winced. "Sorry. Darius did tell me the two of you had been married as kids. I wasn't trying to sound like I know nothing at all about you. I know there's history. I'm more interested in the future."

Whitney's forthrightness caused Maggie to frown.

Whitney winced again. "Sorry. I'm a lawyer. Half of what we say sounds like a cross-examination."

"That's okay. I'm not the kind of person to keep secrets, but there really isn't anything to tell. I work for him."

Whitney harrumphed. "You bought that story about them needing you to take minutes?"

"Yes and no." She toyed with the glass of juice Whitney had insisted she drink before they hit the stores. Whitney was the kind of person who inspired honesty, and, being as confused as she was, she could use a friend to talk to. "I think Nick asked me up here so your husband can check me out."

Whitney tapped her long, slim index finger against her lips. "Interesting. They grew up without each other." She smiled. "Of course, you know that. You went to school with Nick, so you know he didn't even know he had brothers. But the thing of it is, last winter once they decided to be brothers for real, they hit the ground running. They really depend on each other. Trust each other. If Nick asked Darius to check you out, there's a reason. A good reason. A big reason."

"Like a test?"

"No, more like the way a guy brings his girl home to his family to see if she fits—"

Fear fizzed through her. Wasn't that the conclusion she'd drawn herself?

"—so that's good."

She shook her head fiercely. "No! It's not good! I *don't* fit! If that's why I'm here I'm toast."

Whitney laughed. "You're not toast. You didn't bring a ball gown. That's all. And apparently Darius's invitation was deficient, not your packing. So we're getting you a dress." She leaned across the space and patted Maggie's hand. "We're getting you one special dress because once you get in the right dress, you'll belong."

"Really?"

"Trust me. My parents were very solidly upper-middle class. Then my dad scored a few really big clients and suddenly we were on Park Avenue. I never thought I'd fit. Especially at my first formal charity event. Then I found the right dress and walked into that ballroom with my head high, knowing I was just as good as everybody else in the room, and—*poof*—I was fine. Sometimes all you need is a little bit of confidence."

"I hope you're right."

Whitney settled into her seat and smiled. "I know I'm right. Plus, the right dress might just be the push Nick needs to admit what he's up to."

"So we're getting this dress to impress Nick?"

The driver opened the door. Gorgeous, sophisticated Whitney stepped out into the hot July sun. This time, she wore white pants and a black shirt with her wide-brimmed black sun hat and black sunglasses.

The picture of sophistication and knowledge, she said, "The right dress can do many things."

That night Maggie felt stupid for spending hundreds of dollars she didn't have on a dress to impress a man. She could say Whitney had been overly persuasive, except she knew in her heart of hearts she desperately wanted Nick to take the next steps. He definitely cared for her. He unconsciously looked out for her. He'd out-and-out offered her money to help her. And he'd asked his brother to check her out.

He had to have some feeling for her. But if she didn't get him to admit it here, where they were just themselves, when they got back to Ocean Palms, where everything was stiff and stilted and too many memories blocked them, he'd go back into his shell and never admit it.

Because she'd packed so sparingly, dinner had been informal in a small dining room that looked out over the ocean.

Darius pulled out Whitney's chair. Nick pulled out Maggie's. She smiled over her shoulder at him. "Thanks."

He returned her smile. "You're welcome."

Maggie's heart swelled like the waves rolling up to the shore. She didn't think this dinner was the be-all and end-all of opportunities for Nick to realize his feelings and be able to voice them. But it was one step in many steps she'd have to take with him this weekend. Everything had to go well.

Darius set his napkin on his lap. "So did you girls have a good day shopping?"

Whitney's eyes sparkled. "The best. Maggie has excellent taste."

Darius laughed, but Nick picked up his water glass and said, "So what happened with the people from London?"

"The group that wants to buy into Andreas Holdings?"

"Yes."

"I shut them down. But we're not the only ones who own Andreas stock. We've got to get to Dad's old secretary before London does. Otherwise they could end up owning one-third of our company."

And with that, Darius broke into a long, detailed explanation of problems that would cause, and Nick listened intently. They talked business through dinner, while Whitney and Maggie discussed how Whitney juggled her life, raising Gino and working. Everything seemed fine. Almost normal. Two couples chitchatting at dinner. Until Darius suggested they retire to the game room to play pool or cards.

Suddenly Nick glanced at her, glanced at the door and said, "I think I'll just go to my suite. In fact, I think I should walk Maggie to her suite, too."

Happiness burst inside her. He wanted to be alone with her. If that wasn't a good sign, she didn't know what was. "Yes. I am a little tired."

He took her elbow and led her through the maze of halls in the downstairs and finally up the spiral staircase to her room.

At the door, he met her gaze. "Can I come in for a second?"

Nerves and joy attacked her simultaneously. "Yes. Sure."

"Great."

He opened the door for her and she walked into the sitting room.

He pointed at the sofa. "Have a seat."

She smiled. "Uh, since this is my room, isn't it me who's supposed to say that?"

He chuckled. His eyes crinkled at the corners when he smiled and Maggie's heart sang. He was the older, wiser version of the boy she had loved, but she loved him every bit as fiercely as she'd loved Nick Roebuck. If he was here, in her room, to spend time with her, to tell her he was beginning to have feelings or even just to kiss her again to test the waters, she wanted it.

She facilitated it. She sat on the sofa instead of the chair so he could sit beside her.

He did.

Her heart thumping in her chest, she set her hands on her lap to still them.

"Maggie, there's something I have to tell you."

"Yes?" She pried her nervous hands apart, giving him the chance to take them.

He didn't, but he did gaze into her eyes. "By now I guess you've figured out that I didn't just bring you here to take notes."

Telling her pounding heart to calm down, she smiled. "I'd have to be pretty thick to have missed the signs."

He winced. "Darius isn't very good at being sneaky."

She laughed. "No."

"I'm amazed he didn't tell Whitney what was going on."

"Don't underestimate Whitney. She has her suspicions."

He laughed nervously. "Right." He sucked in a breath.

"Anyway, since there's no point in hiding this anymore, I've decided to just come right out and tell you what's going on."

As a prelude to telling her he loved her, or even was only interested in her again, that left a lot to be desired. He'd been a lot more romantic as an eighteen-year-old.

"Sunday and Monday, I talked about you at length with my brothers. Cade, my younger brother, suggested that it was time I see the truth."

Her hands shivered with the need to take his. Her tongue nearly said the words he was taking so long to say. She had to clamp her teeth together to stay silent.

"I need to move here to New York to take some responsibility from Darius. And I'd like to make you my general manager of Andreas Manufacturing."

She managed to prevent her mouth from dropping open, but for thirty seconds silence reigned.

Finally Nick broke it. "I thought you'd be pleased."

"Yes!" She bounced off the sofa, desperately trying to shift her brain to work mode and to blink away the tears flooding her eyes. But frustration and disbelief rose up in her. He'd kissed her. He was attracted to her. Whether he knew it or not he'd brought her home to meet his family—

She spun to face him. She couldn't quell the disbelief that roared through her and demanded clarification. "This has all been about a job?"

"Not just any job. I want you to take over my company. This is a big step for me. For both of us." He paused. "What did you think it was about?"

She swallowed, turned away again. Dear God, if she cried, she would kick her own butt.

"Maggie?"

When she wouldn't face him, he put his hands on her shoulders. The warmth of them seeped through her simple T-shirt, and tried to warm her heart. He might not love her but he cared about her enough to make sure she had a really good job. More, though, he now trusted her.

He turned her around. "You wanted this to be about us?"

She wouldn't look at him.

"There is no us." His voice was a soft whisper. "There can't be an us."

She swallowed.

"I loved you fifteen years ago."

Definitely unable to meet his gaze for this, she mumbled, "And you're still attracted to me now."

"That's physical." He chuckled sadly. "I'm not sure that's ever going to go away. But you're right. It's always been about more than sex with us. You were the one person I was absolutely positive believed in me."

For that she caught his gaze, searched his dark, dark eyes. "I did."

He shook his head. "No. You didn't. You left. You might as well have said you didn't believe I would make it unless I got help from my dad. You broke that trust."

She frowned, confused that he was laying all this at her feet as if he'd had no part in things. "I was young and exhausted. I'd just lost a baby. I wasn't thinking about trust. Only about need. About you and your mom going without—"

"I needed you. Not money."

His voice was soft, calm. But anger had begun to brew inside Maggie. The arrogant confidence in his tone trembled through her like the first shakes of an earthquake. He might not have been the one to leave, but he was far from innocent.

She didn't stop the fury that seeped into her tone when she confronted him. "Oh, yeah. You needed me? So why didn't you try to find me? Why did you simply let me go? I was home for a week before I left for university. Yet, you never came after me. Never once recognized I might not have been in a good enough emotional state to make the choice I'd made. You simply let me go."

"Maggie, no man goes after a woman who doesn't have faith in him. Especially not the one person he always believed was his number one supporter."

"You think I don't have faith in you?" Shaking her head, she sniffed a laugh. "When I needed a job, who did I come to? When I was pregnant, alone, abandoned by the husband who simply walked away for greener pastures, who did I come to? I didn't think we'd get back together. I gave no thought to the fact that we might still have chemistry. I was in trouble and I knew the one person in the world who could help me was you…and that's who I trusted. Who I came to. You."

The truth of that hit Nick in the gut and totally disarmed him. "You came to me because you knew I could help?"

"I might have come for a job, but it was because I knew for sure I could depend on you to help me. You were always the only one I knew I could depend on."

Her admission didn't change the fact that she'd left him. But she was right. He'd never gone after her. He'd let his blasted pride stop him. Pride so thick it had taken him years to grow up and out of it. Still, he wasn't that boy anymore and she wasn't that frightened girl. She was a smart, successful woman, who when she'd fallen on hard times had turned to him. And he was a smart successful man, who, when she'd come, couldn't turn her away.

"Wow."

"I'm sick of paying for something that happened fifteen years ago," Maggie said, her voice thick with tears. "I'm sick of thinking about it, talking about it—"

"So am I." Hands already on her shoulders, Nick yanked her to him. The truth of the present didn't merely override the events of the past, it obliterated them. They were adults. Two different people. Two people who'd both made mistakes. Two people who could only find longed-for redemption with each other.

He pressed his mouth to hers and kissed her the way he'd wanted to kiss her when she'd first walked into his office. He slanted his mouth over hers, taking, not asking, not caring that he might be rough or crude. He'd waited fifteen long years to kiss her again. And he intended to indulge, enjoy.

She opened her mouth on a gurgled sound of pleasure that seeped into his skin and set fire to his blood. He couldn't get enough of the feel of her, the taste of her. When his hands skimmed down her arms and back up again, he redirected them to her waist. He cruised the slight indentation, then shifted upward until he met her breast.

Her breathing changed. So did his. The fire in his blood became an inferno of need that totally shut off his thought process. This was what he wanted, what they both wanted.

And it was time.

But Maggie pulled away. "No. Wait. Stop." She gulped in air, obviously trying to get her bearings. "Everything's happening so fast."

It was true. Even through his passionate haze he could see her fear. And why not? They might have been lovers fifteen years ago, married fifteen years ago, but they were now interacting as two new people. And the new person he'd become barely bore any resemblance to the boy she'd loved.

He stepped back.

She blinked up at him. "So now what?"

"I'm not sure." He wasn't. He'd never even considered a permanent relationship with any woman but Maggie. Part of him wanted to pick up where they'd left off. The other part knew that couldn't happen. No one can really pretend fifteen years hadn't happened. Worse, Nick Andreas didn't have permanent relationships.

"We can't just ride off into the sunset."

"No. We can't." He peered over at her, chuckled. "Maggie, I'm way different from the guy you married."

"I know."

"I've done my share of running around."

"I guessed that."

"The thing is…I'm not sure I can settle down."

Her head tilted. Then she laughed. "Maybe that's our problem. Maybe we look at each other and don't see a potential partner, we see instant marriage. Maybe what we need to do is pull back, sort of start over." She walked over and slid her hands around his neck. "Actually date."

"We never did date."

"No. We didn't."

"We went right from friends to lovers to a married couple in a few weeks."

She kissed him lightly. "Exactly."

He slid his hands around her waist. "So, what do we do?"

"Well, I'm going to kiss you good-night and you're going to leave."

He frowned. "I'm not sure I like this."

"Which is probably why we skipped the dating step." She kissed him again. "You can be very persuasive."

One more kiss.

"But good night."

CHAPTER ELEVEN

Two minutes before nine o'clock on Saturday morning, Maggie found the downstairs office and slipped inside, trying to appear cool, calm and efficient. She was here to be an assistant. So what if she could have easily made love with Nick the night before? So what if she and Nick hadn't just cleared the air, they'd cleared a path to be together? She was just about certain neither one of them wanted to announce that to his brothers. At least not until they themselves understood what they were doing.

Plus, she still had to take notes.

She knew her calm attitude was the right choice when Nick said a pleasant, but restrained, "Good morning," and introduced her to his brother Cade—a typical Andreas with dark hair, broad shoulders and shrewd dark eyes.

As soon as she was settled, Darius started the meeting.

The morning passed quickly in a flurry of discussions and the kind of arguments only brothers could have. Maggie was amazed at how close they'd become, considering that Whitney had told her they'd only decided to be brothers for real the past January.

They broke for lunch and then picked up where they left off for another two hours of discussion.

When the meeting was over, Maggie went to her room,

intending to begin inputting the minutes in her laptop but she fell asleep. She didn't awaken until someone knocked on her door. Fearing it was Nick, she fixed her hair when she passed a mirror and raced to the sitting room.

"Come in," she said as she opened the door, only to find Whitney on the other side.

She held out a simple gold necklace with a small diamond pendant and diamond earrings. "I brought these for you to wear."

Maggie gasped. "I couldn't."

"Don't worry." She smiled. "You're only borrowing them. Besides, you have to. If you wear anything else with that dress, you'll overpower it. These are perfect."

Staring at them, Maggie had to admit they were perfect. And she did want to look good for Nick. "Okay."

"Okay." Whitney turned away, then faced Maggie again. "And breathe. Darius said the meeting went well, you were a star and Nick told them he'd already given you the general manager's job."

"Really?" In everything that had happened, she'd forgotten about the job, about the fact that Nick wanted to move to New York.

"Really. You're set. So just relax and enjoy."

When Whitney was gone, Maggie pressed a hand to her stomach. Relax? Enjoy? They weren't even officially dating and already she had to face a problem. She'd finally, finally come home and he was leaving. Moving to New York.

Ten minutes after the official start time of the ball, Nick headed for Maggie's suite. He knew what he was doing. When he and Maggie walked into that ballroom together tonight, they'd be a couple. But that was good. He didn't want to give himself any way out or any way to finagle himself and Maggie into something less than what she needed. She wanted to date for real. To give them a real shot. And he agreed.

Still, nerves jangled. His tie felt too tight. Hell, his skin felt too tight.

Two seconds before Nick would have knocked on Maggie's suite door, she opened it. The scent that was so uniquely Maggie greeted him first, nearly paralyzing him with wicked thoughts. Then he looked at her.

Her long red hair had been pinned up in a bundle of curls. Some hung loose and danced along her neck, pulling Nick's gaze there, then to her shoulders. The sleeves of her pale yellow gown draped to her biceps, leaving her shoulders and chest bare, taking his gaze to her breasts. They peeked out over the satiny yellow material, but not a lot. Just a peek. Just enough to whet a man's appetite and maybe even make him thank his maker.

He took a step back. The gown skimmed her trim, toned body and glided over her baby bump. It hugged her hips and caressed her thighs and fell to the floor with a loose grace that made it all at once sexy and elegant.

"Wow."

She smiled sheepishly. "Your sister-in-law has good taste."

Though he let himself be a little mesmerized, something inside his gut told him to stop. To hold back. Because he was sure it was the playboy inside him, he ignored it. He'd loved this woman and she was working her way back into his life. This was the thing he could do with Maggie that he hadn't been able to do with any other woman. Be smitten. Charmed. Hypnotized. It was the first step to being able to commit and he told his panicky feeling to settle down, and he just let himself enjoy.

"No. You have one hell of a body. I think you could make sack cloth and ashes look good."

He held out his arm and she slid her hand into the crook of his elbow.

"Shall we?"

She drew in a quick breath. "Yeah. I'm as ready as I'll ever be."

"You'll dazzle them."

"Right. I'm a small-town girl who really wasn't all that successful in the big city. I was lucky to get a job with you, Nick."

Her voice was so soft, so serious, that he stopped. Guilt welled inside his chest. They'd screwed up their lives royally. Her by leaving. Him by letting her go. Not finding her once he'd refused the money. Not realizing she'd been in no state to make their big decision. They'd talked this all out the night before. He wouldn't let it hold her prisoner.

"We were lucky to find each other."

As soon as the words were out of his mouth, he realized how true they were, but that itchy little shadow of doubt nudged at him again. Again, he ignored it.

They glided down the spiral staircase into the front foyer where they were greeted by Darius and Whitney. Dressed in a pale blue strapless gown, Whitney was the kind of beautiful that could stop traffic. But to Nick she didn't hold a candle to Maggie.

"You look fabulous!" Whitney said, bussing a kiss on Maggie's cheek. "I told you you would be fine."

Maggie laughed. Darius kissed her cheek, told her she looked fantastic and more or less handed her and Nick off into the ballroom.

Within three seconds Cade was at their side. He pulled at the collar of his white tuxedo shirt. "I hate these things."

Nick laughed. "They're not so bad."

"Not to you, Mr. Party Guy." He yanked on his collar again. "I live on a ranch, spend time on oil rigs. I don't do things like this."

Once again, Nick felt a nudge of something that made him feel odd, uncomfortable. Cade hadn't necessarily meant anything by his comment. But it gave Nick that too-tight skin feeling again. He was well-known for dating starlets, sophisticates and even a princess or two. He didn't commit. Yet, here he was with a pregnant woman—a woman he shouldn't hurt—

That's when he understood. The feeling racing through him wasn't about his fear that he couldn't commit, it was the knowledge that he shouldn't even try this unless he was sure. Because if he wasn't, Maggie was the one who would be hurt.

But, knee-deep in the conversation with Cade, Maggie laughed. "Well, if it's any consolation you look great. I'll bet all the available women are salivating at the possibility of dancing with you."

"Was that an offer?"

Maggie froze, but Nick stepped between her and Cade so quickly she wouldn't have had a chance to answer anyway. "She's spoken for."

"So what? She's not dancing."

Taking her hand, Nick turned to the dance floor. "She is now."

They twirled out onto the floor in a waltz. Her gown flowed around them. He caught her gaze and she smiled at him. This was right. This was what he wanted. He twirled her until they reached the French doors, then he twirled her one more time, taking them out to an empty terrace.

Silver moonlight enveloped them. Her skin glowed. Her eyes sparkled. Contentment settled over him. They moved around the terrace to the waltz, gazing into each other's eyes. Happy. When the song ended, Maggie stepped fully into his embrace, but before Nick could kiss her, Cade appeared in the doorway.

"Darius sent me to find you. Dinner's about to be served. We're on the head table with him."

Nick took Maggie's hand and led her to the door. Cade slapped his back. "I hope you brought your checkbook because I'm not even going to tell you how much Whitney hit me up for."

Nick laughed, too. *This* he understood. "My checkbook's at home. But I was thinking of doing a wire transfer anyway."

Cade laughed. "Always one-upping everybody."

A weird sensation stole through him. It was as if Cade's words turned him back into Nick Andreas. "I don't one-up."

"Of course, you do." Cade casually headed into the ballroom. "We all do. It's part of being an Andreas."

They found the head table and Nick pulled out Maggie's chair. Dinner was served. Whitney made a sweet plea for money from the nearby podium. And the band began to play again.

A few minutes later, Darius returned to the table where Nick and Maggie sat, lingering over dessert.

"Cade, Whitney and I are going upstairs to say good-night to Gino. Would you like to come along?"

Maggie all but jumped out of her chair. "I'd love to."

Nick laughed. "I'd also love to."

They met Cade and Whitney in the foyer, eased up the circular stairway and back a long hall to the nursery. Darius opened the door.

Baby cries, toddler shouts and laughter poured out like the roar of a lion. Chaos reigned.

"Come in!" Working hard to be heard above the noise, Gino's nanny, Liz, a pretty blonde who looked to be about twenty, motioned them inside.

Whitney and Maggie entered first, then Cade and Darius.

Nick followed his brothers in. Two little boys about Gino's age played on a mat on the floor. Three little girls who looked to be a year or two older than Gino sat at the small plastic table and chairs having a tea party. A baby lay in a bassinette.

"Who are all these kids?"

"Play date," Liz answered simply. "When the parents party, I volunteer to hold a play date for Gino."

Whitney laughed. "I tell her she's crazy."

"But the kids love it," Liz insisted. "They always sense when their parents are out for the evening and it makes them unhappy. This way they feel like they're part of things."

Nick noticed Cade looking uneasily at the three little girls currently arguing over a teapot, as if the noise of their argument slithered like a rattlesnake along his skin.

He felt the same weird pressure building up in him. Kids were cute. He was around them all the time at his mom's daycare. He'd simply never gotten this close to them. He was always kind of looking at them through a doorway. Or waving as he drove past his mom carrying one. He wasn't accustomed to being with kids who weren't old enough to play Wiffle Ball.

Liz continued talking. "After they've run out of steam, I read a story and they fall asleep."

"Maybe we should take Gino into another room to say good-night?" Whitney suggested, pointing to a door to the right.

Darius scooped Gino off the mat, but he immediately leaned out of Darius's arms, begging Nick to take him.

Nick beamed and realized that his former thought process was incorrect. He *had* gotten very close to a kid who wasn't old enough to play Wiffle Ball. Gino. He adored this little boy. He couldn't define or describe the feelings that welled up in him every time Gino sought him out. Or hugged him. Or gave him one of those sloppy kisses only a baby could give. He wasn't quite sure why the other kids scared him, except maybe there were so many of them.

They trooped toward the master bedroom door, but suddenly the baby in the bassinette began to yelp. The tea party girls' fight intensified. The two abandoned boys on the mat burst into wails.

Everybody but Liz and Maggie froze.

"I've got this," Liz insisted.

But Maggie pulled the baby from the bassinette. "I'll take him. You settle the others and I'll bring him back when we bring Gino."

Liz said a quick, "Okay, thanks," as she headed over to break up the tea party scuffle.

They walked through the sophisticated brown and aqua master bedroom into the sitting room in front of it. Nick sat on the sofa with Gino, who playfully slapped his face.

"I think you have too much energy to go to sleep."

Gino yelped.

Everybody laughed. Cade snagged him from Nick's lap. "Hey, kid. I'm going downstairs to see if I can't find a little entertainment tonight with a willing woman. So I'm going to kiss you and hug you and bug out of here."

"That's not something you tell a baby," Darius scolded.

But Whitney laughed. "It's fine." She turned to Cade. "But next year it won't be."

Cade said, "Yes, ma'am," kissed Gino's cheek noisily and handed him back to Nick before he left the room.

Nick also gave him a quick kiss. The nursery noise had fallen off to almost nothing, which probably meant story time was in progress. He wasn't surprised when Darius hoisted Gino off his lap.

"I hear Liz reading. It's best for Gino to already be in his crib for this."

Nick rose. "Right."

Whitney faced Maggie. "You can bring little Bruce in, too, now."

"Can I have two more minutes?"

Whitney's eyes softened with love, but something puckered in Nick's chest. In a few short weeks, Maggie would give birth to a little one like that.

Whitney and Darius took Gino into the nursery and Nick rose from the sofa. He walked over to Maggie.

"Let me see Bruce."

She handed the baby over with a smile and Nick looked down at the kid. Because he was a baby, just a little younger than Gino had been when he came into their lives, Nick expected to feel the rich, deep emotion he'd felt the first time he'd held Gino, but he felt nothing. No surge of love. Or joy. Or even slight happiness.

He supposed it made perfect sense. He loved Gino. He was his blood. He could do no wrong. Nick didn't have that connection to any of the other kids here so he didn't feel the love.

It wasn't a big deal. It certainly wasn't something he'd even mention now that he'd figured it out. But even as he thought that, his gaze fell to Maggie's growing belly. And suddenly he realized this horrible feeling wasn't just about some nameless kids attending his half brother's birthday party.

What if he didn't feel anything for Maggie's baby?

CHAPTER TWELVE

WHEN they returned to Ocean Palms, Maggie could feel the change in Nick. He was lighter. Happier. So much like the old Nick that sometimes it was hard to believe fifteen years had passed since they were married as kids.

With the bid in, her training period began, and so did their dating. They went to movies, concerts, took walks on the beach. Though Nick began spending two days a week at Andreas Holdings headquarters, they never discussed his moving to New York. And soon Maggie realized why. He wouldn't talk about anything permanent because no matter how much she loved him or how much he seemed to love her, there were no guarantees. So he wouldn't make any specific plans. That way if things didn't work out between them, moving away could be his fallback position.

Which was fine. Great actually. If things didn't work out between them personally, she'd still have a job and he could get far enough away that each could get over the breakup. But Maggie was supremely confident things would work out. She and Nick had always fit like two puzzle pieces. And they definitely still had sizzle.

Recognizing the change in their situation, her dad shamelessly asked Nick for help getting in his hay. Since he was spending half his weekend at the farm anyway,

Charlie figured he might as well work. And Nick happily agreed.

Friday in the second week of August, when the air was thick with late summer heat, the town kids chatted about going back to school, and her training period was coming to an end, Maggie arrived at work feeling like the boss.

Driving up to her private parking space in her shiny new red SUV, the work and rewards finally came together for her. Nick was returning from two days in New York and she'd been running the show for over a month. People respected her. She knew the ropes. She had some experience, not just theory.

"Good morning, Janette," she said, smiling at *her* new assistant, a thirty-something single mom, who wasn't afraid to get her hands dirty or dig in and do difficult work.

"Good morning, Maggie. Mail is open and on your desk."

Maggie said thanks and breezed through to her office. She plopped into the chair and immediately began returning phone calls.

Though Nick was supposed to fly home that morning and come to Andreas Manufacturing in the afternoon, he strode into the office about twenty minutes after she did. His hair was still wet from the shower. He wore jeans and a big sloppy T-shirt. He walked around the desk, spun her chair around, leaned in and kissed her.

Delight danced through her. "Thought you were flying back this morning."

He kissed her again. "I flew home last night."

"At?"

He winced. "About midnight. We finished up at ten and by the time I got packed and to the airstrip, it was... late."

She laughed.

"Hey, I missed you."

"I missed you, too."

And she hadn't forgotten that tonight was supposed to be *the* night. They'd had several close calls with making love, but for one reason or another it had never actually happened. Pretty soon she'd be too big and too tired to even consider it and she wanted it to be special, perfect. So when he'd left on Tuesday, she'd promised and he'd made her pinky swear that tonight would be the night.

"My dad's driving to Ohio today."

"Oh, yeah?"

"Yep. Gonna go see Charlie Jr."

"Really?"

"So now we don't have to worry about asking his permission for me to spend the weekend."

He laughed. "It's just like when we were kids."

Framing his face with her hands, she laughed. "Not quite. This time we know what we're getting into."

A shadow passed across his face. Quickly. But she'd seen it. Something serious was troubling him. "What's wrong?"

He pulled away. "Nothing."

"There's something."

He shook his head. "Yeah, we have to work eight hours before we can go home."

Though his answer was meant to reassure her, he was having doubts. Big or small, it sent a warning spiraling through her.

She told herself to forget it. They'd make love tonight and maybe another time or two over the next week, but soon she'd have to abstain. She didn't want to lose this chance by pushing him to talk about something that might be nothing.

* * *

At five o'clock, Nick listened for the sounds of Janette leaving. Drawers closed. Her computer wound down. She popped her head inside the office.

"See you on Monday, Maggie." She glanced at him. "See you Monday, Nick."

Maggie said, "Good night."

Nick smiled and waved.

One. Two. Three.

The door closed.

He leaped off the sofa. "I thought she'd never leave."

Leaning back in the tall chair behind the desk, Maggie laughed. "It's actually two minutes till five." She rose. "You're impatient."

"Not arguing that." He grabbed his keys and cell phone from the coffee table, motioned for her to precede him. "Let's go."

"Wait!" She laughed. "We haven't even discussed logistics yet."

His brow furrowed. "Logistics?"

"Do you want to come with me to my house while I pack a bag so you can drive me to your house?"

"Yes." Sheesh. He was a moron. If he were any more eager, he'd take her right here on the sofa.

He sucked in a breath. Smiled. "We'll both drive to your dad's house. You can pack a bag and leave your car, and life will be good."

"Great."

She drove to the farm and he followed a safe distance behind her. In the car, he reminded himself that she was a pregnant woman. Perhaps not physically delicate, but certainly not agile. And let's not forget emotional. Tonight had to be special.

He pulled the Porsche in beside her new SUV, jumped out and headed up the porch steps like a calm, sane man.

Walking into the dark foyer, he assumed she was upstairs and he went into the kitchen for a glass of water. But he stopped dead in the doorway. Her dad sat at the kitchen table, head in his hands.

"What's up?"

Maggie sent him a pleading look, as Charlie said, "I can't go."

"You can't?"

"He's missing Vicki."

"Not just missing Vicki," Charlie corrected. "I'm having trouble with the whole situation. Every time I get to the highway, I remember driving to Charlie Jr.'s with her and somehow or another that takes me back in time to when I found her."

Nick eased over to the table, pulled out a chair and sat. "I think that's probably normal."

Charlie dragged his fingers through his hair. "I was so lonely after your mom died and Vicki walked into my life and suddenly I wasn't alone anymore."

Nick's gaze shot to Maggie's face. The way Charlie was talking it was as if Maggie hadn't even existed. He could see from the question in her eyes that Maggie felt it, too.

Still, she patted her dad's arm and said, "I know. Vicki coming into your life was a good thing."

"And Charlie Jr., too." He shook his head. "Man, she loved that baby. She was such a great mom."

Maggie stiffened. She said, "Yes, she was," but Nick could see the hurt on her face.

"She loved doing school things with him, loved taking him to the beach. And bake? Every time he sneezed she baked him cookies."

Maggie swallowed, but she quickly pulled herself together and snuggled against her dad's shoulder, comforting him. "I know. She was great."

But Nick wasn't a daughter struggling to comfort her dad, and he knew the truth. Vicki hadn't been a great mother. At least not in Nick's memory. She might have been mother of the year to her own child, but the child who'd come to her by default, Maggie, had largely gone ignored. Maggie had felt like an outsider in her own home. Worse, her father had never noticed. And maybe Vicki hadn't, either. They were both nice people, good people. Especially Charlie. He wouldn't deliberately ignore anyone. Yet, he hadn't noticed that his second wife had never taken to the child from his first marriage.

Maggie rose to get her dad a drink and Nick glanced at her protruding stomach. Fear skittered through him. He felt nothing for her baby. Except maybe jealousy. Nick might have been the first man to make Maggie pregnant, but another man had given her the child she'd hold. Another man had given her the baby she'd become a mother to. How could he not be jealous?

How could he guarantee he wouldn't be like Vicki, not quite able to love her child?

How could he say he wouldn't unintentionally hurt Maggie's baby the way Vicki had hurt Maggie?

Nick stayed another twenty minutes and helped Maggie start supper. But when she asked him to set the table, he rubbed his hand across the back of his neck. "I think I'm going to head home. Let you and your dad have some privacy."

She nodded, walked over and brushed his lips with a kiss. "As soon as he's sleeping, I'll come over."

Nick smiled before he left, but the seeds of discord that had been growing inside him had begun to sprout into full-blown doubt. No matter how much he loved Maggie, if he put her baby into the same kind of home life that she'd had, she'd never forgive him.

Hell, he'd never forgive himself.

He had to figure out a way to fix this.

Maggie finally got her dad into bed at about nine. She hastily packed a bag, showered, dressed in a pretty, airy sundress and headed to Nick's.

As was her practice, she didn't knock. She parked her SUV in the garage beneath the house and headed up the stairway into the butler's pantry and to the kitchen.

"Nick?"

"I'm out here."

She turned to face the French doors, which were open. But the deck light wasn't on. Confused, she set her bag on a close counter and walked outside.

"Hey."

He didn't turn from the railing. "Hey."

So she met him there, mimicking his position by leaning her forearms on the wooden rail and looking out into the darkness. "What's up?"

"The stars are pretty tonight."

She glanced up. "They are." The stars were bright, the ocean nothing more than a comfortable roar a hundred yards or so beyond Nick's house. Only the white foam of an occasional wave was visible in the darkness.

Nick stayed silent and the odd, unnamed fear she'd had that morning resurrected. She'd seen the shadow cross his face while they were chatting in the office. He'd also left her to deal with her dad alone. Normally he stayed around. Talked her dad through his sadness. Tonight, he'd gone.

She bumped his shoulder. "So why'd you leave me all alone with my dad?"

He still didn't look at her, didn't say anything and the unnamed fear took hold, took meaning. All along it had seemed too good to be true that they could pick up where they had left off. And she knew—she just knew—he was having second thoughts. Making love the first time had taken them from friends to a married couple. It had been a lightning-fast change. No chance to think things through or look back.

And today they were going to make love again. For the first time in this portion of their relationship. Undoubtedly he knew there'd be no turning back. And maybe he wasn't ready?

She eased away from the railing. "If you don't want me to stay—"

He pivoted to face her. "No. God. No. I'm sorry." He scrubbed his hand across his mouth. "It's just—I just…" He sucked in a breath. "I've been having some weird thoughts lately."

"What kind of weird thoughts?"

"You know how I—you—" He stopped, huffed out a breath. "All that talk about Vicki being a good mom tonight floored me."

"She was a good mother."

"To Charlie Jr."

She laughed as relief rippled through her. "I told you all that was resolved."

He took her upper arms in his warm hands and caught her gaze. "That's not what I saw on your face tonight."

"A momentary lapse."

"Really?" He studied her eyes. "Because it's been fifteen years since you and Vicki supposedly found your footing, yet thinking about your childhood hurt you."

"A bit." She might as well admit it. Nick had been her best friend through that time. He knew how alone she'd felt. How abandoned. She might not have thought about it in a while, but being home had brought a lot of it back. And, tonight, her dad's words had cut like a knife. "But I've decided to treat it as only a momentary lapse. She might not have been there for me. But she had been for Charlie Jr." Unconsciously she rubbed her hands along her swollen tummy. "But I now understand why it happened. I wasn't her blood child."

She stopped herself because the color had drained from Nick's face and his gaze had fallen to her stomach.

And suddenly his fears made sense.

He didn't love her baby. Didn't *want* to love her baby.

"Oh, my God."

She turned to go but Nick stopped her. "Wait! Wait!" He shook his head in regret. "It's not what you think. Things are just confusing for me right now."

She searched his eyes. "How confusing?"

"I'm involved with a woman who's pregnant with another man's child. But I've also seen the life you've led, being that child, the child from a different relationship. I didn't just see Vicki ignore you. I saw the end result. I saw you cry." He raked his fingers through his hair. "I know how you hurt."

She stepped back, out of his reach. "You don't want my baby."

It was a statement, not a question.

"I don't want to *hurt* your baby and I feel—"

"Feel what?" she demanded as the blood in her veins chilled to just above freezing. She now had proof Nick didn't want her baby. Nick Andreas never stammered. He didn't get confused. He always knew what he wanted. If he thought he was confused now, it was because he was arguing with the answer he already knew.

"That's just it. I don't know."

She squeezed her eyes shut.

"I'm afraid we're going to do to your baby what Vicki did to you."

She took another two steps back. "I'm not. I'm not even close to fearing that. You know why? Because I know you and I know the huge capacity you have to love. If you're worried that you can't love my baby…it's because you don't, because you know you won't."

She spun away and headed for the French doors. She grabbed her overnight bag and raced down the stairs.

"Wait! Maggie!" Nick was on her heels. "Damn it, Maggie! I thought you said we could talk about anything. We have to talk about this."

She jumped into her SUV. "We just did."

And Nick watched her go. Once again, she'd made a decision for them. He wanted to talk. She ran. And maybe that was what was fundamentally wrong with their relationship.

CHAPTER THIRTEEN

"Let me get this straight. You're working on a Monday?"

Nick rolled his eyes and headed for the silver coffee service in his New York office. "Maggie's trained now. She doesn't need me."

"She's about to give birth. I think she needs you."

"She has six weeks."

"So you're here?"

"Yes. Full-time."

Darius just stared at him. But Nick gave him a look. The look. The one that said *don't cross this boundary.*

Darius shrugged. "Fine." He tossed a stack of papers on Nick's desk. "That's the email trail for my discussion with the group of private investors in London who want to buy into Andreas Holdings. They know there's another shareholder."

"And you want me to...do what?"

"Just familiarize yourself with the backstory. Because if we don't find that shareholder before the people in London do, we may be going to war."

Darius left and Nick settled down at his desk. Picking up the papers Darius had left him, he forced himself not to think about Maggie. Half of him understood why she'd balked, been appalled, about his worry over not being able to love her baby. The other half was angry. He was only human. He hadn't asked for the weird feelings, for the fear. Yet, she'd acted as if he'd calmly, rationally decided not to love her child.

He ran his hands down his face. She'd been hurt.

Hell, he'd been hurt!

But he'd tried to call her. Had tried to see her. And she wouldn't answer the phone or see him. Maybe that's why he hadn't gone after her the first time. She was stubborn.

Pain rippled through him at the thought. She wasn't stubborn…well, maybe a little… She was hurt. He knew she was hurt and she wouldn't let him help her, wouldn't let him try to fix this.

Of course, he'd been the one to make the problem.

Which took him back to the fact that he hadn't asked for his feelings.

He just had them.

He still had them.

And maybe she was right not to want to see him. Maybe there was no way to work this out.

The only thing he could do was work. Get his mind off this. So he put his attention on the email trail Darius wanted him to read and started in. He worked until five o'clock, then realized he hadn't even taken a break for lunch. Without a word to anyone, he left Andreas Holdings and went straight to Darius's penthouse apartment. Normally he'd stay at the house in Montauk, but he wasn't ready for that yet. Whitney would know he and Maggie had split. If she didn't know today, she'd know soon because she and Maggie had become friends. And then Nick would face a million questions that he'd prefer not to answer right now.

How would he explain to Whitney, lovable Whitney, who'd lost a baby, that he didn't have an ounce of feelings for Maggie's little one? He'd tried. He'd honest-to-God tried to feel something for Maggie's baby. But when he did, the only emotion that registered was horrible jealousy. Maggie had no trouble carrying this baby. But she'd lost theirs. He wasn't pointing fingers. He knew nature was nature. Maggie was not at fault. So, he supposed he was railing at nature. Angry with fate. Disgusted with destiny. Why had his baby died?

A million emotions washed through him as he entered the penthouse. Rich buttery hardwood floors and a sky-line view of the city greeted him as he entered. He barely noticed them. One minute he shook with rage. The next he was a puddle of sadness, of loss.

He grabbed a bottle of twelve-year-old Scotch and headed for the TV room, where he planned to drink him-self to sleep.

It took two weeks before Maggie stopped crying herself to sleep. Nick no longer came to the plant. He stayed in New York. Every Friday morning, he called Janette who filled him in on any phone calls or correspondence that needed his attention. But he never spoke to Maggie.

She could think that he was still angry and didn't want anything to do with her, but she had a feeling that, like her, he knew talking would only be painful and slow their recovery from their breakup.

Which meant he wanted to recover. He wasn't coming home so there'd be no risk that seeing her would make him long for what they'd had. What they had was deficient. He really and truly believed he couldn't love her child and if he couldn't love her child, then there was no future for them. Because he was right. She would not let her child be raised by a parent who couldn't love him.

Him.

Her baby could be a boy. And if it was he would need

a male influence. Not someone who loved his mom, but didn't love him. But someone to teach him. Someone to guide him along the road to being a man. She'd learned firsthand from Vicki that if the same sex parent had no interest in a child, there'd be no teaching. There'd be no bonding. And that would leave a huge hole. A void. Her child would live a loneliness that couldn't be described.

She wouldn't do that to her baby.

So she spent the next three weeks telling herself that Nick walking away had been the right thing.

That Friday, she hadn't even watched the door hoping Nick would stroll through, as she had the first few Fridays of her tenure as general manager. She didn't linger until six, thinking he might pop in after he thought she was gone, so that she could catch him, and if nothing else see him.

She was beyond all that. Strong now. Getting ready for her baby.

As she drove home, a storm began rolling in. Dark clouds gathered, filling the blue sky with inky blackness.

Dressed in a suit and a crisp white shirt, her dad glanced over her head as she walked inside. She could see from the worried expression that clouded his eyes that he didn't like the look of the sky.

"Are you sure you don't mind me going?"

She set her briefcase on the kitchen table and smiled. "Positive."

This time, the expression on his face said he didn't believe her. He shrugged out of his jacket. "You know what? I don't really need to go to bereavement group tonight."

"You do!" Maggie crossed the room, picked up his jacket and handed it to him. "I'm fine."

He laughed. "Okay. Okay. I get it. I'm a mess without the group. I'm going."

Walking across the kitchen to the door, he shrugged into his jacket again. One foot on the back porch he hesitated. "Wow. That storm's going to be a beaut."

She glanced at the dark, angry clouds. "You know what? I think you'd better take my SUV."

"The truck's fine."

"The truck is a piece of junk." She laughed and for the first time in weeks actually felt human. Normal. Grabbing her keys from the counter by the door, she said, "Take the SUV."

He smiled as if hearing her laugh had been worth the insult to his beloved truck. But he glanced worriedly at her belly and set her keys on the counter again. "You can't drive the truck. It's a standard. If I take your car, you're stranded."

She pointed at the sky. "As if I'm going out in this."

"Right."

"So go."

Still, he hesitated.

Impatience crawled up her spine. She was tired, achy and just wanted to be alone. Specifically, she wanted a nice shower and two hours of mindless television so she could forget her backache, forget that she had another week of carrying this baby, forget that she and Nick weren't really a match.

He looked down at the keys, then back up at her. He studied her face for several seconds. "Okay. Fine. I'm going."

Though it was difficult, she mustered a smile.

He stepped out into the wind.

Grateful for the reprieve and knowing she had at least twenty minutes before the storm actually broke, she climbed the stairs, turned on the shower and stepped into the warm spray. Her back had ached all day. Her feet thumped with the weariness of having to support her burgeoning weight. But most of all her heart hurt.

She might have spent the day not looking for Nick, but now that she was alone, in the quiet, quiet house, she couldn't get him out of her mind. Losing Josh had been nothing compared to losing Nick. She should have known that. She should have realized that getting involved with the man who'd stolen her heart at six and let her leave him at eighteen, would end in the kind of heartbreak that tore through her soul, leaving tattered, unmendable pieces in its wake.

She forced her head under the spray as tears pooled in her eyes. She wasn't feeling sorry for herself. She was angry with herself. She'd been through this before. And though she'd been the one to leave Nick the first time, she'd always known she wasn't quite right for him. He was smart, strong, gorgeous. She had to force herself to do things, push herself to be bold. She wasn't even sure how to behave in the world he now lived in. And she certainly wasn't gorgeous.

Hell, today she looked more like a whale than a woman.

The tears in her eyes spilled over and ran down her cheeks. Again, she didn't try to stop them. Her entire body ached, but her broken heart shimmered with misery. Because she hurt so badly she decided not to fight it. She'd take this night and grieve the loss of her one true love, then tomorrow morning she'd be fine. There would be no more reason for her dad to worry about her. She'd pull herself together and no matter how intense the pain that sneaked up on her, no matter how lonely she'd get for the one person who'd ever made her genuinely happy, she would put on a smile and she would get through her life as if she were the luckiest, most blessed woman in the world.

Actually, once she had her baby she would be the luckiest, most blessed woman in the world. She'd have her dad. She'd have her baby. She would have the family she'd always longed for as a child but never quite fit into.

When she knew her skin would prune if she spent any more time under the spray of water, she hauled herself out and wrapped herself in a towel.

The first swipe of lightning raced across the sky. Were she in a better mood, she would have smiled at her timing. Instead she groaned when pain filled her back. This was awful. She'd known she'd be uncomfortable the last week of her pregnancy, but she hadn't expected this kind of torture.

Another flash of lightning streaked through the thick black clouds as she waddled to the bedroom. This was not looking good.

Still, what did she care? She had four hours till midnight. Four hours left in her self-declared night of mourning. She intended to use them.

But the next lightning bolt hit close. Her room filled with light, and a crack and boom immediately followed. She didn't even get seconds to count in between the lightning and the thunder. They were almost simultaneous, which meant the strike had been within a mile of her home.

The bedroom light flickered.

No. No. No! She could not lose the electricity. If she had to grieve in a dark house, she'd be beyond pathetic. Just let her keep the lights.

They flickered again then blinked off completely.

Light from the candles she'd left in the bathroom sent a wink of a glow into the hall. With a groan and a hand on her aching back, she made her way to the bathroom. She picked up the two scented candles she'd had sitting on the vanity and carried them back to her bedroom.

She really wasn't in the mood to wrestle into pajamas, so she drew a nightgown over her head. Her plan had been to make herself some hot cocoa, sit on the porch and cry. But the storm had brought a heavy humidity, making it too hot and humid for cocoa. The wind was too strong for her to sit on the porch. The lightning too close.

And as for crying, she could do that in her bedroom. On her bed.

She lay down. Suddenly the ache that had been in her back, raced around her sides to her tummy.

Dear God. What if she was in labor? A week early. With no car.

She settled herself. She'd simply call 9-1-1. It wasn't a big deal.

Except that her purse with her cell phone was downstairs and she now ached so badly she didn't think she could move.

Nick's lightweight shirt blew in the wind whipping across his deck that overlooked the ocean. Normally he loved to watch storms wreak havoc miles out over the water and wait for the resultant crash of the waves on his shore. But this storm was here. Any second now sheets of water would drench the happy little tourist town and anyone foolish enough to be standing on his deck.

Yet he didn't feel like going inside.

He ached so much he pressed his hand to his chest and rubbed the spot where he believed his heart to be.

Lightning streaked through the billowing black clouds, followed by a roar of thunder. Only an idiot tempted fate by making himself a target for lightning, no matter how awful he felt. He turned to go inside and found himself face-to-face with his brothers. Darius looked worried. Cade carried a case of beer.

His spirits lifted, and for the first time since discovering he wasn't the only Andreas son, he was abundantly glad he had siblings.

"Are we in a hurricane?"

Cade laughed at Darius. "Greenhorn, where I come from this isn't even a really big storm."

With his hands on both of his brothers' shoulders, Nick turned them and urged them inside. "This might not be a big storm where you come from but where you *are* it's a dilly. So move."

He closed the French doors behind them, two seconds before the first wave of rain hit. It pelted the glass like a million tiny diamonds. A continuous clicking sound filled his kitchen, as the lights flickered then went out.

"Great."

"Well, since there's no power for the refrigerator, it looks like we'll have to drink this beer."

Nick couldn't help it. He laughed. Cade was nothing if not pragmatic. A night with two stupid brothers was exactly what he needed to forget that he'd lost Maggie again. And this time it was his fault.

"Toss me a can."

"It's bottles. Walk over and get one."

Nick first went for the flashlight he kept in the top drawer of the cabinets. He hit the button and illuminated the room in an eerie beam of light.

Darius took a beer from Cade. "Too bad we can't sit outside and watch this."

"Yeah." Cade cast a longing glance out at the ocean. "That's some storm."

"Thought you were used to bigger?" Nick said, also accepting a beer from Cade.

"I am. But I'm also landlocked. I don't get to see anything like this on the water."

"We can go downstairs. Sit under the house."

Cade was already on his way to the stairs. "I forgot about that."

In two minutes, they were under the house, on rickety lawn chairs, drinking beer, watching the storm.

"I hope Maggie's not out in this."

And with those words from Darius, Nick suddenly realized why his brothers had come. He'd thought they'd noticed his apprehension when he'd left Andreas Holdings that afternoon. He had to be at the plant on Monday and he would see Maggie for the first time in six weeks. They knew he still hurt over her. They also knew he believed he'd made all the right choices. But he still hurt. And he still worried about seeing Maggie.

So he'd suspected they'd hopped on Cade's plane and followed him. To support him. But they weren't here for him. They were worried about Maggie.

"She's fine. She has her dad. Her friends. People at the plant took to her like bees to honey. She's got at least eight mother hens who fawn all over her."

Darius took a slug of beer. "She doesn't want her dad or a mother hen. According to Whitney, she's probably curled up in a ball of despair, wondering what the hell she did wrong."

"She didn't do anything."

Cade leaned around Darius and nudged Nick's arm. "Yeah. We get that part, genius."

"So, what? You're mad at me, too?"

"More like confused." Always calm and in control, Darius spoke with the air of authority. "You can't tell us that you don't love her. We see it on your sappy face. Yet you walked away when she needs you the most."

"She doesn't need me."

Cade barked a laugh. "Ah, poor, Nick. The love of his life doesn't need him."

"Shut up."

Darius turned to Cade. "Yeah, Cade. That's not helping."

Cade faced the ocean. "Okay. Fine. I'll just drink my beer and wait for waves to start splashing across our toes."

They were silent for a minute as the wind and rain, lightning and thunder put on a grand show.

Finally Nick said, "Power's probably going to be out all night." He sucked in a breath. "But Maggie's not alone." He told himself he'd only said that to alleviate his brothers' concerns. Not because a tiny spark of panic had welled up in his gut. "She's got her dad. And a car. And a cell phone."

"Right," Darius agreed. "She's probably fine."

"I mean…what could happen?" Nick took a quick drink of his beer, feeling odd tentacles of fear crawling up his spine with icy fingers. "She's due but not till next week." He sucked in a breath. "Though the last time I saw her she looked really big. So big that I'd wondered if she'd miscalculated her due date."

Darius groaned. "I hope you didn't tell her that."

He was digging, trying to get Nick to tell him about their fight, but horrible self-loathing and disappointment filled him. After the way they'd all taken to Gino, he'd never tell them. He couldn't tell them. They'd think him as crazy as Maggie did.

Instead he said, "I don't have a death wish."

Cade laughed, but much to Nick's relief didn't say anything.

Nick settled back in his chair. Rubbed his hand over the

day-old stubble of beard on his chin and cheeks. Maggie was fine. The power was out, but she was with her dad.

He squeezed his eyes shut. "Janette told me her dad has bereavement group every Friday night." Shooting out of his chair, he headed for the steps and his SUV keys. "She's alone in this."

He wasn't surprised that neither of his brothers argued when he bolted out into the night. He wasn't even surprised that he was going to check on her. He dialed her cell phone, but she didn't answer.

And suddenly he needed all his concentration for driving. Tree limbs had broken off. Water washed across the road. So he tossed his phone to the seat beside him and kept going.

He loved her. There'd never been any doubt in his mind that he loved her. He might be a fool who was so torn up about her baby that he couldn't accept him or her, but he'd never doubted his love for Maggie.

Ducking rain, he raced up the front porch steps to her house. He pounded on the door. "Maggie!"

She didn't answer. He tried several times and gave up. Though it wasn't late, she could be in bed, sleeping. And he was being foolish. So they were having a storm. She'd probably gone wherever she needed to go before it started. She might have driven her dad to bereavement group and decided to stay with him rather than ride home in the storm alone.

That was probably it.

Feeling foolish, he raced back to the SUV, accompanied by the roar of thunder, the pounding of the rain. His hand stalled above the door handle.

What if she was inside but just plain couldn't hear him?

What if she was afraid?

Lightning hit a nearby tree. Thunder roared like a hungry lion.

Hell, he was afraid.

He ran up the porch steps again, and, this time, tried the front door. It was unlocked. She wouldn't leave her house unlocked if she wasn't here.

He searched the downstairs first, calling her name. "Maggie! Maggie!"

But no answer.

He bolted upstairs, taking the steps two and three at a time as panic rolled through him.

Bursting into the room, he said only, "Maggie." She lay on the bed, curled up in a fetal position.

She turned to him. Tears streamed down her cheeks. Her eyes were glassy. "The baby's coming. I can't move. I couldn't even get to my cell phone."

Panic seized Nick. Trees and power lines were down. Even if she'd gotten to a phone, and called 9-1-1, there was no guarantee an ambulance could have gotten here.

He sat on the edge of the bed, trying to remember the books he'd read fifteen years before when she was pregnant with his child.

Sobbing, she said, "I'm so glad you came."

He blinked back his own tears. He was worthless. Ridiculously worthless. Always worthless when it came to Maggie.

He caught her hand. "I'm glad, too—"

She moaned suddenly and squeezed his hand. "Oh, God, Nick. This baby is coming right now."

Not giving himself time to think, he jumped up and grabbed the covers, tossing them off the bed.

She rolled to her back, her knees up, her legs spread, as if nature had taken over.

Which was good. He was going to need more than a

little help from Mother Nature, if they were going to get through this.

"Where are your scissors, towels and a basin for water?"

Grabbing her knees, she reared up and groaned through a pain that had to have been excruciating. "Towels are in the bathroom closet. Scissors are in the top drawer of the bathroom vanity. Basin is in the kitchen, beneath the sink."

"Okay. Hang on. I'll be back as soon as I can."

Taking one of her candles with him, he raced to the kitchen and found the basin. He flew back up the stairs, hurled himself into the bathroom and grabbed an armload of towels and the scissors.

When he returned to the room, Maggie was panting. Her gown had worked its way up her tummy.

Sweat beaded on Nick's forehead, but he didn't stop or take time to think. He grabbed two towels and slid them under her before taking the basin to the bathroom and filling it with hot water. While there, he grabbed some alcohol.

He pulled out his phone to call 9-1-1, hoping they'd reach the farm before the baby was born, but Maggie groaned.

"He's coming!"

Nick doused his hands in alcohol then rinsed them in the water before he raced to the foot of the bed. As she'd said, the baby was coming. He watched the head crown, then the shoulders ease through one at a time and caught the baby before it hit the bed. He grabbed another towel and wrapped the baby, laying him on Maggie's stomach so he could cut the cord.

Maggie's eyes filled with tears. "Oh, my God, Nick. It's a boy! Look at him. He's beautiful."

Nick paused. Actually looked at the baby. A boy. He swallowed. Tears filled his eyes. "He is beautiful."

"So tiny."

He glanced at the absolutely perfect miniature fingers and toes. An unexpected smile formed. "He's probably the smallest person I've ever seen."

Unnamed emotions skittered through him. He blamed it on coming down from the adrenaline that had spiked in his blood. After handling the rest of the birth, he washed his hands and called 9-1-1. He explained the situation to the dispatcher and she said she'd send an ambulance immediately.

When he disconnected the call, the silence in the room was deafening. He didn't know what to say. What to do. He'd known Maggie was in trouble and raced to her. But now that the trouble was over, they were still the same people.

She patted the bed beside her. "Sit."

He ambled over. Sat on the bed. Glanced at the baby. "He's so beautiful."

She smiled. "Yes. He is. Thank you. I don't know what would have happened without you."

His chest ached. He pictured her on the bed, alone, scared, not able to handle the situation for herself. Still, he said, "You would have been fine. It was a very easy delivery."

She gaped at him. "Do you not get it yet? Nick, I need you. Everybody needs somebody sometime and every time I've really needed somebody you have been there."

He smiled reluctantly. "Sort of like fate."

"Sort of like destiny."

He looked at the baby again. So tiny. So perfect. Then he glanced at Maggie. So content. So perfect. "I can be an ass."

"Or maybe it just takes you a while to think things through and come to terms with it all."

Wrapping his fingers around the baby's middle, he lifted the towel-clad bundle from Maggie's tummy. "Welcome to the world, kid."

Maggie laughed.

"My God. I thought Gino was small when we got him at six months. This kid is like one-tenth his size." He caught her gaze. "He really needs us."

"Yes, he does." She smiled slowly. "And I really need you."

The joy of hearing that enveloped his heart, warmed it enough that he could take a risk. "I need you, too."

She caught his fingers and squeezed. "I'm so sorry I got angry that you were afraid you couldn't love him."

"Shh. It's fine. We're fine." He glanced at the baby. "Maybe better than fine. My God. He's so adorable. I can't believe I was afraid."

"I can understand. I—"

"No, Maggie. I was jealous." He closed his eyes in misery. "My brothers and I made a pact when we decided to become brothers for real. No secrets. So no secrets here, either. I was jealous." He swallowed. "You had lost our baby. Another man had given you this child…this child that you'd get a chance to hold and love. I couldn't get past that."

"Nick—" His name whispered to him as she slid her hand across his. "Have you ever really grieved our baby?"

He sucked in a breath. "I'm not sure."

"You need to do that. You need to let yourself feel all the pain of his loss and put him in a special place in your heart."

"I wonder what he would have looked like."

"Well, seeing how the Andreas genes seem to dominate, I'd guess he'd have been dark-haired with dark eyes."

Nick smiled.

"And a devil. Ornery, but fun."

This time Nick laughed. "Yeah. That's how I saw him, too."

"So keep him in your heart."

He swallowed hard and nodded.

"And take care of me and Egbert."

His head snapped up. "Egbert?"

"Sure. It's an old family name that no one's used in decades."

He rose, rocking the brand-new baby boy. "There's a reason it hasn't been used in decades. As names go, it sucks."

She laughed.

The noise of the ambulance pulling into the farm rolled into the room a few seconds before red and blue lights flashed through.

"So, you don't like Egbert. What do you think we should name him?"

He looked down, love filled his heart until he thought his chest would explode from it.

He caught her gaze. "Michael Nicholas Andreas."

She smiled. "That's a great name."

"He's a great kid."

"He is."

He paced to the window, saw the ambulance crew getting out and faced her again. "And you'll marry me."

"Well, I'll have to if you're adopting my son and giving him your last name."

He laughed. The ambulance crew hustled in. Took the baby. Cared for Maggie.

And Nick leaned against the windowsill. For fifteen years he'd cursed fate. Now suddenly he didn't hate the old bat so much. He had Maggie back. For real. For good.

And he had a son.

EPILOGUE

WHITNEY and Darius had insisted on bringing Gino to North Carolina for the baptism. While the waters had become too cold to swim in New York, the beach in North Carolina was still warm and sunny.

Still, they'd held the baptism dinner at Maggie's dad's house. *He'd* insisted.

"All right. All right," Charlie yelled, calming the noisy group. He'd gotten out Vicki's good china and her crystal for wine and set the big table in the formal dining room. "Turkey will be carved in about two minutes. There's no reason to get restless."

Gino yelped, pointing at the mashed potatoes and gravy on Whitney's plate.

"Yes, they're yours," Whitney said with a laugh.

"What's his?"

All eyes turned toward the arched entryway, when Cade walked in.

Maggie was about to jump up and give him a hug since he'd said he wouldn't be able to make it, but Nick said, "You missed the actual baptism."

He strolled to a seat at the table. "Had to fly myself over," he said, pulling out a chair and straddling it. "Can't fly in a suit, can't go to church in jeans."

Charlie harrumphed. "Lots of people go to church in jeans."

"That's just an excuse," Whitney said, handing him a plate and some silver.

Darius shook his head. "I just think he's so accustomed to being with cattle that he sometimes forgets how to be human."

Cade threw a fresh dinner roll at him. "At least I'm not so pampered that I use bath salts."

Whitney gaped. "Bath salts are good for the skin."

And so it went. Charlie passed out slices of juicy turkey. Nick, Cade and Darius teased. Gino ate his mashed potatoes. Maggie and Whitney talked about caring for infants as Maggie cuddled her newborn baby.

Things weren't perfect. But life rarely was. But, finally, finally, she had a family. The family she'd always longed for. The family Nick had promised at eighteen that he would give her.

are proud to present our...

Book of the Month

Come to Me
by Linda Winstead Jones

from Mills & Boon® Intrigue

Lizzie needs PI Sam's help in looking for her lost
half-sister. Sam's always had a crush on Lizzie.
But moving in on his former partner's daughter
would be *oh-so-wrong*...

Available 15th April

*Something to say about our Book of the Month?
Tell us what you think!*

millsandboon.co.uk/community
facebook.com/romancehq
twitter.com/millsandboonuk

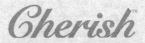

Meet the three Keyes sisters—in Susan Mallery's unmissable family saga

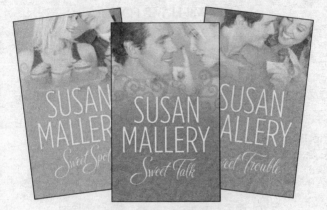

Sweet Talk
Available 18th March 2011

Sweet Spot
Available 15th April 2011

Sweet Trouble
Available 20th May 2011

For "readers who can't get enough of Nora Roberts' family series"—Booklist

Everybody loves a royal wedding!

AND WE HAVE FOUR...

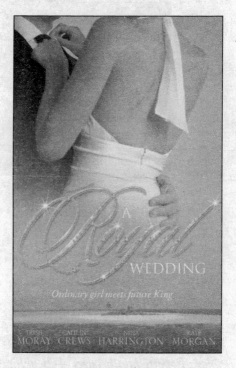

OUT NOW!

One innocent child
A secret that could destroy his life

Imprisoned for a heinous crime when she was a just a teenager, Allison Glenn is now free. Desperate for a second chance, Allison discovers that the world has moved on without her…

Shunned by those who once loved her, Allison is determined to make contact with her sister. But Brynn is trapped in her own world of regret and torment.

Their legacy of secrets is focused on one little boy. And if the truth is revealed, the consequences will be unimaginable for the adoptive mother who loves him, the girl who tried to protect him and the two sisters who hold the key to all that is hidden…

"Deeply moving and lyrical…it will haunt you…"
—*Company* magazine on *The Weight of Silence*

www.mirabooks.co.uk

2 FREE BOOKS
AND A SURPRISE GIFT

We would like to take this opportunity to thank you for reading this Mills & Boon® book by offering you the chance to take TWO more specially selected books from the Cherish™ series absolutely FREE! We're also making this offer to introduce you to the benefits of the Mills & Boon® Book Club™—

- **FREE home delivery**
- **FREE gifts and competitions**
- **FREE monthly Newsletter**
- **Exclusive Mills & Boon Book Club offers**
- **Books available before they're in the shops**

Accepting these FREE books and gift places you under no obligation to buy, you may cancel at any time, even after receiving your free books. Simply complete your details below and return the entire page to the address below. You don't even need a stamp!

YES Please send me 2 free Cherish books and a surprise gift. I understand that unless you hear from me, I will receive 5 superb new stories every month, including two 2-in-1 books priced at £5.30 each, and a single book priced at £3.30, postage and packing free. I am under no obligation to purchase any books and may cancel my subscription at any time. The free books and gift will be mine to keep in any case.

Ms/Mrs/Miss/Mr _____ Initials _____

_____

Surname _____

Address _____

_____

_____ Postcode _____

E-mail _____

Send this whole page to: Mills & Boon Book Club, Free Book Offer, FREEPOST NAT 10298, Richmond, TW9 1BR